BLOOD HUNT

Applause for L.L. Raand's *The Midnight Hunt*

"Thrilling and sensual drama with protagonists who are as alluring as they are complex."—Nell Stark, author of the paranormal romance *everafter*

"An engaging cast of characters and a flow that never skips a beat. Its rich eroticism and tension-packed plot will have readers enthralled. It's a book with a delicious bite."—Winter Pennington, author of *Witch Wolf* and *Raven's Mask*, the Kassandra Lyall Preternatural Investigator paranormal romance novels

"'Night's been crazy and it isn't even a full moon.' Who needs the full moon when you have the whole of planet Earth? L.L. Raand has created a Midnight otherworld with razor-cut precision. Sharp political intrigue, furious action, and at its core a compelling romance with creatures from your darkest dreams. The curtain rises on a thrilling new paranormal series."—Gill McKnight, author of *Goldenseal* and *Ambereye*, the Garoul paranormal romance series

"L.L. Raand's vision of a world where Weres, Vampires, and more co-exist with humans is fascinating and richly detailed, and the story she tells is not only original but deeply erotic. A satisfying read in every sense of the word."—Meghan O'Brien, author of the paranormal romance *Wild*

While *The Midnight Hunt*…is a gripping story [with] some truly erotic sex scenes, the story always takes precedence. This is a great read which is not easily put down nor easily forgotten."—*Just About Write*

Acclaim for Radclyffe's Fiction

2010 Prism award winner and *ForeWord Review* Book of the Year Award finalist *Secrets in the Stone* is "so powerfully [written] that the worlds of these three women shimmer between reality and dreams... A strong, must read novel that will linger in the minds of readers long after the last page is turned."—*Just About Write*

Lambda Literary Award winner *Stolen Moments* "is a collection of steamy stories about women who just couldn't wait. It's sex when desire overrides reason, and it's incredibly hot!"—*On Our Backs*

Lambda Literary Award winner *Distant Shores, Silent Thunder* "weaves an intricate tapestry about passion and commitment between lovers. The story explores the fragile nature of trust and the sanctuary provided by loving relationships."—*Sapphic Reader*

Lambda Literary and Benjamin Franklin Award Finalist *The Lonely Hearts Club* "is an ensemble piece that follows the lives [and loves] of three women, with a plot as carefully woven as a fine piece of cloth." —*Midwest Book Review*

ForeWord's Book of the Year finalist *Night Call* features "gripping medical drama, characters drawn with depth and compassion, and incredibly hot [love] scenes."—*Just About Write*

Lambda Literary Award Finalist *Justice Served* delivers a "crisply written, fast-paced story with twists and turns and keeps us guessing until the final explosive ending."—*Independent Gay Writer*

Lambda Literary Award finalist *Turn Back Time* "is filled with wonderful love scenes, which are both tender and hot."—*MegaScene*

Lambda Literary Award finalist *When Dreams Tremble*'s "focus on character development is meticulous and comprehensive, filled with angst, regret, and longing, building to the ultimate climax."—*Just About Write*

By L.L. Raand

Midnight Hunters

The Midnight Hunt

Blood Hunt

By Radclyffe

Romances

Innocent Hearts

Promising Hearts

Love's Melody Lost

Love's Tender Warriors

Tomorrow's Promise

Love's Masquerade

shadowland

Passion's Bright Fury

Fated Love

Turn Back Time

When Dreams Tremble

The Lonely Hearts Club

Night Call

Secrets in the Stone

Desire by Starlight

Honor Series

Above All, Honor

Honor Bound

Love & Honor

Honor Guards

Honor Reclaimed

Honor Under Siege

Word of Honor

Justice Series

A Matter of Trust (prequel)

Shield of Justice

In Pursuit of Justice

Justice in the Shadows

Justice Served

Justice for All

The Provincetown Tales

Safe Harbor	Storms of Change
Beyond the Breakwater	Winds of Fortune
Distant Shores, Silent Thunder	Returning Tides

First Responders Novels
Trauma Alert

Erotica

Erotic Interludes: *Change Of Pace*
(A Short Story Collection)

Radical Encounters
(An Erotic Short Story Collection)

Stacia Seaman and Radclyffe, eds.:
Erotic Interludes 2: *Stolen Moments*
Erotic Interludes 3: *Lessons in Love*
Erotic Interludes 4: *Extreme Passions*
Erotic Interludes 5: *Road Games*
Romantic Interludes 1: *Discovery*
Romantic Interludes 2: *Secrets*
Breathless: *Tales of Celebration*

Visit us at www.boldstrokesbooks.com

BLOOD HUNT

by

L.L. Raand

2011

BLOOD HUNT
© 2011 By L.L. Raand. All Rights Reserved.

ISBN 10: 1-60282-209-3
ISBN 13: 978-1-60282-209-2

This Trade Paperback Original Is Published By
Bold Strokes Books, Inc.
P.O. Box 249
Valley Falls, NY 12185

First Edition: March 2011

Excerpt from *Firestorm* © 2011 By Radclyffe.

CREDITS
Editors: Ruth Sternglantz and Stacia Seaman
Production Design: Stacia Seaman
Cover Design by Sheri (graphicartist2020@hotmail.com)

Acknowledgments

Series work is a double-edged sword, offering familiar characters to work with while demanding fresh new stories and an ever-expanding world. The Midnight Hunters series is filled with possibility, and I hope I can continue to explore the complexities and challenges of these characters through many books to come. In the end, the readers will decide. Many thanks to each of you for all the encouragement in this new adventure.

Endless gratitude to: editors extraordinaire, Ruth Sternglantz and Stacia Seaman, for finding the wrong turns—those that remain are all mine; first readers Connie, Diane, Eva, Jenny, Paula, Sandy, and Tina for suggestions and support; author Nell Stark for insightful feedback and inspiring discussions of Weres and Vampires; Sheri, who knows what I want when I say "smokin'"; Cindy, who gets the work out month after month; and never last—all the readers who stand by me.

And to Lee—whose patience is legion. *Amo te.*

Dedication

For Lee, my Alpha hero

CHAPTER ONE

D rake's nostrils flared at the stench of torn flesh and congealing blood. The dirt floor of the abandoned warehouse soaked up the splattered body fluids of the dead wolf Weres, the corpses gleaming wetly under the slivers of silver moon lancing through the holes in the dilapidated roof. Her mate panted beside her, Sylvan's dusty blond hair matted with sweat and her bronze skin streaked with blood. Sylvan's lean, muscular body glistened with a damp coating of adrenaline and pheromones. Four deep, ragged claw marks gouged her side. Ragged rents from the rogue's teeth covered her chest and shoulders. The rogue leader had not died easily.

How bad is it? Drake didn't speak aloud. She wouldn't let the others know of her worry, but she didn't need to. Their mate bond connected them emotionally, physically, and psychically.

They'd all been in pelt during the battle and had shifted back to skin at the end of the fight. Sylvan's wounds should have healed already, but she wasn't at full strength. Not twenty-four hours before, Drake had plunged her claws into Sylvan's abdomen and extracted multiple silver-bullet fragments. The silver still circulated in Sylvan's system, poisoning her. Drake shuddered. She'd come so close to losing her, and her mate wasn't out of danger yet. Someone still wanted Sylvan dead.

Sylvan? How bad?

The muscles in my side are torn. He missed my hip joint. I'm already healing.

You need to shift. You'll heal faster. Drake leaned against Sylvan, needing the contact. Needing much more than that, but waiting until Sylvan had given her orders to the hunters. The *centuri*, Sylvan's elite guard, formed a semicircle behind them, protecting their flanks. Sylvan had led them on a hunting raid in retribution for the assassination attempt against her that had nearly killed Lara, one of her *centuri*. She'd accepted the rogue Were's challenge and fought to the death.

Drake understood why Sylvan had accepted the rogue's challenge and why she had faced him alone, but standing by and watching the larger, mad wolf rip and tear at her mate had nearly driven *her* mad. She'd wanted to throw herself into the fight, to put her own body between Sylvan and the rogue, to tear his heart from his chest. She'd done nothing. Sylvan was Alpha, and she could not rule her Pack if she could not stand to a challenge. The Timberwolf Pack respected her, loved her, but they would not follow an Alpha who could not protect them. Without a strong leader and a clear hierarchy, a social order of predators that was ruled as much by instinct as intellect would descend into chaos. Drake knew all that, but her instincts, her very soul, railed at her to protect her mate. The urge still made her guts churn. *You should be healed by now. Shift, Sylvan.*

After I get my hunters home.

Niki will safeguard your centuri. *Please, love.*

Trust me, mate. I am more than strong enough to do what needs to be done. For my wolves, for you. Sylvan clasped the back of Drake's neck, her still-extruded claws lightly scratching the thick muscles along Drake's spine.

Drake suppressed a shiver of pleasure. Battle released a flood of neurotransmitters that blocked pain, but once the threat had passed, the chemicals morphed into sexual stimulants. All the hunters with Sylvan were aroused. So was she, even more than the others. She and Sylvan were newly mated, and the mate bond demanded near-constant physical connection and sexual release in order to fuse the chemical and hormonal markers that defined them as a mated pair. *Then hurry and finish. We don't know how many more rogues may be on their way, and you've fought enough this night.*

You worry too much. Sylvan's thoughts held a hint of laughter and the pride that ran in the blood of a long line of Alpha Weres. With no hint of a limp, Sylvan strode to the two cowering rogues who knelt in pools of blood and submissive urine, their heads bowed, limbs trembling. Drake and the hunters had killed the other rogues, leaving these two alive to bear witness to the outcome of the challenge and to spread the message that Sylvan was alive—not only alive, but deadly and without mercy.

"Tell your masters the Alpha of the Timberwolf Pack says these streets are mine. This city, this territory is mine. If you sell drugs to poison my wolves, I will come for you. If you threaten my Pack, I will come for you. If you break the laws of my Pack land, I will come for you. The challenge is issued." She kicked the lifeless corpse of the rogue whose throat she had torn out. "And I will not be as quick as I was with this cur. Now go."

The two hesitated for an instant, then spun around, still on their knees, and crawled out of sight. Within seconds, the sound of fleeing footsteps echoed through the cavernous building. Sylvan turned to Niki, her second and the leader of her *centuri*.

"Burn it."

"Yes, Alpha," the auburn-haired Were said. Smaller and fuller-breasted than Drake, Niki's muscular body was a fighting machine. The Pack *imperator*, Sylvan's enforcer, she lived to protect Sylvan. "Andrew—get the Rover. Jonathan—the accelerant is in the compartment under the floor. Max—take Jace and patrol the access road. We don't want this mongrel's lieutenants taking us by surprise if they come looking for him." She spat on the naked body of the dead rogue.

Jonathan, one of the newest *centuri*, rushed off with Andrew. Max, a craggy-faced, shaggy-haired Were, grunted his assent and loped away with Jace, a lithe blond female and Jonathan's twin.

Sylvan slid her arm around Drake's waist. "Happy now?"

Sylvan was trembling, and Drake instinctively drew her as close as she could without appearing to be supporting her. Watching Sylvan dominate the rogues aroused her even more than the fight, and she hadn't thought that possible. Her skin tingled with pheromones and shimmered with sex sheen that mirrored Sylvan's. Her clitoris pulsed and her sex clenched rhythmically. Her inner muscles pounded, and her sex glands, the olive-sized nodes buried deep at the base of her clitoris that produced the unique Were sexual neurotransmitters, were hard and ready to burst. "I won't be happy until I have you alone and under me."

Sylvan laughed. "Not until I've had you under me, and I've come in you."

"You're not strong enough for that yet."

"I was strong enough a few hours ago."

Drake needed Sylvan so badly her blood burned. "That was before you had to fight, and now you're injured again. We'll wait to tangle until you've shifted and finished healing."

"I'm strong enough to take my mate." Sylvan nipped Drake's

neck, her bite searing through Drake and making her hips jerk. "And I'm going to come on you very soon."

"I'm ready."

Sylvan kissed her, her hand in Drake's hair, tilting her head back. She thrust her tongue deep into Drake's mouth, her kiss a claiming, a demand—hot and hard and furious. Heat flared in Drake's belly, tightening her clitoris, filling her pelvis with blood and *victus*, the Were life-essence. Her glands pulsed, and she growled into Sylvan's mouth.

Niki said from behind them, "The incendiaries are set, Alpha."

Sylvan's blue eyes shimmered to wolf-gold and bored into Drake's with the promise of their mating. "Do it."

Leaving the *centuri* to ignite the blaze, Drake and Sylvan headed out to the heavily fortified black SUV. Drake filled her lungs with the cool, clean scent of the night—animals in the brush, pollen on the breeze, fish in the nearby river. Life. "I want you in the infirmary as soon as we—"

"No." Sylvan stopped and gripped Drake's shoulders. "I told you that's not what I need."

"I know—"

"No, you don't." Sylvan yanked Drake close, her mouth against Drake's throat. "You. I need you."

Heat roared through Drake's blood, spiking her clitoris so hard she almost came. She needed to claim Sylvan as badly as Sylvan needed her. She ached to touch her, taste her, and know in her bones that Sylvan was alive and well and hers. Groaning at the surge of need, she pressed against Sylvan, rubbing her bare chest over Sylvan's. Her nipples hardened, her breasts tensed, and her skin sparked. Her claws and canines extruded. Before she surrendered to the mating call, she pulled away, whimpering at the painful separation. "No, you're injured. We shouldn't—"

Sylvan snarled and her face shifted, the starkly beautiful planes edging into the sharp edges of her wolf. She was an Alpha Were, and denying her was dangerous.

Drake caressed Sylvan's chest until Sylvan's taut muscles eased. Too softly for anyone else to hear, she whispered, "Don't snarl at me, love. You don't scare me."

The corner of Sylvan's mouth twitched. "That was one of the first things I noticed about you when you were still human. You should have been afraid. Even now, you should be. But you never have been."

"I love your fury. I love your strength." Drake ran her fingers through Sylvan's hair. "I love your power. I'll never fear it."

"But you won't let me control you, either, will you?"

Drake opened the rear door of the Rover and they settled onto the benches bolted lengthwise to the sides of the compartment. "No."

Sylvan laughed.

"I'd like to speak to Detective Jody Gates, please," Becca Land said when the phone at police headquarters was answered by a laconic voice she recognized as the night dispatcher. For crying out loud, was he the only one who ever worked nights?

"Like I told you last time, lady, she ain't working. And no, she ain't called in for the five messages you already left. Maybe you should take the hint."

Becca flushed. *As if.* "My interest is professional—" And why was she explaining something that was no one's business to a man she didn't even know? "Can you tell me when she's scheduled—"

"She was due in at twenty-two hundred. Yesterday. She's late."

By about twenty-four hours. "Surely you have procedures for—"

"Her lieutenant don't seem too worried. Maybe *she* should take the hint and look for another kind of work." He snorted. "Don't really need Vampire cops, now do we?"

A click was followed by empty air. Becca stared at the silent phone. Since when was it okay for city officials not to even pretend to hide their prejudices against Praeterns? Or had the discrimination always been this blatant, and she was just now noticing? God, she hoped she hadn't been that blind.

This plan to track down the elusive Detective Gates wasn't working—time to try something else. She'd been watching Jody's town house almost nonstop since someone shot the Were Alpha there following a meeting with Jody. Jody had given her own blood to revive a dying Were guard and nearly died herself. Talk about a huge scoop, and she hadn't called it in. She'd been right there—really right there. Kneeling in blood and praying that someone didn't die. She'd held off reporting the shooting because she didn't have the bigger story—she wanted to know what was behind those gunshots. And if she reported an assassination attempt on the U.S. Councilor for Were Affairs, the

AP would bury the city in TV newscasters and there'd go her chance at the *real* story. Nope, something big was brewing and Jody was her best source. Sort of a sad statement, considering how the Vampire detective wasn't speaking to her at the moment, but hey, a reporter worked with what she had. Detective Jody Gates. God, what a pain in the ass.

She didn't even like the damned Vampire, but she hadn't wanted to see her die either—or whatever living Vampires did before they reanimated as Risen Vampires. She hadn't even known that a Vampire could die from giving up too much of her own blood, but then who knew what the rules were anyhow? It wasn't as if the Vampires—or any of the Praeterns—let humans in on their secrets. Well, okay, maybe that was understandable, considering that humans had done a pretty good job of wiping out the Praetern species something like a millennium ago, and they'd all gone into hiding and hadn't resurfaced until two years ago, when Sylvan's father more or less announced to the world, "Hey, everybody, there are a whole lot of preternatural species who have been living among you for forever, and we are tired of hiding." The great Exodus had pretty much turned the world upside down, and humans, outnumbering the Praeterns by thousands to one, weren't so sure they really wanted to share living space with species like Vampires and Weres who just might consider them prey, or the Fae who had all kinds of magical powers, or the Psi who might be influencing minds, or the Magi whose incantations and spells and wizardry were better weapons than anything humans had been able to construct. Humans, despite their numbers, often built their cultures based on fear, as Becca came to realize more every day.

Well, she wasn't afraid. She was pissed off. She'd tried to help Jody—she'd offered her *blood*—and what did she get for her efforts? Jody had practically tossed her out on her ear. She'd left Jody's house, but she wasn't going to stay gone.

She was an investigative reporter, and she wanted to know who had taken shots at someone as high profile as Sylvan Mir, and while she was at it, she wanted to know what was going on with the mysterious girls who were showing up in ERs with deadly fevers no one wanted to talk about. Not quite true. *Someone* wanted to talk about them because he—she thought it was a he, she couldn't really tell from the muffled voice on the phone—had been calling her to tell her about these cases. Why? Why did someone want to alert the press to these infections? Were they, as the caller claimed, instances of Were fever being transmitted to humans? If that was true, she needed to alert the human population.

Didn't she? Wasn't that her responsibility—to report the stories that made a difference, to expose the dangerous secrets that ultimately cost lives? She hadn't written anything about it yet. She told herself it was because she didn't know enough, but how could she know enough if no one would tell her anything?

Feeling like a stalker, she'd waited and watched and waited some more, from before dawn the day before until well after sunup, for Jody to return. When the Vampire hadn't shown, she'd figured Jody was spending the daylight hours somewhere else, and she'd gone home for a few hours' restless sleep, then back on watch before sundown. As the hours passed with still no sign of Jody, she'd started to worry. Maybe Jody hadn't recovered from nearly bleeding out, or the Vampire equivalent of it. Maybe Jody was at the hospital, although come to think of it, she'd never seen a Vampire patient in the ER. Like Weres, they didn't seek conventional medical care. After giving the Were her blood, Jody had said she'd needed to feed. And she'd said to Sylvan Mir, *You may not thank me when your* centuri *wakes up hungry. I need to be there when she does. When I've taken care of my needs, I'll come.*

Becca pulled her laptop from underneath the front seat and ran a Google search on Sylvan Mir. She'd read enough exposés and editorials about the Were Alpha and the Adirondack Timberwolf Pack to have a general idea where their Compound was located. After scanning a few articles, she clicked Google Maps and punched in the coordinates on her GPS. Time to hunt. First stop—the private headquarters of the most powerful Were Alpha in the Western Hemisphere.

CHAPTER TWO

Niki vaulted into the Rover along with Jace and Jonathan. Everyone grabbed pants from the pile on the floor. Max climbed in front, Niki pulled the doors closed, and Andrew gunned the motor, rocketing them away. The warehouse erupted into flames that licked at the undersurface of the low-hanging clouds. The sound of approaching sirens cut through the roar of the fire.

Still naked, Niki knelt on the floor and tugged her cell phone free from the waistband of her black cargoes. Instead of pulling on her pants, she opened her phone.

"Who are you calling?" Sylvan asked.

"Elena, to let her know you're injured," Niki said.

"No," Sylvan said. "I don't need a medic."

Niki, her eyes still hunter green, growled low in her chest and gripped Sylvan's shoulder. "Alpha, you've barely recovered from the wounds you suffered yesterday, and now the claw marks are not healing as quickly as they—"

"Enough!" Drake said before Sylvan could answer. A black haze of fury narrowed her vision until all she saw was Niki's throat. Another female had put hands on *her* mate. She grabbed Niki's wrist and yanked her away from Sylvan. Shoving Niki back across the space between the two benches, she loomed over her. "You forget yourself, *Imperator*."

Drake's claws emerged along with her wrath and dug into Niki's bare shoulder. Thin rivulets of blood ran over Niki's collarbone and onto her naked breasts. Niki's claws and canines shot out, and she snarled, the bones in her face sliding as she started to shift. The air grew pungent with the scent of sex and rage.

Drake didn't think, she didn't wonder at her own actions. Instinct drove her, a primal need to establish order and protect her mate. She gripped Niki's neck and threw her onto the floor of the moving vehicle. Crouching over Niki's nude body on all fours, she scraped her canines over the bounding pulse in Niki's throat. "Do not question the Alpha's judgment. And don't touch her. She's mine."

Niki thrashed, struggling against Drake's hold. Her eyes rolled, saliva gleaming on her bared canines. Drake bit Niki's throat, and scarlet ribbons welled from the punctures. Straddling Niki's thighs, she forced her pelvis into Niki's, crushing Niki's sex under hers. Niki arched and whined. Drake bit deeper. Shuddering, Niki turned her head away, submitting.

Drake kept her canines buried in Niki's neck and ground her pelvis into Niki's until Niki's breathing slowly eased and she lay docile. Drake growled low in her chest. *The order in the Pack has changed. I am Sylvan's mate. I am Prima now.*

She was second only to Sylvan in rank and dominance now, and she would prove she deserved that place if she had to fight every dominant Were in the Pack. She would never give up her right to stand by Sylvan's side, not while she still breathed.

When Niki was completely subdued, Drake eased her canines free and pushed up on her hands to allow Niki a breath. Slowly, Niki licked Drake's neck.

Drake whispered, "If the Alpha needs care, I will give it to her."

"Yes, Prima." Niki whined and licked her again. Drake rumbled comfortingly. She'd had to discipline Niki, swiftly and clearly, for challenging Sylvan. Now she had, and the Pack bond had to be reestablished. She nuzzled Niki's neck and traced the bite marks she had made with her tongue. "I trust you to guard her in my absence."

"With my life, Prima." Niki's back arched, and her clitoris lengthened and pulsed against Drake's leg.

Drake rolled off before Niki released in a show of sexual submission. Niki had already submitted in every other way, and any further surrender would humble her unnecessarily. Niki loved Sylvan, and Sylvan loved her. Drake was not threatened by their affection, and she needed Niki to protect Sylvan. She yanked on a pair of jeans, but her sex was too swollen to close them. Sylvan had pulled on jeans, too, but left them open. She leaned with her head back and her eyes closed, her posture approving all Drake had done.

"Are you all right?" Drake covered the gouge in Sylvan's side with her hand, hiding from the others the blood that seeped between her fingers. If they had been alone, she would have drawn Sylvan into her arms, but she could not do that in front of the others.

"Just tired," Sylvan murmured. "I'll be all right."

"We're almost to Pack land," Drake said.

Sylvan smiled, the stark planes of her face softening. "Home."

Drake kissed her, wanting to mark her as hers. First Sylvan's fight had unleashed every protective and aggressive instinct she had, and now her tussle with Niki had excited her even further. Her clitoris was tense and swollen, her sex glands full and ready to burst. Sylvan sensed her need and arched on the seat, her nipples hardening, her silver pelt line thickening on her lower abdomen. Drake traced the soft strip of pelt between the hard columns of muscle with her fingertips. She didn't care they were not alone. Weres frequently coupled within sight of others. Displays of sexual dominance and claiming were as normal as hunting together or the young sleeping in a tangled pile of Packmates.

"Wait, Prima," Sylvan whispered, her words strangled. "I am close to losing control."

"Good." Drake licked the purplish mark on Sylvan's chest, her mark, and Sylvan jerked. She needed to taste her. The need was so strong she whined softly and pressed a hand between Sylvan's legs. She rubbed her cheek over the bite on Sylvan's breast. "I want you."

Sylvan turned her head toward Andrew at the wheel of the Rover. Adrenaline and endorphins were driving her wolf to ascend, and she was close to shifting. She battled down her wolf, but Drake's call was so strong her sex glands tightened painfully, the way they did right before she released. She needed to be inside Drake, needed to empty into her. "Head to my quarters. Hurry."

Andrew slammed the Rover to a halt in front of Sylvan's secluded log cabin, and Sylvan, one arm around Drake's waist, shoved open the rear double doors. "Convene the war council. We'll be there soon."

She dragged Drake from the Rover onto the wide front porch and down into the shadows. She ripped Drake's jeans open and shredded the material loose. Drake tore open Sylvan's jeans, and before she could throw them aside, Sylvan thrust between her legs. Sylvan notched her swollen clitoris into the wet channel of Drake's sex.

"I'm ready to come already," Sylvan groaned.

Drake's claws dug into Sylvan's shoulders, and her black eyes gleamed with shards of gold.

"Come in me, come in me," Drake gasped, her legs clamped around Sylvan's hips, her mouth on Sylvan's chest.

"Bite." Sylvan needed her mate's bite to trigger total release. Neurotransmitters and sex kinins boiled in the glands buried deep at the base of her clitoris. She threw her head back, canines erupting. "I need to come in you now. Please." Her vision fragmented, and the world shifted to sharp planes of gray. Her wolf was winning. "Drake! Bite me!"

Sylvan's anguish drove every thought from Drake's mind except giving Sylvan what only she could give her. Snarling, she bit her mark on Sylvan's chest, releasing the hormones that would make Sylvan empty. Sylvan swelled at Drake's opening, and the pressure pushed Drake to release. Canines still buried in her lover's flesh, she arched her neck, exposing the vulnerable vessels. Sylvan roared, her hips pumping, and bit into the curve of Drake's neck.

With Sylvan's essence filling her, Drake orgasmed instantly. Her stomach convulsed, and she poured her release over Sylvan's sex. She'd never come so hard for so long. The relentless contractions continued even after Sylvan collapsed against her. Shivering, trembling, she stroked Sylvan's damp back and kissed her neck, her jaw, her mouth. "Sylvan? Love? Are you all right?"

Sylvan panted, her chest heaving. Her hips twitched, and her clitoris, still swollen erect, rolled against Drake's, sending Drake into another spiral of climaxes.

"I love you," Sylvan said.

Drake's heart seized. She could no longer imagine an existence without Sylvan. She couldn't imagine taking a breath without her, and war was coming. Sylvan would be at the heart of the battle. Tears welled in her eyes, and she fought to contain them. She would not burden Sylvan with her fears. Sylvan was Alpha and would die before forsaking her destiny or her duty.

"I love you." Drake wrapped her arms around Sylvan. "I need you."

"I need you," Sylvan whispered. An admission that no one but Drake would ever hear.

Drake cradled Sylvan's face against her neck. "You don't believe the rogue you killed was the only one behind the attempt on your life, do you?"

"No." Sylvan eased onto her side and stroked Drake's abdomen. "He had his own agenda, but he was following someone else's orders.

Someone with a larger plan. I suspect we'll know what that is soon enough."

"You can't fight again until all the silver is purged from your system. You need to shift."

"Soon. After we convene the war council. Don't worry, mate."

"Asking me not to breathe would be simpler," Drake said.

"If I could spare you what's coming—"

"No." Drake feathered her fingers through Sylvan's hair. "We fight together."

Sylvan nodded and relaxed in her embrace. Drake didn't fear death. She only feared losing Sylvan, and she would never let that happen. Never.

❖

At three in the morning, traffic on the Northway was light, and Becca piloted her Camaro north from Albany at eighty miles an hour. If she got stopped by one of the ubiquitous state troopers, she'd play her investigative reporter card and tell them she was on the trail of a hot story. She wouldn't be lying either. Of course, she had no idea what the story really was, but she was damn well going to find out.

She exited the Northway and drove slowly down a one-lane road into the Adirondack forest, searching for signs of the boundaries of the 700,000-acre wolf Were territory. Flipping on her high beams, she peered right and left as the road progressively narrowed, changing from pavement to gravel and, finally, to dirt. A deer bolted from the forest into her path, standing with spindly legs spread, its liquid eyes more curious than frightened. She slowed even further. If she killed a deer tonight, she would totally lose it. She'd spent too much time on her knees in Sylvan's and Lara's blood to tolerate one more ounce of pain and suffering. Just when she was about to give up, headlights blasted into her rearview mirror and nearly blinded her. She slammed on her brakes, her breath rushing from her chest. Okay. She was alone in the middle of God knew where, and she hadn't the slightest idea how to shoot a gun. If she'd had a gun. She did have pepper spray, and she scrambled in her bag for it.

A rap on the window sent an icy hand squeezing around her heart. Her fingers closed around the canister, and she palmed it as she turned and squinted into blackness. A light shone into her face and she blinked furiously.

"Please identify yourself," a female voice demanded in the brusque tone used by every cop Becca had ever met when they wanted to be intimidating.

"You first," she yelled through the closed window.

"You're encroaching on Pack land."

"Says who?" Becca called. "I didn't see any signs."

"You drove past one a mile and a half ago."

"You ought to make them bigger, then, because I was looking for it. Who are you?"

The light flickered out of Becca's eyes and briefly illuminated the face of a gorgeous redhead with green, green eyes. Becca recognized the sculpted cheekbones and carved jaw of every single Were, male or female, she'd ever seen. Did they all have to be so beautiful? The light was back in her eyes.

"I am Lieutenant Dasha Baran. May I see your ID, please."

"You first."

Becca thought she heard laughter, although the low resonant rumble could've been a growl. Goose bumps broke out on her skin, but her fingers relaxed a degree on the pepper spray in her hand. Something slapped against her window, and she flicked on the overhead lights. A laminated ID. The same gorgeous face. Rank and name underneath. Dasha Baran, Lieutenant. Taking a deep breath, Becca slammed her press ID against the glass next to Baran's with her photo facing out.

"Becca Land," she said. "I want to see the wolf Alpha."

Baran laughed. "The Alpha does not see visitors on demand, particularly in the middle of the night. Her office number is listed in the telephone directory. Call for an appointment."

Becca rolled her window down. "Wait. What about Detective Jody Gates. Is she here?"

The Were's lip curled at one corner. Becca's goose bumps grew goose bumps.

"I'm sorry I can't help you. Please turn around and exit Pack land."

"I know what happened to your Alpha last night. If you don't want a story in the newspaper about someone shooting her, then I suggest you take me to see her."

Baran snarled and thrust her face into the window, and the gorgeous Were wasn't gorgeous anymore. She was fucking terrifying. Becca choked back a scream and instantly flushed at her reaction. God damn it. She'd seen Weres shift before. Just not right in her face. The gleaming canines and shimmering gold eyes and the warning growl chilled her to the bone, but she had a job to do too. One that mattered a hell of a lot. And she'd had plenty of practice standing up for herself. Straightening sharply, she glared at the Were and snapped, "Don't threaten me. I'm on your side. Now back *off*."

The Were lieutenant made a visible effort to stop her shift, if that's what she was doing. The muscles in her face tightened, her elongated jaw tensed, and as her throat rippled, her snarls quieted. She actually ducked her head. What the fuck was that all about?

"My apologies, Ms. Land," the lieutenant said, her gaze sliding just to the left of Becca's ear. "If you'll wait here, I'll call the Compound."

"Thank you." Still shaking inside, Becca slipped the pepper spray canister back into her bag and quickly checked to be sure she had her essential tools. Digital recorder. Digital camera. Cell phone. Good old pad and pencil. Pepper spray. Backup pepper spray. Breath mints, wet wipes, and a protein bar. She closed her purse and gripped it in her lap. She was ready.

She had to tell herself that because she had no idea what to expect if and when she breached the Were Compound. Reporters never got through the gates. Hell, reporters rarely had an opportunity to interview Councilor Mir in her offices in Albany. They sure as hell did not demand an audience with her in the heart of Pack territory. She figured her chances of getting inside were zero to minus a hundred, but she was going to sit here in her car until *someone* talked to her.

"If you'll come with me."

Becca jumped. Damn it! She needed to stop reacting like she was afraid of the Weres. But they walked so damn softly, although nothing like the way Jody glided invisibly from one place to the other, too quickly for the eye to follow. The Weres prowled, swift and lethal, like the animals some people felt they were. They weren't animals. They weren't humans who sometimes became animals either. They were what they were. They were Weres, with a fascinating combination of humanoid and animal traits. She wasn't yet sure how to characterize the Vampires, and she couldn't seem to stop thinking about that. About who and what Jody was. About who and what Jody needed.

"Why should I get out?" Becca asked.

"I'll drive you to the Compound."

"Thank you," Becca said in her coolest, calmest voice. She gripped the door handle and pulled it up with determination. As she stepped out, she said, "I could drive and follow you—"

"In my vehicle, please," Lieutenant Baran said, and from her tone, the conversation was over.

The Were quickly disappeared into the darkness, obviously thinking Becca could see as clearly in the dense forest as she could. The narrow dirt road was heavily overgrown, or more likely had been left that way to conceal it, and the little bits of moonlight filtering through the trees gave her barely enough illumination to stay on the cleared track. A dark shape loomed ahead and she hesitated. A Humvee, or something like it. Bigger. Like armored-tank big. Jesus. What were they expecting? A war? Becca's throat went dry.

Lieutenant Baran suddenly loomed in front of her, switched on a flashlight, and aimed it across the front of the vehicle. Becca trailed her fingertips along the hood for balance as she squeezed between the matte black vehicle and the underbrush. When she reached the passenger door, she hoisted herself into the high seat. No roof. Just a roll bar. Baran was already behind the wheel, and Becca had barely gotten the door closed when the vehicle shot forward. She gripped the handhold next to her shoulder and strained to see where they were headed. She couldn't see a damn thing. North. East. West? Not a clue. Hell, they could take her anywhere out here, leave her, and she wouldn't have the slightest chance of finding her way out.

"You're in no danger," Baran said in her low, throaty voice.

"What do you mean?"

"I can smell your fear."

Wonderful. Becca twisted on the seat to face the Were behind the wheel. "I'm not afraid of you. I just dislike not knowing where I'm going."

"You don't like not being in control."

"Oh, and you do?"

"I'm a Were."

As if *that* answered everything. Becca's eyes had adjusted enough for her to see the smile that flickered at the corner of the lieutenant's mouth. She was back to being gorgeous again. Not only gorgeous, but downright incredibly sexy. Becca caught her breath. Maybe Weres had the same ability to attract prey with a sexual thrall that the Vampires did. Oh my God. Was she going to start throwing herself at the Weres the way she wanted to with Jody?

"Are you married?" Becca said. "Mated, I mean?"

Slowly, Dasha Baran turned her head and met Becca's eyes for the first time since she'd left her to call the Compound. Little flecks of gold flickered behind the dense curtain of her lashes. "Are you inviting me to tangle?"

Becca played that word through her mind. It wasn't difficult to decipher it. "No, I was making conversation."

A rumble that might've been laughter churned upward from Dasha's chest. "Weres might think of that as something other than a casual remark."

"I see. Well then, you can just pretend I didn't—"

"I am not mated. Even so, as I said, you are safe."

"Actually, what I am is really embarrassed. I'm quite sorry for—"

"Do you mind when a human male finds you attractive or invites you to...have a personal interaction?"

Becca's face felt warm despite the cool breeze streaming through the open top of the vehicle. "Ah, no. Depending on the circumstances, I might be flattered. Well, not if it was a man. But if it was a woman? Yes, probably. But I wasn't—"

"I'm teasing."

Of course she was. Weres, like all Praetern species, had lived side by side with humans for thousands of years. They'd remained invisible by learning to fit in, by hiding their essential natures. What had she expected? That in their natural habitat the Weres would be less civilized, unable to control their basic urges? "I'm incredibly sorry. I didn't mean to insult you."

"You didn't." Dasha laughed. "Just for your information, Weres rarely have human partners. Although I'm not mated, my interest is only in other Weres. I hope *you're* not insulted."

"Not insulted. Absolutely not. Embarrassed? Absolutely. Are we almost there?"

"Nearly. I would have blindfolded you, but the *centuri* said to extend you the utmost courtesy." Dasha looked from the road back to Becca, and the gold glowed brighter in her eyes. "Please do not make me regret that."

"I won't," Becca said, hoping she wouldn't discover any reason to change her mind.

CHAPTER THREE

I feel the dawn," Michel said. "The dog tests you, Regent."

"Don't fret, darling, I trust you'll have me home well before sunrise." Francesca, Chancellor of the City and Viceregal of the Eastern Vampire seethe, reached across the space between the buttery, tan leather front seats of the Rolls and caressed the slim, leather-clad thigh of her *senechal*. Michel's slender, deceptively strong body tensed, and her fiercely elegant features hardened. Michel never completely relinquished her responsibilities as Francesca's enforcer, not even when she was in the throes of bloodlust. Another time, another place, Francesca might have teased her oh-so-serious protector into relaxing her hypervigilance, even coaxed a smile from her. But not tonight, not when she'd received a call from Bernardo, a wolf Were and one of her fellow Shadow Lords, informing her of an emergency meeting less than an hour to full sunlight. Michel was right to worry.

Unlike younger Vampires, she wouldn't succumb to circadian torpor as soon as the sun rose, but eventually she would fall into moribund coma even well protected underground from ultraviolet radiation. And she would incinerate nearly as quickly as a newly animated Vampire if exposed to full sunlight. She didn't have much time, and Bernardo knew that. She didn't entirely trust her fellow Shadow Lords—they might join forces to increase their strength, but undoubtedly each of them had a private agenda. She certainly did.

Michel fixed her Adriatic blue eyes on Francesca. Her midnight hair bled into the night and made her pale, stark features even more hauntingly beautiful. "I don't trust any of them. They'll turn on you if it's to their advantage."

"Of course they will. But it's better to be close to your enemy."

Francesca laughed, thinking of Cecilia Thornton, the Fae Queen and one of the five Shadow Lords in addition to herself, Bernardo, Nicholas Gregory—the only human, and another Vampire whose identity remained a secret even to the other Lords. She intended to stay very close to Cecilia, whose golden beauty hid a ruthless soul. It was rumored that Fae blood bonded even more potently with Vampire ferrin than that of Weres and produced an exquisite orgasm. She grew wet thinking of what pleasures the Fae Queen might deliver. The muscles in Michel's thigh quivered, and Francesca rasped her nails over the tightly stretched leather at the apex of Michel's legs. Michel was the highest-ranking Vampire in her house, closest to her in lineage, and acutely attuned to her hunger. Her lust awakened Michel's. "When we're done here, we'll feed together."

"Yes, Regent," Michel whispered, maneuvering the Rolls under an abandoned railroad trestle over a deserted stretch of the Hudson River north of Albany. She pulled into line with a Harley hog, a Lincoln Town Car, and a silver Lexus SUV. Human bodyguards, Were *sentries*, and Fae Royal Guards ringed the vehicles, staring at each other with varying degrees of distrust and animosity. Francesca's sight and hearing were ten times that of a human and even more acute than a Were's. She had no trouble picking out the gunboats filled with the same mixture of armed guards with automatic weapons patrolling the murky waters under the bridge.

"You see," she said lightly to Michel, curling her fingers around Michel's forearm as they walked side by side. "Perfectly safe here."

"Do not jest, Regent," Michel said with a low growl. "You are not immortal, merely nearly so."

Francesca stilled and Michel halted instantly. Francesca framed Michel's face, her thumbs tracing the sharp arch of Michel's cheekbones, and kissed her. She let her incisors unsheath and scraped the inner surface of Michel's lip until she drew blood. She sucked the tiny tears, rhythmically stroking the tip of her tongue over Michel's. She bathed Michel in the full spectrum of her sexual thrall and felt Michel tremble. "You worry too much, darling."

Michel breathed heavily, but her expression remained resolute. "Let's hear what the rabble has to say. I want you secured before daybreak."

"I do love it when you're forceful," Francesca said. "I suppose we should."

As they drew near to the three Shadow Lords hidden in darkness beneath the underpass, Nicholas Gregory, the behind-the-scenes leader of HUFSI, Humans United for Species Integrity, jabbed a manicured finger at a heavyset, russet-haired wolf Were.

"Your orders were to eliminate the wolf Alpha," the silver-haired, patrician human shouted. "Not only did you fail, your underlings involved the Vampire detective and the very same human reporter we chose as an information conduit. Now you tell us Sylvan Mir—the one you were supposed to destroy—has killed the leader of your drug distribution network. Could you be any more incompetent?"

With a growl, Bernardo, the Alpha of the Blackpaw Were Pack, leapt across the six feet separating them in the blink of an eye, forcing the startled human to stumble in retreat. Three-inch canines flashed in the Were's snarling mouth. "I do not take orders from you, weakling."

"Perhaps you should," Nicholas said, his expression filled with disdainful condescension. "Don't think you're indispensable. Your drug money bought you a seat on our council, but you can easily be replaced."

"Now, boys," Cecilia, the Fae Queen, chided, her lilting voice filled with laughter and lust. "There will be time for you to measure your penises when we control North America. Until then, let's concentrate on our Grand Plan, shall we?"

"Yes, we need to focus on the first order of business." Francesca glided up to the voluptuous blonde's side. "We must block the Coalition's attempt to secure legal protection for the Praetern species. Legitimizing our rights will force us to reveal more about our power base. Disclosing our financial holdings, exposing our species' strengths and weaknesses, allowing the humans to insert themselves into our affairs when they outnumber us will eliminate the advantage we have as the stronger species."

"That's not enough," Nicholas insisted. "The present Coalition needs to be destroyed. We must eliminate the wolf Alpha. With her gone, the Praetern Coalition will need a new leader, and we can put our own representative in her place. Someone who will guarantee that the bill to protect Praetern rights never makes it out of committee."

"We all want to see the Coalition fail." Francesca wondered if Nicholas really appreciated that his loathing for all Praetern species extended to his fellow Shadow Lords. She would never have agreed to work with the human if Nicholas hadn't commanded considerable political and financial resources. For now, he was useful. Ultimately, he would not be. "We must wait until our numbers are stronger and we are prepared to infect the human population with the synthetic fever toxin."

Nicholas nodded with obvious reluctance. "I agree that exposure at this point would be disastrous. That's exactly why we can't afford the kind of sloppy work our dog friends have been doing."

"I will kill you, human," Bernardo growled at the ultimate insult. He dropped to all fours, his body shimmering on the edge of shifting.

"We don't have time for this," Francesca said, moving between the two males. "Sylvan Mir is well respected among humans and commands the largest wolf Pack in this hemisphere. We might consider winning her over to our cause"—she gave the still-snarling Were a contemptuous glance—"especially now that she and the authorities have been alerted to the possibility of an attack on her life."

"Sylvan Mir is her father's daughter," Nicholas said. "She won't turn her back on his vision of Praeterns living openly among humans."

Bernardo rumbled in agreement. "If it weren't for Antony Mir instigating the Exodus and exposing us all, we wouldn't be negotiating with humans."

"And we wouldn't be negotiating with animals who barely have a conscience," Nicholas snapped.

"I'm afraid where Sylvan is concerned, Nicholas is right," Cecilia murmured, languorously tracing her fingertips along the edge of Francesca's diaphanous camisole as it dipped between her breasts. "The ever-so-beautiful wolf Alpha is quite incorruptible."

"Perhaps not," Francesca mused. "Not if we have leverage over her."

"She needs to die," Bernardo said. "Her lands rightfully belong to me."

"She won't be easy to eliminate," Cecilia noted in a reasonable tone edged in steel, "but with her gone, the Coalition will be far more malleable. If we make it appear she was assassinated by humans, the others in the Coalition will soon see our only hope is to create autonomous nations where we can rule as we see fit without interference."

"Why not attempt to sway her while work continues on refining the fever toxin?" Francesca suggested. Sylvan would not be easy to kill, and she would make a formidable ally. Sylvan had become the public face of the Praetern species, representing the Coalition in Washington. Blond and beautiful, Ivy League educated, she was the perfect spokesperson, and the media loved her. Besides, the gorgeous Were Alpha was as intoxicatingly powerful in bed as out, and Francesca was quite fond of her. At least, she was very fond of the sex they shared. "We can always eliminate her, and letting some time pass may make her think the threat is over."

"You have a point," Cecilia said, her fingertips slipping beneath the camisole and stroking the curve of Francesca's breast. "When we have raised our armies and driven a wedge between the Coalition and the human governments, we will be in a much stronger position to assume control and divide the lands among us. Do you have a plan, dearest Francesca?"

Francesca laughed softly. "What is a Were's greatest weakness?"

"Other than silver?" Nicholas said. "Their mate."

"Sylvan is unmated, but there are others in her Pack she would die for." Francesca kept her gaze on Bernardo and caressed Cecelia's neck. "Sylvan is likely to think differently of her father's quest if she begins to lose those closest to her. In the meantime, we can concentrate on synthesizing the fever toxin."

Cecilia turned to Nicholas. "What do your researchers say about their progress?"

"We have scientists in multiple labs working twenty-four hours a day to synthesize the toxin capable of inducing Were fever in humans." Nicholas sighed. "They report inducing the fever in twenty percent of subjects. Unfortunately, they can't predict the severity of the symptoms or who will be affected. Mortality rates among the subjects has been very high."

"I haven't seen any public reports regarding the subjects you released," Francesca said.

Nicholas shrugged. "I had hoped the reporter would alert the public to the potential menace, but thus far, she has not." He sneered at Bernardo. "Now that we've involved her in the attack on Mir, she may be searching in places we would rather she not look."

"Your laboratory experiments appear to be failures," Bernardo said smugly.

"Since the Were traits are only transmitted through females, we're limited in being able to only use human female test subjects," Nicholas said. "If Were males were not impotent—"

"We are not impotent," Bernardo snarled.

"Don't bait him, Nicholas," Cecilia said with a long-suffering sigh. "You know as well as the rest of us Were males are capable of impregnating females, they simply can't produce Were offspring on their own."

Francesca cut into the argument. "Dominant Were females can also induce pregnancy, and that's one important reason we need to control the Were Alpha. She will only gain strength among the Were Packs if she mates and produces an heir."

"You just want Weres for food," Bernardo said, his canines flashing. "Were blood makes you come harder than a human's, doesn't it, bloodsucker?"

"You dream of me taking your blood," Francesca crooned, drawing him into her thrall. His eyes glazed and an erection bulged behind the fly of his dirty blue jeans. She forced one sexual image after another into his mind. "You hunger for my bite, for the scent of my pleasure coating your skin, for the heat of my mouth closing over your co—"

Bernardo's hips jerked, and a damp stain spread over the front of his pants.

Laughing, Francesca released him with a casual flick of her fingers, and he staggered, shaking his head in a daze. "But I'm afraid you're just not enough for me."

"Bitch," he muttered, but his eyes burned gold with lingering frenzy.

"We need more subjects," Nicholas said, turning away from the sexual display with a look of displeasure.

"I've had my street crews searching," Bernardo said. "Finding human females who won't be missed is not easy."

"In the meantime," Francesca said, "let's delay further attempts on the wolf Alpha. If she was to bring the Timberwolf Pack into our camp, we would have a formidable army when the time comes to exert our dominance."

"Very well, we'll wait." Nicholas Gregory turned to Francesca. "You have two weeks to bring Sylvan Mir over to our side. Then she must die."

Chapter Four

Becca braced both hands on the dashboard as the vehicle bounced over a progressively more rutted track. After what seemed like miles of twisting trails, Dasha slowed in front of an eight-foot-high, razor-wire-topped chain-link fence. A male and a female, both tall and muscular and wearing the same black BDUs as Dasha, appeared in the headlights in front of the gate. Dasha leaned out of the vehicle. "I've been cleared to bring a visitor to headquarters."

The male, heavy boned and blond, stalked to the side of the vehicle. *Stalked* was the only word Becca could bring to mind. The way his long legs covered the ground and his eyes never wavered in the harsh halogen light reminded her of the way predators hunted in the nature shows she'd seen. He drew abreast of Dasha and peered into the truck, his eyes slowly coursing over Becca's face and down her body. "Who is this?"

"A reporter."

A snarl curled his full, almost-beautiful upper lip.

"She has clearance to enter." Dasha straightened in the seat, appearing taller and broader all of a sudden. The air around Becca shimmered as if one or both of the Weres emitted electricity. This couldn't be good.

"From who?"

"Callan."

The male rumbled, and the sound would have been terrifying had Becca not heard Dasha make a similar growl not that long ago. Whatever was happening at the Compound, the Weres didn't want anyone witnessing it. Deciding silence was the wisest course, she clamped her tongue firmly between her teeth.

Dasha gestured toward the gate with her chin. "Open it."

For a long moment, the male hesitated. Dasha emitted a full-throated rumbling growl. A challenge. The hairs on Becca's arms stood up. The male remained motionless as Dasha's growl grew louder. Finally, he shrugged with the smallest dip of his head and turned away. "Make sure she doesn't wander."

Dasha engaged the clutch and drove deeper into the forest.

"What is it that no one wants me to see?" Becca asked after a few moments had passed and the churning, grating sound emanating from Dasha's chest had stilled.

"The Compound is our home. We do not like outsiders here."

"I'm not a spy or anything."

Dasha glanced at her. "Interesting choice of words."

"I just meant—"

"It doesn't matter. If you are, you'll never leave here alive."

"And how will you decide if I'm an enemy?"

Dasha smiled with just the corners of her mouth. "We'll know."

Becca couldn't decide if that was just an empty threat designed to frighten her, or if the Weres were sensitive to every human physical and emotional cue. If that was so, her years of living with a controlling father would come in handy. She'd learned early how to hide her feelings about what really mattered.

A stockade fence even higher than the chain-link they'd passed through earlier rose out of the darkness, denoting the final barrier to the interior of the Compound. To the heart of Pack land.

Becca rubbed her palms on her pants, suddenly struck by the enormity of where she was. Apparently, these guards knew she was expected, because as Dasha maneuvered the vehicle across the flat, bare ground toward the barricaded gate, it slowly opened. She took a deep breath.

Game on.

Once inside, a group of interconnecting two-story log and stone buildings came into view, dominated by a massive three-story structure with block-long stone steps and a front porch as wide as a two-lane highway. The ground between the buildings was hard-packed earth, and other vehicles like the one in which she rode were parked near each of them. Here and there shadowy figures garbed in BDUs passed from one building to another through the thin fingers of light cast by security lights hidden under the eaves of the heavy slate roofs. Dasha brought the vehicle to a halt in front of the central building, and a dark male with thick black hair that fell to his shoulders bounded down the stairs and strode toward Becca's side of the vehicle. Dressed in the same body-hugging black T-shirt and black BDUs as Dasha, he was as gorgeous as Dasha. Thankfully, Becca didn't feel the slightest twinge of desire. Maybe she'd been wrong in presuming that Weres, like Vampires, exuded some sort of sexual attractant. Of course, terror did tend to dampen the libido even when the source was preternatural. He grasped the handle of the door and yanked it open, and her pulse jumped. His eyes might have been beautiful if they hadn't been as hard as the stones in the building behind him.

"I am Callan, captain of the guard. I'm afraid your trip has been for nothing. The Alpha is not here."

"I'd like to wait."

He shook his head, and his chest flexed beneath the shirt. Oh, he was striking, all right. Powerful and domineering. No wonder you rarely saw more than two Weres together in public. The sheer physical force of them would make humans nervous. Even the Alpha's guards kept out of the public eye as much as they could. Well, they had before tonight, but she bet that would change. The lengths to which the Weres, the Vampires—all the Praeterns—must have gone to remain undetected was staggering. And depressing. But that wasn't her battle, at least not tonight. Over twenty-four hours had passed since the assassination attempt. She hadn't heard a single word from Jody or any of the Weres. She'd been cut out, cut off, and she couldn't allow that to continue. She couldn't pretend she hadn't witnessed what she'd witnessed. And what about the next call she received from her anonymous source, telling her another girl was on her way to the emergency room with a lethal fever? If no one would answer her questions, she was going to be forced to report what she knew. She didn't like being without choices, and the closed ranks of the Weres and the Vampires were leaving her with none.

"It's imperative that I speak with your Alpha."

"I'm afraid that won't be possible. I asked Dasha to bring you here because you didn't seem to understand the situation. Either you leave our territory immediately, or I will be forced to detain you."

"Excuse me. You seem to be the one who doesn't understand the situation." Becca climbed down from the vehicle to face him on equal ground. Never mind that he was a foot taller than her and twice as wide.

She could never best him physically. She couldn't stand up to any of them, even if she'd had a gun in both hands. But she didn't fight with her hands, she fought with her brain. At least when it was working, which she couldn't always count on around Jody Gates, at least.

Dasha slipped around the front of the vehicle and stood midway between her and the captain. Dasha's presence was oddly comforting, although she wasn't foolish enough to think she'd found an ally. But at least Dasha had stood up for her when the perimeter guards had not wanted to let her pass, and she didn't feel quite as alone as she had just a few minutes before. "I was with the Alpha when she was shot. For all I know, she might be dead. Either you prove to me otherwise, or tomorrow's headlines will force you to tell the world where she is."

Beside her, Dasha tensed. Callan's eyes blazed, and the bones in his face morphed from handsome to deadly. A menacing sound rolled from deep in his chest, and Becca sucked in a breath. Her insides quivered, and she prayed her legs would hold.

"I see you're still instigating trouble," a cool voice remarked from the shadows close by.

Becca tried like hell to contain the surge of excitement that just hearing Jody's voice stirred, because the damned Vampire would sense the racing of her blood. The last thing she wanted was Jody Gates to know the sound of her voice jacked her temperature up ten degrees. Slowly, she turned, and Jody stepped into the small circle of light. She looked terrible. Always thin, she'd still exuded *katana*-like strength— slender, razor-edged, graceful, and utterly deadly. Now she appeared emaciated and verging on fragile, her pale skin drawn tight over the sharp bones of her face, her eyes deep pools of fathomless darkness above cratered cheeks. An unfamiliar hollowness filled Becca's chest.

"I thought you might be here," Becca said. "How did you know I—"

"I sensed a human in the Compound." Jody smiled wryly. "I couldn't think of anyone else foolish enough to come here. This isn't a safe place for you."

Becca hadn't let anyone tell her where she belonged in a very long time. She'd had a lifetime of someone else telling her what she should and shouldn't do. Becca folded her arms beneath her breasts. "Oh really? And just why is that?"

Jody glanced at Dasha and Callan. "Would you give us a few minutes, please."

Callan growled, and Dasha moved over next to him.

"She threatened the Alpha," Callan said. "She's not going anywhere. I'm taking her to the detention—"

Suddenly, Jody was inches from Callan, her face close to his, her eyes a brilliant crimson. "I claim blood rights. Touch her and I will drain you, Wolf."

Callan growled. The air around Dasha's body shimmered like heat waves over blacktop, and in her place stood a huge black-and-brown wolf, lips drawn back and gold eyes narrowed. Oh, this wasn't good. Jody did something, Becca had no idea what, but Callan shuddered, his face contorting as if he'd been stabbed. Dasha emitted a high-pitched whine and slumped at Callan's feet. Oh fuck. This was bad. And what the fuck were blood rights?

"Jody," Becca said urgently. She wanted to touch her but wasn't sure how aware the Vampire was of her presence. Jody's expression vacillated between fury and desire. Oh crap. She'd seen that look before. Jody needed to feed, and now she had two Weres in her thrall. "Jody. Stop. They're not going to hurt me. Let them go."

Jody's gaze slid from Callan to Becca, and the fire in her eyes struck Becca with such force her stomach clenched. Her skin flamed, and her breath caught in her throat. She stifled a moan. Jody's need was so fierce Becca felt it in her own core. How could Jody stand it? "I'm fine. They're not going to do anything to me. Now stop it. Whatever you're doing to them, stop it."

Dasha whimpered softly and Callan groaned. Jody's eyes flared again, then she shuddered, and the Weres sagged backward. Dasha whined unhappily, and Callan cursed most inventively.

"A moment alone, please," Jody said.

"Five minutes," Callan snapped. "Then she leaves with a promise not to endanger the Alpha, or I take her."

Jody grasped Becca's arm and pulled her away. "You don't seriously think you can threaten to expose the Were Alpha and just walk out, do you? With their Alpha in danger, the Weres will kill anyone they sense is a threat."

"You look horrible," Becca said. "What are blood rights?"

Jody's mouth twitched. "Thank you, and nothing you need to worry about."

"Says you." Becca sighed. Choose your battles. Right. With Jody that's all there was. "Why are you here. Is it Lara? Is she all right?"

"It's too soon to tell. Did you hear what I just said? You should not be here."

"What's wrong with you?"

Jody shook her head impatiently. "Nothing. Transitioning a newling is difficult. I'm fine."

"What about Sylvan? Is she—"

"She's alive, that's all I can tell you."

"Then why can't I see her? Where is she?" Becca jammed her hands on her hips.

"I shouldn't have let you witness the meeting last night. You wouldn't have seen what you saw. You need to forget it."

"Oh really? What do you expect me to do? Just forget someone tried to kill Sylvan Mir? It doesn't matter who she is, that's news. But she is who she is, and someone trying to *assassinate* the U.S. Councilor—"

Jody gripped Becca's shoulders, her eyes hot flames. "You don't know what you're getting into here. We could be on the verge of war. You need to stay away from us. Away from Sylvan. Away from me."

"Let go of me," Becca snapped, jerking her shoulders free. "I'm not staying away from the story. If you don't tell me what I need to know, I'll find someone else who will."

Jody's face tightened. "I could compel you to do as I say. I could make you think what you witnessed was merely a dream."

Becca's heart turned to ice. "If you do that, I will hate you for the rest of my life."

"You may end up feeling that way anyhow, but at least you would still be alive."

"You forget I'm already part of this. Someone tipped me off about those sick girls. Someone wants me to know, wants the world to know. You're going to need my help."

"Why do you care?"

Becca struggled for words. Jody's question resonated with something she'd never heard from her before. Bleak resignation. She much preferred the arrogance, but she couldn't let herself be sidetracked by emotions that might not even be real. Jody could probably make her feel anything. "Someone almost killed Sylvan. Someone is doing something that's killing those girls. I don't believe those two things are random occurrences."

"I forgot. You're after the story."

"Of course I am. I'm a reporter. That's what I do. But—" But what? What could she say? How could she explain what she didn't understand herself? Just a few days ago, the story had been everything.

But now, now it was the individuals who mattered. Those nameless girls mattered. Sylvan mattered. So did Jody, damn her. Becca didn't know how she felt about that, so she said nothing.

"I have to go," Jody said. "I can't leave Lara with Marissa—"

"Marissa? Marissa's here?" Becca regretted the question as soon as she voiced it. Nothing like announcing she was jealous, which she wasn't. Just because the attractive—all right, admit it, beautiful—doctor had a massive case of the hots for Jody and practically offered her a vein the instant she saw her didn't matter to her at all. Not one tiny bit. "Good, you look like you need to feed."

"She's here for Lara."

"What about you?"

"I'm not your concern. You need to learn to stay away from places you don't belong."

"I've heard that all my life," Becca said, and the ice around her heart turned to stone. She'd been told way too many times she was the wrong sex, the wrong color, the wrong everything to let anyone or anything tell her what she could think or feel or do. "I don't let anyone tell me where I belong. Least of all someone with something to hide."

"Then you and I have nothing else to discuss. Good-bye, Ms. Land."

The night was instantly cooler, emptier, as if some vital force had suddenly disappeared. Jody was gone, and Becca stopped herself from looking around for her. She wouldn't see her. Jody was a master at disappearing. Just another reason not to give a damn about her. She strode to the vehicle where Dasha waited, thankfully no longer in wolf form. "I'm done here. For now."

Chapter Five

The roar of a powerful engine shattered the predawn quiet, and Sophia Revnik rushed outside onto the wide flagstone porch of the *sentries'* barracks. Vehicles had been rolling in and out of the Compound all night, but this one was different. The Rover was back. The Alpha and her *centuri* had returned. Sophia's blood rushed as the heavy vehicle rumbled closer and the vibrations from its oversized wheels coursed through the ground and into the stones beneath her bare feet. She'd been trying to sleep and hadn't been able to, not while Niki and the others were on a hunt. She couldn't rest with injured in the Compound either. She was a medic, and even if she didn't understand what was happening to Lara, she'd sensed the unrest in the Pack. One of their own was in danger. She'd waited to be called, choking dread filling her chest, but no word had come.

Sophia paced, every step stirring the queasy feeling in her stomach. Her wolf prowled with her. Flight. Fight. Tangle. Her instincts warred with her reason, and her body pulsated with need. She gripped the porch column and pulled the night into her chest. Her wolf clawed at her, tested her resolve, more restless than she'd been since the last awful heat. She shivered. The moon rode low, and the sky shimmered with an orange glow in the east. Almost dawn.

The Rover careened into the Compound's central courtyard, and the doors flew open. Andrew, the twins, and Max jumped out. The muscles in Sophia's throat closed, and a surge of adrenaline electrified her skin. Niki, where was Niki? She vaulted the railing onto the hard-packed dirt.

"Max, where's—"

"There." Max jerked his head toward the rear of the vehicle.

Finally, finally Niki leapt down—shirtless, sex-sheened, powerful and wild. Sophia breathed her in—earthy and rich, redolent with battle lust. Like the others, Niki wore only unbuttoned jeans. The sleek thin line of red pelt bisecting the lower portion of her etched abdominals drew Sophia's gaze like a magnet. Niki's scent deepened, pheromones flooded Sophia's nostrils, and her sex clenched in answer. She felt herself get wet. She met Niki's hot gaze, compelled to acknowledge her readiness by the thrum of need that had been building in her belly for hours. Wanting to signal her willingness. She struggled so often to contain her instincts, but not tonight. Tonight she wanted. Needed.

Niki's eyes narrowed and a warning growl resonated in her chest. Sophia shuddered and looked away. Why should the rejection surprise her? Niki always refused to take her, even when she was in frenzy. If Sophia wasn't so close to frenzy herself she'd admit it was better this way, but damn, it still hurt.

"Is everyone all right?" Sophia asked.

"All fine." Niki braced her hands on her hips, taking Sophia in. She'd scented her long before the Rover stopped. Sunshine and saplings. Even in the semidark, Sophia's shoulder-length platinum hair shimmered around her delicate features. Her full breasts beneath her white tank top were tight-nippled, and her eyes, normally deep indigo, glinted with chips of white diamonds. Niki's clitoris jumped and her stomach cramped. Sophia never tangled with Weres more dominant than her, venting her sex frenzy with beta Weres unlikely to incite a mate bond. Sophia was a healer, not a killer. She deserved the one thing Niki could not give her. Tenderness.

"Any word of Lara?" Niki winced inwardly at the harshness of her tone, but hiding her need when it rode her so hard had her wolf straining at her throat. She ached to be grounded in Pack. She needed the touch of another wolf now more than ever. Struggling with Drake, submitting to her, had flooded her with hormones. Her skin burned, and the pressure in her depths made her crazy to release. She didn't dare risk going any closer to Sophia. Sophia would tangle with her, willingly by the intensity of her scent, and Niki didn't want that. Her need, not Sophia's. No. That's not the way she wanted it. She rubbed her abdomen, trying to dull the throbbing that grew by the second.

"Sophia?" Niki said. "How's Lara? Did the Vampire take care of her?"

Sophia seemed not to have heard, her gaze following the movement of Niki's hand as she rubbed her stomach.

"Niki, let me—"

"No," Niki growled. She was too close to the edge to be around Sophia now. Sophia would come to her at any second, and she would not be able to resist. Her canines throbbed and her claws shot out. She backed up a step. Sophia slipped closer. "No!"

"Niki," Sophia murmured, "you need—"

"I *need* to see Lara." She took another step back. In the span of a few days since Sylvan had taken a mate, the order of the Pack had shifted, and the changes had left her feeling displaced and impotent. Now one of her closest Packmates might be dying. She wanted to rip and tear her enemies to shreds, and she wanted to fuck. She was so close to the edge her wolf prowled her skin.

"The Vampire is with her and won't let anyone in," Sophia said.

"She'll let me in," Niki snarled. She didn't want Jody Gates in the Compound, even if the Vampire detective *had* come to look after Lara. Gates might have saved Lara's life by offering her blood while Lara's heart healed, but now…now Lara would probably turn—and be what? Part Were, part Vampire? Whatever she was, to survive she'd need Gates, a Vampire Niki did not trust. Niki's breath caught, remembering what had happened after the detective had become so depleted feeding Lara. Gates had been in danger of dying herself. To keep the Alpha, badly wounded, from giving her own blood to revive the Vampire, Niki had torn open her own jugular and let Gates feed from her instead. The erogenous chemicals in the Vampire's bite had made her orgasm. Instantly, continuously, releasing time after time until she was hollowed out and empty. The thought of baring her neck to the Vampire filled her with loathing, but her glands swelled in anticipation.

"I have to go," Niki said.

"Your call is so strong," Sophia said. "It's all right, Niki. I wan—"

"You don't want this." Niki wouldn't use her, even if the want was mutual. She hungered for more than pleasure, she craved the ecstasy, the mindless oblivion of a Vampire's bite. "And neither do I."

"Niki—"

"No." Niki wrenched her gaze away from Sophia, bleeding from the pain in Sophia's eyes, and loped away.

❖

Gray strained in her shackles, the rough surface of the cinder-block wall scraping her bare back. She counted the approaching footfalls, ignoring the burn and the wet, thick blood pooling in the hollow at the base of her spine. Three men, one light and quick, one stumbling, one heavy and steady. She sniffed the air, her nostrils flaring at the acrid odor of sick sweat, cigarette smoke, and testosterone excitement. Her six-by-six cell was windowless, but the pull of the moon was inexorable, calling to her even in the dark, dank confines of her prison. Not yet sunrise. Early for the first test of the day.

Deep within the fabric of her being, her wolf paced restlessly. She never rested anymore. The weeks of captivity, the constant torture, the unrelenting hunger kept her close to the surface. Gray had barely learned to shift at will before the humans with hoods hiding their faces had caught her running alone in the forest and had thrown nets of woven silver and steel over her, dragging her from Pack land to this place. Once, shifting had been her greatest joy. Now she struggled not to. She wouldn't let them have her wolf—it was bad enough they forced her to give them her *victus*. She would die before she would surrender her wolf to their probes and machines.

The thin light from the naked bulbs hanging from the ceiling in the hall outside her cell barely reached the back wall where she was shackled. The last of the light disappeared as the guards approached her cell, and she drew herself up on shaking legs. When had they last brought any food? She hadn't shifted, hadn't run in weeks. She was dying, but she would not let them see her weakness. Then the fingers of light crept back into the cell, and the guards moved on. They had come for Katya, not her.

That wasn't right! They always took her first for the testing, not Katya, and strapped her into an elaborate restraining chair with her arms stretched out at ninety degrees and her legs held wide apart by horizontal braces attached at the ankle by silver-plated cuffs. The toxic burns on her wrists and ankles from her futile thrashing to break free never completely healed. Sometimes, more frequently lately, they took them together—and they tried to make Katya force her to breed by exciting her with her hands and her mouth.

Gray shuddered. The change in routine sent a shiver of unease down her spine.

"Gray?" Katya whispered under cover of the keys clanging in the lock on the adjoining cell.

"I'm here, Katya. I won't ever leave you," Gray subvocalized. The humans would hear only a growl, but her Packmate would understand her. She couldn't project her mind the way the Alpha could, but she could communicate in a range too low to be intelligible to anyone other than another wolf Were.

The three human guards in rumpled khaki uniforms dragged Katya down the hall, through the windowless steel doors at the end of the corridor, and out of sight. Gray pressed her ear to the thick stone wall. Usually, Were hearing was acute enough to penetrate several floors of a building, and mere walls were no obstacle. But she was rewarded with only silence. Maybe they had found a way to impregnate the walls with silver. Would silver block sound? The Alpha would know.

The Alpha's face filled her mind, and with the image came a longing for home and Pack so acute her stomach twisted, and she slid down the wall. Dizzy and weak, she rested her head on her knees. She would never let her captors see her anguish. She wouldn't let Katya see her fear. She was a dominant Were, she needed to be strong, she needed to protect her Packmate. Katya was not nearly as dominant as Gray in the order of the Pack, and that made her Katya's protector. But how could she protect her Packmate when she had no idea how to free herself? She'd reached out psychically over and over again, hoping to find some hint of the Pack, some sense that she was not as alone and isolated as she felt. Days, weeks had passed, and no answer came.

She drifted in a black haze until the sharp clink of metal followed by the grating of steel on stone warned her the guards were returning. Now they would take her. Her groin tightened in preparation for the coming pain. The response was automatic after so many sessions in the laboratory. Her body was conditioned now to anticipate pain with every touch. She didn't mind. The pain made her mind sharp and her spirit strong. They would not break her. She would not embarrass her Pack by crying out. She would not disappoint her Alpha by showing weakness to those who tried to destroy her.

The three men appeared in front of her cell.

"Watch that one," the thin, balding one with the scent of decay floating around him said. Elliot, he was called. "She likes to use her teeth."

"Too bad the pretty ones are so nasty." The young one, Ames, held the restraint collar at the end of a long flexible rod in one hand. His mouth split into a smirk, and he gripped his crotch with his free hand. Gray snarled, jutting her head forward and letting her canines slide out over her lower lip.

"Stay back and behave," ordered the third, a large, shaggy-haired male with pockmarked skin and angry eyes, as he unlocked the cell.

Gray jerked her head away when Ames pushed the restraint collar toward her neck with the rod, but the wide cuffs that held her shackled to the wall allowed her little movement, and he was practiced at placing the collar. Within seconds, the broad silver-plated collar snapped around her throat, and burning pain tore down her neck and into her chest. Her back arched, she couldn't stop it, but she bit down on her tongue to prevent the slightest whimper from escaping. Blood filled her mouth, and she swallowed it. Her wolf's screams of rage filled her head.

Through the haze of agony tearing at her mind, she heard laughter.

"Where is Katya?" Gray growled, happy that her voice did not tremble.

While the big guard, Martin, controlled the long rod attached to the collar, Elliot joined Ames. The two of them inserted keys into the shackles on her wrists and quickly re-cuffed her arms behind her back.

"Seems your girlfriend's not as feisty as you are," Elliot said, straddling her thigh as he worked. The stiffness in his pants brushed against her naked pelvis.

"Where is she? What have you done to her?" Gray's heart hammered in her chest, and she trembled on the verge of shifting. She hungered to taste their blood, to tear their flesh from their bones, to make them pay for every moment of pain and humiliation they had inflicted on Katya. Inside her wolf raged, clawing at her guts, ripping at her psyche. Sweat broke out on her forehead and chest, the muscles in her stomach turned to stone, and her sable pelt line erupted low in the center of her belly. Rage and pain stiffened her clitoris.

"Looks like she's ready for us." The guard who smelled like death gripped her sex, twisting until her swollen sex glands hardened from the unrelenting pressure, and she snarled, thrashing her head from side to side. She would rip his throat out.

"You better ease up on that until we get her in the lab," the big man with the furious dark eyes said, pushing the controlling rod into Ames's hand and loosing Elliot's hold on Gray's sex. "If we have to stun her and she loses that stuff, the bosses won't be happy."

"This one's got plenty to spare," Elliot said with a sneer. "With the amount of jizz she makes, she could probably populate the whole countryside with those fucking mutants."

"Yeah, well, the bosses want it in a test tube, not all over the fucking floor. Leave her alone."

"You turning into a wolf-lover all of a sudden, Martin?" Elliot said.

"What I love is my ass in one piece," Martin said. "You guys got her? Let's go."

As soon as the cuffs on her ankles opened, Gray reared back and jerked at the rod attached to the collar, just as she did every time they came for her. Just like every one of the dozens of times before, Ames triggered the electric shock and flames shot along her nervous system. Her muscles convulsed and she fell to the floor, unable to stifle the whine wrenched from her throat. The surge of current made her clitoris jerk, and her hips pumped helplessly. One more jolt like that one and she'd release. A boot struck her hip.

"Get up, bitch."

No way would they break her. No way. Staggering to her feet, Gray clung to the image of Sylvan and home. The Alpha would come for her. She believed that with all her heart.

CHAPTER SIX

Niki vaulted onto the porch of the rambling L-shaped infirmary and barreled toward the door.

"You can't see her," a quiet voice said from the shadows.

Niki stopped, regarding the petite brunette curled up in an Adirondack chair. Elena's dark eyes swirled with unhappiness. "She's alive?"

Elena sighed and, rising from her seat, drew Niki into a tight hug. She ran her fingers through Niki's hair and stroked her back. Niki relaxed into the *medicus*'s embrace, Elena's gentle caresses soothing some of the sharp edges of her lust and calming the acrid dread she'd endured while watching Sylvan fight the rogue. All her life, she'd been by Sylvan's side—playing dominance games when they were pups, tussling with her as an adolescent, fighting beside her as an adult. She'd rather die than see Sylvan suffer a single injury, and she'd failed completely to protect her twice in as many days. She'd urged Sylvan to take a mate, knowing she couldn't give the Alpha the soul-deep protection she needed, but she would never have chosen Drake. The doctor was a newly turned Were—a *mutia*. Not everyone in the Pack would accept her, and she would be sterile, unable to give Sylvan an heir. She was a political liability, physically inferior, and not worthy of the Alpha. But nature and Pack law dictated Niki bow to Drake's will, and she had. She'd submitted, and prior to this day she'd only gone to her knees for Sylvan. The burn of humiliation simmered in her belly, and she growled.

"What happened?" Elena continued to stroke Niki's shoulders and arms.

"Nothing." Niki pulled Elena's sweet scent deep into her lungs. The *medicus* was mated, and her caresses did not incite Niki's need to tangle, but Niki was nearly as dominant as Sylvan, and her frenzy would eventually stir Elena. Neither Elena nor her mate Roger would mind that, but she broke free and backed away. For the first time in her life, her needs set her apart from the Pack. "Tell me about Lara."

"She's…" Elena kept hold of both Niki's hands. Her voice vibrated with anger and worry. "I've heard her crying out. I don't know how aware she is. I can still feel her ties to the Pack, but I don't know… what she is."

Bile churned in Niki's stomach. Lara's heart had been shredded by a fusillade of silver bullets meant for Sylvan, and even the Alpha's treatment of her wounds had not been enough to save her. She'd been dying, *had* died, and the Vampire had kept her from passing beyond anyone's help by giving Lara her blood. Blood that would colonize her organs, infest her system, *turn* her from the dominant Were *centuri* she'd been into something…other. Something, perhaps, not Pack.

"I don't care what she is," Niki said. "I intend to see her."

"Be careful, *Imperator*," Elena said. "The Vampire is powerful, and the Alpha has given her leave to be here. We are in her debt."

"I know what we owe her," Niki said, the quick hard pulsations in her sex a potent reminder she couldn't, and didn't want to, ignore.

❖

Jody watched Dr. Marissa Sanchez orgasm for the third time in as many hours. Lara pulled from the punctures she had made in Marissa's neck, and Marissa moaned, her hips undulating faster and faster. Marissa's familiar, ecstatic cries ignited Jody's bloodlust. Until recently, she had been the one to feed from Marissa's neck. She had been the one to release the hormones that made Marissa come. She couldn't stop the rise of her bloodlust, not when she hadn't fed all night and the heavy scent of blood and sex thrown off by Lara and Marissa permeated the air, but she was strong enough not to join them. No matter how much she lusted to bury her mouth in Marissa's groin and drink her.

Like all her species, she orgasmed in the throes of bloodlust when she fed, but the release was purely physical. When humans, and on rare occasions Weres, showed signs of wanting more than the shattering orgasms her feedings induced, she moved on. Ever since Marissa had shown signs of becoming emotionally attached, she'd rarely let her host. She wouldn't tolerate an emotional connection with her hosts, not when the next step was blood addiction. She didn't want the responsibility.

First they'd be dependent on her for the hormones her bite provided to achieve sexual satisfaction. Then they'd want to blood-bond and be turned. And turning more often than not resulted in death for the human hosts. The spiral was inevitable.

Marissa cried out, clutching Lara's back and riding the hand buried deep between her thighs. Jody's stomach roiled and her vision shimmered. Her hunger pounded in her loins, and the rich aroma compelled her incisors to unsheath. Across the room, Marissa's eyes snapped open, searching for her.

"Jody," Marissa whispered, her voice a plea. She stretched out an arm in invitation, then abruptly, her eyes rolled back, and she went limp in Lara's arms.

"You've taken enough," Jody warned. When Lara kept feeding, Jody leapt to the bedside and cupped one hand beneath Lara's chin, pulling her mouth away from Marissa's neck. "Stop."

"No!" Lara whipped her head around, her eyes an inferno of red and gold. Vampire and Were. Like all newly turned Vampires, she was ravenous and unable to control her bloodlust. Those urges accelerated the inherent sexual frenzy provoked in Weres by danger or challenge and made her lethal. She should probably let Lara die now. If she helped her live, she'd be responsible for seeing that the newling didn't run amok while she learned to feed without tearing her hosts to pieces.

"She's unconscious. You took too much too quickly."

"I want her," Lara growled.

"She needs to recover." Jody still didn't know why she had offered her own blood to save the Were. She had no particular fondness for Weres. Unlike the Fae, the Magi, and the Psi, Vampires and Weres did not rely on magic and extrasensory abilities to stay alive. Vampires and Weres were predatory creatures whose survival depended upon physical power and dominance. They were more often rivals than allies.

Lara had acted instinctively when she'd thrown herself in the path of the bullets meant for Sylvan—any Were would have done the same. But Jody hadn't expected to see Sylvan risk her own life trying to save one of her guards. Sylvan, with blood pouring from multiple wounds in her torso, had fought for Lara's life. No Vampire would have chanced their existence for an underling. Probably not even for a family member. So she'd offered her own blood to keep Lara alive long enough to heal, but Lara had been too close to death and hadn't been able to replenish her own blood stores. She'd incorporated Jody's blood and had become a rare chimera, both Were and Vampire. Lara, like

Jody—like all Vampires living or Risen—was now dependent on the ferrous carrier compounds in human and Were blood to supply oxygen to her tissues. Without it, her own blood would slowly empty of the essential elements needed to sustain life, and she would suffocate—one cell at a time.

Jody stroked Lara's damp face. "The hunger will not kill you. You're stronger than your urges."

Lara jerked her head away. Her incisors gleamed. "She agreed."

"She'll die."

"I don't care."

"You will." *And so will I.* Lara was her responsibility now—hers to protect *and* control while Lara learned to satisfy her needs. Even for powerful, experienced Vampires like Jody, the urge to absorb every ounce of heat and strength a host could provide was hard to restrain. For a newly turned Vampire, the bloodlust was so exquisitely painful, the need to feed so overpowering, they would leave a trail of bodies behind them before they were hunted down and destroyed. Jody would not allow one of her line to devolve into an animal.

Jody tightened her grip on Lara's jaw. "You will do as I say."

"I need more." Lara's thick chestnut hair clung in wet strands to her corded neck, her pale bronze skin stretched tight over knife-edged bones. The muscles in her torso rippled, and a faint dusting of brown pelt exploded down the divide between her carved abdominals. Her nipples tightened into small, hard stones. Aggression in Weres was always accompanied by sexual arousal, and she was doubly dangerous with all her drives demanding satisfaction. "I *want* her."

"It's almost dawn. We're going hunting after you sleep." Jody held Lara in place with the force of her gaze. "We'll find you another host."

"Now." Lara lunged for Jody's throat, and Jody tossed her across the room. Lara crashed into the wall and fell onto her back.

Before Lara could regain her feet, Jody leapt atop her. Driving her thigh between Lara's legs, she simultaneously grabbed Lara's wrists in one hand and pinned them to the rough wood floor. Lara roared, her eyes blind pools of fire. Jody twisted Lara's hair in her fist and pressed her mouth to Lara's ear.

"Don't make me kill you," Jody warned, the weight of her body magnified a dozen times by the power of her mind thrall.

Lara whimpered, and sanity surfaced through the agony of endless hunger and searing sexual need. Wrapping one leg around Jody's thigh, she ground her swollen sex into Jody's hip. "Help me. Please. Please."

"I will." Jody relinquished her grip on Lara's hair and pushed the flat of her hand between their bodies, skating over the stone plains of Lara's abdomen to her sex. She palmed the swollen clitoris and pressed down rhythmically, milking the glands on either side. She brushed her mouth over Lara's. "Come in my hand. Let me feel you spend, Wolf."

Lara arched like an overdrawn bow, only her head and heels touching the floor. Her abdomen contracted, her pelvis jerked, and she released in a howling fury of pleasure and pain. Jody, shuddering with need, held her down until the spasms stopped. Lara was still Were enough to excite her bloodlust, but not Were enough to satisfy her. If she tried to feed from Lara, she would likely kill her and poison herself. Vampire blood was too ferrous-depleted to sustain another Vampire.

When Lara quieted, Jody rolled away, panting. Hunger stripped away her control—relentless and unstoppable—but she wouldn't have fed from Lara even if she could have. She hadn't imagined Lara's face dissolving in pleasure at her bite, but that of a human female she had no intention of ever tasting. Becca Land awakened more than her hunger, incited more than her bloodlust. She stirred a longing she couldn't afford to feel, a need for connection that only harbingered pain. She'd seen firsthand the inevitable result. She'd watched her mother die because her father had been too weak or too selfish or simply too uncaring to resist momentary pleasure. Vampires had millennia to indulge their needs. Humans had only a fleeting lifetime and a fragile hope for immortality. She might be a predator, but she would not become a murderer.

Pushing herself to her knees, Jody buttoned her shirt with trembling hands and tucked it into her pants. Lara lay curled on her side, her knees drawn up, her hips and thighs slowly flexing as her orgasm waned. Jody leaned over and skimmed her fingers through Lara's hair.

"Get dressed. We're leaving."

Jody didn't wait for an answer, but proceeded to cover Marissa with a sheet and lift the semiconscious woman into her arms. The bites in Marissa's neck were already fading, but she was hovering on the brink of serious blood loss. Marissa always did push the envelope when she hosted.

"Did I hurt her?" Lara whispered, standing now, her whiskey eyes hollow with torment and lingering hunger. She'd pulled jeans and a shirt from the closet and dressed mechanically.

"Dr. Sanchez will be fine after a day's rest and some nutritional supplements," Jody said. "Don't forget she volunteered. She wanted the pleasure of feeding you."

"The pain won't go away."

"Your body is seriously oxygen deprived." Jody opened the door and gestured for Lara to precede her down the hall to the main lobby of the infirmary. "What you're experiencing is severe lactic acid poisoning. You need to replenish the ferrous carrier compounds frequently, or the pain will become debilitating. If you don't feed, your cells will break down, and your muscles and organs will disintegrate. You'll become paralyzed, lose consciousness, and die within hours."

"Aren't I dead already?" Lara said bitterly.

"No, you're not dead. You're pre-animate—a living Vampire."

"I am a wolf Were!" For an instant, Lara's wolf surged again, and her eyes shifted to amber gold. The bones in her angular face sharpened. A deep rumble of warning resonated in her chest.

Jody slowed, untroubled by Marissa's weight. Although others frequently misinterpreted her slender form and pale complexion as delicate, she was stronger than any human and even some Alpha Weres. Her lineage was ancient, and when she rose after death, if she rose, she would be among the most powerful Vampires in the world. At any other time she would not have tolerated Lara's display of dominance, but she didn't want to subdue her again. Lara was still too unstable, her system in chaos, fluctuating wildly between her Were and Vampire urges. Most Weres who were turned, and who survived the turning, were more Vampire than anything else. Many could never shift form again. But Lara was not just any Were—she was one of the strongest Weres ever turned. Where she would fall on the spectrum, the eventual extent of her power, was unknown. She was likely to be one of a kind.

"You should thank me, Wolf, not challenge me." Jody captured Lara's gaze in her thrall. "We don't have time for this rebellion tonight. Dawn is coming."

Lara shuddered, unable to break completely free. Her face was luminous with pain, but still she managed to speak. "When will the hunger stop?"

"When you've fed enough."

"Who?" Lara's gaze fixed on the rapidly bounding pulse in Marissa's neck. "Can she…a little more?" Her incisors dropped, and as if feeling her call, Marissa's lids fluttered open.

"Let me feed her," Marissa whispered, writhing in Jody's arms.

"No," Jody said. "Any more and you'll never break the blood addiction. I won't turn you into a whore."

"I'm burning." Marissa's eyes were pleading, her lips moist and swollen. Her nipples hardened against Jody's arm. "Let her make me come. I need her."

"No."

Lara snarled. "Let me taste her."

Elena's voice cut through the hallway like a whip. "That human needs attention. At least allow me to give her some fluid."

Lara spun into a crouch. "Stay out of this."

Niki vaulted through the doorway and landed between Elena and Lara, her canines and claws extended. "Stand down, *centuri*."

"I don't answer to you." Lara's eyes flamed Vampire red.

"You answer to me." Jody ensnared Lara's mind and eased Marissa, unconscious again, into Elena's outstretched arms. "Take her. Some intravenous fluids—"

"I know what to do." Elena looked from Lara to Niki, who growled at Lara's challenge. "Don't let them fight."

"My Vampire needs to feed." Jody struggled to hold Lara back by force of will. She'd misjudged how strong she would be so soon after turning. Lara was not like any other pre-animate Vampire—she was more like a newly Risen, very strong and very hard to control. "I don't have time to get her back to the city and find another host."

"I'll feed her." Niki's gaze shifted from Lara to Jody. "I'll feed you both."

Jody studied her and Niki held her eyes.

"Come with me," the Vampire said and dragged Lara away.

❖

"Let her go. I'm ready." Niki tensed, ready to leap if Lara lunged at her. Lara didn't look like any Were in the grip of sex *or* battle frenzy she'd ever seen—Lara's eyes didn't gleam wolf-gold, but simmered with crimson flames. Lara was all Vampire, a stranger in a Packmate's body.

"She'll tear your throat out," Jody warned.

"I can handle her." Niki's wolf braced to fight.

"I want the wolf under me," Lara growled.

Niki almost whined in need, but not from Lara's call. Lara's Vampire part was ascendant, but her sexual pull was nothing like the magnetic compulsion that emanated from the slim, pale Vampire who now rested her hand lightly on Lara's neck. Jody's thrall hammered Niki with another wave of sexual power, and her clitoris jerked erect.

"You'll take her the way I say you'll take her," Jody told Lara mildly. "When I say." She looked at Elena. "We'll need to stay here. After Lara feeds, this close to dawn, she'll sleep."

"Bring the human to the treatment room," Elena said. "There are empty rooms down the hall you can use."

"Secure?" Jody asked.

"You'll be safe. The Pack will guard you." Elena stopped outside the treatment room and stroked Niki's cheek. "Be careful."

Niki nodded curtly, frenzy eating at her insides. She'd fought down the lust too many times since the hunt with the Alpha. She wanted to empty, mindlessly, endlessly. She wanted a Vampire's teeth in her throat. She shoved through a door and didn't see the Vampires move, but suddenly they were on the other side of the room, flanking the bed. Waiting for her. She pushed the door closed and did something she'd never done within the Compound before. She locked it.

Take off your pants.

Niki didn't hear the Vampire's words, she felt them in her head. Jody still gripped the back of Lara's neck and seemed to be holding her back, not by physical restraint, but with the force of her mind. Lara's sweat-soaked T-shirt clung to her chest, outlining her tense, swollen breasts. She hadn't shifted, didn't even seem to be morphing under the pressure of sex frenzy the way most dominant Weres did when they needed to tangle. Niki couldn't detect her scent, didn't feel the prickle on her skin of a Were broadcasting her need. All of the usual signals that marked Lara as Were, as Pack, were muted or gone. Lara's eyes were opaque red pools of fire, devoid of recognition or connection. Her lips curved not in a snarl of wild Were sexual demand, but in a seductive curl above glistening incisors.

Niki's chest constricted. Lara wasn't Lara, and the loss weighed so heavily on her heart she nearly went to her knees. She was blood-bonded to Lara just as she was to Sylvan and the other *centuri*, and losing one of their own was worse than losing a body part. A black chasm of despair threatened to swallow her, and she roared in agony. No more. She couldn't bear any more. She grasped the edges of her open fly with both hands and ripped the heavy canvas from her thighs. Her wolf clawed at her to shift, but she clung to her shredded control.

"Let her loose," Niki demanded, her voice roughened by her thickening vocal cords.

"Not yet." Jody unbuttoned her shirt with one hand. Her smooth, pale body gleamed like carved marble. With a quick flick of her wrist she tore Lara's T-shirt down the center. Lara ripped away the remnants of the shirt and pulled off her jeans. Smiling faintly, Jody whispered to Niki, "Come join us."

Lara strained in Jody's grip, a keening whine reverberating in her chest. Her eyes fixed on Niki's neck. A wave of sexual longing hit Niki, and her sex tightened. Whose call had captured her? Jody's? Lara's? What did it matter?

Come here, little Wolf. Let us taste you.

Niki's canines and claws erupted, her pelt line flared, and her clitoris throbbed. Like all dominant Weres, sex and aggression were two points on the same spectrum. If she didn't release soon, she would fight the first Were who even smelled like a challenge, and Lara was the closest candidate. Niki bounded across the room, landing lightly in a crouch in front of the two Vampires.

Lara struggled in Jody's phantom grip, the muscles in her chest and neck straining. Niki's wolf bristled at the challenge, and Niki snarled.

"Don't fight her," Jody said. "She can't help herself. Her hunger is ruling her. All she knows is pain."

Niki's heart seized, and the urgency in her loins receded. She straightened and cupped Lara's cheek. "Lara, I'm here."

Lara arched as if an electric current shot through her spine, and her keening became a howl. She gripped Niki's arms and yanked her onto the bed, covering Niki's body as they fell. Niki's back slammed down, and Lara's thigh drove between her legs, crushing her sex. White-hot agony ignited in her core, and her wolf surged past her restraints. She was under attack! She had to defend herself. She bit Lara's shoulder, burying her canines deep into the muscles. Lara bucked and spent herself on Niki's stomach, coating her with hot, thick *victus*. Lara reared back, incisors bared to strike. Niki struggled, but Lara was strong, so strong.

Niki saw death coming. Would that really be so bad? Her death would be fast, and she'd be drowning in pleasure. She could let go. Let go of it all. She had only to surrender.

No! If Lara killed her, Lara would be lost forever.

Niki drove her hands into Lara's hair, twisting Lara's head away, preventing her from feeding. Preventing Lara from giving her what her soul screamed for. She would never believe that Lara was lost to her, lost to the Pack. She sobbed when the pressure in her groin made her stomach cramp and her mind cloud. She didn't want to think. She just wanted a few minutes of peace. But Lara needed her more than she needed to escape. Lara was Pack, and Pack was everything.

"Lara. Lara. It's me."

The crimson blaze in Lara's eyes dimmed, and uncertainty flickered over her face. "Niki? What?"

"It's okay. You need to feed. I want to feed you."

Lara looked down at herself, at her hands pinning Niki to the bed, at the pool of vital fluid glistening on their stomachs. "What did I…" She shuddered, her face contorting, and reason left her eyes.

Jody climbed onto the bed, straddled Niki's hips behind Lara, and jerked Lara against her chest. She held Lara's head on her shoulder. Lara seemed not to struggle, but her skin rippled continuously as if she were shuddering inside. Jody said, "She needs to feed. Her periods of lucidity will get shorter and shorter. If you don't feed her, she'll die."

"She won't die." Niki turned her head, exposing her neck. Her clitoris pulsed against Jody's pants. "Tell her to take what she needs."

Jody eased Lara down until Lara lay on the bed next to Niki and guided Lara's face against Niki's throat. "Feed."

Lara struck hard and fast, her bite like a knife cutting into Niki's throat and down into her chest. Then a tidal wave of erotic power enveloped her, as if a thousand hands, a thousand mouths, caressed her simultaneously. Jody's voice flowed over her, low and warm and soothing.

Don't worry, little Wolf. You're ours now.

Jody knelt between Niki's legs, and Niki gripped Lara's shoulder, her claws digging into muscle. Lara pulled at her neck and each pull pounded in her groin. Growling, sobbing, Niki arched off the bed. Jody took her into her mouth, her incisors piercing her sex on either side of her clitoris. Pleasure more intense than anything Niki had ever experienced burst inside her. Twisting under Jody's slender weight, she whimpered and came in Jody's mouth. The searing release drove the breath from her chest and burned away every fear, annihilating loneliness and uncertainty in utter oblivion. Her wolf receded and she stopped struggling.

Jody held Niki's writhing body down on the bed with one hand pressed to her rigid abdomen. She drank, absorbing the power of blood and *victus*. Her body, nearly starved, flushed with the rapid infusion of life. Powerful Were blood bonded with hers, more potent than any drug. Her hips bucked, and she orgasmed in the throes of bloodlust. She drank and came, swallow after swallow, until Niki's glands were empty and her clitoris softened. The satisfaction coiling through her was so electrifying she didn't want to stop. Distantly, she heard a savage growl, and Lara spent again in a thick flood against the Niki's hip. Jody dragged herself away from Niki's sex and gripped Lara's shoulder.

"Let her go."

Niki's neck and chest glistened with a sheet of red. Lara's eyes were closed, her throat working convulsively as she sucked at the stream of blood slowly trailing down Niki's throat. One hand held Niki's breast, squeezing as she swallowed. Niki's hips pumped steadily in synch with the rhythm of Lara's feeding, her thighs drenched with her release. The scent of blood and sex made Jody's stomach cramp, and her groin throbbed. After turning Lara, she'd fed from four hosts before rushing to the Compound to tend to the newling. She still didn't feel replenished. She still needed more. She needed more of the Were. But even as strong as this Were was, if they took any more they'd kill her.

Jody gripped Lara's jaw, squeezing until she forced her offspring to open her mouth, and dragged her away. Bracing her back on the wall, Jody held Lara in her arms. Lara trembled and whimpered, her eyes open but unseeing. Jody stroked her hair. "It will pass. You'll survive. Sleep now."

Lara shuddered and went completely still. Dawn was breaking.

Niki groaned and rolled onto her side, squeezing a hand between her legs. Her hips rocked as the hormones Lara injected into her system continued to stimulate her.

Jody closed her eyes, savoring the languor of feeding and climaxing. The Were was powerful. Niki's blood filled her with more strength than any host she'd ever had. She stroked the Were's head as the Were pressed against her thigh. She could get used to this. The Were rumbled, crawled over her thigh, and stretched out between her legs. A warm mouth moved on her sex. With fresh Were blood circulating in her veins, she would be able to orgasm again. Maybe then she could banish the sound of Becca's voice and the hot rush of desire Becca ignited every time she saw her. She lifted her hips and let the Were take her between her lips. She could be satisfied with this. Very, very easily.

CHAPTER SEVEN

Becca reached Club Nocturne when the first whispers of dawn glowed above the mountains across the river to the east. Bouncing over the cracked concrete parking lot with foot-tall weeds growing in the crevices, she cruised down the first row of closely packed vehicles and tried not to think about Jody. About who she was with or what she was doing.

Jody Gates epitomized absolutely everything that pissed her off—she was cold, remote, patronizing, and arrogant. Never mind she was god-awful sexy without even trying—that was the whole point, remember? Vampires didn't have to *try* to be sexy—they just were. It was all biology, and Becca knew that. She *knew* that. Why her body couldn't catch up to her head, she didn't know. She'd gotten good at ignoring the constant all-over buzz whenever she was around Jody, but she couldn't stop herself from thinking about her, or from worrying that she hadn't recovered from saving Lara. Her stomach lurched at the Technicolor images of first Lara, then Jody almost dying. Red, bright red. So damn much blood.

She cringed at the memory of offering herself, offering her blood for crying out loud, to save Jody's life, and being turned down flat. How many times did she have to hear the word no? Jody had made it perfectly clear she didn't want her or need her. Fine. She got the message. She was an investigative reporter, and Jody Gates was a detective and a potential source in a developing story. That's what she needed to remember. That's all that mattered between them. And if Jody didn't want to tell her what had happened to the Were Alpha? Fine. She had other sources to tap.

She squeezed her Camaro into a tiny space between a pickup

truck and a BMW, cut the engine, and sat watching the unadorned, windowless door of the hottest Vampire club in town while the engine ticked like a fading heart. Club Nocturne looked as dead as most of its inhabitants—no sign, painted-over windows, and bare security lights that did little but laugh at the dark dangling from loose fixtures. There might as well have been a notice saying "Condemned—Keep Out" plastered on the front. She willed herself to get out of the car, but her arms and legs were as heavy as the concrete chunks underfoot.

The last time she'd been inside, she'd nearly given in to the enticing thrall of a female Vampire and her male lover. Jody had come to her rescue that time, and after berating her and calling her an idiot in not quite so many words, Jody had gotten her to promise she wouldn't go inside again without an escort. As if an escort was going to be easy to come by. Especially now—Becca squinted at her watch—at 4:40 a.m. Less than half an hour until sunrise.

The risen Vampires would all leave soon, needing to be sequestered in their lairs before sunrise. If she waited until then, she'd be safe enough. Well, maybe not safe. But safer than she would be right now, when every Vampire in the club would be in a feeding frenzy, sating their blood needs before sleeping. Well, Jody said *she* slept during the day—Becca wasn't certain what the Risen did exactly. Did they sleep, become comatose, die? For real?

Like the Weres and all the other Praeterns, the Vampires didn't disclose much about their biology or their society. Jody said the pre-animates, living Vampires like herself, could tolerate short exposures of ultraviolet radiation. As to the Risen Vamps, no one—no human, at least—really seemed to know. She'd read reports from human scientists insisting that Risen Vampires really were dead and only appeared to be reanimated. The fundamentalists and xenophobes latched onto reports like that as proof that Vampires did not deserve legal protection or civil rights or much of anything at all.

The more time she spent around Jody, the less she realized she knew. She didn't know how often Jody needed to feed or how much blood she needed to sustain herself. She didn't know what happened when Jody died, but that idea scared her. All she knew was that Jody was capable of enthralling her blood host, and that when she fed, everyone orgasmed. Nice side benefit. She knew that much, and she knew that Jody didn't want her.

"Not going there again," she muttered. Why in the hell had she ever promised Jody she wouldn't enter the club without an escort?

Nocturne was the most popular Vampire club in the city and was filled every night with Vampires and Weres and humans. This was where she would find the information she needed. Or at least a lead. About the infection that had shown up in five human teenagers. An infection that had *killed* five young girls. And about Sylvan Mir and who wanted her dead. She hated to go back on her word, even though Jody had practically coerced her compliance. Jody was very persuasive.

She had a quick snapshot memory of Jody enthralling Callan. *I claim blood rights.*

Something else she didn't know. The air in the car suddenly seemed too hot, too close, and Becca opened the door for some ventilation. Blood rights. What the hell? Like she was just free for the claiming. Damn the ego of the wom—Vampire.

Jody had been so adamant about her not going inside the club alone, as if she were helpless. She wasn't helpless. She'd been fending for herself and doing a damn good job of it for years. So okay, she could cop to being clueless, but she wasn't helpless. She drummed her fingers on the wheel, looking for a loophole. None occurred to her. She pressed her fingertips to her eyes and reminded herself that she was an investigative reporter following a hot lead and nothing, nothing and no one, prevented her from getting a story.

"Especially not an arrogant Vampire who pretty much told me she wanted me out of her life." Becca snatched up her purse and automatically checked inside to be sure she still had her pepper spray— which wouldn't do her a damn bit of good if some Vampire wanted to bite her neck. She jumped out of the Camaro just as a silver Rolls-Royce glided up to the club.

Two females emerged, including one she didn't recognize but who reminded her of Jody in that ethereal way of all Vampires—lean, dark-haired, pale, painfully beautiful. Every movement graceful, fluid, and utterly powerful. The other she knew from the media. Francesca, Viceregal and Chancellor of the City.

Becca rushed toward the pair as the Rolls pulled away. She thought fast and shot from the hip. "Excuse me. Excuse me, Viceregal. Do you have a comment about the assassination attempt on the wolf Alpha last night?"

The dark Vampire she didn't know suddenly appeared inches from Becca, her disdainful expression pricking Becca's already sensitive ego. "Who are you?"

"Becca Land, *Albany Gazette*." She tried to sidestep to speak directly to the Viceregal, but the other Vampire blocked her way again without seeming to have moved at all. Becca craned her neck, trying for eye contact. Maybe not so smart with a Vampire but, hey—points for balls. "You're aware the attack occurred in a prominent Vampire's home?"

"Call during business hours tomorrow," the Vampire who had to be a bodyguard said in a voice that reminded her way too much of Jody. "Our media director—"

"Why? We're all here now."

The Viceregal rested a pale, slim hand on the dark Vampire's arm. "That's all right, Michel. Let's be good hosts, shall we?" She held out her hand. "I'm Francesca."

"Becca Land." Becca took the Viceregal's hand, and when Francesca smiled, heat rolled through her belly, and she nearly swooned. Thank God for the shadows, because her face must be flaming. "Thank you for seeing me."

"The pleasure is all mine. Shall we go inside?"

"Yes. Thank you." Becca followed the two Vampires on none-too-steady legs, deciding they would do very well as the escorts she'd promised Jody Gates she would have the next time she entered Club Nocturne.

❖

Drake's fingers sifted through Sylvan's hair, gently scratching her scalp and massaging her neck. The soft caresses were comfortingly possessive. Sylvan rumbled and hitched her thigh a little higher over Drake's, pressing her center to Drake's hip. If she could, she would drench Drake with her essence just to make sure everyone recognized Drake as hers. The mate bond joined them in every way, but knowing her claim was irrefutable wasn't enough. Not when Drake was everything. Deep down in her core, Sylvan's wolf settled with a contented sigh and closed her eyes. Sylvan rested too, in the only place she'd ever been safe, ever felt completely at home.

"You can sleep for a few minutes," Drake said.

Sylvan nuzzled Drake's neck. "We have to meet with the war council."

"I know. Just for an hour or two, enough for you to shift and heal."

"I'm all right." Sylvan caressed Drake's chest, stroked her breasts and her belly. Her mate was worried. She worried too much. That part of Drake that had been human, that had never lived in hiding, that had never had to fight adversaries she thought were friends, face foes who saw her only as a creature to be eradicated—that part of her didn't yet trust the strength and cunning of her wolf. Or of Sylvan's. "I promise never to leave you."

Drake stiffened for an instant, then began stroking Sylvan again. "I'll need time to learn how to love you."

Sylvan pushed up on her elbow and clasped Drake's chin in her palm. She let her wolf rise and called Drake's. Lightning shards of gold slashed through the black depths of Drake's eyes, and the planes of her face sharpened and grew bolder. "You know how to love me. Never doubt that."

Drake's canines forced their way out, and she rubbed against Sylvan, her skin shimmering and hot. Sylvan's mating frenzy spiked. Snarling softly, she rolled on top of Drake and grasped a wrist in each hand, pinning her. She flexed her hips and pressed hard between her mate's thighs. An ache, harder and sharper than any she'd ever known, settled in her loins, and she felt herself swelling, getting harder and larger than she'd been in the heat of their first mating. Flames licked at her core, and she shuddered.

Drake whined and thrashed, acid scouring her insides. She scored her claws up and down Sylvan's back. "Sylvan? God. What is it? I feel…I need you again." She whimpered, her breasts so tight her nipples burned. Her stomach clenched, one fiber after another contracting until the hard surface of her abdomen knotted into cords. An aching chasm opened inside her. "I hurt. Sylvan…what's happening? Please…"

"You'll be all right. I'll take care of you." Sylvan pushed her pelvis between Drake's thighs and edged her clitoris between the hot folds of Drake's sex. When the swollen head settled in the shallow depression of Drake's opening, her hips pumped involuntarily.

Drake dug her claws into Sylvan's ass and wrapped her legs around Sylvan's hips. She tilted her pelvis, locking Sylvan into her. Her gut clenched, the muscles in her stomach squeezing down on the tense receptacles buried deep between her thighs. "I'm burning. I'm burning. God, Sylvan. Do something."

"I need to come in you again." Sylvan groaned and licked the bite on Drake's shoulder. "I'm going to come soon. Hold on."

"I'm trying. Ah God…hurry." Sylvan's hormones flooded her and Drake bucked, milking Sylvan with her tight inner muscles. "I can't stand it. I need you to come."

Sylvan snarled and pulled Drake's face to her chest. "Now. Now."

Drake bit her and Sylvan exploded, hips pumping, blood boiling in her veins. Her essence coated her mate. Her mate. *Hers*. Sylvan sank her canines into Drake's shoulder, and Drake howled, coming over her in hot waves. Sylvan couldn't stop emptying, didn't think she'd ever stop, until finally her arms gave out and she dropped onto Drake.

"Jesus, what was that?" Drake gasped, clutching Sylvan with both arms around her shoulders.

"You don't know?" Sylvan said with a shaky laugh.

"I love you. I want you constantly, but I've never felt anything like that before." Drake shivered. "It felt like I was on fire inside. It hurt, Sylvan. I still hurt."

Sylvan sighed. "Everything is happening so fast."

"What do you mean? Everything? What's wrong with me?"

"Nothing. Nothing is wrong with you." Drake's uncertainty tore at Sylvan's heart. She didn't want her mate to fear what was natural for a Were, but Drake still didn't believe she wasn't somehow dangerous, that the fever—the turning—hadn't damaged her.

"What are you afraid to tell me?" Drake asked.

"I think…I think we are breeding. What you're feeling—what *we're* feeling—is breeding frenzy."

Drake sucked in a breath. "The pain, the burning up inside to couple—you feel that too?"

"Yes."

"But Niki said I can't—"

"Niki doesn't *know*," Sylvan said. "None of us know. All we know is your wolf is strong and healthy, and she wants to breed."

"What does that mean? And what do we do about it?"

Sylvan rolled onto her side and settled Drake against her. She stroked Drake's dark hair back from her face, and ran her thumb along the bold edge of Drake's jaw. "I don't know why it's happening so fast. Maybe…"

"Don't keep things from me," Drake said. "I don't need that kind of protection."

Sylvan's wolf bristled at the command in Drake's voice, and Sylvan rumbled. At Drake's soft growl, she brought herself to heel.

"Maybe your wolf senses the Pack is in danger and I don't have an heir."

Drake's eyes darkened. "Nothing is going to happen to you."

"I know," Sylvan said quickly, "but our wolves don't think that way. All they know is that the Pack needs a strong leader, and we are the Alpha pair."

"And now that you're mated, your wolf wants to breed. Breed with me."

"Yes."

Drake tried to sit up, and Sylvan clasped her around the waist. "Don't. Don't run from me."

"I can't give you offspring."

"We don't know that. We don't know anything right now."

"Then we have to find out. Sophia's parents may have discovered something in the samples I gave them already."

"When they do, they'll call me." Sylvan caressed Drake's face. "We've been searching for these answers for a long time."

"And what do we do about this breeding frenzy? We just keep…" She paused and gestured to the two of them still on the porch, naked and exposed and vulnerable. "I haven't been able to think of anything except having you since the hunt. We're practically defenseless."

Sylvan laughed. "You can't sense Max and Jace?"

Drake raised her head, sniffed the air. The *centuri* were close. "Hell."

Sylvan grinned. "Are you complaining about coupling?"

"No, God no. I hurt like hell until we do, and then—I'd stay connected like that with you forever if I could. But what happens when I don't conceive? What will your wolf do?"

"It doesn't matter what my wolf *wants* to do," Sylvan said. "You are my mate."

Drake rested her cheek against Sylvan's shoulder. "This is a terrible time for this to be happening."

"Breeding frenzy is never convenient. It can, however, be pleasant."

"Tangling with you twenty-four hours a day is a lot more than pleasant." Drake grinned and rubbed her cheek on Sylvan's chest.

"It won't be twenty-four hours a day." Sylvan nipped Drake's chin. "I have Pack business to attend to."

"And I have a job."

Sylvan's skin prickled. "What do you mean?"

"I'm a doctor, remember?" Drake frowned. "I might not keep my job at the ER now, but I—"

"You're my mate now."

"And what? I'm supposed to warm your bed and nothing else?" Sylvan growled. "You want to fight me now, Prima?"

"Maybe. Maybe I do." Drake broke Sylvan's hold and sat up. "No, damn it. No, I don't want to fight. But we need information. About what's happening to us and why a handful of human girls had Were fever or something close to it. We need to know why I turned after one of them bit me."

"And how do you want to do this?" Sylvan sat behind Drake and extended her legs on either side of Drake's hips, clasping Drake against her chest.

"I want to work at Mir Industries with the Revniks. With their experience and my tissue samples, we can—"

"No!" Sylvan roared, and Max burst out of the woods. She snarled at him, and he disappeared. "You will not be a test subject. You are my mate. You are Prima of the Timberwolf Pack."

Drake rubbed Sylvan's arms, lightly scratching the tops of her clenched hands. "I *am* your mate. And that makes the Pack my responsibility too. And we need to know what we face. If whatever happened to me happens to other humans and we can't counteract it, the humans will try to contain the threat by containing us. Imprisonment would be the easiest solution, if they stopped at that."

"They would hunt us." Sylvan's throat thickened as she started to shift.

"We can't let that happen," Drake said. "You must let me be your mate and do my job."

Sylvan rested her chin on Drake's shoulder, breathing deeply to center herself in the scent of her mate. Every instinct pushed her to keep Drake safe within the Compound, guarded by her *sentries*. "I'll assign guards. You'll take them whenever you leave the Compound."

Drake sighed. "If that will make you feel better, all right."

"You'll promise to be careful."

Drake laughed softly. "Yes. I will."

"If I'm right, and we're on the brink of breeding frenzy, I won't be able to be away from you for very long."

Drake twisted in Sylvan's arms and searched her face. "What do you mean? What will happen?"

"If we don't couple, the pain will incite our wolves. We could be dangerous. Especially me."

"I understand. You're Alpha, and the biological imperative to breed is strongest in you." Drake combed her fingers through Sylvan's hair and kissed her. "I'm here. I'm yours, and I want you just as much as I need you."

"Are you ready to meet with the war council?"

"I'm ready for whatever we must do to protect our Pack."

Chapter Eight

Inside, Nocturne looked pretty much the way Becca remembered it from her last visit. The converted warehouse had high ceilings lost to view behind ductwork and gloom, rows of horizontal windows rendered impenetrable to daylight with black paint, and shaded wall sconces throwing off just enough light for bar patrons to make their way between the sprawling leather sectionals and occasional tables and chairs to the massive chrome-and-granite bar occupying one entire wall. Becca peered into the thick murk, hoping not to step on anyone, figuring most of the patrons had superhuman eyesight along with everything else. Vampires and Weres outnumbered humans by at least five to one. She was used to being in the minority—most investigative reporters were still men, she was African American, and she was a lesbian. She'd felt the subtle and not-so-subtle barbs of prejudice, but no one had tried to kill her for her differences. Yet.

"If you want to host," Michel said dryly, "you haven't much time before the Risen will depart."

"No," Becca said, hoping she didn't sound too, too hasty. "I'm here to speak to Viceregal Francesca."

"Then I suggest you stay close."

"I will."

Like she was going to wander away when everywhere around her Vampires were feeding. Every spare inch of horizontal surface was occupied with pairs and threesomes or groups in more varied combinations of genders and species than a random-number generator could predict. A few humans and Weres leaned more or less upright against the bar, some appearing dazed, probably having just hosted and still in a post-orgasmic bliss. Others were being fed upon by Vampires who knelt between their spread legs or drank from their necks or breasts.

Sometimes two or three Vampires fed at a time from a single host. She remembered Jody's warning from the last time she'd been here. *Do you want to be compelled to have sex?*

Caught in a Vampire's thrall she'd go willingly, and she'd enjoy it. If the sounds and sights surrounding her were any indication, she'd enjoy it a hell of a lot. And chances were she'd want to do it again and again. Pleasure kept the humans and Weres coming back to offer their bodies and their blood night after night at Nocturne and half a dozen other clubs just like it all around the city. Vampires argued their interactions with their hosts were perfectly safe. After all, they didn't kill their blood hosts—quite the opposite. Why would they intentionally eliminate the source of nourishment they needed to survive? No, on the contrary, they offered exquisite rewards.

A day ago, she'd held a Were in her arms while Jody fed from her. Their arousal, their orgasms, had excited her, even though she'd been kneeling in a pool of blood. She shuddered. She hadn't even been the focus of Jody's thrall, and she'd been ready to give her blood. What would she offer if she really were compelled? No freaking way. When she gave her body, she'd do it with her mind clear and with full knowledge of the consequences. Oh no, she wasn't going to stray.

A hand reached out of the darkness and caressed her neck, cool fingertips trailing down her throat to the exposed skin between her breasts.

"Oh!" Becca gasped and immediately regretted it. A flood of odors engulfed her—the tang of fresh, adrenaline-spiked blood, the thick alluring spice of sex, and the wild rush of earth and forest that could only be Were. Even worse, she felt herself get wet and knew there was no way in hell that every Vampire within fifty feet of her wouldn't know. She stumbled to a halt.

"On second thought," Becca said, "maybe my timing is bad. I'll come back—"

"You have nothing to fear, my dear." Francesca took Becca's arm, tugging Becca close to her side. "No one here will bother you."

"Sure, because everyone probably thinks I'm your next meal." Becca's skin tingled, and if Jody hadn't demonstrated exactly how subtle and persuasive a Vampire's thrall was, she wouldn't have recognized the rush of power that blasted from the Vampire Viceregal. Despite the lack of light, Francesca's camisole was remarkably translucent. She had gorgeous breasts, milky white and rosy tipped. The pressure in Becca's loins grew heavier. She'd love to run her tongue along the curve of—

Jesus, she was losing it! She disengaged her arm from Francesca's grip as nonchalantly as possible. Offending her hostess would be a really bad idea at the moment. "I mean, I'm sure I'm safe with you."

"I rarely mix business with pleasure," Francesca said, her voice an amused purr. "At least, not until we know each other a little better."

Becca felt her face flush. Change of subject. She was a reporter, damn it. Ask a question! "What about you? I mean, it's almost dawn, and don't you have to—"

Michel growled, "You needn't concern yourself with the Regent's needs. I am here to take care of that."

Francesca threaded her arm around Michel's neck and kissed her. "And you always exceed my expectations."

Michel's eyes closed and her slender body trembled. Becca stifled a whimper. Her hand was only inches from Michel's breast. Horrified, she yanked it away. Mouth dry and heart pounding, she ached to stroke the hard points of Michel's nipples tenting her dark silk shirt. Michel's hips rolled, and instantly, Becca envisioned herself on her back, the lean, muscular Vampire thrusting rhythmically between her legs. She folded her legs around the slim hips, opening her center to the hot, slick glide of the Vampire's sex. Ripples of pleasure streaked along her spine, and she arched, twisting her fingers in the Vampire's hair, dragging the dark head down to thrust her tongue into her lover's mouth.

Jody's eyes bored into hers, glinting pools of black fire. Oh God, she wanted to come screaming in those eyes. Jody. If only Jody would— Becca shuddered. Not Jody. Not Jody, not Michel. She dragged herself a few feet away from Francesca and Michel, panting for breath and unspeakably aroused. Focusing on Jody helped her gather the shreds of her tattered control. Jody could be with Marissa right now, feeding from her, pleasuring her, coming with her. Wherever Jody was, she wasn't thinking about her. *And I'll be damned if I'll think about her.*

She searched the room, half hoping the scenes of bloodlust would put an end to her unwanted fantasies about Jody and help her fight the arousal accosting her inside and out. Through hazy eyes, she took in the carnal tableau playing out in rapid flashes of naked flesh, contorted faces, and orgasmic cries. Directly in front of her, a naked male Vampire with flowing blond hair knelt on a black leather sectional, thrusting his penis between the thighs of a boyishly beautiful female Vampire who fed from the groin of a standing male Were in half-shift, the heavy bones of the Were's face elongated and his canines jutting out over a full lower lip. The sculpted muscles in the male Vampire's ass contracted harder and harder, while the female Vampire's abdomen undulated with wave upon wave of orgasm. Becca jerked her gaze away. Francesca and Michel stood with their arms around each other observing her. Michel's elegant mouth sneered, but Francesca's smile was playful.

"Surprised?"

"I thought you couldn't..." Becca blurted and immediately bit her tongue. Jody said feeding triggered orgasm, but those two Vampires weren't feeding from each other and they were damn sure coming. So did that mean Jody—not Jody, Vampires—could have regular sex? Not that she knew what regular sex actually was anymore. She so wished she'd asked Jody about a million more questions.

Francesca stroked Becca's hair, her cool fingertips brushing the back of Becca's neck. "You thought what, darling? That we weren't interested in sex with each other? That sex was nothing more than a casual side effect of a good meal?"

Becca's face flamed. That was exactly what she'd thought. "No, of course not. I haven't spent a lot of time thinking about your sex life at all."

"That's unusual," Michel said sarcastically. "That's the only thing most reporters want to talk to us about."

"Well, I'm not your typical reporter." She was just as curious as anyone else, but she wasn't about to admit it, especially now.

"Well, for the record," Francesca said, her voice rippling down Becca's spine as smooth and warm as a caress, "some of us enjoy sex even when we're not feeding, although usually the experience is infinitely more pleasurable when blood and sex are combined."

"Of course," Becca said, trying to sound casual and informed. Nearby, a human male, who reclined in a large leather chair with a crystal glass of amber liquid in his right hand, groaned and ejaculated into the mouth of a male Vampire. His grimace of pleasure shot straight through her, and her stomach clenched. She averted her eyes in time to see a woman masturbated to orgasm by a leather-clad female Vampire who held her in her lap and fed from her neck. The woman's stunned expression and her cry of ecstasy ran over Becca's skin like fire. Enough. God, she couldn't take another second without going up in flames. "Is there somewhere quieter we can talk?"

"Let's go somewhere more comfortable." Francesca extended one arm, and a man and woman materialized out of the gloom, their rapturous gazes fixed on her as she briefly caressed each one. "If you don't mind giving us a moment, Michel and I will just make a brief stop to"—a sensuous smile turned Francesca's face from merely beautiful to breathtaking—"take care of our more pressing needs."

The tip of Francesca's tongue lightly moistened her lower lip, and Becca swallowed a moan. Her nipples tingled, and the steady drumbeat that had started in her groin the minute she'd walked in the door escalated to a pounding reverberation. "Happy to wait. Whatever you need to do."

Francesca was suddenly very close. She trailed her fingertips down Becca's throat and lightly along the outer curve of her breast, a caress that might have been innocent if they were anywhere else. But they weren't anywhere else, were they. Becca tried not to shiver and failed.

"One day I'll remind you of saying that." Francesca kissed her lightly on the cheek. "I promise you won't be sorry."

Becca kept her gaze firmly fixed on Michel's very nice ass as she followed close behind the two Vampires and their blood hosts. Hopefully, Francesca couldn't read minds, because sorry didn't cover the half of what she was feeling right now.

Sylvan and Drake vaulted up the stone stairs to the headquarters building in the center of the ten-acre walled Compound. Guards patrolled atop the heavily fortified log walls that framed the outer perimeter. Sylvan had doubled the *sentries* after the attack and increased patrols throughout the hundreds of miles bordering her territory. The air in the Compound was heavy with the scent of aggressive Weres on high alert.

Sylvan pushed open the double wooden doors and, with Drake by her side, strode down the hall and into the council room that occupied one entire side of the building. The windows, as usual, stood open, and the early-morning breeze cut through the room, carrying the scent of forest and prey. Her wolf rumbled, wanting to run. She needed to shift so her metabolism would heal her lingering wounds. The gashes on her flank and back had closed, but the muscles beneath were still raw and weak. Beside her, Drake stiffened, and a second later, the press of Drake's hand warmed her lower back.

I'm fine.

Of course you are. I just need to touch you.

She leaned into Drake's caress and scanned the room. Max occupied his usual place just inside the door, his legs spread and his arms folded across his massive chest. The twins, Jace and Jonathan, young and lithe and blond, occupied opposite ends of a brown leather sofa. Their smooth, eager faces belied their speed and cunning. They were quick and agile in the field and utterly fearless. Andrew, wiry and outwardly calm, leaned against the fireplace. He was slow to anger, steady in a fight, and stealthily lethal. Callan, the captain of her *sentries*, paced in front of the open windows while his second, Val, a dark-haired, hard-bodied warrior much like Niki, leaned against the wall nearby, her deep dark eyes brooding. Both *sentries* were agitated and coated in stress hormones. Val had recently coupled with Lara, but they were not mated. Callan's mate, Fala, was breeding, and his need to be with her permeated the air. If Drake hadn't been standing beside her, Sylvan would have felt the same way.

"Where's Niki?"

Max and Andrew exchanged glances.

Sylvan growled, a low warning deep in her chest.

"We think she's with Lara."

Sylvan advanced on the sofa, and Jace and Jonathan abruptly sat upright, as near to attention as they could be without standing. Sylvan pulled off the T-shirt she'd donned after a quick shower.

"Rise," she said.

The two young Weres jumped up. Jace's eyes, a shade darker blue than her brother's, shimmered with excitement and a burst of pale pelt shot down the center of her abdomen below her cropped white T-shirt. Jonathan whined, his skin shimmering as pelt coursed just below the surface.

"From this day forth," Sylvan said, "your loyalty and your lives belong to me and to the *centuri*. By serving me, you serve the Pack, and the Pack is all."

"Yes, Alpha," the twins said breathlessly.

Sylvan extended her forearm. "Bite."

Jace hesitated only a second, then grasped Sylvan's forearm in both hands, her canines bursting forth as her face flickered between wolf and Were. She bit down and her eyes closed, her body shuddering as Sylvan's blood forged the bond. Sylvan stroked her hair, and after a second, guided her face away. Jonathan followed, and once released, he and Jace bowed their heads and brushed their cheeks against Sylvan's chest. She folded them in her arms and let them breathe her in, giving them her strength and her power. Both shifted, unable to absorb her call in Were form. The two white-and-gray wolves whined and rubbed against her legs.

Sylvan stroked their backs. "Welcome, *centuri*. Come with me while we collect our *imperator*."

Spinning on her heel, she stalked out and bounded into the courtyard. Drake joined her and the two wolves flanked them. The door to the infirmary stood open and Sylvan followed the scent of her *medicus* to the treatment room. Elena and Sophia bent over either side of a stretcher, tending to the dark-haired human she'd seen with the Vampire and Lara the night before. The human's neck and breasts were scored with puncture marks. She'd been fed on, ravenously. Lara. Her *centuri* had done that.

"How badly is she hurt?" Sylvan asked.

"She's weak," Elena said as Sophia adjusted an intravenous drip. "She's exhausted, but I think she's just sleeping. We're giving her some fluid. I don't have any of the drugs the Vampires use to help replenish human host blood stores."

"We should get some," Sylvan said.

Elena glanced past Sylvan to the empty hall beyond. "Yes. I'll take care of that."

Drake said, "Do you need my help?"

"You're more familiar with human physiology than I am," Elena said. "If you wouldn't mind, Prima, I'd feel better if you examined her."

Drake glanced at Sylvan. "Will you need me right away?"

Sylvan stroked the back of Drake's neck, then kissed her. "Go ahead. She came here to aid our *centuri*. We need to take care of her. We are in her debt."

"All right." Drake caressed Sylvan's back. "Where will you be?"

"Reminding my *imperator* of where she belongs."

"Last night was difficult for all of us," Drake said quietly.

"She forgets her place."

"Perhaps she doesn't know it."

"Then she will."

Sylvan bounded into the hall and cast out for Niki. She scented blood, a great deal of blood, and her wolf awakened with a growl, seeking the danger. Sylvan pushed against the closed door to the room where she sensed Niki, and found it locked. Snarling, she shouldered it hard and the door banged against the inner wall. When a warning growl greeted her, she partially shifted and leapt into the center of the room. Niki, covered in blood and sex-sheen, crouched on the bed in front of Lara and Jody. Niki's neck was torn, her chest crisscrossed with claw marks, her sex bruised and swollen. All three were nude. Lara appeared unconscious and Jody slumped against the wall, awake but barely alert.

Niki snarled, "Don't come any closer."

"You would challenge me, *Imperator*?" Sylvan whispered.

Niki whined, her claws and canines extended but her gaze downcast.

Jody grasped Niki's forearm. "It's all right, little Wolf," she murmured, her words slurred. Even in the diffuse light from the hall, her ordinarily pale skin was flushed.

"Come with me." Sylvan flooded the room with her call. Her wolf was battered and injured, weaker than she should be. If Niki sensed weakness in the Alpha she might issue challenge, and Sylvan could not afford to accept when she might lose. She had to control Niki now, before Niki's instinct overruled her loyalties. "Leave them."

Niki shuddered. "No."

Sylvan launched herself across the space between them and took Niki to the floor. Straddling her, she clamped her hand around Niki's throat and squeezed Niki's throat closed. Niki's eyes rolled in her head and her entire body trembled, but rather than resist as Sylvan expected, she seemed eager to submit. Sylvan growled, and Niki arched under her, offering more of her throat. Sylvan released her and crouched over Niki's belly.

"What are you doing?"

"I don't know," Niki gasped. "I can't leave them."

"Both of them? Not just Lara?"

"Either of them."

Sylvan pressed her palm between Niki's breasts. "You are mine, Wolf."

Jody said slowly, "We exchanged blood. She senses the bond and wants to protect us."

"How long will that last?" Sylvan asked without looking away from Niki.

"Until sunfall." Jody sighed. "This time."

Sylvan knelt and pulled Niki up into her arms. "Stay here today, *Imperator*. Rest. Keep them safe."

"I'm sorry." Niki nuzzled her neck and rubbed her breasts against Sylvan's.

"No." Sylvan kissed her forehead. "Lara is Pack, and the Vampire saved her. You're right to be here."

Niki kissed Sylvan's throat and straddled her thigh, her pelt line flaring. Her hips flexed and she whined plaintively.

From across the room, Drake growled, "Niki, that's enough."

Sylvan lifted Niki and guided her back to the bed. "I'll be back at sundown."

"Yes, Alpha," Niki murmured, stretching out so her body blocked the two sleeping Vampires from anyone who might come through the door.

"It's all right." Sylvan kissed Drake and pulled her from the room before her mate's territorial drive spurred her into a fight with Niki.

"Niki needed me. My wolves need to touch me."

"Not like that," Drake said. "Niki has always wanted you."

"She's blood-bonded to me. The ties are very strong."

Drake growled. "I don't care. No one touches you that way."

Sylvan smiled. She felt the same way about Drake. "I smell your need."

"I want your mouth on me. Finish your meeting, Sylvan. Then we will run."

Sylvan's heart beat hard in her chest, and a hot flood of desire anointed her thighs. "As you command, Prima."

CHAPTER NINE

Becca's heart rate accelerated with every step as Michel led the way around the end of the bar and into a narrow passageway invisible from the main lounge. The hallway was windowless like everything else in Nocturne and illuminated only by a few floor-level lights. Apparently, she was the only one having any trouble seeing. Francesca, Michel, and the human hosts strode confidently forward as if they were in a hurry. They probably were. Both Francesca and Michel were Risen Vampires and were likely driven to feed before dawn as urgently as all the other Vampires inside the club. The man and the woman were dressed similarly—dark trousers and fitted black silk shirts unbuttoned to reveal her braless breasts and his sculpted, hairless chest. The eager pair—brother and sister? lovers? strangers?—crowded against the two Vampires, stroking and caressing anywhere they could touch. She was the fifth wheel, all right, and fine by her.

By the time they reached the end of the corridor, her eyes had adjusted. A massive steel door like one on a bank vault blocked the end of the passageway. Michel placed her palm against some kind of sensor plate and entered a long string of numbers into a touchpad. The door swung silently open onto a wide marble staircase leading downward into darkness. Becca looked back over her shoulder and saw nothing but more darkness. Talk about a rock and a hard place. She could go below ground with two Vampires—and who knew how many more might be waiting down there—or she could dive back into the freaking feeding frenzy in the club. All things considered, she'd take her chances with the Viceregal. Hopefully, Francesca wasn't interested in creating any kind of negative publicity, and feeding on an unwilling reporter would definitely generate bad press. Becca was the last one through the door, and as she felt for a handrail, praying there would be one, the door closed behind her with a solid thud, and blackness descended.

She gasped and wondered if Vampires responded to fear the way other predators did to helpless prey, culling out the weaker members of the herd. That wasn't going to be her. No way. She straightened and started down into the darkness with a determined step. She brushed against someone's back and stumbled. Her hand slid over cool, smooth skin and silky hair. Electricity coursed up her arm, and her breasts tingled.

"Michel darling," Francesca said. "Turn on the light for our guests, won't you?"

Becca breathed out as dim overhead lights flickered on, and she could make out a perfectly ordinary-looking hall at the bottom of the staircase. Polished wood floors, cream-colored walls, a series of closed walnut doors. Francesca led the group to the far end of the hall and grasped an ornate brass handle on a massive dark door.

"Come," Francesca said, pushing the door wide. "I trust you'll be comfortable here for a few minutes, Ms. Land?"

"Ah…" Becca tried for a nonchalant expression. If she weren't locked in the lair of the most powerful Vampire in North America, she wouldn't have any trouble getting comfortable. The huge drawing room could have been transported directly from a French manor house—high ceilings, luxurious carpets, and elaborate wall hangings framed the space. Plush leather sofas and an opulent maroon settee faced a marble fireplace where a low fire burned. The temperature had dropped as they'd descended, and the warmth was welcoming.

A sterling silver tea set, of all things, sat on a low table in front of the hearth. Fragrant steam—hinting at oranges and dark spices—emanated from the pot. A gleaming platter contained artfully cut and perfectly arranged petits fours. A bowl of clotted cream and a basket of scones completed the culinary array. High tea at dawn.

Apparently, the staircase she'd walked down was something akin to a rabbit hole, because she'd certainly fallen from one reality into another. Francesca had her arm around the young brunette's waist. The woman, who looked in her early twenties, but who knew what a steady infusion of Vampiric hormones did to a human—another question she'd have to ask Jody—nuzzled at Francesca's neck, kissing her throat as she caressed Francesca's breast with one hand inside her camisole. Michel's face was a study in stone. She clasped the enraptured man with her hand around the back of his neck, her fingers white against his dark skin. If the state of his trousers was any indication, even her nonsexual touch was all the invitation he required. But then again, maybe Michel was bombarding his mind with promises of pleasures to come.

"Thank you," Becca said, sounding completely absurd to her own ears. "This is fine. I'll be fine here."

"Good." Francesca's incisors gleamed behind her full ruby-red lips, more visible than they had been a few seconds before. Her eyes were no longer pure turquoise, but splintered with crimson and maroon. Her nipples had deepened to a dusky rose and were so hard they threatened to pierce the sheer fabric of her camisole. She skimmed her mouth down the brunette's neck, and the woman, heavy-lidded and dazed, whimpered. "We won't be long."

Francesca and Michel guided the humans toward another door on the far side of the room, leading to what Becca suspected was the bedroom, and she wanted to follow. She wanted Michel and Francesca and even the two strangers to run their hands over her body while she caressed Francesca's milky-white breasts and worshiped her flushed nipples with her mouth and her tongue. Becca clasped her upper arms and dug her fingertips into her skin, focusing on the crescents of pain and willing her feet not to move.

Francesca looked back over her shoulder with an indulgent smile. "Next time. I promise."

And then they were all gone, and the door was closing, and Becca sank onto the sofa, her legs trembling and her stomach in revolt. She finally understood the expression *sick with arousal*. She was so keyed up her whole body verged on meltdown, and she was afraid she would be literally ill. She drew her legs up on the sofa and hugged her middle, closing her eyes and forcing herself to breathe deeply, in and out, in and out.

Eventually, the terrible arousal subsided, and she poured herself some tea. Her throat was dry, her hands still trembling. When she heard the first keening cry, she jumped. The brunette climaxing. Then a deeper groan like that of a mortally wounded animal—the man. Laughter, light and airy and utterly satisfied. Francesca. A low murmur, sensuous and redolent with desire. Michel. Becca no sooner wondered who was pleasuring Francesca than she got a crystal-clear mental image of Francesca and Michel facing one another on a huge oval bed, their clothes open, their legs entwined, their hands and mouths caressing throats and breasts and the sweet clefts between ivory thighs. The somnolent man and woman lay nearby, naked and abandoned, their limbs sprawled and blood trails wending over their chests—cast aside like the remains of a forgotten meal. Michel's worshipful eyes glowed like lava erupting from the earth's core as she brought her mouth down on Francesca's, devouring her like a starving animal. Francesca raked her nails down Michel's slender back, leaving rivers of blood in her wake. Michel arched, the muscles in her neck corded, her mouth open in a scream of unbearable ecstasy.

Becca whimpered and tried to force the images from her mind. How naïve she'd been to think she understood Vampire sexuality after witnessing Jody feeding. Jody had taken the blood she needed to survive and given pleasure in payment. Jody had orgasmed, true, but there'd been none of the passion Becca had just seen, if what she'd seen was real. And who could know reality from projected desire with Vampires? Could she believe anything she saw or felt?

Becca picked up the teacup and cradled it in her hands, wishing desperately that the faint warmth would penetrate the terrible chill in her body and melt the icy band around her heart. She'd watched Jody make a woman come in the throes of bloodlust, and she'd never seen a lonelier sight. Why, *why*, couldn't she stop wanting to take away that loneliness?

Sylvan leaned with her back against the huge stone fireplace with Drake resting against her chest and her arms around Drake's middle. She couldn't let her go any farther away. The breeding frenzy that ruled them both surfaced in Drake as relentless estrus, a sexual heat that could only be stanched by an infusion of her mate's *victus*. Heat poured from Drake's body, scorching Sylvan's bare chest and abdomen, literally boiling her blood. Drake's call kept her constantly aroused, forcing blood into her turgid tissues, pumping hormones and sex kinins into her glands. The constant drive to explode between Drake's thighs filled her belly with pain. The absence of physical connection now would rip out her guts. At least with Drake this close she could think. For a few minutes, before the frenzy overtook her reason and she had to have her.

Knowing Drake needed her was pushing her control to the limit. Sylvan rumbled restlessly, scraping Drake's stomach with her partially extruded claws. Her wolf paced in frantic circles, poised between rage and running. Her pelt line was thick and broad, and her skin etched with the ripple of pelt just beneath her skin. Drake whimpered quietly, too quietly for anyone else in the room to hear, and pushed her ass into Sylvan's crotch.

Sylvan kissed her neck. "Soon, mate. Soon."

"I'm all right," Drake said hoarsely. "Take care of Pack business."

"Breeding with you is the most important Pack business I have."

"Does everyone know?"

"Yes." Sylvan kissed her neck again and nuzzled her ear. "Any wolf in breeding frenzy telegraphs their need, but when the Alpha is breeding, the entire Pack feels the call."

"Hell," Drake muttered, sensing the rising agitation in the room. Callan, already in a heightened state because he and his mate were breeding, rumbled steadily, an erection straining against his fly. Val, stoic as always, stood ramrod straight with a trickle of sweat running down her cheek and dripping from the angle of her jaw. Max growled and paced, Andrew worried a spot in the floor with one foot, and Jace and Jonathan, barely out of adolescence and least able to control themselves, lay at Sylvan's feet in pelt, whimpering and occasionally licking her legs. "We're disturbing everyone."

"No. Those in the Compound and closest in the forest will be stirred by our call, but it's no hardship for them. They'll be happy. We celebrate all our young, but especially the Alpha pair's. Our breeding makes the Pack feels secure."

Drake dropped her head against Sylvan's shoulder and sighed. Great. Now her most private experiences belonged to everyone. Everyone depended on her and Sylvan to produce offspring. A few weeks ago she'd been human, with no lover, no family, and no desire for either. Now she was not only an essential part of a huge community, interconnected physically and psychically, she was wed—mated on a true physical level—to the most important member of the Pack. The most important Were in North America. And her body was demanding she contribute in the most fundamental of ways, ways that for her might be impossible. Human females had the biological urge to procreate once a month when the eggs in their ovaries matured. That increase in libido was nothing compared to what she was experiencing—a terrible nonstop pressure deep in her pelvis that consumed her every thought, a pounding, driving need for Sylvan to be over her, inside her, soul deep. She was just this side of crazy. "Do what you have to do. I'll be all right."

Sylvan lightly bit her shoulder. "I love you."

"Work, Sylvan."

"Callan," Sylvan said. "Status of our borders?"

"Six Blackpaws crossed into the far northeast corner of our territory just after dusk last night. My *sentries* challenged, and they turned tail and ran." He sneered. "Mangy cowards."

"Were they hunting?"

"Scouting, it looked like. Niki ordered extra *sentries* posted two days ago. We're secure."

"Good. Take the senior recruits if you need more bodies. Max," Sylvan said, "we need intel from our Pack members working undercover in the rogue ghettos. Find out if there's a price on my head or if the hit was privately sanctioned."

Drake's muscles tensed, and her claws and canines erupted. She'd kill anyone who threatened her mate. Jace and Jonathan crowded closer. Andrew sucked in a breath, and Val twitched.

Sylvan smoothed her palms over Drake's shoulders and down her arms. "You have nothing to fear, Prima."

Drake tilted her head so Sylvan could kiss her neck. "I love you."

"Max"—Sylvan curled her fingers in Drake's hair—"find out if the rogues are organizing. We need to know how they get orders, who leads them, how they're armed. If Bernardo is moving against us, he'll need soldiers." Sylvan tightened her hold on Drake. "His Pack isn't that large. I don't think he'll risk an all-out attack. He'll want to distract us and divide our forces with skirmishes, ambushes like the one on my mother—"

"The Alpha is the logical target," Drake said, focusing on Max. "She'll be most vulnerable in the city. Double her guards."

"Yes, Prima," Max said.

"You think I can't defend myself?" Sylvan whispered. "You want my wolves to think me weak?"

"I think you're my mate, and I'll do what needs to be done to see that you're safe. Live with it."

Sylvan laughed softly. "Remember you said that."

"Alpha," Callan said, "Fala reports an increase in the frequency and size of drug shipments being moved in and out of the city. No one knows who is purchasing it, but a lot of it is getting into the hands of young Weres. Some of them ours."

"Call Fala. I want her input on something else too."

Callan pulled his phone off his belt, pushed a single digit, and spoke in a low voice to his mate. "She just returned from her tour of duty. She'll be right here."

"Until further notice," Sylvan said, "no one leaves the Compound alone. Jace and Jonathan are now the Prima's personal guards."

The young wolves perked up, eyes glistening and tongues lolling.

"Any unmated females currently living outside the Compound need guards. Val, you take care of that."

"Yes, Alpha."

A knock on the meeting-room door sounded and Sylvan called, "Come."

A statuesque brunette in a city police uniform—black pants, knee-high motorcycle boots, and pressed khaki shirt—strode in, her glittering eyes immediately tracking to Callan. Her lips lifted in a seductive smile, and Callan took a step forward, a deep rumble rolling from his chest.

"Fala," Sylvan said sharply, "the quicker we finish, the quicker you can have him." The brunette ducked her head, and Callan settled back where he was.

"I'm sorry, Alpha," Fala said. "You need me?"

"I don't think the rogue attack on Misha was random. She would be the third dominant female involved in an incident in the last two months. Do the police have any reports of attacks on Weres, attempted abductions, anything out of the ordinary?"

"Nothing official." Fala shrugged. "But then not everything makes it into a report, especially not when it involves us. I'll tap my street informants."

"And the female missing from the university? Katya Styles? Her parents don't believe she would disappear, even for an unsanctioned mating. Have you been able to trace her?"

Fala shook her head. "We tracked her scent markings as far as the parking lot outside her dormitory. Then, nothing. It's as if something wiped out her scent."

"That's impossible," Sylvan said. "Even if she got into a car, there ought to be some residual trail."

"Not necessarily," Drake said quietly.

"What do you mean?" Sylvan asked.

"The medical basis for argylosis is probably a chemical binding of the silver ion to certain receptors in Were blood and tissue that inhibits normal cell function. That's why even a small amount of silver is so deadly. A sublethal dose could significantly disrupt multiorgan systems in ways that we don't yet understand. If Katya was poisoned or even cloaked in some way with a silver compound, she might not leave any scent markers behind."

"You mean she could be nearby, and we wouldn't be able to detect her?"

"That's possible, theoretically at least. If I could get into the lab and run some tests—"

"Soon enough," Sylvan grumbled. "What about the adolescent we presumed buried in a rockslide? We still haven't found any remains?"

"No, Alpha," Callan said, "but we don't know exactly where she was. She roamed, like all the adolescents."

"But, Alpha," Max asked quietly, "shouldn't you sense them, if either of them is alive and anywhere in the territory?"

Sylvan snarled, and Drake's skin prickled in response to her mate's aggression. "Sylvan, love, he's not challenging your ability. If something is interfering with Pack bonds on a fundamental level, we need to know."

"I can't feel them," Sylvan said, her frustration turning her words to gravel.

"Which means," Andrew said, despair in his eyes, "Katya and Gray are gone."

"Maybe," Drake said. "But if they're drugged, if they're being slowly poisoned with silver, or shielded with it somehow, even the Alpha's psychic connection might be disrupted."

"If it is possible to break the Pack bonds," Sylvan said, "our entire Pack will be at risk. We cannot allow our enemies to have such knowledge."

"I need to get into the lab," Drake said. "We need to know a lot more about a lot of things. Silver is just one of them." She reached back and stroked Sylvan's face. "You should stay in the Compound until we have a better handle on all of this."

Sylvan laughed. "I head the Praetern Coalition, remember? I need to meet with the committee members, draft resolutions, speak to the media—I can't just disappear."

"Just temporarily—"

"No," Sylvan growled.

Drake spun in Sylvan's arms and drove both hands into Sylvan's hair. She locked eyes with Sylvan and felt the *centuri* converge behind her, encircling them. "You cannot be risked. *We* will not let you put yourself at risk."

Sylvan glanced past Drake's shoulders, then nipped at Drake's lower lip. "You like to take chances, mate."

"Maybe. Maybe I do." Drake kissed Sylvan hard on the mouth. "But not with you. Never with you."

CHAPTER TEN

Gray twisted like a fish on a line as the guards dragged her down the hall on her knees, the six-foot rod attached to the control collar preventing her from shredding them with her claws. She was still too weak to stand up, but what really scared her was losing control of her wolf. Another jolt through the collar and she'd be too weak to hold her back. Her wolf was so hard to control under the best of circumstances, and being chained and beaten and taunted and starved was pushing her to break free—to run or kill. If her wolf won the battle for dominance and she shifted, she was pretty sure she'd surrender completely and go feral. Her wolf would never surrender to a cage, and they'd have to kill her to control her. Hell, maybe that would be for the best. She wouldn't mind tearing out the hearts of a few of these humans before they destroyed her.

At least if they killed her, she would be free, and they couldn't use her to hurt the Pack. She was so damned tired of fighting to hold on to her sanity. Maybe, maybe if Katya hadn't been in here with her, she would have given in to the demands of her wolf long ago. But if she died, who would protect Katya? Who would divert the attention of the guards when they showed up outside their cages with their stun darts? Who would roar and challenge until they all turned on her, not Katya, for their fun? Who would they shoot with the Taser darts over and over again, not enough to render her unconscious, but enough to paralyze her, enough to cause her nervous system to discharge, enough to make her writhe on the rough cement floor while her body twitched and her sex swelled and burst?

Katya would be alone, and total isolation for a wolf, cut off from Pack, was worse than death. Gray stopped struggling and let them pull her toward the torture chamber. She couldn't afford for them to stun her again. She had to stay alive, for Katya.

"That's a nice doggy," Elliot said, his tone a crooning mockery. "You know you're going to like this. Can't hide how good it feels, can you?"

Double solid-steel doors slid opened soundlessly, and she tripped and stumbled into the laboratory, a gleaming white room lit with huge, bright surgical lamps suspended from the ceiling and dominated by a shiny steel restraint chair in the center of the room. They forced her into it and clamped her shock collar to the headrest with locks on either side of her neck. Two guards grabbed her arms, and lab technicians pulled her legs apart, securing her limbs to boards with silver shackles around her wrists and her ankles. Naked, arms and legs spread, she was completely vulnerable. Turning her head as much as she could, she searched for Katya. Naked like her, Katya lay bound to a surgical table across the room. Her eyes were open, but she didn't seem to be conscious.

The smaller blond female was not yet seventeen, two full years younger than Gray, and even though Katya was dominant, she didn't have the warrior traits Gray had inherited from her *sentrie* mother. Katya was brave, and she would fight them, but even at her most aggressive her body didn't produce the same chemicals Gray's did. The chemicals these humans wanted. And the more they shocked and tortured Katya trying to get her to produce them, the closer they drove her to the brink of insanity.

Gray snarled, fury hazing her vision. "What have you done to her?"

A human male wearing a maroon surgical scrub suit appeared in her line of vision, his dark gray eyes roaming over her body. She recognized him as one who didn't seem to enjoy torturing her—he just looked at her as if she were an animal whose sole purpose was to provide him with information.

"She's sedated." He rolled a stainless steel cart, holding a test tube rack with a row of empty vials, Vacutainers, and blood tubes, and several syringes filled with clear liquid, over next to the restraint chair. He asked casually, "Why doesn't she produce the same motor proteins in her ejaculate as you do?"

She wasn't sure what he meant, but she wasn't about to tell him that two females' chemoreceptors naturally adjusted to match the dominance balance between them—at least, she thought that's what she'd learned in school. She hadn't really been listening all that carefully in that class because she wasn't planning on mating anyone for a long time, if ever. She wanted to be a *sentrie* like her mother. The tech swabbed her forearm with alcohol, and she jerked away.

"It won't do you any good to struggle," he said calmly, inserting the needle of one of the syringes into the big vein in the bend of her elbow and plunging the clear fluid into her.

"What is it?" Flame streaked up her arm and she snarled.

"A chemical distillate harvested from your young friend over there." He looked up at her, his expression quizzical. "Why not just stop fighting us? It would be easier if the two of you would just perform for us. It's not as if the sex would be all that unpleasant. Then we wouldn't have to artificially stimulate you to get the samples we need."

"I'll never help you." These humans didn't seem to know that the hormones released from a sex bite would make a female release the *victus* they wanted. When her captors had tried to force her and Katya to tangle by electrically stimulating them into sex frenzy, neither of them would bite the other. Neither of them released completely, and she never would, at least not voluntarily. The fire spread through her chest and down into her abdomen. She couldn't stop her stomach from contracting when the wave of heat surged lower. She didn't want him to know what was happening to her and concentrated on keeping her breathing even. Her canines throbbed, and the tips of her fingers tingled. Her claws would erupt in a second. She felt her clitoris stiffen, and she growled.

The human made rapid entries into an electronic notebook and took pictures of her.

The more she thrashed, the more intense the boiling pressure became. When he probed between her legs with a gloved hand she arched and snarled, her wolf so enraged she felt herself shifting. She wanted to tangle—no, no, she didn't, that was just the drug, just the electrodes pulsing under her skin—but the need was huge, and she heard herself whimper. Humiliation made her wild, and she jerked harder at her restraints. The scent of her blood drifted to her.

"She's ready. Get me the collection vial," she heard him say through the roaring in her head. He fit something cold and hard over her sex. "Start at one-twenty."

The first pulse of electric current shot through her, and her body convulsed. The silver shackles cut into her skin. The throbbing in her glands was so intense she moaned.

"One-fifty." His voice was calm and cool and she wanted to tear his throat out. The second jolt brought her pelvis lurching into the air, and spasms began deep inside her. She thrashed, trying to contain the blood and fluid pumping into her center.

"Turn on the suction in the collection container."

A rhythmic pulsation began in her groin, and Gray whined.

"One-eighty."

Another jolt of electricity shot through her and the pounding in her groin doubled. The suction device worked at her like a cold, mechanical mouth.

She was going to release, going to empty, and oh, *oh*, she wanted to. She couldn't stand it, couldn't fight it, and her canines burst out, her claws tore though her fingertips, and pelt flared on her stomach. The next jolt came and her clitoris pumped, her glands emptied, and she filled their containers with what they wanted. She roared with pleasure while her heart hardened with hatred.

❖

Becca tried not to stare when Francesca appeared on the threshold of the bedroom. She'd thought Francesca was beautiful before. Now she was glorious. Her cheeks were rose-tinged, glowing from within and more splendorous than the sunrise. Beneath her dressing gown—a flowing, silky white affair loosely belted at her waist—her breasts rode full and firm, her nipples a seductive blush beneath the diaphanous material. Michel, the dark knight, appeared in the doorway behind the queen, her black silk shirt open down the front. Her small breasts were hard, her nipples tight stones above her granite abdomen. Her eyes, the clearest, deepest blue Becca had ever seen, glittered feverishly as they followed Francesca across the room.

Becca swallowed. Maybe the Vampire's thrall could alter her perceptions, because she sure wasn't thinking like herself. Sunrises and queens? Not hardly. She wasn't given to whimsy. She didn't look at the world and see dreams come to life. She surrounded herself with facts, with truths. She'd pulled reality around her like a cloak of armor since she'd been young and had learned that only the things she could see and feel and touch were real. Promises were made to be broken. Love was often a lie. Nothing was forever. These Vampires—Francesca, Michel. Jody. They challenged the very foundation on which she'd built her life. Around them, she couldn't trust what she saw, and she sure as hell couldn't trust what she felt.

She knew one thing for sure, though. Michel and Francesca— she hadn't imagined them having sex. She'd *seen* it. First of all, she couldn't have imagined anything quite as erotic. Okay, maybe she could have if sufficiently motivated, but she wasn't in the habit of imagining strangers getting it on. If she let herself go there, she might be able to put herself in that picture with someone, but other than watching Jody have sex, she'd never gotten off on voyeurism. Jody. Why did it always come back to her?

Never mind. She hadn't made that little scene up. One of them, probably Michel, had sent her that image. She glanced from Francesca to Michel, and Michel smiled, a triumphant lift of her sinfully sensuous mouth. Damn her. Becca almost asked if she'd enjoyed taunting her but thought better of it. She wanted to get some information, one small lead, anything, something to help her unravel the puzzle. What she didn't want to do was spend any more time than she needed to with Francesca or Michel or any other Vampire. Not when simply being in the same room with them tied her stomach into knots and made it impossible for her to think of anything except sex. She wondered about the humans in the other room. If they would stay. If they would host again. If they were all right.

Francesca settled into a deep navy armchair across from Becca. "Hosting can be quite exhausting. They'll sleep until this afternoon."

Becca felt her face flame. "It's really not polite to read someone's thoughts when you haven't been invited."

Francesca curled her legs beneath her, the movement causing her robe to part along the length of her thigh. She was nearly naked. "Ah. So you *were* thinking about them. I merely guessed." She extended an arm languorously. "Michel, darling. Join us."

Becca knew she didn't blink, but she still couldn't capture the movement. Michel was beside Francesca before she had the slightest impression that Michel had moved. She didn't believe for a second that Francesca hadn't been reading her mind. Jody had even said at Sylvan's Compound that she could make Becca believe that something she'd experienced had only been a dream. Clearly, Vampiric mind powers were much stronger than anyone knew. Another secret. She'd grown up with secrets. Secrets and lies and emotional violence. The animal part of her brain, deep down below the civilized cortex, screamed danger.

Screamed for her to run far, far away from the very creatures who fascinated her. She forced herself not to move, to keep her expression completely blank. She needed to remember why she was there, and it wasn't to ogle the Vampires.

"The night before last," Becca said, "someone tried to assassinate Sylvan Mir. I was hoping you'd have some information about that."

Michel's slender body vibrated like a fine blade slashing through the air. "Why would we?"

Becca kept her gaze on Francesca. She'd often found that leading off an interview with a provocative statement or accusatory question yielded a telling response. Catching a subject off guard frequently got her closer to the truth. Clearly, that technique wasn't going to work here. The Viceregal appeared relaxed and unperturbed. In fact, she appeared enviably sated and supremely unconcerned.

"The Alpha was visiting Jody Gates at the time," Becca said, glancing for an instant at Michel. "She's the daughter of the U.S. Councilor for Vampire Affairs. I'm sure the Viceregal knows him."

Francesca's brow quirked. "I know all the Vampires in my territory. I'm very fond of Detective Gates, although I don't see as much of her as I might like these days. She's here frequently to entertain a host, of course, but I haven't had the pleasure of sharing one with her for quite some time."

Becca clenched her hands and tried doing multiplication tables in her head. She was not about to let Francesca read her mind, not when she was fuming over the idea of Jody anywhere near Francesca in bed. The idea of Jody pleasuring Francesca was so infuriating her skin itched. "I also understand that the Vampires and the Weres are allies. I doubt there's anything in the entire Eastern territory that happens you don't know about."

"Why should we share any information with you?" Michel said.

"Why would you want to hide something that would garner public sympathy?" Becca sighed. "Assassinating Sylvan Mir would likely disrupt the Coalition."

"Why should we care about the Coalition?" Michel's eyes were hot coals. "Humans do not dictate what we do."

Francesca took Michel's hand and tugged the slender Vampire down onto the broad arm of the chair. She curled her arm around Michel's neck and kissed her, one hand inside her open shirt, caressing her. Becca tried not to stare, but it wasn't as if she could look anywhere else in the room and not see them. Michel kissed Francesca hungrily, her hand cupping Francesca's breast, her thumb slowly stroking the nipple into erection. Becca felt like a voyeur. She *was* a voyeur. Even worse, the display excited her. Just when she was contemplating getting up and leaving the room, Francesca released Michel. She trailed her fingers over Michel's cheek. "Darling, diplomacy is really not your strong suit."

Michel gave a disdainful snort. "You don't keep me for my diplomatic skills."

"No, darling." Francesca caressed Michel's thigh, her fingertips lingering over her crotch. "I keep you because you're so good at what you do."

Michel's eyes flared, and the heat singed Becca's skin. What the hell was in the tea?

"Then let me do my job, Regent," Michel murmured.

Francesca leaned forward and poured tea. Cradling the cup and saucer, she sat back in her chair as if they had been discussing nothing more serious than the weather. She sipped her tea and regarded Becca over the rim. "I don't sit on the Council, as you know. I am acquainted with the Were Alpha. I think highly of her. If there's an alliance between Councilor Gates and Councilor Mir, I'm not privy to it." She took another sip of her tea and set the cup down. Then her gaze intensified, and Becca felt as if a heavy hand lay on her shoulder, holding her in place. She didn't think she could get up even if she wanted to.

"But I will offer you one observation, and you can do with it what you'd like. Not everyone believes that our species should be absorbed into human society. It's entirely possible that Councilor Mir does not represent the popular opinion of the individuals she stands for."

"What about you, Viceregal?" Becca asked, her mouth suddenly dry. "Do you believe in peaceful cohabitation?"

Francesca smiled, her incisors glittering. "I've been living peacefully with humans for centuries. None of the Praetern species could have existed this long without learning to compromise and adapt. But I have no desire to disrupt a peaceful political process."

"Are you trying to tell me that another Were was behind the assassination attempt on Sylvan Mir?"

"My dear, however would I know?" Francesca smiled, her eyes sliding down Becca's body. Becca's nipples tightened, and she had to work not to squirm. "Are you here as an envoy for the Weres?"

"No. I'm a reporter. I don't choose sides. I report facts."

Francesca laughed and Michel grunted.

"That's a wonderful sentiment," Francesca said. "I wish you luck adhering to it."

"One last question," Becca said, figuring she might as well cast her line into the void, because she had nowhere else to go. "Have you heard anything of humans—girls—who've gotten sick? Maybe they were with some of the Weres who frequent the club?"

"Sick. In what way?" Francesca's question was controlled and cool.

"Never mind," Becca said. If the Viceregal didn't know about the deadly fevers, it might be best not to tell her. "You've been very kind. I appreciate your time."

"I'd like you to give the Alpha a message," Francesca said.

Becca had a great deal of practice at hiding her surprise, and she hoped she'd managed it. Michel looked decidedly unhappy. "What would that be?"

"Tell the Alpha she has enemies in several camps. That perhaps she should look to her friends before it's too late."

"Um. Perhaps you could be a little more specific," Becca said. "Somehow, I don't think that message is going to get me very far."

Francesca laughed and her face lost its soft sensuous glow, growing hard and sharp as a dagger unsheathed from a bejeweled case.

Tell Sylvan to remember the days when Vampires and Weres hunted together.

The room grew hazy and Becca's head swam. She grasped the carved wooden arm of the sofa until her stomach slowly settled. She wasn't sure what she'd heard, if she'd heard anything at all. "What? I'm sorry…I…"

"You look tired, my dear." Francesca rose effortlessly and paused in the doorway of her boudoir. "I'll arrange for someone to take you home."

"No!" Becca blushed. "I mean, I have my car. I'm fine."

"Michel will escort you out. The club is likely to be…raucous… for another hour or so. And do send my regards to the Alpha."

Becca so didn't want to walk back into the dark with Michel, but she couldn't think of a way out of it. She squared her shoulders, metaphorically at least, and decided to make the most of the opportunity. As soon as they were in the hall leading to the stairs up to the club, she asked, "What is it that you do exactly? Are you the Viceregal's, ah, consort?"

Michel laughed, and the sound rippled over Becca's skin like a flood of kisses. She knew with absolute certainty she neither liked nor trusted this Vampire, but her body had no such reservations. If she'd been a furnace, the steel would be melting.

"Stop it," Becca said, halting in her tracks. "You can stop it, can't you? I know you can."

"You are either very sensitive or you've been bitten," Michel said conversationally.

"I have *not* been bitten," Becca said. "Wait a minute. You mean once bitten, someone is more receptive to whatever it is you do? To your thrall?"

Michel took Becca's elbow and urged her forward. "Come. If you won't accept a bodyguard, you should not be here now."

Becca couldn't detect anything except genuine concern in the Vampire's tone, but she wasn't idiot enough to trust her. Neither would she dispute the truth of what Michel said. She started walking, but she wasn't about to be sidetracked. "The Risen will have all gone by now, won't they?"

"Yes, but the pre-ans will have waited to feed until the Risen were finished. Whatever hosts remain will be depleted, and the pre-ans will be hungry." She smiled at Becca and her incisors flashed. "Your blood runs thick and warm."

"That is so rude," Becca said.

Michel laughed, and heat coursed along Becca's spine. Not sexual, exactly, but God, she was drawn to her. Excellent practice for the next time she saw Jody. As attractive as Michel was, she wasn't Jody. "Could you just stop with the seduction routine, please. I've seen the show."

"You're either very brave—"

"I've heard that one too." Becca waited while Michel keyed the heavy door at the top of the stairs, then followed her through. The hallway was as dark as it had been before, and she reached out for the wall to orient herself. Michel took her arm again, and she didn't pull away. "Tell me about being bitten. Once you are, does it mean—"

Becca's back was against the wall before she realized she'd been moved. Michel's hands were on her shoulders, and her hips against hers, pinning her. Becca arched into the heat, tilting her head to one side. The fine pinpoints of pain against her throat sent a rush of pleasure scorching through her core. "Oh God."

"Perhaps I should show you," Michel murmured, her mouth moving slowly over Becca's throat. "I'm still hungry."

"Please," Becca whispered, and she didn't know if she meant *please stop* or *please take me*. She was wet, throbbing, her skin prickling as if electrified. She ached, she hungered, she writhed beneath the weight of Michel's power. No. No, God damn it! She would *not* be taken. Not here, not like this. Not with her. She reached for the place deep inside her that had given her the courage to stand up to the father who had discounted her, to the world that ignored her, to all the voices that had said she didn't matter, and pushed that strength into her muscles and her voice. She shoved Michel back. "No."

Michel laughed and caressed Becca's cheek. "You wanted me."

"No," Becca said, hating that her voice shook. Hating that even for a second it had been true. "Compulsion is not desire. Now please, walk me out of here. I've had enough games for one night."

"When you are ready to explore what you really desire, I'll be waiting."

"If desire equals enslavement," Becca said, her voice no longer shaking, "I will never let one of you bite me."

CHAPTER ELEVEN

Drake clasped the back of Sylvan's neck as they left the Council room. As long as she maintained physical contact with Sylvan, the burning pressure in her depths was tolerable. As to how she was going to survive being apart from her, she had no idea. But she had important things to do and couldn't tangle every other minute, as much as she might want to drag Sylvan down and take her every time she looked at her. She wanted to get to the lab. The Revniks might have discovered something in her tissue samples to explain what was happening to her. She wanted to check on Lara and the human in the infirmary. She wanted to stop the god-awful need raging through her system, but most of all, she needed to see that Sylvan was well.

"You're still worrying," Sylvan murmured.

"I'm loving you, not worrying," Drake said, pushing open the great double doors of the Hall.

When Sylvan would have leapt to the ground, Drake stopped her at the top of the stone steps. While they'd been inside, the sun had broken through the clouds over the mountains, a golden saber scattering the fading armies of the dawn. The sky was so crystalline, the air so clear, she scarcely believed the dark violence of the last few days could exist in the face of such beauty. But she had only to remember the bullet wounds in Sylvan's chest to know nothing was safe from hatred and ignorance. "Let's run, Alpha."

Sylvan smiled and wrapped her arm around Drake's waist. "Do you think of me that way?"

The *centuri* and *sentries* streamed around them and down into the yard, drifting far enough away to give them privacy but not letting them out of their sight. Drake rumbled. She'd have thought the guards would at least leave Sylvan in her care while inside the walls of the

Compound. She supposed she'd have to get used to that—never being completely alone with her mate. Part of her resisted, even though she understood the reasons for it. Sylvan was more than her mate, and she would never completely own her. Sylvan owned *her*, but she would always have to share. She rumbled again, and heat poured down her body like liquid fire. Her body demanded she run or mate, but Sylvan needed to heal.

"You're wrong." Sylvan brushed her fingertips over Drake's cheek. "I do belong to you, only to you. In my heart. In the deepest part of me."

"How did you know?" Drake yanked off her sweat-soaked T-shirt and tossed it onto a low wooden bench next to the railing. She flipped open the top button of her jeans, her belly tightening as Sylvan's gaze raked over her chest and down her torso. "Can you read my mind?"

"No, not exactly. But I can feel your thoughts in my head. Not the words exactly, but the sense of them. I know when you question what you mean to me." Sylvan pushed her jeans down. She'd been shirtless all morning and now she was gloriously nude.

Drake's throat went dry and she readied. "You're so beautiful, Sylvan."

"No more than any of my wolves," Sylvan murmured. Silver streamed down the center of her abdomen and pulsed beneath her skin. The claw marks on her flanks and her shoulders still pulsed an angry red. They shouldn't be there. Weres healed at an enormously accelerated rate, but the poison coursing through Sylvan's bloodstream weakened her.

Sylvan was not indestructible. She could have died. Drake's head pounded with fear and fury. The bones in her face slid and thickened. Her canines and fingertips throbbed. Her skin vibrated with the rush of pelt beneath the dermis. "You're about to shift. So am I. It's time, love."

"Can you wait? I scent your need."

Drake smiled and rasped her claws down the center of Sylvan's body, lightly grazing her sex. "Run first. Then we'll tangle."

Sylvan's eyes flashed gold, and she threw her head back and howled, a deep, soul-shaking cry that carried into the forests and struck at the heart of every wolf in the territory. Drake's wolf answered Sylvan's call instantly, and she shifted. She vaulted off the porch a second behind Sylvan's great silver wolf, landing beside her at the far edge of the cleared area. They streaked past the *centuri*, who shimmered in midshift, and plunged into the dense evergreens that grew uninterrupted right up to the borders of the Compound proper. The narrow path through the thick undergrowth glimmered in swaths of gold and black and green. Sunlight angled in broad glittering shafts through the dense canopy. Pine needles and decaying leaves and patches of rich loam cushioned her pads as she loped. Her nostrils filled with the heavy scent of life—moss on the trees, verdant and rich; mushrooms, pungent and sharp; the musk of deer; the gamey odor of fox and bear. Her blood pumped hard, her muscles bunched and stretched, driving her forward. And by her side, Sylvan. Always and only Sylvan.

The air pulsed with Sylvan's unique scent, coating the inside of Drake's mouth, her tongue, her nostrils with the substance that defined her mate. Their hormones meshed and melded—accelerating her heart rate, stimulating her nerve endings, flooding her glands. They were connected, joined, united in body and soul. They ran together, separate bodies, a single heart.

Sylvan brushed against Drake's right shoulder, and a wash of power broke over her. She whined as the urge to mate struck her hard. Sylvan nipped the air in front of her nose, and for the first time since Sylvan had been injured, Drake relaxed. Her mate was healing.

The *centuri* trailed them through the forest, Jace and Jonathan to their left, Max and Andrew to the right. Now, running as wolf, Drake understood in her bones what she'd resented earlier. If she somehow failed to protect the Alpha, the others would be there to take her place. The *centuri*, the *sentries*, the entire Pack, would be certain that nothing happened to Sylvan. With Sylvan secure, the Pack would be safe. As was right. But in this moment, Sylvan was all hers.

Growling, Drake grabbed Sylvan's ruff and shook her. Sylvan lifted her lip, and a deep rumble rose from her chest.

Drake snapped in her face and danced circles around her. *Catch me, mate?*

Sylvan bit at her shoulder, her canines just grazing the muscle. Drake veered away and then rushed back, bumping Sylvan hard, almost throwing her off stride. Sylvan growled and, with a quick twist of her powerful shoulders, clamped her jaws around Drake's muzzle, closing down until Drake whined. Drake panted and stared into Sylvan's glittering eyes. Drake dropped her head, and Sylvan relaxed her grip. Quickly, Drake shook her off and went back to taunting her, running a few paces away, then swiftly swinging back to charge at her, jaws snapping.

Sylvan's eyes glinted, and she lunged at Drake with a full-throated growl, lips pulled back, teeth exposed. Drake vaulted over her and sent her challenge.

If you want me, catch me.

Drake barreled into the underbrush, and Sylvan gave chase. Nose to the ground, heart pounding joyfully, Drake led her mate deeper off the path. Blood hammered in her veins, in her belly, in her loins, and she ran by instinct, drawing her mate to safety in the shelter of the primeval forest.

❖

Marissa moaned and opened her eyes. "Jody?"

Sophia hurried to the side of the stretcher and rested her hand on the human's shoulder. "You're in the Compound infirmary. You're all right."

Marissa's unfocused gaze wavered between confusion and alarm. "Who are you?"

"My name is Sophia Revnik. I'm a Were medic."

"What happened?" Marissa lifted one arm, examining the intravenous line taped to her wrist. "What are you giving me?"

"Just saline. We weren't sure what else you might need."

Elena approached the other side of the stretcher. "Hi, I'm Elena. How do you feel?"

"Tired." Marissa's dark brows drew down. "Otherwise, all right. I've never required any kind of medical attention before. Why did—Jody!" She struggled to sit up. "Is Jody all right? Where is she?"

"She's nearby," Sophia said quickly. "She's being protected. Don't worry."

"What about Lara?" Marissa's eyes widened and her breathing grew short and choppy. "Is Lara with her?"

"Yes. They're both…sleeping, I guess." Sophia glanced at Elena. "We're not really sure what condition they're in right now. We've never had a Vampire here. Or a Were in Lara's situation."

"I need to be with them," Marissa said anxiously. "If Lara awakens, she'll need to feed. Jody will too. She wouldn't let me host for her during the night, and I could see she needed it."

She reached for the IV as if to take it out, but Sophia stopped her. "Your vital signs are still low. You need more fluid. And rest."

Marissa shook her head. "Please. I should be with them. They'll both need me."

Sophia's chest tightened. "Niki is with them."

"Niki?" Marissa looked from Elena to Sophia questioningly. "God, I don't remember much of what happened last night. That's not normal either." She sank back on the stretcher, her face pale and her forehead beaded with sweat. "Niki. I don't know her. I thought I knew all of Jody's blood servants."

"Niki is one of us," Sophia said, trying not to think about what *blood servant* meant. "She volunteered to take care of whatever Jody or Lara might need."

"Weres are very strong," Marissa said, and her voice carried more than a little envy. "The Vampires often prefer them as servants. Jody doesn't usually, but..." She sighed. "Who knows what's happening now that she has Lara to protect."

"Well," Elena said briskly, "you are in no condition to host anyone. Unlike us, you're not going to replenish your blood stores very quickly. You should not host again anytime soon."

"I know. I know, but I'm not sure..." Marissa looked away. "Thank you for all your help."

"Of course." Elena adjusted the IV drip. "Try to get some more sleep."

Marissa sighed. "Yes, but when Jody wakes up—you'll tell me?"

"Of course," Elena said.

Sophia followed Elena to the far side of the room. She folded her arms across her chest, as if that would somehow lessen the ache deep inside. "She seems all right."

"I think she will be," Elena said, "if she doesn't host again right away."

"She seems to want to," Sophia said.

"I'm not sure if she wants to as much as she needs to," Elena said. "Whatever happens when the Vampires feed, it appears to be addicting. At least with humans."

"Yes." Sophia imagined Niki tangling with Lara and Jody. Giving them her blood. A rumble started between her breasts and forced its way through her chest, vibrating in her throat. She quickly turned away, hoping Elena had not noticed. She had no reason to be threatened or angry. Niki had gone with the Vampires willingly, and she'd made the right choice. The entire Pack was in Jody's debt for what she'd done for Lara. Now both Jody and Lara needed care and protection. They needed to feed, and Niki had offered herself. Sophia knew Niki tangled with other females frequently. Why shouldn't she? She was an unmated dominant female and often in the Alpha's company, either running with her or fighting with her. Niki absorbed the Alpha's call even more than the rest of them, and she needed to release. That was only natural.

But this, this was different. The Vampire was not Pack. Sophia couldn't help but think that Niki's offer of her body was driven more by pleasure than duty. Her canines throbbed, and her vision shimmered to wolf. She'd never reacted this way before when she knew Niki was with a female! Breathing hard, she busied herself restocking supplies.

"Why don't you take a break," Elena said.

"I'm all right."

"You're agitated and restless. You're acting like you could use a good tangle."

"Couldn't you?" Sophia laughed shortly. "You must have felt the Alpha's call a little while ago." She rubbed her arms. Her skin was prickling. She usually had very good control over her shifts, just as she could suppress her need to tangle after years of practice. All of her control seemed tenuous today.

"Oh, I felt it." Elena's eyes glinted with humor. "It's a good thing I'm mated or you might be in trouble."

Sophia smiled. "You know very well if you didn't have Roger, you'd be looking for some other male, not to me."

"I wasn't an adolescent all that long ago. I still remember how much fun tussling with some of the females can be." Elena lifted a box of intravenous bags onto the counter and started passing them to Sophia to stack on the overhead shelves. "The Alpha is breeding. We're all going to be frenzied for a while."

"It's only going to get worse the closer we get to moon hunt, if the Prima doesn't conceive. She might not." Sophia's hands shook. Something was wrong with her, something more than the hyperagitated state of the Pack with the Alpha in breeding frenzy.

"So far," Elena said, "there's nothing to mark the Prima as any different from a *regii*. You've seen how fast she shifts. And she can partial shift, just like the Alpha. I sensed her telepathic link as soon as she turned." Elena glanced across the room toward the human on the stretcher. "She's as much Were as any of us. Maybe she will conceive."

"I hope she does," Sophia said softly. "She and the Alpha are mated. It's only natural for them to want offspring."

"That's what all Were mates want. Offspring to strengthen the Pack."

Sophia's throat tightened around tears. "Yes. Every Were wants to give her mate that."

❖

Niki paced the perimeter of the dark room. The Alpha was running, and she wasn't with her. Sylvan's call had pulled her from an uneasy slumber, and now she was edgy and barely able to contain her wolf. Her belly hurt, her sex throbbed, and she wanted to fight. Or fuck. She was the Alpha's *imperator* and leader of the *centuri*. She always ran with the Alpha. Her role, her duty, had been at Sylvan's side since she was born. Sylvan was gathering her wolves to her for the fight that was coming. She was breeding her mate. Niki's body responded instinctively—her blood ran with battle lust and sex frenzy. She needed release. Rumbling steadily, she paced.

"Little Wolf," Jody said quietly. "Lara will sleep until sundown. You don't need to stay."

Snarling, Niki spun around. "What about you, Vampire? You're awake."

"I'm pre-animate. I can't function well during daylight, but I'll rouse if there's danger." Jody, naked except for her unbuttoned, rumpled white shirt, pushed herself up against the wall. Lara lay curled against her side, and Jody threaded her fingers through Lara's hair. "Her system is in shock. Eventually her body will adapt to the solar fluctuations, and she'll be able to protect herself. Right now, she's comatose."

"And helpless."

"No," Jody said, trailing her fingers over Lara's chest. "I'm here to protect her."

"You were so weak a few hours ago you couldn't have protected anyone."

"Yes, but you took care of that, didn't you? With my mouth at your neck."

Niki stalked to the bed, her canines extended. "I could kill you right now if I wanted."

"Could you?" Jody's body was relaxed and her face softer than

Niki had ever seen it. She held out her hand. "That's not what you want, is it?"

A curtain of red shuddered behind Jody's dark eyes, and Niki's nipples tightened. Her pelt line flared and her clitoris erected. The Alpha's call still echoed through her blood, and she panted with need.

"Come to me," Jody murmured, and Niki bounded onto the bed. She straddled Jody's waist, rubbing her center against Jody's stomach. Her guts flamed and she whined softly.

"You taste like the forest, Wolf." Jody pulled Niki's head down and ran her tongue over Niki's mouth, the razor edge of her incisors scoring a line on the inside of Niki's lip. Niki tasted her own blood, and her clitoris pulsed.

"Do it," Niki growled, the pounding in her loins driving her mad. "Do it, Vampire. Drink me."

Jody struck, swift and deep. Niki arched, fire blazing a trail from her throat through her chest and deep into her belly. Jody's hips thrust slowly with each rush of blood through her veins. Niki howled, pain blossomed into a wave of unbearable pleasure, and she released on Jody's stomach.

Jody injected a flood of hormones into Niki's jugular. *Rest now, Wolf.*

Then Niki was running, paws pounding through the forest, the wind in her ruff, the scent of Sylvan in her mouth. Whimpering softly, she surrendered to the Vampire's embrace.

CHAPTER TWELVE

A warm breeze brushed the back of Sylvan's neck. Pine needles cushioned her naked body, and she smelled life teeming in the soil beneath her cheek. Sunlight warmed her hip. She filled her lungs with pure mountain air, and her body pulsed with energy and strength.

The wind on her neck became a kiss. Fingers skimmed her stomach and cupped her breast.

"You're awake." Drake's deep voice was warmer than the sun. The heat of Drake's body curled against her back was as comforting as the sense of Pack she'd carried with her all her life. When she'd been lonely or afraid, she'd drawn the Pack around her like a shield. Now Drake was Pack, Drake was her shield. She quickened, her blood tingling.

"Very awake." Sylvan pushed her ass into the curve of Drake's belly. "Did you sleep?"

Drake rubbed her cheek over Sylvan's shoulder. "A little."

"You could have. The *centuri* would guard us."

"I know." Drake massaged Sylvan's nipple with the pad of her thumb, making Sylvan coil tighter inside. "I like guarding you. I so rarely get the chance."

Sylvan rolled onto her back and settled Drake against her side, circling Drake's shoulders and threading her fingers into Drake's hair. "That's not your job."

Drake propped her chin on her elbow and traced the line of Sylvan's jaw with her fingertip. She kissed her, slicking Sylvan's lower lip with the tip of her tongue. "And what would my job be, Alpha?"

Sylvan grinned. "To bear me many young, to warm my bed, and to—"

With a growl, Drake rolled onto Sylvan, grabbed her wrists, and pinned her arms to the ground. Leaning down, she nipped her chin. "You're going to be disappointed. You should have picked a submissive mate."

Gold splintered through the deep blue of Sylvan's eyes, and a rumble reverberated through her chest. "*You* chose *me*, remember?"

"How so?"

"You bit me first."

"You gave me no choice." Drake slid her tongue deeper into Sylvan's mouth. Sweet pine and cinnamon coated her tongue, the thick tang of ancient forests flooded her senses. Sylvan's strength, Sylvan's essence, filled her mouth, her chest, her core. She slid her thigh between Sylvan's legs, rubbed her breasts over Sylvan's. She was wet, so was Sylvan. Her breasts were tight, her clitoris aching. She wasn't driven by breeding frenzy now. She was driven by pure and simple desire. "I fell in love with you the first time I saw you."

"Did you?" Sylvan arched and flipped Drake over, coming to lie with her hips between Drake's legs. She leaned on her forearms, her sex cradled against Drake's, and kissed her. "The first time I saw you, you challenged me. I wanted to claim you right there in the ER."

"Good thing I bit you, then. You were awfully slow getting around to it." Drake licked Sylvan's throat and nipped at her earlobe. "Of course, no one told me I'd never be rid of you if I did."

Sylvan grinned and rocked her hips, sliding her clitoris over Drake's. Her eyes shimmered, brighter than sunlight. "That's why we guard Pack secrets."

Drake fisted Sylvan's hair and dragged her head down, kissing her again. She was ready for Sylvan, had been ready since she'd held Sylvan while she slept. Sylvan's clitoris pulsed along the length of hers. Sylvan was ready too and was holding back. Letting Drake lead, letting her needs guide them. The longer they kissed, the more the pheromones sheening their skin blended, enclosing them in a cloud of neurostimulants and hormones. Drake's glands pulsed, her claws extruded, her canines dropped. Her sex pounded as Sylvan slowly thrust between her legs.

"I love you," Drake said, her face becoming more angular and stark, her voice roughening. Sylvan licked her mark, the shadow of her bite on Drake's shoulder that would never completely disappear. Drake arched as Sylvan's mouth triggered a surge of erogenous chemicals.

Sylvan whined softly in the back of her throat when Drake's slick heat enclosed her.

Drake smiled. "You like that, don't you, when I hold you inside me."

"More than I love life." Sylvan's chest heaved and her muscles trembled. "Take all of me."

"Soon." Drake drew her hips away, denying Sylvan the breeding lock.

"Don't play with me, Wolf," Sylvan snarled. "I've been patient."

"I know." Drake caressed her face. "I know you have."

"Then let me answer your call. Let me make you come."

"You always do," Drake gasped, her stomach tightening.

Sylvan thrust, her face taking on the fiercely possessive look she got when she was claiming her—the look Drake loved. Too soon, too soon to end.

"Wait!" Drake bucked her hips, rolled Sylvan onto her back, and sat astride Sylvan's hips. Her center settled onto Sylvan's, but Sylvan would not have enough pressure to spend.

"Drake," Sylvan warned, her hips thrusting automatically. "I can't stop now." Her canines flashed. She was already on the path to release. "I need you to bite me."

"Maybe I want slow," Drake panted, her insides an inferno. Her breasts were tight, her nipples puckered and hard. The thin line of midnight pelt bisected her carved abdominals, and her chest and thigh muscles vibrated with tension.

"You're close to release," Sylvan growled. "So am I."

Drake grabbed Sylvan's hands and carried them to her breasts. "I don't want it to be over too soon. God, touch me."

"It doesn't matter how quickly it's over, we can do it again." Sylvan massaged Drake's breasts, flicked her nipples.

Drake's vision shimmered. "Harder."

Sylvan reared up and caught Drake's nipple in her mouth, her arms coming around Drake's waist, trapping Drake in the cradle of her lap. She bit down on Drake's nipple, and Drake arched and whined. Sylvan scraped her claws lightly up and down Drake's back, licking her way from one breast to the other while Drake writhed and thrust against her stomach.

"I need to come," Drake moaned. She thrust her hands into Sylvan's hair, tugging fitfully, and rubbed her breasts over Sylvan's face. Her glands were so full, so tight, her stomach bunched with pain. She couldn't wait any longer. She needed to empty. Sylvan sucked her nipple, and her claws shot out. "Bite me, Sylvan. God. I can't stand it."

"We're not locked," Sylvan groaned. "I shouldn't come yet. Your breeding frenzy…"

"I don't care. I don't care. We'll do it again. Just make me come now."

Sylvan gripped Drake's hair and pulled her chin back to expose her throat. She scraped her canines over the pounding vessels in Drake's neck, and Drake quivered in her arms.

"Please," Drake keened, and Sylvan's control snapped. She bit into the thick muscle in the angle of Drake's shoulder, and Drake exploded in her lap, bucking and groaning, coating her skin with her essence. Sylvan's clitoris pounded and her stomach cramped. Then Drake's mouth was on hers, and Drake's tongue was sliding between her lips, wet and warm and strong. Drake slid her palm down the slick slope of Sylvan's belly and squeezed her sex. When Drake's fingers closed around her clitoris and tugged, Sylvan forgot about breeding, forgot about Pack imperative, forgot everything except the sweet ecstasy of Drake's touch. She released with a roar, flooding Drake's hand.

"God," Drake murmured, sagging into Sylvan's arms. "I love when you do that."

Sylvan clasped Drake tightly and guided her down to the forest floor, their arms and legs entwined. "That was supposed to be inside you." Sylvan gently bit Drake's jaw. "You need me that way, or your mating frenzy won't be quieted."

"I know. Good thing for me you're so potent." Drake grinned. "After all, what good is it being mated to the Alpha if she's only good for one shot? You do have something left, don't you?"

Sylvan snarled, her eyes going completely gold for an instant before she pushed her hips between Drake's legs and slotted her still-erect clitoris into the cleft in Drake's sex. Drake's eyes rolled back, and she clutched Sylvan's shoulders hard enough to draw blood.

"Yes," Drake gasped, feeling herself close around Sylvan. "Now. Fill me now." She held Sylvan's eyes for an instant of perfect union, then buried her canines in Sylvan's chest. Sylvan arched, hips pumping, and surrendered to her mate.

❖

A high-pitched whine woke Becca. She figured out pretty quickly she'd been sleeping, but it took her a few more seconds to figure out where she was. Her bedroom. She got the where part, but not the when. She hated waking up and not knowing if it was early morning or late afternoon. A good bet was morning, because she never took naps. But she couldn't be sure, and a quick look out the window didn't help any. The watery gray sky could have harbingered the arrival of dusk or dawn.

When had she fallen asleep? She hadn't meant to, but two days of little sleep, high stress, and unwelcome sexual arousal had worn her thin. She'd barely managed to finish typing up her notes before she'd collapsed onto the bed in her clothes. Sometime during her unplanned nap she'd obviously roused enough to pull off her pants and her shirt, because she was wearing nothing now but her bra and panties.

The whine came again, and this time she recognized the vibration of her cell phone on the bedside table.

She grabbed the phone and held it up in the semidark. Five thirty p.m. She swiped the green receive call bar. "Hello?"

She got empty air and cleared her throat. She probably sounded like she'd been sleeping under a bridge. "Hello? This is Becca Land."

"Tell the Alpha her missing females aren't gonna last much longer."

Becca shot up in bed, totally alert. "What missing females?"

Asking the caller to identify himself was pointless. She'd received enough anonymous tips in her life to know that. If he—and it was definitely a he this time—wanted her to know his name, he'd say so. And if experience was any indicator, she had about sixty seconds to find out as much about the five critical Ws as she possibly could before he got cold feet and hung up. Who, where, what, when, and if it all possible, why?

"Who are they? What are their names?"

"They won't tell us." The guy's words tumbled over each other, like they were being spewed out of a pressure cooker. He was nervous or scared. "They get numbers, not names. They're not exactly cooperative."

"When was the last time you saw them?" Maybe the anonymous informant had direct contact with the victims, but it was possible he'd only heard about them. If he was only passing on a rumor in the hopes of making a few bucks, the tip was a lot more iffy.

"A few hours ago. Tell Mir she doesn't have much time."

"How many? How many are there?"

"Two that I know of. There could be more somewhere else."

"And they're both still alive?"

"Not for long."

"Who has them?"

"You think they tell the hired help? Just tell Mir to look for them."

"Wait," Becca said, her heart pounding. "Meet with me. Anywhere you say. I'll come alone. I'll pay. You wouldn't be calling me if you didn't want someone to find them. Help me do that. I promise you—"

"No fucking way. I'm risking my ass doing this much. But I didn't sign on to torture anybody, keeping them chained up like animals."

Like animals. Becca felt sick. She sucked in a breath. Focus. Focus. "Where are they? Tell me where to send the Alpha."

"They move them around. They won't be here much longer."

"Where is *here*? Address. Give me a location."

"I can't. I don't even know for sure."

"What do you mean? You must know—"

"Everything is locked down twenty-four hours a day. Guards. Surveillance. All of us...*shit*—"

"Hello? Hello?" The dead silence filled her with cold dread. God damn it. Why her? Sure, her number was listed, but she wasn't the only reporter in the city. Okay, maybe she was one of the few reporters giving more copy space to the Praetern side of the issues than to the rabid human separatist factions, but still, there had to be another reason she was the go-to girl for hot—and exceedingly vague—tips all of a sudden. Frustrated, she pushed *69. Nothing, of course. Blocked call. Most likely a prepay. God, was it really possible someone was kidnapping Weres, and Sylvan didn't know? But why? Why kidnap someone, and then not use them for ransom or political leverage? Why keep it a secret?

I didn't sign on to torture anybody.

Becca's stomach dropped. The only reason to keep kidnap victims in a fortified laboratory would be to study them. Experiment on them, maybe. She didn't want to believe that was possible, but it was her job to consider the horrific, to uncover evil, to expose depravity. She thought of the human girls with Were fever. Was all of this related? Maybe. It seemed plausible.

Becca kicked aside the sheet and swung her legs to the floor. Why call her? Why not call Sylvan? A trap? Maybe. But she wasn't a threat to anyone.

She was used to working with more questions than answers, but one thing was certain. She needed to talk to Sylvan Mir.

❖

Good thing she'd saved the route back from the Compound in her onboard GPS the night before—all she had to do was reverse her course until she reached the spot where she'd stopped and Dasha had found her. Then she waited. Six thirty p.m. A few minutes after sundown. Jody, wherever she was, would be awake. She'd be hungry. Would Marissa be feeding her tonight, or would Jody find some stranger, or several of them, to fill her needs while she fulfilled their fantasies?

"Lost again?" Dasha leaned on the open window frame of Becca's door. She wore the same regulation black BDUs, but tonight she had an automatic rifle slung over her back.

"Don't you get any time off?" Becca's pulse pounded in her throat. She hadn't seen Dasha approach.

Dasha smiled. "What are you doing here, Ms. Land?"

"I came back to see the Alpha." Becca twisted in her seat, and her face ended up only inches from Dasha's. "You didn't have a rifle last night."

"You're observant."

"That's my job. You're expecting armed combat, aren't you? With who? Rival Weres?"

Dasha's brows snapped together and her eyes glinted. "You're walking a dangerous path. Callan was generous, but the *centuri* may not be. You should leave now before you're taken into custody. Even your Vampire Liege will not be able to help you then."

"She's not my Liege."

"I heard her claim blood rights."

"Well, you didn't hear me agree," Becca shot back. It might've been nice if Jody had clued her in on what the hell all of this meant before she made public proclamations. Asking permission would have been nice too. "I need to speak to your Alpha about missing Weres."

"Missing." Dasha's voice dropped dangerously low, gold cascaded through her emerald irises, and a growl reverberated in her throat.

Becca inched back from the window, keeping her gaze steady on Dasha. Somehow she didn't think it would be a good idea to cower when Dasha was on the verge of shifting, although a huge part of her wanted to curl up in a little ball on the front seat and put her arms over her head. "I'll wait here until you can get a message to someone. Preferably Sylvan. She'll want to talk to me."

"Please stay in the car."

Becca surveyed the slowly darkening woods around her. Where exactly would she go? There was no way she could find the Compound by herself. Still, she nodded. "Whatever you say."

A minute passed. Another. Her stomach rumbled. She hadn't remembered to eat. After a quick shower to clear her head, she'd pulled on whatever was handy, which happened to be jeans, a scoop-necked green cotton tee, and plain black low-heeled boots. She'd hurried out with just the essentials she always carried in her purse. She didn't even think she had a PowerBar in the glove compartment. Good thing she wasn't planning on surveillance.

"Come with me, please," Dasha said.

Déjà vu. Becca grabbed her purse. "Why can't I drive in?"

"Your vehicle is not built for the terrain, and we do not allow outsiders to drive in the Compound."

Outsiders. The term stung, no matter how apt. Becca slammed her door and dropped her keys into her bag. "Right. Okay. Back in your chariot, then."

Dasha grinned, but she didn't seem amused. "You're very persistent."

"So I've been told. Among other things."

"You should be more cautious where you go alone. Or more afraid."

Becca gritted her teeth. She was really tired of being warned off. "What exactly do you get out of fostering this Big Bad Wolf façade?"

Dasha held open the door of the Hummer-on-steroids. "Sometimes, a warning works as well as blood."

"Fine. Consider me warned." Becca climbed in and yanked her seat belt across her chest. Jody warned her off to prevent her from giving up her blood. The Weres warned her off so they wouldn't have to shed it. She'd never thought of her blood as so valuable. Maybe she should start. Maybe she'd been missing the most important point all along.

CHAPTER THIRTEEN

Veronica Standish clicked off the scanning electron microscope and slammed closed the notebook next to her right hand. She instantly regretted the small show of frustration but didn't bother to chastise herself since there was no one else in the lab. She never lost her temper and didn't tolerate displays of emotion in those who worked under her. Maintaining the appropriate professional distance was particularly important now that they were working with live subjects. Everyone involved in Project Apex needed to keep the ultimate goal of preserving the integrity of the human species in mind and to remember that any means were justified. Only those who were able to display logical thinking and emotional distance could be trusted to generate reliable data. Unfortunately, none of her dozen project heads were generating data that brought her any closer to the answers she sought. She snatched the wall phone from its place next to the sealed chamber doors and punched in an extension. She tapped her foot, waiting.

"Adam Sullivan."

"In my office. Five minutes. Bring the gel filtration results."

"They're only preliminary. Nothing conclusive."

"I'll make my own determination." She hung up without bothering to say good-bye. Why waste words by stating the obvious?

She pressurized the airlock isolating the Level 4 lab and adjoining holding cells from the rest of the building and stepped into the control chamber. She stripped off the heavy green cover gown, shoe covers, and cap and tossed everything into a biohazard bag. After she retrieved her burgundy suit jacket from the peg she'd hung it on earlier, she reversed the pressure and let herself out into the adjoining hallway. She waited a few seconds until the door clicked closed, assured herself the computerized locks had engaged, and headed down the dim hallway to her office.

Most of the other rooms along the corridor were dark, the technicians and scientists having left hours previously. She glanced at her watch. Precisely 1900. Early yet. Her office at the end of the hall was the largest on the floor, but seemed smaller due to the overflowing bookcases and the huge partner's desk crowded with folders, journals, and stacks of printouts. She walked to the window and watched the headlights streak by on the distant highway to the west. The mountains surrounding the sprawling complex rose like forbidding shadows against the horizon.

Somewhere out there right now, hundreds of Weres hunted, mated, and bred. They'd been doing it for centuries. How had the human race let that happen? How could they have been blind to the presence of soulless predators in their midst? In their arrogance, the Praeterns had made a fatal mistake. In attempting to secure the future of their species by negotiating for the same rights as humans, by declaring their right to exist simply by existing, they had surrendered their greatest weapon. Invisibility. Now she and others like her around the world could right the wrong that had gone unattended for millennia.

The Weres were the greatest danger to human civilization of all the Ptaeterns—largest in number, well organized, and with a charismatic and intelligent leader. Sylvan Mir was a formidable adversary, but ultimately, she was still just an animal. The newspaper photograph of her losing control in a hospital ER showed just how different she really was. Ultimately, no one would complain about containing and controlling—or eliminating—a dangerous predator, any more than they complained about shooting rabid dogs. Oh, the other Praeterns were of concern, but their numbers were smaller and their reproductive capabilities even more limited.

She laughed, tracing a line through the condensation left by her breath on the window. Evolutionary mistakes happened all the time. As a result, some species were destined for extinction, and rightly so. The Praeterns had escaped the natural order of things through a perversion of biology.

Their unique adaptive reproductive capabilities had allowed the Praeterns to survive, but the limitations of the process would also be their downfall. Come to think of it, considering that some of them were actually dead already, *reproduction* might be a scientifically inaccurate term. The idea that Vampires could actually *have* offspring was ludicrous, but somehow they managed to find humans willing to provide biological material. The idea disgusted her. Any human male or female who squandered their genetic legacy to enable a Vampire to pass on their affliction should be imprisoned. That Vampires could somehow compel humans to host for them was reason enough to destroy them, but to seduce humans into creating more monsters? She had no doubt other humans would ultimately agree and exterminate the Vampires. If not, the armed divisions of her organization would see to their eradication.

The Weres, though, they offered a far greater challenge. Unlike the Vampires, who were usually solitary or loosely organized into families and ruled by a Clan sovereign, the Weres were well organized, well armed, and ferociously aggressive. Those traits combined with their longevity made them very, very dangerous. They needed to be subjugated, but they wouldn't be easy to control or eradicate.

Hence Project Apex. Her master plan. The first order of business in controlling any species in danger of becoming a major evolutionary threat was to understand how they bred and then to neutralize their reproductive capability. Sterilize the females first, then contain the remaining population, and if control wasn't possible, exterminate them. A logical algorithm for dealing with aberrant species that threatened the natural order.

A knock sounded behind her followed by a male voice. "Dr. Standish? You wanted to see me?"

Veronica turned from the window and studied the sandy-haired man in a maroon scrub suit standing in the doorway of her office. He had been one of her first recruits when she'd accepted the position as head of Project Apex shortly after the Exodus had informed the world of the presence of mutant species. Recruiting scientists to study new species at a biochemical and subcellular level hadn't been difficult. She hadn't told them of the ultimate goal, and she was careful that none of her project heads worked on anything other than a small piece of the project. None of them knew enough to jeopardize the project if they defected or were compromised.

"Adam," she said, indicating a visitor's chair in front of the wide desk. She casually moved away from the window and rested her hip against the edge of the desk. With him sitting, she was looking down on him. Gold stubble glinted on his jaw and purplish shadows deepened the hollow crescents beneath his eyes, making him look older than the thirty-six years listed on his résumé. They were the same age, but her olive skin and dark hair and eyes, compliments of her Greek mother, hid the ordinary signs of fatigue. Or would have, if she was tired. But she wasn't. Work invigorated her. The cause filled her life with purpose. And right now, she needed more ammunition for the coming fight. "I just looked at the cell cultures. Everything is dead. The cell membranes are disintegrating. We've got to have better preparations."

"I don't think it's the preparations." Adam scrubbed a hand over his face. "None of the standard culture mediums support growth, and we haven't been able to determine exactly what is missing."

"How much difference can there be?"

He laughed bitterly. "Far more than we anticipated, and we're picking up more variations at a subcellular level every day. We need more subjects."

"With their muscle mass, you should have plenty of tissue for biopsy." She wasn't about to tell him she'd been demanding more test subjects for months to no avail. She accepted that procuring live specimens was difficult, considering how treacherous the Weres were and how difficult it was to separate them from the Pack. She'd argued that capturing grizzly bears and killer whales was also risky and difficult, but big-game hunters managed it. Surely trained soldiers could do it. She'd been promised two more females in reproductive prime for her selective breeding experiments. She was still waiting. "How are you doing with sequencing the motor protein in the ejaculate?"

"We're still running samples through the high-pressure liquid chromatograph. The problem is, the chemical mix changes all the time. We can't isolate a predominant neurotransmitter." He passed her the histograms of the most recent gel filtration runs and shook his head. "Besides the complex chemical mix, degradation is extremely rapid. That's probably one reason why their reproductive rates are low."

"Which is offset by their excessive sex drive and unusual potency." Veronica took a slow breath, suppressing the swell of rage that simmered between her breasts and tightened her nipples. "You have two prime subjects. Surely you have enough test material. How often are you collecting?"

"Every three days on average. The process is physiologically traumatic—"

"Adam—no one dies from forced ejaculation. Animal breeders do it every day."

"It's possible the hormonal stimulants we're using to induce production of the specimen are altering the chemical balance of the ejaculate. We know that not every sexual encounter between Weres results in glandular secretions capable of inducing reproduction. Maybe something else triggers the appropriate chemical dispersion."

"Then induce intercourse. Let me repeat—animal breeders do it all the time when artificial insemination is unsatisfactory or they aren't able to collect appropriate specimens. Get them stimulated, and get them to fuck."

He sighed and shifted in his chair. "We've tried that. They're very resistant—"

"I don't want to hear excuses, Adam. I want results. Step up the collections, and run the HPLC continuously until you isolate the primary initiator. I want the reproductive cascade sequenced." What she didn't tell him was that she couldn't begin to produce an immunoglobulin that would act as a chemical sterilizer in the Weres until she had a specific protein to use as a template. She could try a shotgun approach with a mixed antibody, but the chance of killing the Were and not just sterilizing her was higher. Of course, if she had a ready supply of subjects, she wouldn't be as concerned about that. "I'll expect you to deliver something usable within the next week. Don't disappoint me."

"I'll do everything I can to see that I don't."

She smiled, eased off the desk, and braced her hands on the arms of his chair. "I'm sure you will more than satisfy."

His green eyes glazed as she kissed him. Nothing blunted her frustration and restored clarity of thinking like a quick, hard orgasm, and after she judged him more than ready to provide one, she straightened and opened the button on her pants. "You can start now."

The gold wedding band on his left hand glinted as he opened his fly and drew himself out. She'd already pushed her pants off and straddled him quickly, taking him all the way inside with one long slide. He groaned, and she kissed him again, mostly to silence him. She had one purpose, to come. She wasn't concerned with his pleasure, although her very disinterest seemed to be what kept him always available. She couldn't be bothered analyzing why that might be. She rode him in fast hard strokes, one hand braced on his shoulder, the other manipulating her clitoris. She jerked back as the first intense contraction jolted through her pelvis and her vision blurred. *Ah God.*

A wave of heat followed the first crush of pleasure and she bit her lip to stifle a groan. She peaked again, her thighs trembling, and distantly registered Adam had climaxed. She worked herself on his erection until the spasms inside her subsided and then she pushed off him, using the tail of his scrub shirt to blot herself dry.

"Schedule your next simulation for tomorrow at eleven. I want to observe." She pulled on her pants, tucked in her shirt, and tidied herself. "I'd like fresh coffee too."

She didn't wait for him to fumble himself together and let himself out, but left her office through the rear door into the utility hallway that circled the core of the building. She punched in the security code on the pad next to the windowless metal doors, noting her hands were steady. She smiled, doubting Adam's were. The overhead lights cast a thin, sickly yellow glow over the flat gray walls as her footsteps echoed hollowly on the dingy tile floor. She stopped in front of the first cell and regarded the subject chained against the wall.

"If you care about your Packmate, you'll cooperate with us tomorrow. We're more likely to get what we need if you provide the samples voluntarily, and then we can let you both go." Veronica ran her finger up and down the silver-impregnated steel bar. Her clitoris still throbbed pleasantly. "After all, it's just sex, and there's nothing special about that for you, is there?"

❖

"You can open the windows," Jody said. "The sun is low enough now."

Niki didn't answer but pushed up the glass and released the outside shutters. She leaned against the window frame and breathed deeply, her back to the room.

"Stay with Lara." Jody rose and buttoned her shirt. "I want to check on Marissa."

"Won't Lara wake soon?" Niki asked without turning around. "You're up already."

Jody walked over to the window. "She won't respond instantly to the change in UV levels until she has adjusted to her turning. I will feel her when she begins to wake and return before she is fully aware. Until then, I don't want to leave her unguarded."

"She is safe in the Compound."

"I'm not worried about anyone attacking *her*. When she emerges, she won't be lucid. She won't know where she is. All she'll know is hunger. Your blood is strong. She is still sated, but she will need replenishment soon."

"How long is this going to last?" Niki said. "This mindless hunger you've created in her?"

"I don't know."

Niki snarled. "How can you not know? You must have seen hundreds of turned humans and Weres."

Jody laughed. "Not nearly as many as you think, Wolf. First of all, I'm not that old. Secondly, we turn far fewer than legend suggests. Our food supplies are not endless, and we live…" She laughed again, the bitterness welling in her chest. "Let's just say we live a long time. There are reasons, I suppose, it is so difficult for us to create offspring."

"All predators have small litters."

Jody didn't see the distaste in Niki's eyes she was used to whenever the subject of Vampires reproducing arose. "You don't find it unnatural for us to want what every other species has? Progeny to carry on our species? Offspring to carry on our heritage?"

Niki turned away, her face feral and hard. "I don't usually concern myself with Vampires. I only care about the Pack."

"Not necessarily a bad thing," Jody said softly. "Although I'm afraid we must all become concerned about other species than our own, or we may find ourselves standing alone."

Niki shot her a surprised look. "You believe the humans will rise against us?"

"I think they may have already. Maybe not just the humans." Jody sighed. "I'm not sure. But I'm uneasy about the attempt on your Alpha. If she had died—"

Niki's face morphed and her canines dropped. She snarled, her eyes wide and wild.

"Easy, Wolf." Jody brushed her palm over Niki's chest, Niki shuddered, and sanity returned to her eyes.

"How do you do that?" Niki demanded. "How can you do that to me when we have no bond?"

"We have a bond, little Wolf. For a while, your blood fills my body and my essence runs in yours. It's not the mate bond you experience with another Were, but a blood bond nearly as powerful."

"I don't want it, I never asked for it," Niki roared.

Jody shrugged. "There is no way to stop it from happening when I feed. I could draw blood, yes, without creating any kind of bond. But once I feed? Then we are joined."

"Even now, I hunger for you," Niki said, sounding desolate.

"I know." Jody was careful who she chose for blood servants and how frequently she used them. Some hosts came to desire more than just the erotic satisfaction induced by feeding, developing such an acute addiction to the erotostimulants Vampires secreted that they would literally go insane without it. She didn't know where on the spectrum Niki fell, and she wasn't going to find out. "I don't plan on feeding from you again. As the hormones in your system dissipate, the bond will diminish."

"What about Lara?" Niki asked.

"She'll need to feed as soon as she awakens. If Marissa can't host, we should find another Were who is willing."

"I will feed her." Niki thumped her chest. "She will not suffer."

"No, she won't. Once I get her into the city, she will have ample opportunity to feed. I have blood servants who will see to her needs later tonight. Tomorrow, when she is not quite so mindless, I will teach her to hunt."

Niki scraped her claws down the wall, leaving gouges in the roughhewn wood. "She *knows* how to hunt. She is *centuri*. One of our strongest, one of our best."

"I know what she *was*. But now she is Vampire, and she must learn another kind of hunt or I will be forced to destroy her."

"Harm her, and I will kill you," Niki said.

"You could try, little Wolf. You could try." Jody ached for Niki's blood with the same relentless fervor that drove the Were to give it to her. But she would wait. She had to wait. She couldn't risk Niki becoming a thrall.

And now, her senses registered another reason to wait, one even more compelling.

She let her mind stretch out beyond the confines of the Compound. The beat of a human heart pulsed in her head and echoed through her body. Bloodlust burned in her core. She would be forced to feed soon, but first, she would see Becca.

CHAPTER FOURTEEN

Becca sighed inwardly as the tall stockade gates closed behind them. Dasha parked the vehicle in a turnaround in front of the central building. The Compound was even more crowded than it had been before dawn that morning. Pairs and groups of uniformed *sentries* crisscrossed the courtyard between the buildings. In the flat white light cast by the security lights, everyone looked youthful and in fighting form. Becca doubted they were all as young as they appeared, but she'd never actually seen a Were who appeared even middle-aged, let alone elderly. It really wasn't fair for a species to have both longevity and beauty, and now that she thought of it, all the Praeterns had those qualities. Maybe humans were just jealous.

"Sylvan is here, isn't she?" Becca asked. She'd made it through the door. One hurdle down, about ten to go. Relaying the information she'd gotten from her anonymous caller was only part of her agenda. She didn't intend to be used as a go-between—a passive conduit to funnel information that someone wanted Sylvan or someone else to know. She wanted to be part of the investigation. She was going to have to bargain, and she had probably sixty seconds to figure out how to bargain with a Were. And not just any Were. The Alpha.

"A word of advice," Dasha said.

Becca grasped the handle of the door, waiting. "I'd appreciate it. Thank you."

"If you want to see the Alpha, come as a friend. Not as a reporter."

"I am a reporter, but if I wasn't also a friend I would have run with the story I already have. Believe me, it's big news."

Dasha studied her for so long, Becca wondered if the lieutenant could read her mind. She didn't think Weres had that capability, but the more she was around the Praeterns, the more she realized she didn't know. And boy, that really frustrated her. A trickle of sweat dripped down her neck, but she waited while Dasha sat with such stillness she might have been a statue.

"Wait for me," Dasha said, jumping out of the truck. She skirted quickly around the front, opened Becca's door, and cupped Becca's elbow. "I'll take you inside. Stay close."

They hadn't even reached the stairs when Callan appeared on the porch, blocking their way with his legs spread and his thick arms crossed over his broad chest.

"I've allowed you this far," Callan said, "because you said you had information about some of our Weres. If you're lying—"

"I'm not," Becca said. "What I have to say, I want to say to your Alpha. She knows me. Tell her I'm here. Please."

Callan shot Dasha an angry look. "You stand for her now?"

"I stand for Pack, just like always. But it should be the Alpha's decision to hear her or not."

Callan growled, his features darkening as his gaze locked on Dasha's. The aggression pouring from them was so thick Becca's skin tingled.

"Look," Becca said sharply, trying to get them to look at her and not each other for a few seconds. "I didn't come here to start a fight. Can we try being on the same side for a while?"

"It's been a difficult few days," a lithe blonde with a voice as melodic as a symphony announced as she crossed the Compound to them. The female stepped between Dasha and Callan, as if she actually thought her slender body would provide some deterrent if the two of them decided to tear into each other.

Oh, this was getting worse by the second. She'd be persona non grata if her very presence started a rumble between Pack members. "Don't you have some sort of protocol for getting a simple message to Sylvan?"

The blonde smiled but kept her eyes on Callan and wrapped her delicate fingers around Dasha's forearm. "Lieutenant, you don't want to challenge him." Her voice was light, almost cajoling. "You know how unreasonable breeding mates can be about everything."

Callan snarled. "That has nothing to do with it."

"Doesn't it?" The blonde laughed softly. "I bet half the reason you're snarling right now is Fala is calling you."

His mouth flickered, his expression fluctuating between pride and nervousness. "Her heat is more intense this time. We've tried before and…"

He looked away from Dasha, and the lieutenant stopped snarling.

The blonde tilted her head toward the barracks. "Go find your mate, Callan. Dasha has this under control."

"Lieutenant?" Callan addressed Dasha but didn't lock eyes.

"I will stay with Ms. Land until the Alpha decides to see her, or not. I'll be personally responsible for her as long as she is within our borders. Sir."

"I'll inform the Alpha she's here." He nodded abruptly, spun on his heel, and stalked away.

"Cranky, isn't he?" Becca muttered.

Dasha laughed. "His mate is in heat."

"You'd think that would make him happy." Becca held her hand out to the blonde. "Thank you. Are you the official peacekeeper?"

"I'm Sophia Revnik, one of the Were medics." She shook Becca's hand. "The Alpha is not in the Compound at the moment. I don't know how long she'll be."

"I'm happy to wait."

Sophia turned to Dasha. "Don't leave her alone. It's after sundown. I'll be in the infirmary checking on our visitors."

"Jody?" Becca asked. "Is Jody still here?"

Sophia regarded her with surprise. "You know her."

"I wouldn't say that," Becca said wryly, "but we're acquainted. I'd like to speak to her. Detective Gates and I are working together on the investigation." Okay, maybe that was spinning the truth a little, but she wanted to see Jody, and this beat sitting in front of Jody's house all night.

"All right. I'll take you over, although I don't know if she's able to leave…"

"I know what happened to the Alpha's guard."

"You know quite a lot, it seems." Sophia's tone was curious, not critical.

Not enough. Becca smiled. "Thanks for the help."

"Dasha," Sophia said, "if you want to come—"

"Where she goes, I go," Dasha said, her voice deeper and more gravelly than it had been moments before. Her skin glimmered as if she were drenched in sweat all of a sudden, but the night was cool. Her eyes glittered strangely as her gaze swept over Sophia. "The Alpha ran tonight."

"I know." Sophia took an unsteady step back. "Dasha—"

"If you're looking for Val or the *centuri*…maybe Niki—"

"No," Sophia said quickly. "None of them."

Becca was usually good at deciphering unspoken conversations, but whatever messages they were sending, they weren't verbal. She could have sworn Sophia was purring—no, not purring, rumbling very quietly. And her rapid breathing was unmistakable. Dasha's jaw was so tight she was going to crack a tooth. Holy hell, these two were seconds from jumping each other!

"Ah, you mentioned taking me to Jody?" Becca said, surprised at how dry her throat was.

"Yes," Sophia said, her eyes still on Dasha.

"Great," Becca said. Just great. Dasha's canines were definitely longer. And Sophia's eyes were gold now.

"Right this way." Sophia turned away abruptly. "They're in here."

Becca hurried to keep up with Sophia's long, swift strides. God, whatever was stirring everyone up around here had better not be catching.

❖

"How are you feeling?" Jody stroked damp strands of Marissa's dark hair away from her pale cheeks.

Marissa grasped her wrist, smiling weakly. "I've felt better, but I'm all right."

"I'm sorry. I let things go on too long."

"No, you didn't." Marissa entwined her fingers with Jody's. "I wanted to be with her. I wanted to be with *you* too."

Jody smiled. "I always knew you were ambitious."

Marissa laughed, her eyes still deeply shadowed, but clear. "How do you think I got to be chief medical examiner?"

"Not by letting someone nearly bleed you dry," Jody said bitterly. She should have seen how powerful Lara had become. Unlike most newly turned, Lara had the strength to match her urges, and she'd fed like a fully Risen Vampire but without the same control. She was all the more dangerous in her mindless state.

"But you didn't let me die, did you." Marissa looked across the room to Elena. "Would you please tell this one that I'm fine?"

Elena set aside the chart in which she'd been recording lab results.

"She's anemic, but you'd know that. Her blood pressure and pulse are fine. She needs heme stimulants, iron supplements, and probably a few days' rest. But she's quite stable."

"Good." Jody caressed Marissa's face. "I don't have to tell you not to host again for several weeks, do I?"

"Several weeks!" Marissa sat up suddenly, her eyes widening then blurring out of focus. "Oh."

"Damn it." Jody caught Marissa as she slumped sideways and cradled her against her chest. Behind her, the door opened, and her senses sharpened. Becca.

"At *least* two weeks." Carefully, Jody laid Marissa back down and drew the sheet up over her bare breasts.

Marissa's eyelids fluttered, and she mumbled, "Too long. Too long to go without. Without you."

Jody turned, knowing Becca was watching, expecting censure. Even the most supportive humans became uncomfortable when faced with the reality of Vampire survival. Ordinarily, she didn't concern herself with human opinion, but she couldn't so easily relegate Becca to the faceless, nameless masses. She hadn't planned on the swift kick of pleasure at seeing Becca's smile.

"How are you?" Becca said softly.

"I'm surprised they let you back in." Jody nodded a greeting to Sophia, who edged around Becca and crossed the room to join Elena at the workstation.

Becca shrugged. "I'm persuasive."

"Among other things." Jody grasped Becca's elbow and drew her outside into the hall. "What are you doing here?"

"Working." Becca ruthlessly expunged the image of Jody tenderly stroking Marissa. Jody looked worse than she had that morning. She was always pale, but Becca was starting to distinguish what was a healthy pallor and what wasn't. When Jody hadn't fed, she developed a tightness around her eyes and mouth, as if her skin adhered more tightly to the bone. As if her substance were contracting, pulling in on itself. As if she were dying. Becca's heart clenched. She knew if she touched Jody now, she'd be cold. "What are *you* doing?"

Jody frowned. "What are you talking about?"

"You need to feed again. You've been here for two days. Who's been—" Becca glanced into the treatment room. Marissa appeared to be asleep. She was bone white, her neck riddled with jagged bite marks and deep purple bruises. "You didn't—"

"No," Jody said quickly. "Lara is voracious, and Marissa is insistent. I let Marissa host for Lara one time too many."

"But she didn't feed you."

"I'm all right." Jody's eyes were flat, unreadable.

Becca knew what that meant. Someone else had given Jody what she needed. A swift spear of jealousy cut through her, and she impatiently brushed the feeling aside. "Well, whoever it was didn't give you enough. You still need—"

An earsplitting roar shook the air, and the floor vibrated beneath Becca's feet, as if someone had dropped a huge weight from a great height. Another crash was followed by a wild cacophony of growls and snarls. The closed door to the room opposite where they stood shuddered as if a battering ram had struck it from the other side.

Jody grasped Becca's arms and pushed her toward the open doorway of the treatment room. "Get inside with Marissa and the others. Lock the door and don't come out, no matter what you hear, until I—"

Another deep-throated, enraged growl shot through the air, and the heavy wooden door across the hall splintered with a resounding crack. Wood fragments flew everywhere.

Jody grabbed Becca, threw her against the wall, and covered her with her body. Becca stifled a scream, more surprised than afraid. Her back was against the wall, her face pillowed against Jody's neck. Jody's throat was soft and cool, but she was very much alive. Absurd to register that now, when her heart was pounding so loud in her ears she could barely think.

Jody jerked and grunted as if surprised.

"What—" Becca exclaimed.

"No questions," Jody snapped.

"Hey!" Becca was lifted into the air, spun around, and deposited bodily in the doorway of the treatment room. Sophia and Elena had pushed Marissa's stretcher into the far corner and were crouched in front of it.

"Inside. Close the door," Jody ordered and turned toward the commotion in the hall.

"Oh my God." Becca stared at the foot-long jagged chunk of wood, easily two inches thick, that protruded from Jody's back between her left shoulder blade and her spine. Jody's white shirt was already soaked in blood so dark it looked black. Becca's throat closed, and her stomach threatened to revolt. She took a step down the hall after her. "Jody!"

Jody spared her one furious glance. "Get inside with the others."

But Becca couldn't. She couldn't run and she couldn't hide. Running and hiding was a victim's solution. She'd learned never to run. The punishment never stopped until you proved you couldn't be hurt, until you proved you were stronger than any ammunition used against you. Even if every instinct *hadn't* demanded she stand her ground, she couldn't have escaped to safety while Jody was wounded. Because of her.

Sophia appeared beside her and grasped Becca's arm. "Go back inside. I'll watch the door."

"No." Becca reached around Sophia and yanked the door shut, closing Marissa and Elena inside. She put her shoulder against Sophia's and stood guard in the hall. "We'll both watch it."

The crashing in the room opposite continued, as if bodies were careening against the walls. Suddenly Lara bounded into the center of the hallway and crouched on all fours, her eyes flaming pools of fire, her incisors dripping blood. Her bare chest and abdomen were awash in crimson.

Becca's heart leapt into her throat, but before Lara could strike, Jody materialized and blocked Lara's path. Jody's back was to Becca, and the horrible stake was still there, an obscenity Becca wanted to pull out with her own hands. She didn't dare move, didn't dare try to help, afraid she would only draw Lara's attention and precipitate a battle.

"No more," Jody said to Lara. "You'll not feed again until I say you will." Lara's hot gaze swung from Jody to Sophia and Becca. Her lips pulled back and she snarled.

Niki staggered out of the room where Lara had been kept, her chest and shoulders covered with teeth and claw marks. At the far end of the building the front doors flew open, and Dasha raced toward them.

"Her," Lara growled, her ravenous gaze locked on to Sophia as she stalked slowly forward. "Her."

"Lara, no," Sophia shouted. "Lara, it's Sophia. Lara. You don't—"

Lara vaulted onto the wall and seemed to run up the vertical surface, careening out of Jody's reach, and lunged at Sophia. Dasha and Niki, racing from opposite directions, launched themselves at Lara and dragged her to the floor. The three Weres tumbled in a mass of writhing limbs, slashing claws, and flashing teeth.

Lara whipped her head around, slashing Dasha's chest and left shoulder with her canines. Dasha roared and her grip loosened. Lara pulled her arm free and smashed Niki in the chest hard enough to catapult her against the wall. Niki's body struck so hard the wood cracked, and she fell to the floor, stunned.

"Get behind me. Don't move," Sophia ordered, pushing Becca against the wall and crowding close against her front, shielding her.

Becca's legs turned to jelly. Lara was loose again and would be on them in a second. She readied herself for the agony she knew was coming, but the pain never arrived.

Jody, a slender, dark blur, caught Lara by the throat and threw her twenty feet down the hall. Suddenly, the hallway was filled with Weres—Niki, Dasha, Sylvan, Drake, a pair of blond Weres Becca had never seen before. She scarcely took note of the Weres; her attention was riveted to Jody. God, she was still bleeding so much. Her shirt and the back of her pants were drenched.

"Get back in the room," Jody said, advancing on Lara who crouched on all fours, wild and insane. "Do it now."

"No," Lara snarled, her gaze cutting to where Sophia blocked the closed door to the treatment room. "I want her. I want her. I smell her. She's ready."

"No," Dasha shouted and stepped in front of Sophia.

Jody's gaze on Lara intensified. "You'll feed from no one until I say you will. Do as I say, or you die tonight."

Lara charged, and Becca's heart dropped to her toes. Jody was no match for a wild out-of-control Were, even if she hadn't been hurt. Lara was taller, heavier, and insanely strong. *Oh God, please, please don't let Lara kill her.*

Lara leapt, claws extended, jaws wide, aiming for Jody's jugular. Inches from burying her fangs in Jody's throat, she stiffened in midair, her forward progress halted so abruptly her body vibrated. Jody shot out her right arm, caught Lara by the throat, and pinned her to the wall. Lara's face darkened and her eyes bulged. Her arms and legs convulsed, pinwheeling impotently in empty air.

"Yield to me now, newling," Jody said, her voice as flat and hard as tempered steel. "Yield to me now, or you die."

Sylvan roared. "You will not kill my wolf."

"She is mine now." Jody didn't move, didn't even look at Sylvan, but Lara shuddered as if she'd been violently shaken. "I will do as I like."

Becca swallowed, half-amazed, half-terrified. Jody was hurt and bleeding, but still she held Lara off the floor with one arm. How strong *was* Jody, and how much more had she been hiding?

Sylvan pushed through the crowd of snarling Weres until she was inches from Jody. "Kill her, Vampire, and *you* will die with her."

"Time out," Becca called, pushing out from behind Sophia and inching down the hallway toward Jody and Sylvan. "Everybody needs a time out right now. You've got bigger things to worry about than Lara's adolescent rebellion."

Neither Jody or Sylvan gave any indication they heard her. The air around them was hot enough to ignite at any second. She turned to Drake. "Can't you do something?"

Drake shook her head. "No. This is between the Alpha and the Vampire."

"This is crazy. Lara's under control now."

Sophia slipped her arm around Becca's shoulders. "The Vampire is in the Alpha's territory. There can be only one leader here."

"I don't care. I don't care about territory or ego or whose dick is bigger—"

"It's not about that," Sophia said quietly. "It's about order. It's about survival. You understand those things, don't you?"

"No. Not like this." All she knew was Jody had a wooden stake the size of a hammer handle sticking out of her back, she was bleeding all over the floor, and Sylvan Mir was about to tear her throat out. She'd never been so scared in all her goddamn life. She was helpless, and she hated it.

"Vampire," Sylvan said, "do you want to make this our fight tonight?"

"You can't control her," Jody said. "If you try, she will kill your wolves."

"Then you do what you must do to control her. But you do not kill her."

Jody shot Sylvan a look filled with disdain. "Your soft heart will be your death someday, Wolf."

Drake growled and bounded to Sylvan's side. "Be careful what you say about my mate."

Sylvan cupped the back of Drake's neck. "It's all right, Prima. Our Vampire friend is just frustrated."

Jody half-smiled, her crimson gaze returning to Lara, who hung limply in her grasp. "Are you ready to obey me?"

"I'm hungry," Lara gasped. "I'm hungry. Please, make it stop."

"I'll feed her." Niki staggered toward them.

Jody whipped her head around. "No. Not you."

Sophia stepped forward. "I'll do it."

"No!" Niki roared and grasped Sophia, trying to drag her away.

"Don't touch her," Dasha shouted, her face morphing as she shouldered Niki away from Sophia.

Niki thrust her face into Dasha's, red pelt streaking her abdomen. "Get out of my way."

"No."

Niki drove her claws into Dasha's wounded shoulder. Howling, Dasha raked her claws across Niki's belly and they crashed to the floor, tearing and biting.

"Stand down," Drake growled at the thrashing Weres. She grabbed Niki by the neck and yanked her off Dasha. Whipping Niki around, she pinned her against the wall. "Now is not the time, *Imperator*."

Niki's eyes were wide, wild. "Let me go."

Drake shook her. "Look at me."

Niki shuddered, her eyes rolling.

"Niki," Drake murmured. "Niki, look at me."

Niki's agonized gaze fixed on Drake's, and she moaned. "Prima, I failed. The Alpha, Lara...I failed."

"No, Niki. You didn't." Drake pulled Niki's face against her neck. "You're ours. Don't you know that?"

"Please." Niki closed her eyes and slumped against Drake. "Please let me go."

"Never. Go sleep somewhere. Your job is done tonight." Drake kissed her forehead and released her. "The Alpha will need you soon. Be ready."

Niki turned wounded eyes to Sophia, and Dasha took a protective stance in front of her.

"Go, Niki," Sophia whispered.

"I'm sorry," Niki murmured.

As soon as Niki disappeared, Jody let Lara slide slowly down the wall until she rested on the floor, her head hanging between her knees. Jody ran her fingers through Lara's soaked hair and looked at Sylvan.

"My Vampire needs to feed."

Sylvan nodded. "I will send someone to you."

Jody leaned over, lifted Lara as if she were a child, and cradled her in her arms. She headed toward the splintered door. "I will see that she harms no one."

"I'll feed her," Sophia said. "Lara won't hurt me."

"You don't know that," Dasha growled. "She almost killed Niki."

Sophia paled.

"Not you, Sophia," Sylvan said. "We can't risk injury to one of our medics."

"What about me?" Dasha said.

Sylvan shook her head. "Get Max."

"Jody's hurt," Becca said.

"The Vampire can take care of herself," Sylvan said.

Becca's temper snapped. "She's trying to save your guard! How much blood does she have to shed for you before—"

"I meant," Sylvan said calmly, "she knows what she needs. When she tells us what that is, I'll see that she has it."

"If you wait for her to admit she needs anything, she'll be dead." Becca sidestepped Sylvan and marched toward the room where Jody had disappeared. "You know what? I don't have to play by your rules."

CHAPTER FIFTEEN

Before she lost her nerve, Becca strode down the hall toward the room where Jody had taken Lara. The doorway was ringed in splinters, resembling a gaping maw filled with rows of jagged teeth. A shark's mouth waiting to swallow her or rip her to shreds. Two steps into the shadow-filled room, she halted abruptly.

Across the room, Jody knelt with her back to the door beside a plain metal-framed bed. The rumpled sheets were stained with dark patches of what Becca could only imagine must be blood. Lara was nude and lay curled on her side, her arms wrapped around her middle, her legs drawn up, her face a visage of pain. Jody stroked her hair and murmured something in a low, gentle tone. Jody's shirt was so soaked in blood, only the crumpled white collar indicated what color it had been. The stake was gone. Jody must have pulled it out. How could she still function? She must feel pain. God, was she able to shut out all the emotions that defined humans—fear, pain, need, desire?

Was she truly that different? Could she be immune to those feelings and still be capable of compassion and tenderness? Because Jody *was* tender and caring. She'd been compassionate with Lara from the moment Lara had been shot. And she'd been protective and concerned for Becca in Nocturne. Jody was heir to a powerful dynasty—she didn't have to be a police detective. But she was. She did her job because she cared.

"You need medical attention," Becca said, taking another step closer. She wouldn't believe Jody didn't hurt.

Jody had felt Becca coming before she'd reached the doorway. A brush of warmth against the back of her neck, a bright tingling in her nostrils, a rush of energy in her blood. Human. Prey. Yes. But more. *Becca.* "You can't come in here."

"I'm already in," Becca said. "Let Elena or Sophia check your back. You could be injured inside."

"I'm not."

"How do you know?"

"I know. I can't leave Lara right now." Jody turned Lara onto her back and rested her palm lightly between Lara's breasts, holding her down with the force of her mind. She could have controlled her without touching her at all, but she'd been where Lara was when she'd first come into her power. She hadn't been as mindless, but her control had been erratic for the first few months, and her father had kept her restrained. She had been helpless with hunger and wild with need. She remembered the aching isolation of being abandoned, being a victim of her own consuming urges, immobilized and deprived of any contact. Imprisoned in solitude so absolute the last vestiges of sanity eroded like sand in the wind.

She vowed then never to inflict such agony on another being. She had planned never to turn a human or a Were, and without offspring born or turned, she would never need to torture a Vampire. She'd been so careful to monitor her blood servants for any sign of addiction and to replace them well before they reached the point where she would have to turn them to save their sanity. But she hadn't counted on saving a life and inadvertently altering one forever. Looking at Lara now, she wondered if the newling would thank her when she finally regained awareness, or try to kill her. Regardless of the outcome, she wouldn't leave her Vampire alone and in pain. "You should not even be in the Compound with her like this."

"You're still bleeding," Becca said. "I can tell from looking at you that you don't have a drop to spare."

Jody swiveled away from the bed, keeping one hand on Lara. Becca stood framed in the rectilinear glow of golden light slashing through the shattered doorway. Her body was a dark silhouette, strong curves and gentle promises. Instantly, all Jody's urges converged at once. Hunger gnawed at her insides. Hunger for blood, hunger for the scent that teased her mind and frayed her control. Her clitoris was soft, silent, but she knew the first rush of Becca's blood would make her come. Her throat ached and her gums throbbed. Her incisors unsheathed. She was so hungry, and Becca was so close. "Leave while you still can."

Becca didn't retreat, but knelt beside her, her fingers warm against the back of Jody's neck. "I can't. Every time I turn my back, you're almost getting yourself killed. I get that you're immortal, but..." Becca's fingers drifted into her hair. "You're not all right. You're shaking."

"Becca," Jody whispered. "You don't know what you're risking."

"I know I can't walk out of this building right now. Max is on his way. I remember him, he's huge. Can he feed you both?"

Jody shuddered. She needed the blood, but she wanted Becca. She'd never had trouble separating blood from sex. She didn't feed to come. She fed to live. Orgasm followed feeding, a biological afterthought. Now the promise of sexual satisfaction was as hollow as the act. She needed to feed, but she wanted what she couldn't have. Sex without blood. Without Becca's blood. "Lara is taking every ounce of my control. You're not safe around me."

"Yes, you said that before. Funny, you're the last Vampire I'd ever expect to be all talk." Smiling, Becca touched Jody's cheek with her fingertips. "What would happen if I gave you my blood? Just this once."

Jody groaned and closed her eyes. She couldn't keep looking at the pulse pounding in Becca's throat. Just the few seconds of hearing the blood rush through the great vessels in Becca's neck had filled her mouth with hormones. Chemicals that would keep the bite wound open while she fed, stimulants that would stream into Becca's system— soothing her even as they ignited her nerves. Becca's fears, perhaps even her revulsion, would be lulled while the hormones flooded into her brain and forced her to a shattering climax. They would both come, and it would mean nothing. "I can't."

"Why not?" Becca inched around on her knees until they faced one another. She skimmed her fingers along the edge of Jody's jaw. "You're the first Vampire I've met who resists taking blood when offered. Michel wasn't even invited, and she..."

"Michel?" Jody's mind clouded with fury. "When did you see Michel?"

"At Nocturne this morning."

Jody gripped Becca's shoulder, fear warring with anger. "I thought we agreed you wouldn't go there again."

"No, you pronounced. I never agreed to that. I told you I wouldn't go without an escort, and I tried, I really tried. I needed to get inside, and I was working out how I could do that safely when the Viceregal and Michel invited me in. I was safe with them."

Jody laughed grimly. "You can't be that naïve. Safe with either of them? The most powerful Vampire in the Western Hemisphere and her enforcer? What did Michel do?"

"She didn't do anything. She just assumes too much."

Jody let go of Lara and grasped Becca's chin, turning her face first one way then the other, peering at her neck. "If she bit you, I will kill her."

Becca grasped Jody's wrists and pulled Jody's hands away from her face. "Stop that. Even if she did, what would it be to you?"

"No one is going to bite you." Jody struggled not to claim her then, not to bury her incisors in Becca's neck and inject her essence into Becca's blood. She wanted to drink her, bind her. "You won't be safe in the places you insist on going unless you've already been claimed. I claim blood rights over you. No one will bite you except me."

"Does that mean we're engaged?"

Jody gritted her teeth. "It means exactly what it says. No Vampire will feed from a claimed host, not without risking death."

"Well, I don't intend to belong to anyone. And I'm certainly not going to give up my rights to someone who's not even interested in utilizing them. I refuse."

Jody shook her head. "You can't. The host has nothing to say about it."

"Host? Are you sure you don't mean slave?"

"As soon as I make it known that I have claimed blood rights, you'll be safe. I should've done it—"

"I don't believe in empty threats. You're not going to claim anything, especially something you're too afraid to take." Becca grasped Jody's face in both hands and kissed her.

Jody's senses filled with her. Searing heat, unbearable sweetness, pounding tendrils of power slid into her mouth and down her throat. Her belly heated, and hunger clawed up her spine. She groaned and grasped Becca's shoulders, opening her mouth and allowing Becca's tongue into her mouth. Becca should have been afraid, but she wasn't. Her tongue searched for Jody's, plunging deeper into her mouth, her tongue forcefully stroking over Jody's.

"Be careful," Jody murmured. Her incisors were bared, dangerously sharp. "Don't cut yourself. If I taste you, I won't be able to keep from drinking you."

Becca played her tongue over Jody's incisors. "Maybe I want you to."

Jody groaned and jerked her head away. "Becca, don't."

"You taste so good." Becca caressed her palms over Jody's chest, her fingertips outlining her clavicles and trailing down the inner curves of her breasts. "Just tell me what I'm feeling is real. Tell me you're not doing anything to me, that this is only us."

"I swear to you," Jody murmured, stroking the backs of her fingers over Becca's breasts. "You're not enthralled. But you have to stop."

Becca pressed closer, straddling Jody's hips as they knelt on the floor, her crotch coming to rest against Jody's. "I was so worried outside in the hall. So afraid something would happen to you." She kissed Jody's mouth, her neck, her throat. "I know you're hurt, but all I can think about is having you inside me. Just touch me. Don't bite me, if you don't want to, but God, touch me…"

"I can't touch you and not bite you." Jody's hands shook as she gripped Becca's arms and held her away. "And if I bite you, the next time you want to kiss me you won't know if it's your desire or the call of my blood to yours. What will you think then?"

"I don't know. I don't even know if I care."

"You'll care."

The light from the hall was suddenly blocked, and a thick shadow cast across the floor. Jody snarled and pulled Becca against her side, shielding her with an arm around her shoulders.

"It's Max," Max said from the doorway. "I've come to help Lara."

"Go now," Jody said to Becca, standing unsteadily. She helped Becca to her feet. "Do whatever you came here to do with the Alpha, then leave. You'll be safer."

"Stop talking as if you're the enemy."

Jody grimaced. "Are you sure I'm not?"

"Yes." Becca rested her hand on Jody's hip. "Can you at least go see a medic now?"

"In a few minutes." Jody took a deep breath. Pointless to hide the truth. "I can't go anywhere until I feed."

"Will you feed from Max?"

"Yes, if he'll let me. Please. Go away." Jody shuddered, cramps nearly bending her double. Lara thrashed on the bed, the smell of Jody's need rousing her. Jody motioned to Max. "Take your shirt off. Leave your pants on if you don't wish to couple with her—"

"No," Max said sharply, pulling off his T-shirt as he approached the bed. "She wouldn't want to, if she could choose."

"Then just open them and lie down. Hurry." Jody had trouble

getting the words out, her throat was so constricted. He smelled of earth and forest, filled with power and life. She wasn't sure how much longer she could go without collapsing or attacking someone. Attacking Becca. "I have what I need," she said to Becca. "More than you can give me. Go."

❖

She should go. She knew she should go. Jody had been very clear. *I have what I need.*

Closing her eyes, Becca touched her lips with her fingertips. They were so sensitive, she could still feel Jody's kisses. She ran the tip of her tongue along the inside of her mouth, over her lips. She didn't taste blood. She wished she did. God, what did that mean? She'd kissed her—wanted the kiss. Wanted more. She hadn't lied. She'd been terrified during the conflict in the hallway. Jody had been horribly hurt and could have died any number of ways. So could any of the others out there. Becca wouldn't have wanted any of them to die, but only losing Jody would've torn apart something inside her. Why?

Jody was trying as hard as she could to drive her away. How many times did a girl have to hear she wasn't wanted to get the message? But she couldn't get the feel of Jody's hands on her out of her mind, out of her body. Jody's hands had shaken. She'd never been with a lover who had wanted her that much.

Maybe Jody's desire was just for the blood. Maybe that's all Jody had wanted. But if that was it, why hadn't Jody taken her blood? And why the hell had she offered? She'd never had the urge to share blood in the two years she'd known of the possibility, even though every time she witnessed Vampires feeding she was not only fascinated, she was aroused.

A groan from across the room brought her eyes open wide. Max lay on his back in the center of the bed with Lara crouched over him, naked, straddling his denim-covered thigh. Crimson rivers welled from four long scratches down the center of his massive chest. Lara leaned down and licked the blood, and he groaned again. Jody, her back against the wall on Max's far side, stroked Lara's back, her pale hand seductively delicate against the Were's dark bronze skin. Jody looked across the room, and her gaze locked on Becca's.

Jody's voice whispered through her mind. *This is what I am. Is this what you want?*

Becca's belly tightened as Lara's sex swelled and throbbed. The ache moved deeper, tightening as Max's erection pushed up against his jeans. Jody's incisors gleamed against her lower lip, lava swirling in her eyes. Hunger, aching hunger. Jody's hunger.

Becca's thighs trembled, and she locked her knees to keep standing. She was Max, she was Lara, she was need. She found her voice but could barely whisper. "Stop it."

Go. You don't want this.

She should go, but she couldn't. Couldn't force herself to walk away, not while her heart pounded between her thighs. Not while Jody's need was so huge.

Max growled and pulled Lara's face against his neck. Jody's hand glided down the center of Lara's back and over her ass as she leaned closer and kissed Lara's temple.

Max turned his head toward the door, exposing more of his neck for Lara, and his gaze drifted over Becca's face. He seemed calm, totally unafraid. When Lara gripped his shoulder and drove her incisors into his neck, his body arched and his eyes sparked gold. His mouth parted in a grimace, but his roar was one of pleasure. Lara rode his thigh, her naked breasts against his chest, the sounds of her swallowing loud in the thickly silent room. Max's breathing grew harsh and fast, his chest and belly heaving. Lara snarled, her hips bucking, her claws leaving dark tracks down his belly.

Becca looked beyond them when Jody rose to her knees, her face stark. Max reached out an arm in her direction, and Jody caught his massive wrist in her hand. She shuddered, a blade in danger of snapping.

"Feed," Becca whispered. Jody stared at her, sanity slowly bleeding from her eyes. Becca couldn't bear the pain. "Feed."

With a snarl, Jody bit down into the bend of Max's arm, opening his brachial vein. Her body jerked. The two Vampires fed, and Max moaned. Lara writhed and drenched him in her essence. His face half-shifted and he came.

The intimacy was crushing, and finally Becca had to turn away.

Chapter Sixteen

Becca stepped over the splintered remnants of the threshold and into the hallway. Sophia paced up and down not far away, rubbing her arms as if she were cold, but the infirmary was warm. She looked up as Becca drew near, her elegant features hollowed with worry.

"How are they?" Sophia asked.

"Everyone's still alive." Becca noticed the door to the treatment room was still closed as they walked together toward the front doors. "Marissa?"

"Elena is with her. She's sleeping. She needs it."

Becca laughed wryly. "I can imagine. Lara is…" She shook her head, imagining what it would be like to feed Lara repeatedly in her wild, seemingly insatiable state. Watching Lara career unpredictably from dangerous predator to helpless victim of her own voracious needs had filled Becca with pity. Witnessing her feast on Max had triggered fear and fascination. She could easily understand how hosting for Lara could be addicting. "How long was Marissa with her?"

"Almost a day."

"I'm amazed she survived."

"It's not Lara's fault," Sophia said quietly.

"Of course it isn't." Becca stopped walking and grasped Sophia's arm. "Is that what you think? That I find Lara revolting or repulsive? You think I want her to be punished somehow?"

Sophia sighed. "You haven't seen us at our best today, I'm afraid. I don't know what you must think after witnessing that chaos in the hall." She lifted her hands and let them fall, her expression weary. "First Lara nearly attacking us, then Dasha and Niki fighting over…"

"They were fighting over you, weren't they?" Becca asked. "I was reading that right, wasn't I?"

Sophia pushed her hair out of her face. Her hands trembled. Shadows circled her eyes, making the deep blue surface impenetrable as the surface of a mountain lake cut from bedrock. "Yes, they were. I didn't mean for that to happen. I didn't even say yes to Dasha."

"Do you have to? I mean, I gathered some of it was involuntary."

Sophia smiled. "The attraction part can be rapid and unexpected, especially now with the Alpha…" She caught her breath and smiled again, shaking her head as if to chastise herself. "Everyone is a little agitated, and that often leads to aggression, especially for the more dominant Weres."

"Like Niki and Dasha."

"Yes."

"Aggression and sex go hand in hand sometimes. Not necessarily in a bad way," Becca mused. "Make-up sex is probably a classic example, not that I have all that much experience with it."

"Make-up sex." Sophia smiled faintly. "After a fight you want to be closer, to reconnect, to touch again."

"Yes, sometimes. Maybe more often than we'd like to admit." Becca thought about the kiss *she'd* initiated. She had not walked into that room planning to kiss a Vampire. She'd gone after Jody because she'd been afraid for her. She'd never once been afraid *of* her, even when Jody had been close to killing Lara. And she had no doubt that Jody would have killed Lara if she'd thought that was the only way to keep everyone else safe. Jody would have suffered, but she would have done it. No, she hadn't been afraid of her, but she'd been afraid *for* her.

When they'd first met, she'd been equally seduced and repelled by Jody's effortless charm. She'd hated knowing how easily she could fall prey, literally, to the Vampire thrall. She'd kept her distance, kept her walls up, and resisted seeing Jody as anything other than a sexual predator. The last few days had changed her mind. Her barriers had begun to crumble long before she'd seen that stake sticking out of Jody's back, even before she'd seen Jody almost bleed out, saving Lara's life. Jody had gone out of her way to protect her from being unwittingly enthralled by a Vampire pair at Nocturne, and even when Jody was being annoyingly domineering, she was trying to guard her. Jody risked her life over and over protecting others, and what was really scary, even more than seeing her bleed, was knowing how little Jody cared that she might die.

She'd kissed Jody because she'd wanted Jody to know someone cared if she lived or died. That *she* cared. Oh boy. She did not want to go there for very long. "Sometimes we want sex to remind ourselves we're still alive, that we're safe. And that those we…care about are safe."

"Yes," Sophia said, "when we tangle, we connect with each other and to Pack."

"What happens to a living Vampire when they die?" Becca asked. Right at that moment, she really needed to know. Maybe then she could put the nagging worries about Jody to rest.

Sophia frowned. "They rise. I don't know exactly how long it takes. They don't discuss the process."

"One hundred percent of the time?"

"I assume so, but I really don't know. Maybe the Alpha does."

"God," Becca whispered, suddenly making sense of the hurried conversation in the foyer of Jody's town house the night Jody had revived Lara. Sylvan had asked Jody if she was blood-bonded, and Jody hadn't answered. Then Sylvan told Niki that Jody wouldn't rise without a blood bond. Jody could die. Really die. "How can you keep so many secrets?"

"Sometimes secrets keep us safe," Sophia said quietly, almost as if she didn't mean for Becca to hear.

"And sometimes they can kill us."

"Yes." Sophia grasped the handle on the heavy front door. "Dasha is waiting outside to take you to the Alpha. Are you ready?"

"Yes," Becca said, wishing she were with Jody. What would she do if she were back in that room right now? Would she find some place on that bed with Max and Lara and Jody? Would she want to be part of what she had watched them share? The idea of being so vulnerable, so exposed, was terrifying enough. Sharing something so intimate with anyone other than her lover might be more than she could handle. "Can you see that someone replaces that door before morning? I should take care of what I came here for."

❖

Jody lay on her back in the swiftly darkening room, Lara draped over her and Max asleep beside them, his arm thrown over them both. Lara murmured fretfully, drew her thigh over Jody's, and slid her hand down Jody's belly and between her legs. Jody grasped Lara's wrist and moved her hand away. Max and Lara would rouse in a few hours, and then she would take Lara home.

She listened to Becca's footsteps disappear down the hall, and her insides ached. Becca's taste still lingered in her mouth. Beneath the sharp copper tang of Max's blood, Becca's honeyed kisses soothed her. She'd climaxed the instant the potent Were blood had rushed through her body, but so close after Becca had kissed her, she'd only been aware of Becca as she'd fed. Of her taste and her scent and her heat. So easy to imagine Max's arm had been Becca's throat beneath her mouth, the blood filling her Becca's blood. Her clitoris pulsed now, enlivened by the Were's blood. If Becca was here she could make love to her, and she might even be able to come without feeding again. The aftereffects of the fresh infusion of blood wouldn't sustain her sexual ability for long, not that it mattered.

Becca wasn't here, and she was just as glad. Even if Becca had been willing, she couldn't offer her even the simplest of intimacies—not without endangering her. She couldn't hold her or kiss her or make love to her without biting her. Even now, fully fed and satisfied, she hungered for her. Bloodlust rose like a malevolent storm, sweeping through her until all she knew was pain. Pain and the taste of Becca in her mouth.

❖

Becca had originally thought the broad expanse of the Compound was the heart of Were territory, but as she followed Dasha across the wide porch and into the central building, she realized she'd reached the inner sanctum. A huge double-sided stone fireplace jutted up from the center of the first floor into the open rafters three stories above. *Stone* was probably the wrong word. *Boulders* more accurately described what formed the hearth. Clearly, the rough gray monoliths, some taller than her, had been chiseled from the surrounding mountains. The floors were slabs of wood, each easily a foot and a half wide, carved from ancient trees. The walls were logs, precisely hewn and joined. She doubted a single nail was used anywhere in the construction of the massive building. Despite its size and sweeping floor plan, the headquarters did not appear cold or impersonal. Thick rugs defined multiple seating areas, and the wood-and-leather furniture appeared well used. She wished for a chance to pull her camera out and grab a few snapshots, but Dasha moved quickly down a broad hallway and deeper into the building.

"Are you sure you want to do this?" Dasha stopped in front of two carved wooden doors easily twelve feet tall. The broad wrought iron handles were shaped like enormous claws as long and thick as Becca's forearms.

"Why wouldn't I?" Becca asked, as if she couldn't think of about a million reasons. Starting with the fact she'd just witnessed things no human had probably ever seen before, and the Weres would likely want to keep it that way.

"Sometimes putting yourself in the middle of someone else's fight can be deadly."

Becca grimaced. "I think I'm already in this one. Someone certainly wants me to be." She smiled at Dasha, whose eyes had returned to their warm Mediterranean blue. Her face was still subtly different, though; cleaner, longer, more starkly beautiful if that were even possible. "But thanks. I appreciate your concern."

"You're welcome." Dasha rapped sharply on the door. From inside, Sylvan's voice rolled toward them, and the door vibrated.

"Come."

"How does she know who it is?"

"She knows." Dasha pulled up on the handle and pushed the doors open with her shoulder. Then she stepped aside and allowed Becca to precede her.

This room was every bit as impressive as the rest of the building. Another gigantic fireplace, multiple oversized leather sofas and chairs. A huge desk against one wall, tall French doors opened into the night. Equally tall windows, also open. Becca shivered as a chill wind cut across the room. Sylvan stood with her back to the glowing fireplace, barefoot in blue jeans and a dark T-shirt. Drake was next to her, similarly dressed, an arm slung around Sylvan's waist. The sofas and chairs and wall space were occupied by almost a dozen Weres, most of whom she'd never seen before. Fortunately, even when slightly intimidated—okay, maybe a lot intimidated—she'd learned not to show it. Hiding her emotions had gotten her through childhood with a minimum of criticism and had proven advantageous during difficult interviews.

This was definitely going to qualify as a difficult interview.

"I understand you wanted to see me," Sylvan said. "If you came all the way out here, I assume it's important."

"It is, Alpha." Becca stepped deeper into the room until she stood just in front of the sofa where the two blond Weres she had seen earlier each occupied one end, their sprawling limbs nearly touching. She kept her gaze on Sylvan. "I appreciate you seeing me on such short notice."

Sylvan nodded. She was even more imposing in the jeans and T-shirt she wore like a second skin than she was in the tailored suits she wore when she appeared on television, and she was damn impressive then. Sylvan's power filled the room, and you didn't have to be a Were to feel it. Becca drew a breath.

"I have a message for you from the Viceregal and one from an anonymous caller." Becca tilted her chin up. "And I have a few questions."

Sylvan's mouth flickered. Becca didn't think it was a smile. "Let's start with the critical issue. Callan says you mentioned missing females."

"Yes. I received a call from an unidentified male—species unidentified—late this afternoon. He claims female Weres are being held captive somewhere—"

The room erupted in a thunder of growls and snarls, so vicious and so loud Becca's skin broke out in goose bumps and the hair on the back of her neck stood up. She'd never really thought that was possible. She flinched but managed to suppress the trembling in her arms and legs.

She half expected Sylvan to shout down the unruly Weres, but Sylvan never raised her voice.

"Easy, my wolves." Sylvan's low, calm tones cut through the chaos. "We'll find them. This I promise."

The violent snarls and the growls diminished to a low, anxious grumbling and finally stilled. Becca felt soothed inside, as if a gentle hand had brushed over her consciousness. She narrowed her eyes and regarded Sylvan intently. "I felt that."

Sylvan smiled. "You seem to be quite sensitive. Most humans would not."

"I'm hearing that a lot," Becca muttered. "Is it true? Have some of your females disappeared?"

Sylvan's expression never changed, and she did not answer.

Becca blew out a breath. "Look. You can try to stonewall me as much as you want, but someone wants me to know these things. I'm like a damn clearing station for hot tips. The problem is, I can't make very much out of them without more information. If you're not going to help me, I'm going to start asking around until I find someone who will." Time to play her best cards. "My first call tomorrow morning is going to be to the national offices of HUFSI, because they certainly have an agenda, and they're no friend of the Weres. My second call will be to Senator Weston."

Drake spoke up. "That might not be wise. All those inquiries will do is call attention to the situation."

"Yes, I imagine they will." Becca lifted her shoulder. "No one is leaving me any choice but to shake the trees and see what falls out."

"This is Were business," Sylvan said and the softness had left her voice. "No concern of yours."

"Wrong. It became my concern the first time someone called me, and every day it's more of my concern. Do you really think I'm going to stand by and pretend I didn't see someone try to kill you? Or ignore the fact that young girls are dying from something that might be Were fever? And now there's a rumor Weres are being tortured? I don't think so." Becca tried to keep the challenge out of her voice, because she didn't want to confuse the issue. She didn't for a second think the Alpha could be bullied. But she had to prove she couldn't be either. "So either you let me in or I'm going to start knocking on doors, and you'll have a lot more people asking you questions."

The two young blonds on the sofa in front of her sat up quickly, rumbling in the back of their throats, and heat streaked over her skin. The next thing she knew, Sylvan was next to her.

"Damn it. You're almost as fast as Jody."

"Comparing a Were to a Vampire is probably not wise," Sylvan murmured.

"And why should I start doing anything that's smart?" Becca met Sylvan's eyes and then remembered that was not a smart thing to do either. She held Sylvan's gaze for just a second, and then looked to the side, but not down. Damn it, she was not going to cower in front of anyone, even one of the most powerful Weres in the world.

"What is it that you want, Ms. Land?" Sylvan asked.

"I want to share information with you. I'm good at what I do. I'm not a detective, but I'm a damn good investigator. And I know people." She let her gaze swing back to Sylvan's, and nearly lost herself in the deep, penetrating blue of her eyes. God, she was gorgeous.

"Careful," Drake murmured, sliding in beside Sylvan and casually gripping the back of her neck.

Becca jerked. "My apologies, Alpha."

"No need," Sylvan murmured, brushing her fingers over Drake's cheek. "Associating with us could be dangerous."

"I know. But I trust you to keep my skinny human ass out of the fire."

Someone in the room laughed.

"I'd like to keep these events out of the public eye," Sylvan said. "Do you agree not to report them?"

"I agree not to report an incomplete story, as long as you let me work with you."

Sylvan sighed. "I will assign a Were liaison who will report directly to me. Any information you uncover will be relayed either to her or me. She will also see that your…ah…butt stays in one piece."

Becca smiled. "Thank you. I appreciate that." Now for the tricky part. "I met with the Viceregal this morning. She suggested there were those in the Coalition who didn't agree with your position."

"Politicians rarely agree," Sylvan said with a thin smile. "Even Praeterns."

"I gathered it might be more than just philosophical disagreements. She hinted you might be in danger from someone within." Becca tensed in preparation for the uproar of aggression she expected, but the room remained quiet save for a few low, ominous rumbles.

"Names?"

Becca shook her head. "I'm sorry, no. She also told me to tell you to remember the days when Weres and Vampires hunted together. What did she mean by that?"

"The Praeterns were not always in the minority, and we did not always hide," Sylvan said softly.

"That might be a bit of information you want to keep to yourself," Becca said, suppressing a shiver.

"Yes. I agree." Sylvan looked to the blonds, who quivered at attention on the sofa. "Gather the rest of the *centuri*. It seems we will be visiting the city tonight."

"I'm coming with you," Becca said. When Sylvan's brows rose, she hurriedly said, "A deal is a deal."

"I can understand why the Vampire finds you a challenge."

Becca felt her face flush, and damn it, her heart started racing. Probably every Were in the room could tell. "If you mean she finds me a pain in the ass, you're right."

Sylvan smiled. "Probably that too."

Chapter Seventeen

Becca hadn't thought the tension in the room could get any higher, but that was before every Were suddenly came to alert and fixed on the hall doors. The low rumbles and growls escalated, and she didn't need a translator to tell her something had made the Weres very unhappy. Someone or something was coming, and they weren't going to get a welcome reception.

"Jace, Jonathan," Sylvan said quietly, and the two gorgeous blonds jumped up from the sofa and flanked Becca. Drake sidled almost imperceptibly in front of Sylvan, her body between Sylvan and the door. Dasha loped from her post against the wall and took a position on Sylvan's far side.

Becca was impressed and a little intimidated. In a matter of seconds, both she and Sylvan had been subtly surrounded by Weres. "What?" Becca said quietly.

"Andrew," Sylvan said, "open the door for our guest."

The red-haired Were with the whipcord body stalked to the doors, and Becca's breath stilled in her chest. She wasn't afraid, not exactly. Hard to feel afraid in Sylvan's stronghold, surrounded by the elite of Sylvan's forces. She had all the protection she could possibly need, but that very protection made her uncomfortable. She wasn't used to being guarded, and she certainly wasn't used to needing it. She was very rarely afraid—wary and cautious, of course—but she was always too focused on her goal, even in perilous situations, to register fear. What really bothered her at the moment was that she didn't know enough to interpret what she was witnessing. She was the outsider. She was the one who didn't know the rules. She was the one who didn't belong, and being helpless out of ignorance just plain pissed her off.

She'd spent a lifetime proving there was nowhere she couldn't go, nothing she couldn't do, and no situation where she didn't belong. She belonged because she was too good at what she did to be shut out, because she didn't give up. And because she didn't run from anything.

"What?" Becca said.

Andrew pulled open the doors, and Becca's lungs started working again. She sighed, and the little bit of dread that had been niggling at her insides was instantly replaced by a combination of exasperation and reluctant pleasure. Jody sauntered into the room with her arm loosely around Lara's waist. Max strode on Lara's other side, not quite touching her. They were all dressed in dark T-shirts and pants, standard Were dress around the Compound, which from the few glimpses Becca had caught appeared to be a clothes-optional environment. While the Weres filled out their clothes with tight muscles and strong bone, Jody somehow managed to look sleek and elegant in hers.

Becca was relieved to see Lara appearing a little more like herself. At least she seemed oriented, and some of the wild, haunted unrest had left her face. Her amber eyes were clear for the first time in two days, even though her cheeks were sunken with dark smudges of fatigue and sadness. Max seemed no worse for having hosted two Vampires at once. But Jody was the one Becca studied. Jody looked strong and healthy again, her pallor having been transformed into her usual pale luminescence. The anxious tension that had plagued Becca since she'd left the infirmary drained away, leaving her nearly light-headed.

Jody's gaze traveled over Becca's face, lingering for just a moment before lasering in on Sylvan. For that heartbeat of connection, heat flared in Jody's eyes, and Becca almost smiled. She knew the difference now between the red inferno of bloodlust and plain old desire. Jody hadn't looked at her as if she were a meal. She'd looked at her like she was a woman. Becca allowed herself one second of satisfaction before trying to decipher what was happening.

"We had an agreement," Jody said to Sylvan. "We would work together to identify the assassin and whoever had ordered the attempt on your life."

"Nothing has changed," Sylvan said.

"The agreement did not include civilians. Particularly vulnerable ones."

"Now wait a minute," Becca said. "If you're talking about me—"

Jody spared her another glance, her old familiar arrogance and dismissive expression firmly back in place. Maybe blood made her feel invincible. Having fed certainly made her insufferable.

Becca took a step away from the flanking Weres. She didn't need guards, and she could damn well stand up to one self-important Vampire. "You have no idea what I'm capable—"

"You aren't equipped to deal with Praeterns. I doubt you could protect yourself from a violent human, let alone from an aggressive Praetern."

"Maybe you'd like to test your theory?" Becca stilled her hand in midair, just short of poking Jody in the chest, but boy, she wanted to. And she never got physically violent, so Jody was really pushing all her buttons. She thrust her face into Jody's and tried, more for her own sake than Jody's, to keep her voice low. "You don't own me, and you never will. So stop acting like a…a…horse's ass."

The lingering growls morphed into laughter. Jody's beautiful mouth tightened, and her dark eyes flashed. "Then agree to blood rights."

"Can they be rescinded?" Becca recognized the opening of a negotiation, something she doubted Jody entertained very often. She, on the other hand, was used to it. Finally, something on her own turf.

"Up until the moment I bite you. Once I've executed the blood claim, no."

Why did that sound just a little bit thrilling? Becca ruthlessly ignored the frisson of excitement that skittered down her spine. "And you'll promise to cooperate. Not get in the way of my involvement in the investigation?"

A muscle bunched along Jody's jaw. "You have my word. Under the following provision—you do your investigating with me. From now on, we are partners." Jody flicked a glance at the Weres who had regrouped around Becca. "Then you'll have adequate protection."

Jace snarled. "Perhaps you'd like to challenge *me*, Vampire. We'll see who's capable of guarding her."

"You're young and foolish, Wolf." Jody smiled, and her incisors slid down. She tilted her head toward Lara. "And I already have one wolf in my Dominion."

With a snarl, Jace leapt forward, and just as suddenly, stuttered to a stop inches from Jody. Her expression momentarily blanked, as if she had struck an invisible wall.

"Careful," Jody whispered. "I don't want to hurt you."

"Jace, stand down," Sylvan snapped. Her power lashed through the air, and Jace dropped into a crouch, a whine reverberating in the back of her throat. "Don't challenge my wolves, Vampire. And *don't* enthrall them."

"Not intended. My apologies, Alpha," Jody said, turning from Jace as if she were of no consequence, "but you will *not* put Becca in danger."

"I will protect her."

"No," Jody said quietly, so deadly quietly Becca shivered. "I will."

Becca crossed her arms over her chest. She was so damned tired of these power struggles. "I've had it. I am done with all of this posturing and blustering and everything else. Jody, I'll work with you as long as you don't get in the way of me doing my job. Happy?"

"Ecstatic," Jody snarled. "And blood rights?"

"Yes, fine. All right. Put your incisors away." Becca cheered inwardly when Jody almost smiled. "How did you know that Sylvan had agreed I could work with her, anyhow?"

Jody leaned close, her nose almost touching Becca's. "I heard your discussion."

Becca tried to concentrate on the words but found herself falling into the depths of Jody's eyes. She loved her eyes. Oh hell, was Jody enthralling her right now? She looked away, but couldn't banish the whispers of desire that called to her every damn time she so much as looked at Jody. "What? What do you mean you heard?"

Smiling wryly, Jody ran her fingertips along the edge of Becca's jaw. "Don't you know?"

Oh, that did it. Becca melted inside. Warm heat like thick chocolate rolled through her, a sensation so exciting it had to be addictive. "Tell me that what you're doing right now isn't thrall."

Jody shook her head. "You kissed me. I can still taste you. You created the connection. If it's thrall, *you* created it."

Becca shuddered and stepped back. She wanted to kiss her again. She loved the idea of having some power over her, and now was so not the time or the place. "Everyone in this room can hear you."

"Yes. They can." Jody shrugged.

Becca folded her arms over her middle as if she could create a physical barrier between them. She turned away, hoping if she couldn't see Jody she could get her wits together and not completely humiliate herself in front of a room full of Weres. Not that any of them seemed to mind public displays of affection. "The Alpha has already agreed I could accompany her tonight. I'll call you in the morning and fill you in on anything important."

Jody laughed. "I don't think so." She nodded toward Lara, who stood midway between her and Sylvan, looking slightly dazed. "I'm taking Lara to Nocturne tonight. I believe that's where you were headed to begin with. You can come with me."

"I'll ride with Dasha."

"No," Jody said, "you won't. The club will be full in the middle of the night. Any Were or human inside is assumed to be a voluntary host. Even Sylvan's soldiers. They'll be busy guarding her and protecting themselves. You'll be safer with me."

"She's probably right," Sylvan said, joining them. She cupped Lara's cheek and kissed her forehead. "How are you?"

Lara shuddered and leaned into Sylvan, wrapping her arms around her waist and rubbing her cheek against Sylvan's shoulder. She ducked her head and her body seemed to fold in on itself.

Sylvan lifted her chin. "*Centuri?* How are you?"

"I don't know, Alpha," Lara said, her voice rough and thick with uncertainty. "I can't remember much. Only fragments of…hunger and pain and sometimes"—her voice trailed off, and she glanced at Max, then Jody—"sometimes pleasure. I don't know who I am anymore."

"You are mine, as you have always been." Sylvan ran her fingers through Lara's hair. "You survived. You have done well. I'm proud of you." She drew Lara's hand to her chest, placed it over her heart. "Feel the Pack. Feel me. This is who you are, who you will always be."

Becca half expected Jody to argue or make some kind of claim on Lara, but Jody just stood quietly, her hands tucked into the pockets of her black pants, as if she were waiting for an outcome she already knew.

Lara looked panicked, her gaze flickering between Sylvan and Jody. "Alpha, please, I don't know what to do."

"I do," Sylvan said. "You will stay with Jody until you have learned what you need to learn to be strong and safe. Niki will go with you."

"That's not necessary," Jody said. "Lara will have plenty of hosts. The Were is not needed now."

"Niki isn't going as a host," Sylvan said. "We don't leave Pack to fight alone. Niki will be my liaison with you and Ms. Land, as well as

Lara's backup." She glanced at Dasha. "I'm drafting you to the *centuri* temporarily. You'll see that the human doctor arrives home safely when Elena says she can travel. Max, we'll want Misha tonight also."

Max nodded briskly. "Yes, Alpha. Should I get Niki too?"

"Let her sleep for now. She'll find us when she wakes." Sylvan glanced at Jody. "She's fed you both, hasn't she?"

Jody nodded.

Becca watched the silent interplay between them, guessing that Niki had a connection to the two Vampires because she'd hosted for them. The wolf Alpha knew a lot about what happened when a Vampire fed. Interesting.

Sylvan slung her arm around Drake's shoulders. "Let us discover what the Viceregal knows, then."

Becca hung back as Sylvan and her guards loped from the room, the other Weres following behind. She said to Jody, "My car is somewhere, I'll follow you back."

"We should all ride together. Your car or mine?" Jody said.

Becca wasn't sure how she felt about being locked in a vehicle with two Vampires, one of whom had little or no control over her hunger. Jody waited, as if knowing Becca was making the most important decision of her life. She let the lessons she had learned the hard way guide her.

Control what you could, and when in doubt, trust your instincts. She dug into her purse and came out with her keys. She tossed them in the air and caught them. "I'll drive."

CHAPTER EIGHTEEN

Gray jerked upright in her restraints, peering into the murky half-light, focusing on the figure standing just outside her cell. Born to hunt in the dark, she could easily make out the female form, the shoulder-length hair, the long neck and full breasts. She didn't have a name for the woman, but she knew her scent. A lush, verdant smell like crushed flowers after a heavy rain. A powerful scent, intensely female. She had the feeling the woman had been standing there for a while, perhaps talking to her, but she had been drifting. Not asleep. She didn't think she'd slept since they'd brought her to this place, or the place before this one. Sometimes after she'd been in the lab and they'd given her drugs and done things to her body, she lost track of time. Sometimes when they didn't come for her after hours of hanging suspended from the shackles around her wrists, her mind broke free, and she'd dream of running, of shifting, of smelling the world so fresh and clear, of tussling with her Packmates, of tangling on the forest floor, nude and exhilarated after the hunt. When she found herself back in the cell, unable to shift, locked away from sunlight and the mountain air, those memories nourished her.

"Who are you?" Gray asked.

"You're awake. Good," came the low, sultry voice. Long, elegant fingers wrapped around the bars of her cage. "You're very beautiful—in that dangerous way all wild animals are beautiful. Do you know that?"

"What do you want?" Gray asked.

The woman laughed softly. "Nothing very complicated. Just to understand you. Isn't that what your leaders want? Why they revealed you to us? For humans to know you?"

"Why are you keeping us prisoner?"

"We could move you and your friend to more comfortable quarters if you cooperated. If you didn't fight us."

Anger simmered in Gray's belly, and her wolf raged, demanding to be freed to fight. Holding her down was getting harder and harder to do. She panted with the effort.

"Oh yes," the woman murmured, her voice sliding over Gray's skin like a hot tongue. "You are wild, aren't you? Wild and excited. Do you want to hurt me, or do you want to fuck me?"

The woman leaned her body against the bars, her hips lifting and falling ever so subtly. Gray didn't want to tangle with her. She wanted to tear her apart. Her canines lengthened, and her claws shot out. She growled.

"That excites you, doesn't it?" The woman laughed and brushed one hand over her breasts. "Perhaps that's how we need to prepare you for the lab. You're filling up right now, aren't you?"

Gray snarled, rage and helplessness driving her to the edge of control. She thrashed against her restraints, the pain only inciting her wolf more.

"That's enough now. Enough for tonight," the woman said after watching Gray struggle for a few minutes. "We wouldn't want you to waste any of that precious fluid, would we? Tomorrow you'll be doubly ready." She backed away from the cage and whispered, "Good night, my beautiful animal."

Her footsteps died away in the darkness, and Katya whispered, "Gray?"

"I'm here," Gray said hoarsely.

"Who was that?"

"Their leader, I think."

"Don't let her taunt you into shifting."

"I'm trying not to." Her belly hurt with the effort of containing her instincts. She needed to shift, they both did. Without it, their emotional and physical balance was disrupted. Something about homeostasis, another lesson she hadn't paid attention to. But she didn't need a *magister* to tell her what her body proclaimed loud and clear. She was going to shift soon, and when she did, her wolf would never be chained again. "I'm trying."

"I can't remember what happened today," Katya said, and for the first time Gray heard fear in her voice. "Why can't I remember?"

Gray pictured Katya unconscious, restrained on the cold steel table, tubes inserted into her body. Devices stealing her blood and her essence and her soul. Fury surged through her like a firestorm.

"You were drugged," Gray said.

"What did they do?"

"I'm not sure. I think they were taking samples—blood and hormones."

"They want us to breed, don't they?"

"Yes," Gray said, remembering the injections and the heavy heat coursing through her belly. She remembered the swelling in her loins and the rush of pleasure and the overpowering release that went on and on until she was drained and empty and whimpering for more. She hated them and what they made her feel.

"What did they do to you?" Katya murmured.

"The same as you," Gray said, her voice roughening as her throat thickened. Her belly was hard and her sex rigid. Raw hatred ate through her reason like acid on stone.

"We're not going to let them force us, are we?" Katya said.

"No, we're not," Gray said. "I'm sorry they're making you tangle with me when you wouldn't—"

"Gray," Katya said, her voice at once gentle and strong. "You're Pack. Being with you makes me stronger. Feeling you, touching you, it helps me. I need you. It's okay."

"It helps me too," Gray whispered.

"Why can't I feel the Alpha?" Katya said, her voice shaking.

"I think it's the drugs," Gray said. "I can't feel her either, but I can feel you. Can you feel me?"

"Yes. I feel you in my mind and inside me. You feel warm and strong."

Gray shivered and closed her eyes. She didn't feel strong. Even now, part of her longed for the injections, for the electric current that obliterated thought and fear and pain and delivered only unbearable pleasure. "If it weren't for you, I would be lost."

"We're Pack. They can't take that away from us," Katya said. "The Alpha will come."

Gray nodded, certain of only one thing in the midst of the never-ending nightmare.

"Yes, the Alpha will come."

❖

Sylvan drew Drake close against her side as they waited at the top of the stairs for Andrew to bring the Rover around and for Max to return from the barracks with Misha. She nuzzled Drake's neck and let her canines scrape along the heavy muscle at the top of Drake's shoulder, kissing the shadow that marked her bite. Drake shuddered and rubbed against her.

"How are you, Prima?" Sylvan asked.

"Hungry for you. But I'll manage."

"The pain?"

"Just a constant ache." Drake slid around until they were face-to-face and leaned into Sylvan. "But I ache more for the taste of you."

"That's not what you need." Sylvan growled softly and nipped at Drake's throat. "You need me inside you to quiet the breeding frenzy."

"Maybe. Maybe I do, but I *want* you in my mouth."

Sylvan groaned, her body quickening to her mate's call. "We may be several hours in the city. I would tell you to stay here, but I don't think we can be apart that long."

Drake pulled Sylvan's T-shirt free from her pants and rubbed her belly. Sylvan stiffened and pelt erupted under Drake's fingertips. Drake laughed. "No, not a few hours."

"You're handling this better than most Weres in their first heat," Sylvan said, gritting her teeth against the urge to pull Drake down and take her instantly.

"Maybe because I have no idea what to expect. All I know is I need you. And the only frightening thing about that is I've never needed anyone so much before."

"I want you right now," Sylvan said, "and it's nothing to do with breeding. You take away the pain I never knew I had."

"Always. Always." Drake kissed her. "But we need to do this. If they're out there somewhere—our females."

"Yes," Sylvan growled, and her face grew hard and angular. "I need to know how to find them. If I could sense them—" She growled again, and her canines forced themselves out.

Drake rubbed Sylvan's chest until the rumbling quieted. "In the morning I'll go to the lab and talk to the Revniks. We'll figure out what might be blocking your connection to them." She drew back at the sound of a powerful engine approaching and sighed. "Since I don't intend to couple with you on the floor of the Rover in front of Misha and Max, you'd better let me go."

Sylvan huffed. "You think they haven't seen me couple before?"

"If they have, I don't want to know about it. And they won't be seeing it again."

Sylvan clasped Drake's hips and held her fast. "Prima. Weres couple without worrying about who may be watching, and no one does for exactly that reason."

Drake's claws edged out, and she scratched Sylvan's belly until Sylvan's hips lurched. "I don't care. When you come, you will come for me and no one else."

Sylvan thought of where they were going. Of Francesca. Francesca had drained her, tempered her need, but she'd never pleasured her, satisfied her, the way Drake did. "I have never come for anyone the way I do for you."

"And I intend to see it stays—"

"Alpha!" Niki called hoarsely as she raced across the courtyard. She leapt up onto the porch. "I'm coming with you."

Sylvan looped her arm around Niki's neck and pulled her close. With her mouth against Niki's ear, she said quietly, "I need you to stay with Lara. Lara needs you."

Niki pressed her face to Sylvan's throat. "Please, Alpha. I need to be with you."

Sylvan stroked Niki's head. "I know, I know. I want you to be with me. But I need my best to look after Lara and to make sure we know what the Vampire discovers. I trust Gates, but she's still a Vampire. I need Pack at my back. I need you there, Niki."

"I understand." Niki took a shuddering breath. "I think you can trust the Vampire."

"I can't afford to be wrong," Sylvan said. "Stay close to her. To Lara."

"The Vampires...they're powerful."

"Yes," Sylvan said, stroking the back of Niki's neck. "They are." She gripped Niki's shoulders, holding her gaze. "But you are my *imperator.* You are stronger. Feed them, if you need to. Don't fear your need. You are stronger than your need."

"I'm not you," Niki said.

"You don't need to be."

"And the blood thrall?"

"Trust yourself," Sylvan said. "I do. Stop fighting what you need." She kissed Niki swiftly. "Don't worry, we won't be far away."

"Yes, Alpha," Niki whispered as Sylvan and Drake bounded down the stairs and climbed into the back of the Rover. She wanted to stay with Sylvan. Only Sylvan's call was strong enough to block out every other need. Sylvan had always been her safety net, a safe focus for her passion and her desire, even though she knew she'd never have her. Now with Sylvan mated, she was left alone with her own naked desires, and nothing had ever been as frightening.

❖

Sophia heard the Rover pull away and hurried outside. Across the Compound, Niki stood on the porch watching the Alpha leave. Niki was barefoot in only a loose pair of black BDUs. Her hard stomach and full round breasts glistened in the moonlight. Sophia's blood hummed, and she felt Niki's need vibrate across the Compound. She strode toward Niki, and the closer she got, the stronger she felt her call. She'd stayed away from headquarters when Sylvan had gathered her council. Too many dominant Weres in one place, when she was still so unsettled from the Alpha's breeding call and Dasha's hot eyes. She'd resisted Dasha's offer earlier, and with the Alpha leaving the Compound, the restless demands of her body were lessening. But Niki, Niki was so hard to turn away from.

"Are you leaving again?" Sophia asked.

"Yes," Niki said, thankful now that Sylvan had ordered her to go. Sophia stood at the bottom of the stairs, gazing up at her, her pale hair nearly silver in the moonlight. She was beautiful and good and Niki's touch would only tarnish her. "I'm going with Lara."

Sophia's lips parted in surprise. "With Lara? To feed her?"

"No, to guard her."

"And the Vampire?"

Niki couldn't restrain her response. Her stomach quivered, and she growled softly.

"I see."

"No, you don't," Niki said.

"There's nothing to be ashamed of, Niki."

"Isn't there?" Niki drove her claws into the wood post. "I don't want to want *anything* from the Vampires."

"Maybe you should worry less about what…or who…you want. You're too hard on yourself. Concentrate on what you're best at."

Niki laughed, the bitter taste of failure in her throat. "What would that be?"

"Guarding the Alpha. Safeguarding the Pack. No matter what it takes. If it means you tangle with a Vampire, for whatever reason, then you do. The Alpha needs you. We all need you."

Niki moaned, uncertainty filling her chest. Sophia climbed the stairs and wrapped her arms around Niki's waist. Her breasts were full and warm against Niki's bare skin. Sophia's nipples were hard beneath the thin cotton of her tank top. She smelled like sunshine and wild roses, and Niki growled again.

"I believe in you," Sophia said and kissed her. Her tongue skimmed lightly over Niki's lower lip and just inside her mouth.

Niki stood as still as she could, her claws, her canines, her clitoris all hard and throbbing and ready. Sophia's mouth moved down her throat, and she whined, the need to take overpowered only by her need not to harm. "Sophia."

"I know. I know you don't...we can't." Sophia kissed the hollow at the base of Niki's throat. "We can't...I can't be with you that way either." She stepped back and brushed Niki's hair with her fingers. "But I want you to know I feel safe, the whole Pack feels safe, because of you."

"I'll try not to let you down," Niki whispered.

"You won't."

The door behind them opened, and the Vampire emerged with Becca and Lara. Dasha followed a few steps behind and her eyes went immediately to Sophia. Niki growled and Dasha stiffened, her eyes flashing.

"Wolf," Jody said. "I understand you'll be joining us."

"Yes," Niki said through gritted teeth.

"I hope you're replenished after your rest." Jody smiled. "We've an appointment to join your Alpha at Nocturne."

Niki gently released Sophia, filling her lungs with sunshine and roses and hoping the scent would stay with her in the night. Light flickered at the edges of the darkness that had been so close around her only minutes before. "Then it's time we left."

Chapter Nineteen

It's not your fault, Drake telegraphed to Sylvan as Andrew turned into an enormous lot in front of a dark building. If she didn't know better, she would believe the place abandoned. Beyond the club, the dark waters of the Hudson River were a roiling tempest. She rubbed the inside of Sylvan's jeans-clad thigh. *No one suspected those two females were missing until the attack on Misha. And you were the one who wanted the disappearances investigated.*

Sylvan rumbled, her eyes flashing from blue to gold. *The Pack depends on the Alpha to provide unity. The Alpha is the center, the heart holding all, one to another, no matter where they are. If I can't feel them, I've failed them.* Sylvan's rage permeated the close confines of the Rover, and across from them, Misha whined softly and Jace and Jonathan grumbled restlessly.

Drake slid her hand under Sylvan's T-shirt and stroked her chest. Sylvan's muscles were straining, her body hot. Her wolf was close, and she was angry. The young *centuri* were unaccustomed to absorbing the Alpha's power. They all needed calming. Drake softened her touch even further, forcing her mate to concentrate on the feel of her hands, seducing her beast until she could reason again. *Failure is when you deny your responsibility, avoid fulfilling your destiny. You would never do that. Whatever has come between you and your wolves did not originate in you. I'll find out what it is, I promise.*

I need you. Sylvan closed her eyes and rubbed her cheek on Drake's shoulder. *The Pack needs you.*

And I'm here. Drake lightly traced her bite mark on Sylvan's left breast with her fingertips. The skin was even hotter there, vibrating in tune with both their heartbeats.

Sylvan arched into Drake's caress and nuzzled Drake's neck. *You calm my wolf with one hand and excite her with the other. You make me ready and then tell me to wait.*

Drake let her hand drift down Sylvan's belly, smiling as Sylvan instantly pelted under her fingertips. She looked out the front windows and saw that Andrew had angled the Rover close to the entrance. He cut the engine. Time to go inside. Sylvan's skin was slick with pheromones. So was hers. *I just wanted to make sure every Vampire in this place smells me on you. So there'll be no doubt you're nobody's meal.*

Sylvan laughed and clasped Drake's neck. "No one will have any doubt. Stay close."

Andrew pulled open the rear door of the Rover, and the *centuri* climbed out to form a path to the door for Sylvan and Drake. Drake glanced around the jammed parking lot at the vast array of vehicles squeezed into every available space. Luxury cars, limos, dusty 4x4s, rusted-out junkers, motorcycles. As diverse as the clientele, probably. Praeterns had integrated into every social and economic stratum of society over the centuries. She wondered about the humans who mingled with them for pleasure.

"I've never been inside a Vampire club before," Drake said. "I know what thrall feels like, but is there anything else I should know?"

"Gates." Sylvan snarled. "I knew she'd tried to ensnare you the first day she met you."

"But she didn't." Drake slung her arm around Sylvan's waist. Jace and Jonathan flanked the club's door as Max pushed it open, and he and Misha went inside. "Maybe I won't be susceptible now that I've turned."

"I don't think anyone will try to enthrall you, but if they do," Sylvan said in a calm and reasonable voice, "I will tear them apart."

"Maybe you should let me try saying no first," Drake murmured.

Sylvan's only response was another snarl.

"Besides," Drake said as they walked into the club, "I understood hosting was voluntary. Granted, I don't know any Vampires personally other than Jody. The few I know of who work at the hospital tend to be even more reclusive than we are."

"We? Weres, you mean?"

"Yes." Drake kissed Sylvan. "I *am* a Were."

Sylvan's eyes flashed and Drake saw the wolf shimmer in their depths. "What are you worried about, Alpha?"

"The Vampires don't take involuntary hosts, but they hunt with their minds. Weres are not immune, although our resistance is much higher to their thrall than a human's."

"Then I'll be sure to be on guard. I don't want you fighting, not until you need to. And you will never need to fight because of me. I'm your mate. I'm yours."

"I know that. So does my wolf. But she doesn't reason with her mind. She only reasons with her heart."

"Then your wolf knows the truth."

As they shouldered through the crowd, Drake took in the cavernous club, which appeared pretty much as she had expected given the outside. Huge, dark, packed with bodies. Furnishings surprisingly more elegant than she might've anticipated, but then given the activities— understandable. A heavy bass beat undercut the murmur of voices, although the music wasn't loud. This was no dance club. Vampires and Weres and humans were feeding and tangling everywhere. She wondered if humans would watch the frantic exchange of blood and sex with the same fascination they watched lions hunt on the savanna or elks in rut fight to the death over a female in heat. Humans were as much fascinated by the wild side of nature as they feared it. The humans in this room had obviously overcome their fear, or perhaps they merely gloried in it.

A sleek, dark-haired Vampire appeared in their path. Even in the near darkness, the blazing blue of her eyes was captivating. An androgynous mixture of beauty and strength, she exuded power and subtle menace. "To what do we owe this honor, Alpha?"

"We've come to see the Viceregal," Sylvan said.

Sylvan answered calmly, but Drake felt her wariness. Sylvan wasn't tense, she wasn't anxious. She was simply on guard, the way any dominant animal would be in the presence of another predator. Her power and confidence flowed over Drake like warm rain. She loved this side of her mate, as much as she loved holding her after Sylvan had emptied her heart and mind and soul in the storms of their passion.

The Vampire regarded Drake with a raised eyebrow. "I see congratulations are in order."

"Prima, this is Michel, the Viceregal's *senechal*. My mate, Drake," Sylvan said.

Michel smiled, a cool almost amused smile. "The Viceregal will be very pleased to meet you, I'm sure." She glanced at Sylvan and laughed.

"We don't have much time," Sylvan said coolly. "Would you tell your Liege we're here?"

"Make yourself comfortable, *Alpha*," Michel said with a faint edge to her voice. "I'll let her know you're seeking an audience." She glanced at the *centuri*, who formed a semicircle at Sylvan's back. "Perhaps your guards would like to relax while you meet with the Viceregal. I'm sure they could find amusing company at the bar."

Max snapped, "We will be accompanying the Alpha."

"I'm afraid that will not be possible," Michel said. "The Viceregal sees only privileged guests in her private quarters."

Sylvan said, "Drake and I will be happy to meet with the Viceregal alone. My guards will stay up here."

The *centuri* grumbled quietly until Drake shot a sharp glance at them, and they quieted. She understood their apprehension, but Sylvan could not be seen as fearing for her welfare. If someone had targeted her, now was the time for her to show her strength. And Drake was absolutely certain she could protect her if it came to that. No one would harm her mate while she breathed.

"Wait here." Michel disappeared into the crowd.

Sylvan turned to Max. "Be wary of thrall." She lowered her voice. "Especially with the younger ones. They will not have had enough experience to realize when they're being captured."

"Yes, Alpha. But Andrew could stay here, and I could accompany you—"

Sylvan wrapped an arm around his neck and drew him close. "With Niki gone, you lead the *centuri*. Don't let them see you fear for me."

"I do not fear for you, Alpha. But it is my job to protect you."

"And you will. The entrance to Francesca's lair is behind the bar. Position the *centuri* to watch it, and make sure no Vampires go down in force. Her legions will be young males and females, probably dressed like club clientele. Look for the ones who are not feeding. Francesca will not allow them to until she does, and that will not be until near dawn when all the Risen have left. Even the most powerful of Vampires becomes somnolent after feeding, and Francesca does not make herself vulnerable until there is no danger."

Max nodded sharply. "Yes, Alpha."

When he turned away to instruct the *centuri*, Drake said, "You're very familiar with the Viceregal."

"Before the Exodus, she was our ally. I wouldn't say she and my mother were friends, but they stood together to keep order among the Praetern predators. I've known her all my life." Sylvan stroked Drake's face. *Is there something else you want to know, Prima?*

Drake shook her head. She might be a Were now, might be the Alpha's mate, but there were layers upon layers of Praetern history she had yet to learn. Of one thing, however, she was certain: *You carry my bite, no one else's. There's nothing else I need to know.*

Sylvan kissed her. "Francesca is also an excellent chess player."

"Really?" Drake said. "As it happens, so am I."

❖

Becca glanced in the rearview mirror. Lara and Niki were half lying on the backseat, Niki propped up in one corner, Lara in her arms. Lara's face was buried in the crook of Niki's shoulder, and she seemed to be licking her neck. Their arms and legs were so entwined Becca couldn't tell who was who. Both had their eyes closed, and she might have thought they were asleep except for the duet of rumbles filling the car.

She couldn't help wonder if Lara was going to lose control again, and if she did, whether Niki could restrain her. She was very glad to see Nocturne just ahead and signaled a turn into the parking lot.

Jody had been silent on the forty-minute ride from the Compound, and now she said to Becca as if she'd heard Becca's unspoken question, "They'll be all right. Once Lara feeds, she'll be less agitated. I'll take her home, and she'll sleep until tomorrow night."

"What about you?"

Even in the dark, Jody's eyes glowed for a few seconds like flames dancing at the edge of the forest, a firestorm threatening to flare and engulf everything in its path. "I can wait until morning. I would rather you stayed in the car—"

"No way," Becca said.

Jody grinned, an expression Becca had rarely seen, and she found the fleeting flash of sharp incisors oddly and disturbingly erotic. "What?"

"If one in ten times you'd allow me to finish my sentence," Jody said quietly, "I would have said I would prefer you stay outside, but I can't leave you alone out here."

"Why wouldn't I be safe enough in the car?" Becca asked, more curious now than annoyed.

"If you'd like a demonstration, you can stay here and let me call to you from across the parking lot. I guarantee you will come to me."

Becca's skin erupted in goose bumps, and a blaze ignited in the pit of her stomach. "Damn you. Stop whatever you're doing."

Jody chuckled. "I told you before, I'm not doing anything. However, once we have seen to Lara, you and I will need to see the Viceregal. *She* may very well do something."

"I don't doubt it, not after my experience with her this morning. I can't believe she'll tell us anything useful, though—she seems to speak in riddles and definitely enjoys playing games."

"Of course. She's a Vampire."

Becca snorted. "I can't imagine she'll say very much to Sylvan, and probably less to us."

"I'm sure you're right. However, much can be learned from what is not said. And with Francesca, even more can be learned from who she says it to. But that's not why we're going to see her."

"What haven't you told me?" Becca's pulse kicked up, and she wasn't sure if she wanted to hear what was coming next. It seemed every time she thought she had control, Jody did something to strip it away. She'd never met a woman—let alone a Vampire—who could keep her so off balance so consistently. "I don't like secrets."

"Then you will be very unhappy around Vampires. We survive by our secrets."

"And what if I told you I wanted to know yours?"

Jody slid across the seat until her thigh pressed against Becca's. Her mouth was against Becca's neck before she had a chance to flinch. And then she didn't want to flinch. Jody's lips were warmer than they had been earlier when they'd kissed. Not warm exactly, but more like melting snow. The heat of bitter cold tempered by the slow infusion of warmth.

"Jody," Becca whispered. She slid her hand onto Jody's thigh and felt the slender muscles tighten. "Tell me what you think I'll fear."

Jody's incisors pricked her skin, and Becca felt herself grow wet. The tip of Jody's tongue danced over her skin, and she heard a quiet moan. Her? Jody? A tremor rippled through Jody's body.

"What are you doing?" Becca gasped.

"I'm tasting you."

"Oh God."

"With your blood in my mouth, I can find you anywhere."

"How…How far?"

"If I were risen? The connection would have no boundaries. But I'm not, so my ability is less than it might be. But unless you get into an airplane and cross an ocean, I can follow your signature. I will find you."

Becca had never known how much she wanted to be found. She'd never considered herself lost. She always knew where she was and what she was about and where she would be going the next moment, the next day, the next year of her life. Planning gave her life structure and made her feel secure. Now not only was her life topsy-turvy, but she was presented with the realization she'd avoided all her life. She had never been enough to please her father. Subtle putdowns, deadly disdain, a lifetime of being unseen had made her forget how much she needed to matter to someone, to be appreciated for more than just her abilities. To be loved for herself. For the heart of her. She slid her fingers around the back of Jody's neck and into her hair. She pressed her mouth to Jody's, letting her heat warm Jody's cool flesh. When her tongue slid into Jody's mouth, the sensation was like standing in front of a roaring fire after walking naked through a blizzard. Every cell in her body burst to life.

Jody slipped her hand around Becca's waist and eased her silk shirt from her pants. She let her fingers rest on smooth, warm skin and allowed herself a few seconds of believing she could touch her, hold her, taste her…and nothing more. And then the lust struck. Not blind, not mindless, oh no. Totally focused. She hungered for *this* woman, *this* human. Becca. She wanted her. She wanted her blood, she wanted her body, she wanted her soul. Jody groaned and closed her eyes, and Becca's fingers tightened on her neck.

"I want you," Becca murmured, letting her head fall back against the seat. "Please, Jody. You already tasted me. Take more."

Jody's incisors completely erupted, and enough blood still filled her system for her sex to swell and throb. Her mind reached out, soothed Becca's. She could show her a dream, make it painless for her, make her forget it ever happened. She could have her, and Becca would never hate her for it. But Becca would never know her either.

Jody pushed herself across the front seat of the car until her back slammed into the door hard enough to leave a dent in the frame. "No."

Becca grabbed the wheel, clutching it to hold herself in place. "God, I'm sorry. Talk about throwing yourself at someone."

"Lara—I need to take Lara inside," Jody said hoarsely.

"I know. And now…Now you'll need to feed, won't you?" Becca

had done exactly what she hadn't meant to do. Again. She'd offered herself to Jody and once again been denied. And now Jody would take that passion, that undeniable hunger that Becca had stirred, and satisfy it with someone else. *God, that's going to drive me insane.*

"I won't," Jody said. "I won't feed."

"Don't make that promise," Becca whispered. "I don't even want you to. Please. Let's just go."

"Yes. Let's go." Jody opened the door and slid out.

Becca watched her, her heart in her throat. Outlined in moonlight, Jody resembled a sorrowful statue, glorious and bereft.

CHAPTER TWENTY

Becca recognized the voluptuous blonde even before the woman rushed out of the shadows, her hands grabbing for Jody, her mouth curved into an ecstatic bow. "Jody!"

How could she ever forget stumbling upon Jody feeding in a darkened room in the back of the club, or this woman's seismic orgasm when Jody's incisors had sunk into her neck? The blonde had been with a dark-haired man, but he had seemed an afterthought. Even though he'd been pressed against the blonde's back, fucking her enthusiastically as she lay in Jody's arms, the woman's attention had all been for Jody. When Jody had stroked her bare shoulders, fondled her breasts, and ultimately bitten her, the blonde had come screaming, and her orgasm wasn't triggered by the man moving rhythmically inside her. She'd ignited when Jody had fed from her throat.

Becca didn't even know her, and she didn't like her. A very uncharitable thought and one that was not typical for her. But whenever anything involved Jody, her normal behavior went right out the window.

Becca was a hair's breadth away from pushing the blonde's hand aside when Jody smiled, deftly avoided the clutching fingers, and said, "Tricia. You're exactly who I was looking for."

Says who? Becca clamped down on the tip of her tongue to stifle her protest. The rational part of her brain emphatically extolled, *not your business, not your business, not your business.* The rational part of her brain even understood that Jody needed to feed, would always need to feed or cease to exist. Sex and blood were inextricably connected in the Vampire's body and psyche. She got that, and she actually thought she was okay with it. What she wasn't okay with was the idea of someone sharing something so intimate with Jody. Damn it, she was jealous. She couldn't quite bring herself to believe something so incredibly special meant nothing to the parties involved.

Jody insisted that the bloodlust and the sexual release that followed were byproducts of her insatiable need to feed. Her biological drive to sustain her existence couldn't be denied or altered, and any pleasure derived from the act was secondary and often inconsequential to her. Maybe that was true for Jody—that the orgasm she experienced in the throes of bloodlust had little meaning—but Becca was damn sure that wasn't true for hosts. She'd seen enough of them—human and Were—climaxing in the midst of being bitten to know. And from the imploring look in Tricia's eyes, she was desperate for Jody to take her right now.

Becca had to struggle not to say, "Go find someone else. This Vampire is taken." And what if she did, and Tricia actually left? Jody would still need to feed. Could Becca feed her? Would Jody let her?

"This is Lara," Jody said, drawing Lara to her side with an arm around her shoulders. "She is mine, and she is hungry. I want you to feed her." Tricia's eyes registered surprise for just a second, then blanked, as if all thought had fled. When she blinked again, as if awakening, she instantly focused on Lara. Her smile was back, and so was the throaty purr of pleasure in her voice. "Oh, I'm so happy to meet you. Yes, please. I'd love to feed you."

If Becca hadn't been watching so closely, she would've missed that slight transformation, but now she recognized the thrall. Jody had ensnared Tricia and diverted her attention to Lara. Now Tricia probably believed Lara was the one she had always wanted. She certainly acted that way—sliding her arms around Lara's waist and rubbing her breasts against Lara's chest. Beneath Lara's tight T-shirt, the muscles of her chest rippled, and her breasts tensed. Lara's mouth opened, and white flashed against her dark red lips.

"Oh yes." Tricia clutched Lara, kissing her. "I want to feed you."

Even in the low light, the flames that leapt to life in Lara's eyes were as bright as the sun. She groaned and grasped Tricia's hips, dragging her hard against her body. Lara's incisors rested on her lower lip, larger than Jody's and glistening with the anticoagulants that would allow her to feed from Tricia's vein.

"Wait," Jody said quietly to Lara. "You cannot feed out in the open."

"Others do," Lara said, her hips grinding into Tricia as she licked her neck.

Tricia moaned and bunched Lara's T-shirt up in one hand, scraping her lacquered fingernails over Lara's back and leaving long welts. Lara panted, her body shaking.

"They are fools," Jody said. "You'll find cover before you feed."

"No," Lara rumbled, pinpricks of blood blossoming on Tricia's throat. "Let me drink her now."

Jody jerked Lara's head away from Tricia's neck with a seemingly effortless tug. "You must learn to feed safely. You never feed when you're exposed and unprotected, unless you want a stake in your back. Come with me." Jody signaled to Niki, who'd been standing a few feet away. "You need to guard the door. Becca will stay inside with me."

"All right," Niki said. Her dark shirt was soaked and clung to her shoulders and arms. She'd unbuttoned it, exposing her bare torso, and her breasts glistened. A line of fine red pelt dusted her abdomen. Jody traced her fingers down the center of Niki's torso, and Niki shuddered, a low groan reverberating in her throat.

"The room is filled with pheromones, and every Vampire is casting for an available host. You're already half-enthralled," Jody said. "Can you hold?"

"Yes," Niki said, her face angular and hard. She swept her hand down her body, wiping away the moisture. The muscles in her abdomen rippled under her palm. "You don't have anything to fear. I know how to absorb a call without losing control."

Jody nodded. "Yes, as the Alpha's second you would. Sylvan was right to send you."

Niki's eyes flashed. "I won't fail her. Or you, Vampire."

"Good." Jody glanced at Becca, then met Niki's gaze. "The human's safety first, do you understand, Wolf?"

"I know my job."

A push of power flooded Becca's mind, and she looked around. A circle of Vampires with flaming eyes closed in on them. Urgently, she said, "Jody. We've got company."

"I know."

Tricia whimpered and writhed in Lara's arms. Lara's eyes were blind with bloodlust. She dipped her hand into Tricia's dress and drew out her breast. She licked the nipple, an incisor dimpling the hard core, close to piercing it. Tricia whined *oh yes, oh yes, oh yes* over and over again.

"What do we do?" Becca murmured.

"They're drawn to Tricia's blood and Lara's hunger." Jody grabbed Becca around the waist and yanked her against her chest. "Kiss me."

"Wha—"

Jody's tongue filled her mouth, hot and firm and demanding. Heat surged down Becca's throat and flooded her chest, boiling the air in her lungs. Her breasts instantly swelled, and her nipples pebbled. She moaned, delicious tingling spreading from the pit of her stomach deep into her core. She tasted earth and fire, power so primitive her very cells shuddered. She arched into Jody and swallowed hungrily. So good, so thick and rich. So strong. Blood. Jody's blood.

"Oh my God," Becca gasped, pulling away from the kiss.

"Hurry," Jody said, holding a snarling Lara at arm's length with one hand. A thin trickle of blood coursed from the corner of Jody's mouth. The sight of it stirred a foreign hunger in Becca's belly. "Lara can't control her hunger, and she's exciting the others."

"What did you—"

Jody's eyes flared. "Blood rights, remember?" Jody gripped Lara, with Tricia clinging to her, and grasped Becca's arm. She pulled them all into a dark, narrow passageway crowded with feeding Vampires. "Don't look at anyone. Don't slow down."

Jody shouldered her way down the hallway to the room where Becca had first witnessed her feeding. Niki followed behind them, growling at anyone who came too close.

"Inside," Jody said, propelling Becca forward and following her in.

A bed covered with a plain white sheet stood against the far wall. Several overstuffed chairs and a rug were the only other furnishings. Smoked glass wall sconces provided dim illumination.

"No one enters," Jody said to Niki, who took up a post next to the door with her back against the wall.

"Understood," Niki snapped, and Jody slammed the door shut.

"Now," Lara gasped, an agonized groan reverberating in the back of her throat. "Now."

"You must hold her enthralled," Jody said to Lara. "I'm going to release her from my thrall, and you will hold her mind. If you don't, I will not let you feed."

"I'll try," Lara panted. "I'll try. I'll try. I want her. Please. I want her so much."

"I know, but you must learn to ignore the pain. Feel her mind. Read *her* desires. Feed *her* needs and she will feed yours. If you can't, you cannot feed. Do you understand?"

"Yes." Lara doubled over, the ridges in her stomach contracting spasmodically. "Please. Let me have her."

Jody cast a quick look at Becca. "Sit in one of the chairs. You'll be safe there. Don't come near us until it's done. No matter what you see, stay away."

For a second, Becca considered retreating into the hall. She wasn't bothered by Lara's hunger or Tricia's lust, she wasn't even watching them. She was watching the flames consume Jody's eyes. Jody must have cut her own lip to bleed into Becca's mouth, and now Becca couldn't stop wanting her. She tasted her with every beat of her heart. She'd watched Jody feed from Max when she'd wanted to be the one to feed her. She couldn't watch Jody take Tricia too.

Jody's eyes met hers and held. *I won't feed.*

Did she hear that, or was it an echo, a mere projection of her own desire? She couldn't ask that of Jody. She didn't even want to. She didn't want Jody to suffer, and she definitely didn't want her to go without the blood she needed to sustain herself.

The rational part of her mind, what little was left of it, reasoned that Jody had brought her into the room for her own safety. Not only that, but Niki couldn't guard the door effectively if she was trying to ward off Vampires who wanted to feed from Becca.

So she'd stay, damn it, and she'd watch. This was Jody's life. If she really wanted to know her, she couldn't hide from who Jody was or what she had to do.

"I'm all right," Becca whispered and curled up in one of the big chairs, drawing her legs beneath her and wrapping her arms around her knees.

Jody leaned back against the door and drew Tricia into her arms, Tricia's back to her front. Jody's arms came around Tricia's middle, one just below her breasts, the other slanting across her hips. An intimate restraint. Tricia grew limp for an instant, her body sagging as if a puppet master had cut the lines on a marionette, then her head snapped up, and she glanced around the room as if dazed.

"What?" Tricia moaned.

Lara cupped Tricia's face in her hands, a gesture surprisingly tender, and Tricia's lips parted with a sigh. Lara stroked her tongue over Tricia's mouth and Tricia arched against her.

"Lara," Tricia murmured, her hazy gaze lighting on Lara's face. "Touch me, baby, please. I'm so ready."

Lara's face was in profile to Becca, but she didn't have to see Lara's expression to imagine the hunger in her eyes. She saw Lara's arm move between her body and Tricia's, saw Lara's pants drop to the floor and Tricia's dress hiked up above her hips. The hard muscles in Lara's ass flexed and released as she worked her hips between Tricia's spread thighs. Tricia's face convulsed with pleasure and her head sagged back against Jody's shoulder. Lara reached down and hooked Tricia's thighs over her forearms, pulling Tricia's legs up around her hips.

"Oh my God," Tricia whimpered. "What are you doing to me? Oh my God, you feel so hot. How can you be so hot? You feel so good." Trica's head thrashed on Jody's shoulder, her throat rippling with moans. Lara thrust faster and Tricia's hips heaved. "Oh God, you're making me come. Oh, I have to come. Please. Please. More."

Lara's ass pistoned with such speed Becca could only catch glimpses of Tricia's pale thighs wrapped around Lara's golden buttocks. A growl burst from Lara's throat. Her head reared back, her eyes amber, slashed through with red, above her carved cheekbones and partially shifted jaw. Part Were, part Vampire, she was fiercely and terrifyingly beautiful.

"Oh please," Tricia keened.

Lara roared and struck.

Tricia cried out, an agony of ecstasy, as Lara buried herself in her neck. Lara's hips thrust rhythmically, a hard, steady cadence timed to her swallows, and Tricia's body convulsed in endless orgasm.

The intimacy was raw and powerful, but Becca experienced none of the erotic compulsion she'd felt when watching Jody feed from Tricia. That night, this night, Jody held *her* enthralled, not by her predator's power, but by her effortless strength and piercing vulnerability—by no other act than being who she was. Becca looked from Tricia's dazed face into Jody's, and her breath caught. Beyond the hunger that always burned in them, Jody's eyes were filled with longing.

"Jody," she whispered and Jody's lips parted. Her incisors were completely unsheathed. Blood streamed down Tricia's neck onto her chest as Lara fed, the thick red ribbon inches from Jody's mouth. Jody had to be close to bloodlust, and Becca couldn't bear for her to be in need. She rose from her chair.

"No," Jody gasped. "Too dangerous."

Danger from who? Jody? Lara? What did it matter? She couldn't help either of them. Becca sank back into her chair. She'd never been more helpless in her life.

CHAPTER TWENTY-ONE

D o not stray." Michel opened a steel vault door and led Drake and Sylvan down a narrow flight of stairs into a long dim hallway.

Drake checked out the empty passageway. Where were the guards? The attendants? The Viceregal either was very secure in her power or she had an army sequestered somewhere in this underground labyrinth. Drake suspected both things were true. Their footsteps made no sound on the marble floor, and no sign of life emanated from behind the line of closed doors they passed. The air was thick with the scent of blood and lust. Perhaps those rooms were bedrooms where hosts could recover. Drake's wolf, unhappy descending into the lair of another predator, growled and clawed at her in warning. Sylvan was too exposed here, surrounded by potential enemies.

We should have brought the centuri.

Sylvan rubbed Drake's back. *Don't worry, mate. I would not risk you.*

Drake wasn't worried about herself but had no time to argue. Michel knocked on a heavy, carved wooden door, opened it, and led them into a sumptuous parlor occupied by only one individual. Drake still didn't see any guards, but the Vampire standing by the fireplace was exactly as she had imagined—only she had underestimated the Viceregal's exquisiteness. The Viceregal had all the timeless beauty Drake associated with Vampires: the ethereal countenance, the elegant carriage, the brilliant, piercing eyes, perfect skin, lush features, and shimmering aura of sensuality. The Viceregal was a creature of dreams—glorious scarlet tresses falling in sinuous curves over milk-white shoulders, a long, slender neck without a single blemish, sapphire eyes, ruby lips. Beneath the sheer, silvery gown, full breasts, a narrow waist, and flaring hips invited fantasy. Drake's skin tingled, and languorous warmth spread through her blood. An erotic invitation teased along her nerves, and her clitoris pulsed. A faint pressure built behind her eyes. She rumbled low in her chest. Mind probe. Subtle and disturbingly enticing.

Beside her, Sylvan snarled. "Viceregal. You insult the Timberwolf Pack."

"Alpha," the Viceregal said with a smile lifting the corner of her mouth. Her gaze lingered on Drake, glittering with amusement. "Forgive me. She's quite commanding. I'm afraid I was carried away."

Drake remembered what Sylvan had said. Francesca was a chess player. All Vampires loved games, most especially games of the mind. Their mind control was the true seat of their power, even more than the lust and pleasure they were able to induce in their prey. It would not do for the Viceregal to think she was easily influenced or nonplussed. "I've looked forward to meeting you, Viceregal. Sylvan speaks highly of you."

Francesca's brows flickered and she chuckled. "Does she?"

Drake intentionally took her time clasping the back of Sylvan's neck. The Viceregal would know protocol dictated no one touched the Alpha in public. No one except her mate. She stroked Sylvan's throat, letting her fingertips play over the wild pulse. "Yes, she does."

"Francesca," Sylvan said, "allow me to introduce my mate, Drake."

"Yes, Michel informed me of the happy news." Francesca's gaze followed Drake's fingers moving on Sylvan's throat, her midnight irises shimmering with tongues of fire. "I should chide you, Alpha, for not telling me instantly. We would have honored the occasion in the appropriate fashion. We mustn't forget the old ways."

"No, we mustn't." Sylvan leaned her hip against Drake's. "I appreciate you seeing us on such short notice. I understood you had a message for me. I also was hoping you might be able to help me with some information."

Francesca swept across the room to the divan and settled into one corner, extending her arm toward Michel. "Come join me, darling." She indicated the matching divan opposite her. "Make yourself comfortable, Sylvan. Drake. Would you care for tea?"

"No, I'm afraid we're short for time." Sylvan sat, and Drake joined her. "Forgive my rudeness."

"Darling, I can forgive you almost anything." Francesca laughed and played her fingers through Michel's hair. "I can't imagine how I could help you, but you know we are always friends of the Timberwolf Pack, even when others doubt you."

Sylvan tensed, and Drake curled her fingers around the inside of Sylvan's leg. The banded muscles beneath her palm relaxed. Sylvan's breathing quieted.

"I received a message from Becca Land, the reporter you spoke with earlier today," Sylvan said.

"Yes, the human. She's quite delightful. I do hope we see her again soon."

Drake was certain the Viceregal knew that Becca was currently in the club. There couldn't be much in the Viceregal's territory that she didn't know.

"We're trying to keep this quiet until we have a chance to investigate," Sylvan went on, "but several nights ago, someone tried to assassinate me. At least, we believe I was the target. There's a chance it was Jody Gates, the Councilor's daughter."

Francesca's expression darkened. Michel's lids lowered lazily, and she kissed Francesca's bare shoulder. "I can't believe anyone would try to kill you, Sylvan. What a foolish thing to do. That would completely destabilize the Coalition. And we certainly would not want that."

"Certainly not," Sylvan said dryly. "There are, of course, factions both Praetern and human who would like to see the Coalition's mission in Washington fail."

"Well yes, of course." Francesca sighed. "But I'm afraid those radicals and zealots will always be with us. Now that your father's Exodus has exposed us to the world, violent opposition will become part of our existence."

The muscles in Sylvan's leg jumped under Drake's fingers, and Sylvan's power rose. Drake's blood quickened. Her sex pulsed, and her wolf resumed pacing. She leaned forward, still slowly stroking Sylvan's thigh. "The Coalition presents a uniform Praetern power to the world. Its stability is critical to deterring organized resistance to Praetern independence. I would imagine that's what Sylvan's father had in mind when he proposed the Coalition."

Francesca's gaze drifted over Drake's face. "How is it that I don't know you, Drake? I've seen all of Sylvan's wolves over the years. I would not have forgotten you."

Beside her, Sylvan growled. Drake held Francesca's gaze.

"I am Sylvan's mate, Prima to the Timberwolf Pack. Who I was before is no longer important."

"Well said, Prima." Francesca's hand drifted over Michel's shoulder and down her chest, lingering on her breast before trailing lower and settling between her legs. Michel's face showed no response, but her breathing visibly increased.

A whisper of warm breath caressed Drake's neck, stroking down her throat to her breasts, as if moist lips were feathering over her skin. The caress played along her spine and settled low in her belly, stirring her sex. Thrall. She breathed in Sylvan's scent, pressed her fingers harder against Sylvan's thigh, absorbing her heat. She centered herself, grounded herself in her mate, and the probing tendrils disappeared.

Francesca laughed again. "She's worthy, Sylvan. But then of course, you knew that."

"You intimated to Becca this morning," Sylvan said, her voice having grown deeper and gravelly, "that my enemies might be my friends. I've always counted you as my friend, Viceregal."

Francesca's eyes flashed, and Drake caught a glimpse of fiery depths churning below the brilliant blue surface—hot lava flowing down a mountainside, immolating all in its path.

"These are uncertain times, Alpha," Francesca said. "We are at war, but the battle lines have not yet been drawn. Our enemies may stand on both sides of that line when the conflict begins. I and my Dominion will always stand for the Praeterns. Where will you stand?"

"You know where I stand," Sylvan growled. "The Timberwolf Pack will always be first. I will not turn my back on my Praetern allies, but I won't go to war against humans simply to preserve them as a potential source of prey."

"Humans provide the Weres with no critical resources," Francesca said, her expression blanking. "You aren't faced with the possibility of extinction if the balance of power shifts."

"I just walked through your club," Sylvan said. "If anything, you have more prey now that you are able to hunt out in the open than you ever had before."

"Yes," Michel said, breaking her silence. Her gaze swept over Sylvan with disdainful fury. "But freedom always comes with the threat of chains. The first time humans learn of a host being turned involuntarily or of a newling losing control and killing a host, we

Vampires will bear the brunt of the backlash. Humans outnumber us. Where will you and your wolves stand then?"

"You doubt my allegiance, Vampire?" Sylvan said softly.

Drake let her wolf ascend. If a fight was coming, she would fight in pelt. A rumble of warning escaped her throat.

"Michel is passionate," Francesca murmured, stroking Michel's chest casually. "Would not your second take up your cause as ardently, Alpha?"

"I sympathize," Sylvan said, her tone cool. "If your sovereignty is threatened, Viceregal, or your Dominions endangered, come to me. As you did my mother."

"There are those, Sylvan darling," Francesca said quietly, "who fear you may lead us into greater danger by conceding to terms that will favor humans over us. That what you seek to gain will come at too high a cost. Be careful, darling."

Drake snarled. She'd had enough of the Viceregal's familiarity where her mate was concerned. "That sounds like a threat."

"Not at all, Drake," Francesca said. "A caution from someone who cares for your Alpha." She looked pointedly at Sylvan. "You might do well to reconsider your allegiances."

"What do you hear of my missing females?" Sylvan asked abruptly.

Drake thought she saw the Viceregal tense at Sylvan's sudden question, and then Francesca was her imperturbable self again.

"Nothing, I'm afraid," Francesca said. "You're welcome to speak to Guy, our main bartender. You know him, I believe, Sylvan. Or any of my security. Perhaps they saw some of your wayward…females, did you say? That would be unusual, wouldn't it?"

"Very," Sylvan said evenly. "Our females do not leave the Compound unprotected."

"I'm afraid I can't help you, but I will certainly have Michel instruct our people to be on the lookout for anyone who shouldn't be here."

Sylvan stood and Drake followed. Sylvan encircled her shoulders, and Drake caressed her abdomen. The Viceregal watched them intently, her mouth parting as if in anticipation.

"Why would someone want our females?" Sylvan asked.

Francesca shrugged elegantly. "Darling, how could I possibly know?"

Drake didn't see her rise, but Francesca was suddenly a heartbeat away from Sylvan. Drake's wolf reared up and snarled, and her skin prickled with the rush of pelt under her skin. She didn't realize she'd growled out loud until Francesca turned to her, an indulgent smile on her face. "Don't worry, Prima. I know better than to touch. Now."

Drake's fingertips ached with the press of her claws just beneath the surface, and her sex swelled and pulsed. Francesca surveyed Sylvan with open desire, and Drake's vision hazed. She panted, holding down her wolf. Attacking the Viceregal would not help Sylvan's cause.

"It's always about the power, Sylvan. Consider where your power truly lies." Francesca held out her hand to Michel. "It's nearly dawn, and Michel and I have others to attend to. Don't be a stranger, Alpha."

The door behind them opened, and two dark-haired Vampires in dark trousers and form-fitting silk shirts appeared, apparently to escort them out. When Drake looked back, Francesca and Michel were gone. She had things she wanted to discuss with Sylvan, particularly the thinly veiled threats from the Viceregal. But discussion would wait until she had Sylvan alone and could remind her exactly where, and with whom, she belonged.

I already know, Sylvan telegraphed.

I'm going to enjoy reminding you.

Watching Lara feed and Jody struggle not to, Becca fought to keep her silence. Jody's eyes were opaque black, flat and deadly. Her pale skin had whitened above her hollowed cheeks, and her parted lips were a crimson slash framing her elongated incisors. Her throat rippled as she swallowed the feeding hormones flooding her mouth. She was hungry, so hungry, and Becca ached to see her suffer. She could barely imagine Jody's need, even though the anguish was written so plainly on her face.

Becca knew what it was to be lonely, to struggle with a bone-deep sense of isolation and solitary struggle. But she did not know what it was like to hunger for, *starve for*, life itself, hour after hour, day after day. She could not imagine the price such hunger exacted, or the cost of assuaging it with the lifeblood of others for eternity.

"Release her," Jody said, her voice harsh and tight. She gripped the back of Lara's head, her fingers entwined in Lara's tawny hair, but she didn't pull Lara away from Tricia's throat. "Release her."

Lara shuddered, and Becca's stomach clenched. Would Lara be able to stop feeding? Another thing Becca could only imagine—the control it must take for a Vampire to stop short of destroying the host, when their every instinct clamored for more. But Jody could stop, and Lara must learn to do it. Becca held her breath, silently praying that Lara could obey. If Jody was forced to destroy Lara after saving her, the tragedy would be doubled. Lara's sacrifice would hurt the Timberwolf Pack, and Jody would blame herself for failing. How much more must Jody endure?

"Now," Jody snarled, and Lara's head jerked away from Tricia's neck. Lara groaned, shuddering as if an internal war were being waged. Shoulders heaving, she braced an arm on either side of Tricia and Jody, caging them in against the door.

"It still hurts," Lara gasped.

Jody supported Tricia between them, cradling Tricia's head on her shoulder and stroking Lara's cheek with her free hand. Tricia made faint whimpering noises, her face slack, her hands fluttering over Lara's chest and arms. Jody said, "It will always hurt. You'll learn to live with it."

Lara slumped to her knees, burying her face against Tricia's abdomen. "Tired. Tired."

Becca rose, but Jody shook her head. "Wait."

Jody lifted Tricia into her arms, carried her to the bed, and gently placed her down. After covering her with the sheet, she rapidly gathered Lara into her arms and opened the hall door. Niki immediately appeared, her eyes sharp and wary. Jody held Lara out to her.

"Take her to the car," Jody said. "We'll be there in a few minutes."

Niki sheltered Lara against her chest, surveying her blood-tinged face with an angry expression. "When will she wake?"

"Not until tonight. She is vulnerable to more than the sun now. All Clans have enemies. Guard her carefully."

Niki snarled. "I don't need to be told how to protect one of the Pack."

Jody smiled thinly. "She is also Clan *Chasseur de Nuit*. Now you guard a Night Hunter."

Niki's eyes flashed again, and she turned her back, disappearing down the hall.

Jody closed the door behind her and returned to the bed. Bending down, she stroked Tricia's face. "I will send someone to watch over you. You did well tonight."

Tricia reached for her, her face soft and sensuous. "Stay with me. Let me—"

"No, no more tonight."

Becca wasn't sure how Jody managed it, but the door opened again to admit a sleek female Vampire with short, thick blond hair scooped back from her angular face. She looked from the bed to Jody. "You have need of me, Liege?"

"Guard her until she's recovered. See that she is escorted home. She is not to host again tonight."

The female inclined her head. "Yes, Liege. Do you require me to bring a host for you?"

"No," Jody said tightly. "Your service is noted, Amelie."

Amelie nodded once more and took up a post by the door, arms folded beneath her high breasts, ignoring Becca as if she were a mere ripple in the air.

Jody leaned over Becca's chair and lowered her voice. "We don't have much time before dawn. Are you ready?"

"For what?"

"To see the Viceregal." Jody held the door open, and Becca followed her out into the hallway. The dim corridor was packed with Vampires feeding from Weres and humans, sometimes two or three at a time. A wall of muted groans, sharp cries of satisfaction, and moans of impending orgasm assaulted her. A wave of erotic heat surged through her, and her legs trembled. She grasped Jody's arm. "Oh my God."

"Don't," Jody said, jerking her arm away. "You can't touch me right now."

"You need to feed," Becca said.

"Since when did you become an expert on Vampires?" Jody strode into the melee, and Becca hurried to keep up with her.

"I don't need to be an expert to know how difficult it was for you to resist feeding in there. You think I can't see the hunger in your face?"

"You have no way of knowing what is in my face."

"That's not true. I know you hunger. I know you need. I know you're hurting right now." Heedless of Jody's earlier warning, Becca grasped her hand. Jody's fingers were cold. Trembling. "You said yourself dawn is coming. You need to feed before then, don't you?"

"I'll manage." Jody snarled.

"How? I know I asked you not to, but—"

"I'll manage."

Becca wanted to argue, but every step was becoming more difficult as bodies crowded in on her from every side. Fingers trailed over her shoulders and back. Warm breath played against her neck. Her nipples contracted and her stomach tightened. She wanted sex in a way she never had before. Mindlessly, relentlessly. She moaned softly, and cool, strong fingers closed around her wrist.

Come with me, a voice whispered in her mind. Male, female? She couldn't tell. She didn't care. The words were a soothing caress calming the blaze eating away at her insides, a soft mouth moving over her sex. She whimpered softly and turned to the shadowy figure drawing her deeper into the darkness. She took a step and pulled up short. What was she doing? She did not want what waited in the dark. She wanted the bright, burning power of Jody's kiss, not mindless lust. "No," she whispered, and the magnetic pull evaporated, leaving her weak and panting.

Jody blurred past her, and in the fraction of a second before Jody grabbed the Vampire who had just held her arm, Becca saw animal rage in Jody's face. Jody pinned the male Vampire to the wall with his feet off the floor, her forearm crushed across his throat. She pushed her face close to his as she strangled him.

"She is mine." Jody's voice was barely above a whisper, but it shot through the hallway like a whip cracking, and silence fell like a shroud. "She carries my blood. You dare trespass?"

Becca's skin prickled with apprehension, but she held back her protests. This was not her world. These were not her rules. She might not get the subtle power games, but she didn't need a roadmap to know Jody was enforcing some kind of hierarchy. If she interfered, she'd probably put both of them in danger, and they were way outnumbered and surrounded by starving Vampires. When the Vampire Jody had against the wall stopped thrashing and went limp, Jody released him as if he were no more than a discarded toy. He fell to the floor in a boneless heap. He might be dead. Becca couldn't tell. She didn't know how Vampires died.

The Vampires who had crowded around her before drew back amidst a swell of murmurs and hisses, leaving her and Jody alone in the center of the hall. She brushed Jody's hand. She might have been touching a marble statue.

"Jody? Let's go."

Jody spun around, her eyes empty of recognition, her lips drawn back in a soundless snarl.

"It's okay," Becca whispered, trembling inside. She cupped Jody's jaw, letting her fingers trail down her throat. "It's okay."

"He dared to enthrall you," Jody growled, her voice as foreign as her face. "He would have *fed* from you."

"No. No, he wouldn't have. He tried, but I felt you. You." Becca took a shuddering breath. Her connection to Jody might be borne in blood, but it lived in her heart. "He couldn't pull me away from you. Jody, I—"

"Come." Jody took Becca's hand and led her rapidly down the hallway, the path suddenly clear as figures pressed against the wall as they passed. No one reached for Becca, not a single hand brushed against her. No minds touched hers. More than one voice murmured *Liege* as they passed.

"What just happened back there?" Becca asked.

"A reminder of the rules. Hosts have not always been as plentiful as they are now." Jody stared straight ahead as they walked. "Clan territories were once clearly delineated and hunting across borders forbidden. Now that the Exodus has exposed us and hosts seek *us* out, our natural order has been thrown into chaos. The Clan heads must reestablish order, or we will destroy ourselves."

"They called you Liege."

"I am the Clan heir and carry my father's mantle of power."

"Did you kill that Vampire?"

Jody glanced at her coolly. "Does it matter?"

"I'm not sure how I feel about you killing someone to protect me." Becca followed Jody through one narrow hallway after another, completely disoriented. This wasn't the way she had gone to Francesca's quarters the last time.

"To protect you?" Jody laughed. "You think me so selfless? I am a Vampire. I kill to protect my territory, my Clan, my Dominion. You are part of my Dominion now."

Becca snorted. "Since the day I met you, you've tried to shock me and alienate me. It didn't work then, and it's not working now." She shrugged. "I can't pretend to understand what you don't explain to me. You're not human, so there's no reason to expect human rules to apply. I trust you'll do what you have to do to protect yourself and those who depend on you."

"Just like that?"

"For now," Becca said.

Jody's head whipped around. "Why? What reason do you have to trust me?"

"Because I know you're not heartless. I don't know why you pretend you are. One day you'll tell me."

Jody's jaw tightened. "You are naïve."

"No, I'm not." Becca stopped in the middle of the now-deserted corridor. A vault door was visible at the far end, opening no doubt into Francesca's lair. Once they entered, she wouldn't be able to speak so freely to Jody. She didn't know what they were facing, but she knew Francesca would try to separate them—one way or another. Suddenly, it was very, very important for Jody to know how she felt. "I saw what you did when Lara was dying and what you're doing to save her now. You had no reason to save her, but you did. You have no reason to care why someone is killing human teenagers or to discover what's happened to the Were females. But you do. I *know* what you're capable of. I know what it cost you back there in that room not to feed from Tricia in front of me."

"You think too much of me," Jody said quietly.

"No, I don't. But I do think of you all the time, and it's time you knew that." Becca slid her arms around Jody's neck and kissed her. "I want this. I want all of this."

"Becca," Jody groaned, pulling her close. Too long, she'd waited too long—to slake her thirst, to feed her hunger. Tricia's blood had called to her, igniting her bloodlust, enflaming her need, but she'd held back. Like a battered ship on a storm-ravaged sea, she was slowly sinking beneath the inexorable force of her own passion. Becca filled her mind. Becca was all she could see, all she could feel. All she wanted. "Hold very still."

"Don't enthrall me," Becca whispered.

"I won't." Jody lifted Becca into her arms and carried her into the dark shadows of an adjoining alcove, sheltering her from passersby. Jody kissed her mouth, slicked her tongue over the surface of her lips, played her tongue down the bounding pulse in her neck. The jugular rippled next to the pounding carotid, a siren's call spearing into her depths and dragging her under the waves. Battling to hold on to her reason, fighting the blind ecstasy of lust, Jody gently pierced the skin of Becca's neck, slipping through muscle and connective tissue until the vein opened and hot, thick life flowed into her. The fist of pain lodged beneath her breastbone diminished, and pleasure kicked through her pelvis. She insinuated her thigh between Becca's and heard Becca whimper. She swallowed, and her hips jerked, tendrils of orgasm wrapping around her spine, teasing the surface of her mind. Her fingers brushed over Becca's breast, and she swallowed again.

"Oh my God," Becca moaned, her hands in Jody's hair, her back arched. "Your mouth is so hot, so incredible." She stroked Jody's neck and held Jody's face more tightly against her neck. "I know you. Do you hear me? I know you."

Jody's rein on her reason slipped. She needed more, more of life, more of not being alone. More of Becca. She drove deeper, flooding Becca with hormones, and Becca cried out.

"Don't stop." Becca's fingers twisted in Jody's shirt and her hips thrust into Jody's. "God, God don't stop. I'm there. Oh God, God I'm there already."

Orgasm crashed through Jody with every pull at Becca's throat. Becca shuddered in her arms, caught in the undertow of their shared bloodlust. Some small corner of Jody's reason demanded she stop. She had to stop. Stop or risk hurting Becca. Groaning, Jody braced her arm against the wall and dragged her mouth away from Becca's throat. She panted, holding Becca upright with her arm around Becca's waist, while the ravenous hunger raged for her to take more. To take and take and take. She licked the punctures in Becca's neck and sealed the wound. Becca's eyes were closed, her chest heaving. Her nipples strained against the thin fabric of her shirt. Her hands roamed over Jody's breasts and stomach.

"Becca," Jody gasped hoarsely. "Becca, did I hurt you?"

"No," Becca murmured, her voice languorous and low. She pressed trembling fingers against Jody's cheek. "The bite…hurt a little, and then God, so much pleasure. I want you naked. I want you again."

"You taste so good," Jody whispered, resting her forehead against Becca's. "I could have made it so you didn't feel any pain. If you want me to—"

Becca's eyes snapped open. "No. I don't want anything to stand between us, not even your mind. Promise."

Jody nodded. An easy promise to keep. She could never let this happen again.

CHAPTER TWENTY-TWO

Drake kept her hand on Sylvan's back as the two Vampires led them from the center of Francesca's lair through a winding passageway and up several staircases. She was driven to touch Sylvan as much as she was compelled to send a signal that Sylvan was hers. The Viceregal's many thinly veiled threats aimed at Sylvan and her seductive taunting had ignited a fury of possessive rage. The aching pressure in her loins had climbed to an agonizing level during the meeting, and now a searing pain sluiced through her. How much was breeding frenzy and how much the mate bond she couldn't tell, but even the slightest distance between her and Sylvan made her skin burn as if a caustic solution was being poured over her naked body. She could barely see. Her wolf howled to claim her mate.

How bad is it? Sylvan telegraphed.

I'm all right. Just get me out of here.

You're strong, but not strong enough to subdue this need. I hurt. Your need is mine.

How much farther? If she could just get close enough to Sylvan, she could withstand the urgency pounding in her head, in her blood, in her loins. The Viceregal's sensuous voice played through her mind, and she flashed on the way Francesca had looked at Sylvan, as if she'd wanted her mouth on her. Drake's vision shimmered and her claws extruded. She tore open the back of Sylvan's shirt. The scratches on Sylvan's back bled, and Drake's wolf howled again, calling to her mate. Sylvan's canines shot out, blazing white indentations against her lower lip.

Drake shuddered, a blade of heat sliding beneath her skin, filleting her alive. She moaned softly, and Sylvan spun around to face the escorts who flanked them.

"My mate and I require your service," she said.

The female of the pair nodded. "Of course, Alpha."

"A private room."

"This way," the female said, turning down a narrow, nearly dark hallway that branched off the main artery where they walked.

No, Drake warned. *We are without guards. You're not safe here.* Her skin was clammy with sex sweat, her shirt soaked through. *I can wait.*

I can't. Sylvan pushed open a plain, black door and addressed the guards. "No one enters."

"Yes, Alpha." The two Vampires turned shoulder to shoulder and blocked the doorway.

Sylvan pulled Drake inside and slammed the door. She didn't bother turning on the light. They could both see as well in the dark as in daylight. She grasped Drake's shoulders and spun her against the wall. Within seconds, her mouth was on Drake's, her tongue sliding between Drake's lips, her hands opening Drake's pants. Drake's canines raked over Sylvan's tongue, and the taste of her own blood in Drake's mouth brought Sylvan's clitoris fully erect. Sylvan yanked at her fly with one hand and pushed Drake's pants down over her hips with the other.

"Straddle me," Sylvan growled.

Gasping, Drake kicked free of her pants and wrapped both legs around Sylvan's narrow hips. "Oh God, you're so hard, so hot." Drake's head rocked from side to side, her eyes glazing over. "I'm burning up inside. I need you. Now, now, I need you now." Her stomach tightened, the muscles bunching into hard knots, and her sex readied. "Hurry. Hurry. Oh God."

Sylvan plunged her tongue deep into Drake's mouth, drinking her in, savoring the wild taste of virgin timber and rushing rivers and untamed life. Her loins filled with the essence of all that was Were, and she pumped against Drake's core, needing to fill and be filled, needing to join.

"I'm going to come," Sylvan gasped, burying her face against Drake's neck, panting and shivering as her hips plunged in an ever-increasing staccato rhythm. Drake's claws dug into her ass, forcing more and more hormones into her glands. Sylvan felt the bones in her face shifting, felt the wolf running close beneath her skin in a fury to claim her mate. Drake must have sensed her nearing the edge and ripped her shirt open. Their eyes met, gold flaring into gold.

"I love you," Sylvan groaned.

"I love you." Drake's hips bucked, and she spilled over Sylvan's stomach and groin, drenching her in pleasure. Igniting her. Sylvan roared, and Drake slid her canines into Sylvan's chest. Sylvan's head snapped back and orgasm scorched through her. Her clitoris expanded, filling Drake's opening, and her glands pumped furiously, secreting the breeding hormones deep into Drake's body. She was locked into Drake now, her hips involuntarily thrusting, the crush of their pelvises forcing her glands to empty. Panting, she sagged against Drake while she pumped and emptied, over and over and over.

Sylvan's legs gave way, and Drake eased them down to the floor. Drake braced her back against the wall and cradled Sylvan between her spread thighs. She cushioned Sylvan's head against her shoulder. "I'm sorry I couldn't wait."

Sylvan licked her neck and rumbled contentedly. "Why would you apologize for needing me?"

"This isn't safe. None of the *centuri* are here. Max is going to kill me."

Sylvan laughed and caressed Drake's breast. "Francesca's guards would not let anything happen to me here. That would look very bad for the Viceregal."

"They know you. You've been here before, like this."

"No." Sylvan kissed the mate bite on Drake's shoulder. "Never like this. You are my mate. The only one."

"I'm sorry. I shouldn't have asked."

"Why would I mind you wanting to claim me?"

Drake stroked Sylvan's hair, aware of how exhausted Sylvan was right after they tangled. Sylvan was vulnerable now. Drake's wolf bristled, needing to protect her. "Francesca threatened you. I was tempted to kill her."

Sylvan nuzzled Drake's breast and tugged on her nipple through her T-shirt. "That might be politically inadvisable."

Drake's hips lurched as pleasure streaked through her belly and settled between her legs. "Stop that, or you'll ready me again, and I think you might need a little more time to recover."

Sylvan growled. "Never. I will always be ready when you need me."

"I'm all right now. At least for a while. I want to go see the Revniks."

"Now?" Sylvan rolled her head back until she could study Drake's face. "You thought of something?"

"Something Jody said earlier. The medical examiner said the girls with Were fever looked like they'd been in another hospital before arriving at our emergency room. They showed evidence of multiple intravenous puncture sites, among other things. What if they hadn't been in a hospital? What if they'd been in a laboratory?"

Sylvan stiffened. "And you think our females might be in the same place?"

"The same or similar. The Revniks will know what kind of local facility could handle subjects for a protracted period of time without anyone else knowing. There can't be many in our area. Places like that are expensive to build and maintain. To say nothing of the security needed."

"But that doesn't explain why I cannot feel my wolves."

"I may have an answer to that as well." Drake gathered her energy and pushed herself upright. She held out her hand, and Sylvan took it, rising beside her. They straightened their clothing, although Sylvan's shirt was shredded and Drake's fly wouldn't zip all the way.

"You look like you've been attacked by a rabid wolf," Drake mumbled.

"Not rabid—just the opposite." Sylvan grinned and kissed her. "Healthy and strong. All breeding females are powerful and…"

"What?" Drake caressed Sylvan's shoulders, rubbing the knots at the base of her neck with her thumbs. "What, love?"

"Something Francesca said." Sylvan's eyes glowed wolf-gold in the dark. "She said to look to where our power lies."

"Our power lies with you," Drake said. "Don't you think it was a warning that you may still be a target?"

"But we weren't talking about the attempted assassination then. We were talking about our missing females." Sylvan draped her arm around Drake's shoulder and pulled her close. "We guard our females because only the females carry the Were DNA. Both male and female Weres produce breeding hormones, but only a female Were can produce a Were offspring. The males do not carry Were mitochondrial DNA."

"Ah, God," Drake murmured. "You think someone is trying to force breed females?"

"Or perhaps figure out how to artificially replicate the process. Cross-species breeding has occurred, but it's rare."

"To what end? And who would do this?" Drake's every instinct rebelled against the idea, but it wouldn't be the first time one race attempted to subjugate another by controlling reproduction.

"Our enemies," Sylvan murmured. "Or perhaps our friends."

❖

"You need to give me a minute," Becca said, rearranging her clothing with shaking hands. "I can't face the Viceregal until I catch my breath."

Jody stroked her hair, her eyes still shimmering with lust. "You look beautiful."

Becca's heart tripped. Jody had never touched her, never looked at her, with such tenderness. In that moment, she was lost. "You're a little overwhelming, Detective Gates. I...I'm afraid I'm quite undone."

"No more than I," Jody murmured. She stepped back, averting her gaze. "I didn't mean to do that."

"Which part?" Becca had half expected Jody's retreat. Jody had perfected the art of isolation, and now she had to be thrown by how intensely they'd connected. Becca was still reeling, still stunned by how easily she'd accepted Jody into her body, into her psyche. God, into her heart. How could something so many humans labeled unnatural feel so incredibly right? She touched Jody's arm. "Which part do you regret? Feeding from me? Or feeling me?"

"Becca," Jody whispered, and her voice carried the weariness of ages. "You don't want what you think you want with me."

"Don't presume to know what I want. And whatever you do," Becca kissed her, "don't ever presume to make my decisions for me."

Jody shook her head. "As if anyone could."

"Some have tried. But not anymore."

Jody caught Becca's chin in her hand and stared into her eyes. "Who? Who tried to put out the fire in you? You burn so bright, so strong. Who would ever want to dampen that flame?"

Becca's throat closed, and she wasn't sure she could answer. How many times growing up had she heard *don't be so independent, follow the rules, I know what's best for you, do as I say.* "My father, for one. But I rather thought you found my persistence annoying."

Jody smiled, her thumb tracing back and forth over Becca's lower lip. "I do. Supremely so. But I wouldn't change it."

"If you want to keep whatever appointment we have, you'll need to stop now." The stroke of Jody's thumb stirred need low in the pit of her stomach. She was wet, and her clitoris throbbed, and she wanted Jody's mouth on her neck again. She wanted to swallow eternity in Jody's kiss. "I want you again. Only this time I want to taste you."

"We can't." Jody's face hardened. "I won't risk blood thrall."

"You don't know I'm susceptible." Becca laughed grimly. "Just because you make me come harder than anyone ever has? You think I'll become just another host? A quick meal for you in trade for mind-blowing orgasms?"

"Don't belittle what we shared," Jody snapped.

Becca caressed her face. "I won't if you won't."

Jody caught her wrist and kissed her palm. "Have you no sense of danger? No sense of your own fragile mortality?"

"Of course I do. Far more than you. I've always known I would die. I don't fear death, not at the cost of living. Don't try to make me."

"And how do you think I would feel if I were the cause of your death?"

"Is that what you fear? Why?"

Jody exhaled sharply. "We have no time for this."

"We have no time for anything else," Becca whispered.

Jody entwined her fingers with Becca's and drew her against her side. "We need to see the Viceregal. It is required."

"Fine. But this conversation isn't over."

Jody kissed her. "Is any conversation with you ever over?"

"Not where you're concerned," Becca said against her mouth. She let her tongue slide over Jody's, felt the tips of Jody's incisors, receded now, like a distant promise. The memory of Jody entering her, drinking her, drowning her in hormones made her body pulse with renewed desire. "God, I want you again. In bed, with nothing between us. You'll be…quiescent…today, won't you?"

"Yes."

"But if I stayed with you, you would know I'm there."

Jody pulled her close, a tremor racing through her. "Yes. I would know you're there."

"Then say yes. Say it now before we have to face Francesca. Give me that."

Jody closed her eyes and pressed her forehead to Becca's. "All right. Yes. Yes."

"Then let's go see the Viceregal so we can go home before I have to worry about you and the sun."

Jody chuckled. "You think I am so easily gotten rid of?"

Becca caressed Jody's face. "I'm more worried that you don't care enough to be careful."

"You don't have to worry about me."

"Too late." Becca lifted Jody's hand to her lips and kissed her knuckles. "Way, way too late."

❖

"Forgive the informality, Ms. Land." Francesca lounged on the divan in the parlor, her head in Michel's lap. Michel's shirt was open, her breasts barely covered. Michel's pale skin was flushed a rosy hue, as was Francesca's. Michel's hand rested inside Francesca's gown, her long fingers visible through the gauzy material as she stroked the Viceregal's breast. "I'm afraid you've caught us at a bad time. Had I known you were coming down to see me…" She gestured toward the open bedroom. "They were eager."

"Thank you for seeing us," Becca replied. Through the open door, three naked humans were visible, lying in a jumble on top of the maroon sheets. She didn't believe for a second that Francesca hadn't known they were on their way. She suspected the whole scene was staged, but she wasn't moved by it. All she could feel was Jody.

Beside her, Jody said quietly, "We were delayed, Viceregal. My apologies for disturbing you at this time."

Francesca rubbed her cheek against Michel's bare chest. Michel sucked in a breath, her hips rising indolently beneath Francesca's head. "What is it, Jody, that couldn't wait until tonight?"

"I've come to claim blood rights over the human, Becca Land," Jody said formally, "and to petition that you declare her forbidden to any Vampire in your Dominion."

Francesca pushed herself upright. Her eyes glittered, and her full lips parted seductively. "And do you intend to complete the blood bond? Declaring her sacrosanct would be contrary to our customs otherwise."

"The bond is not required," Jody said.

"No, but it is expected."

Becca sensed Jody stiffen. There it was again. The bond Sylvan had mentioned and that Jody clearly did not want her to know about. "Explain to me. What is the blood bond?"

"Nothing you need to be concerned with," Jody said without looking at her.

"I wasn't actually asking you." Becca regarded Francesca. "Viceregal?"

Francesca laughed as if delighted. "Are you sure you want to continue with your claim, Jody?" Idly, she ran her fingers down the center of Michel's bare torso, as if she were petting a favored animal. A dangerous animal.

"I have made the claim, Viceregal." Jody's voice was tight.

"Have you exchanged blood?" Francesca asked.

"Yes," Becca said.

"No," Jody answered simultaneously.

Francesca's eyes narrowed. "And still you do not complete the bond?"

Jody remained silent.

"Your father's Dominion is at risk as long as you are not a bonded heir, Jody. Now is not the time to destabilize one of our strongest Clans." Francesca rose, and power shimmered on the air. "Accept your responsibility, and do what must be done. Otherwise, I do not acknowledge the claim."

"I can make the claim without your support," Jody said.

"You would challenge my authority in this?"

Francesca was inches away so quickly, Becca almost stepped back. She forced herself to remain still, but her heart was jumping around in her rib cage, searching for a way out. A wave of suffocating heat struck her, as if the air had been sucked out of the room, and a giant fist closed inside her chest, making it impossible to breathe. Her head pounded, and spots danced before her eyes. Jody groaned and dropped to her knees. A trickle of blood flowed from Jody's nose. Her hands opened and closed convulsively. Becca's lungs burned.

"Stop it!" Becca panted, struggling to stay upright as she pushed herself between Jody and Francesca. "Whatever you're doing to her, stop it."

"You are indeed brave." Francesca smiled, her fingers skating along the edge of Becca's jaw. She leaned close and kissed her. Her mouth tasted of honey and ancient seas and timeless skies.

"Oh," Becca gasped. Electricity arced through her, and orgasm swelled in her depths. Exquisite, aching pleasure—and nothing to do with her. Unwilled, unwelcomed. She drew a breath and surrendered to instinct. She stopped fighting the invasion and opened herself to the power. The erotic charge flowed through her and dissipated into the air, like lightning discharging into the earth. Her skin prickled, and the choking in her chest eased. Suddenly, she could think. Her body was her own again. "Please. Let her go."

Francesca cocked an eyebrow and regarded her with interest. "You are no ordinary human, Ms. Land."

"I'm very ordinary," Becca said breathlessly, taking Jody's arm as Jody staggered to her feet. "I just won't stand by and see you hurt her."

"She has already absorbed some of your power, Jody," Francesca said, returning to the divan. She curled against Michel, rested her head on Michel's shoulder, and pressed her palm to Michel's abdomen. "The bond is nearly forged. Do what should be done."

"The blood rights?" Jody asked through gritted teeth.

The Viceregal waved a hand. "Yes, yes. I acknowledge your claim on this human." She opened Michel's shirt and kissed her breast, her incisor glancing over a tight scarlet nipple. "Leave us."

"My Liege," Jody murmured, grasping Becca's hand and pulling her toward the door.

Francesca made no acknowledgment but drew Michel's hand between her legs. Michel locked eyes with Becca, leaned over Francesca, and worked her arm deeper between Francesca's thighs. Francesca moaned, her head thrown back, her hips undulating.

Becca forced her gaze away, and as they escaped into the darkened hall, Francesca's laughter washed over her like a familiar caress.

CHAPTER TWENTY-THREE

"Niki and Lara are here," Sylvan said as she and the *centuri* left the club. She grasped Drake's hand and threaded her way between the vehicles until they reached Becca's Camaro. Niki stood by the side of the vehicle, her arms folded across her chest, legs spread, eyes tracking the lot in all directions. When she saw Sylvan, she dipped her head.

"Alpha."

Sylvan looped an arm around Niki's neck, pulled her close, and kissed her forehead. *"Imperator."* She glanced into the backseat. Lara lay curled in a fetal position, eyes closed. "How is she?"

"Asleep. Or unconscious, I'm not sure."

"She fed?"

Niki's jaw tightened, the muscles along the sharp edge bulging. "Yes."

"And how are you?" Niki's features were drawn and tight, a gold rim burning around forest green irises. Even in the moonlight, her skin glistened. Sex sheen. Nocturne was always a sea of sex and blood, but in the hour before dawn when the Vampires feasted, the very air bled. Weres weren't captives to blood like the Vampires, but their wolves became aggressive when surrounded by so much of it. All the *centuri* were aroused. If Niki had been a witness to Lara's feeding, she would need to tangle, and she'd just been in a club full of Vampires. Sylvan knew very well what a powerful draw a Vampire could be when the frenzy hit. "I can leave Andrew with Lara if you need—"

"No," Niki said quickly. "I can do my job, Alpha. As you ordered."

Sylvan stroked her face. "There is no one I trust more. You know that. But if you need—"

"No," Niki repeated, her gaze lowered, holding no challenge. "I need only to safeguard the Pack."

"Stay with Lara, then—protect her. And the Vampire and the human, too, as much as you can." Sylvan lifted her head and scented. "They're on the way. Bring Lara to the Rover—we'll follow them to the Vampire's lair and brief you on the way. I want Lara with me for a few minutes. I want you both to feel me. To feel the Pack. You're ours, Niki. Don't ever doubt that."

"Yes, Alpha." Niki's eyes flashed, and she rubbed her cheek against Sylvan's neck.

"Don't worry, my wolf." Sylvan caressed her cheek. "I will bring you home soon. Both of you."

❖

"You should drive," Jody said, skirting around the front of Becca's car to the passenger side.

"I was planning on it." Becca looked at Jody across the roof. "Are you all right?"

Jody glanced to the east where the sky was lightening. "Yes, just a little tired."

"We'll be home soon."

Jody smiled at the word. She rarely thought of her town house as anything other than her lair. The place she went to avoid the sun, where her blood servants gathered to nourish her at sunrise and sundown. The seat of her power was not a place, but existed in her mind. Ironic, for beings who lived forever, to care so little for the physical. Watching Becca drive, the way her hands held the wheel, her fingers sliding now and then along the curve, reminded Jody of just how pleasurable the physical could be. Touching Becca, absorbing the heat of her skin, was a pleasure that far surpassed the countless orgasms she'd experienced in the years since she'd come into her maturity and first fed.

Becca glanced over at her, then reached across the space between them and took Jody's hand. Jody wondered at the bright swell of pleasure in her chest from the all-too-human action. She tightened her fingers around Becca's and rested their joined hands against her leg. She very rarely sought or welcomed touch. When she fed, she caressed her hosts in the way she knew would excite them, but she did not require their attentions, only their blood. The orgasms she experienced as the life-enriching ferrous compounds infused her system had nothing to do with intimacy.

All that had changed with Becca. When she'd fed from Becca, she'd held herself back, keeping the bloodlust at bay so she could taste Becca, feel Becca's body pressing against hers, hear Becca's cries of pleasure. She'd managed until the very end to maintain her sanity, to preserve a thin patina of awareness, and then she'd had to succumb to the mindless need. Becca's blood had filled her, and the lust had claimed her consciousness. She did not want that emptiness with Becca.

"Whatever you're thinking," Becca said quietly, "you can stop. Some things can't be controlled by reason." She laughed, a warm sound that sluiced over Jody's skin, banishing the chill that always lingered beneath the surface.

"What?" Jody asked. "What do you find humorous?"

"I'm telling a Vampire, whose mind is like a steel trap, not to think." Becca laughed again. "Everything about us—you and me—is a contradiction."

"Yes," Jody said, surprised by a sudden surge of exhilaration. "That makes it interesting, don't you think?"

"Interesting. Yes. It does make it that."

The heaviness of the coming day settled over Jody, making her limbs sluggish and her mind dull. She did not want to sleep. She did not want to leave Becca unprotected.

Sylvan's Rover pulled to the curb in front of her town house, and Becca parked behind it. Jody climbed out, unlocked the door to her town house, and held it open for Niki, who carried Lara inside. Becca followed.

Sylvan remained outside on the landing. "Do you require extra protection?"

Jody shook her head. "I have soldiers who will guard the lair during the day. What do you intend to do?"

"Search out the possible locations where our females might be held."

"And if you discover where they are?"

Sylvan's canines flashed. "We will free them."

"You could be going up against significant firepower. If whoever is holding them also attempted to kill you, they're going to be firing silver. You should let me put together an attack force of Vampires. We are the superior advance team."

"Tell me, Vampire," Sylvan said conversationally, "if you had to guess, who do you think is holding our Weres?"

"Humans," Jody said immediately. "Vampires have no need to capture Weres. Our two species know more about each other than anyone else."

Sylvan nodded. "Even the Fae, with their powers, and the Magi with their spells could not hold one of us."

"What about other Weres?"

Sylvan snarled. "Possible, but why?"

Jody shook her head. "One of the things we must discover."

"I have given you two of my best," Sylvan said, looking past Jody into the house. "It seems we are together in this. For now."

"For now." Jody backed up as a ray of sunlight shot across Sylvan's face. In another few seconds, the foyer would be flooded. She was weary and she was hungry. "Wait for me, if you can, Wolf. We may be stronger together than apart."

Sylvan smiled. "An odd admission for a Vampire."

"Times have changed."

"Yes, they have." Sylvan clasped Jody's shoulder. "We'll meet you at sundown, then."

❖

"Come with me," Jody said and headed briskly down the center hallway.

Becca and Niki, with Lara in her arms, hurried after her. Becca wondered where Jody's hosts were. Did they live in the house with her? Did they arrive at some prearranged time? Did they sleep with her? That thought soured her stomach. Maybe she'd better just wait and find out before she made herself crazy.

Jody unlocked a heavy, oak-paneled door and turned on a light, revealing a wide wooden staircase. Jody stood aside while they passed her and started down the stairs, then entered and locked the door again. Becca surveyed the large room at the bottom of the stairs. Except for the absence of windows, the room resembled the parlor directly above it—bookcases, leather sofas and chairs, thick carpets, and dark wood wainscoting. Three doors led off from the space, and Jody indicated one to the left. "Put Lara in there."

Niki nodded and opened the door onto a bedroom. She placed

Lara in the center of a double bed, arranged a pillow beneath her head, and rejoined them, closing the door.

"What if she wakes?" Niki asked.

"She won't," Jody said. "Not before me."

"How many other entrances are there to this place?" Niki asked.

Jody smiled. "There is a tunnel that connects the lair to a host house, which is guarded twenty-four hours a day. There are multiple checkpoints along the way."

Niki snorted. "Two entrances—one by the stairs, one by this tunnel. You have no guards here?"

"Not usually," Jody said.

"You're foolish, Vampire." Niki shook her head.

"I have no reason to fear for my…life," Jody said.

Becca spoke up. "Maybe you didn't previously, but your involvement with the Weres changes things. If someone is attempting to destabilize the Coalition by killing Sylvan, they may also be targeting your father or, as his heir, you. Or both of you."

Without looking at Becca, Jody said, "In the case of an attack, if I am unable to respond, protect Becca first, then Lara."

Becca sucked in a breath. "You do expect trouble. What aren't you saying?"

"I agree that my association with the wolf Weres is known or will be soon. Everyone in the club saw me with Lara and Niki and you. I can protect myself. I want Niki to protect you."

"Oh, all right," Becca said sharply. "And do you mind telling me how you're going to protect yourself in the middle of the day when you can't even move?"

"I'm not comatose. I can move around if I have to."

"Inside, maybe." Becca waved her hand around the room. "But what if someone breaches your lair and drags you out onto the sidewalk? What's going to happen then, Jody? How long can you survive in direct sunlight?"

Jody's jaw tightened. "If I'm at full strength, I can survive long enough to do what I need to do."

"At full strength." Becca glanced at Niki, then back at Jody. "You should feed."

"And you should be blood-bonded," Niki rumbled. "I can feed you."

Jody shook her head. "We need you at full strength too."

"I am not diminished by giving you blood," Niki said.

"No," Jody said softly. "But you are in danger of becoming ensnared. Go watch over your Packmate. I have no need of you now."

Becca grabbed Jody's hand. "Which room is yours?"

When Jody indicated the door opposite Lara's, Becca dragged her over, opened the door, and pulled her inside. She slammed it.

"Stop keeping secrets from me," Becca demanded. "After what happened at Nocturne, don't you think I deserve to know what you need? What makes you vulnerable?"

"The more you know, the more you are in danger. Knowledge is dangerous."

"Ignorance is more dangerous." Becca grasped Jody's shoulders. "What makes you think it's all right with me for you to sacrifice yourself? You don't get to make those decisions, Jody. Not where I'm concerned."

Jody's eyes darkened, and Becca felt the press against the surface of her mind, as if a heavy weight were bearing down on her from above. "Stop that. Don't you dare try to influence the way I feel about this."

Instantly, the pressure receded. "I'm sorry."

"You damn well should be." Becca stroked Jody's face. "Where are your hosts? Shouldn't they be here?"

"I haven't called them yet."

"Why not?"

"You said you wanted to stay with me."

Becca's heart twisted. "I do. I will."

"Then I'll feed when I wake up."

"You don't want me to see, is that it? I already have, remember?"

Jody feathered her fingers through Becca's hair. "That was before. Before I touched you."

"Oh boy," Becca whispered, turning liquid inside. "You do really, really scary things to me." She leaned against her, tightening her arms around Jody's neck, and kissed her. Her tongue immediately brushed over Jody's incisors, and they were no longer a promise. They were fully unsheathed, sharp and dangerous, eroticly powerful. She tightened, swelling and throbbing. "What is the blood bond?"

Jody stiffened and would have pulled away, but Becca held her fast.

"No more secrets," Becca whispered against her mouth.

"This is not something humans can know."

"I'm human," Becca murmured. "But I will never betray you."

Jody rested her cheek against Becca's hair. "When a living Vampire—a pre-animate—dies, blood stops circulating, the heart stops beating, the brain goes into a suspended state. Unless ferrin-rich blood is provided within a few hours, the Vampire cannot rise. Death is permanent."

Dread settled in the pit of Becca's stomach. There was more, she knew it. "So someone needs to give you a blood transfusion?"

Jody averted her gaze.

"Well? What?"

"Not just anyone. Someone whose blood is compatible. A blood mate—someone whose blood has been prepared. Otherwise, the organs reject the new blood. The result is the same. True death."

"Prepared. Prepared how?"

"Unlike in the living state, the organs of a Vampire who has died have no barrier against the foreign blood. If unprepared blood is used in the animation procedure, a massive transfusion reaction, for want of a better term, will occur, and the Vampire dies."

"That's why you need a bonded host," Becca said. "To prepare the blood somehow? How?"

"A series of blood exchanges, small amounts between the Vampire and the bonded host over time. The Vampire's immune system becomes accustomed to the foreign antigens, the blood mate builds up stores of compatible ferrin-compounds, and when the blood mate provides the transfusion after death, the organs will accept the blood. Revitalization occurs and the Vampire rises."

"We've exchanged blood," Becca said. "That's what Francesca was asking about, isn't it?"

"Yes, but not enough. You are not responsible for me."

"What if I want to be?" Becca whispered.

Jody pushed away. "You don't understand. The more blood we exchange, the more you will be tied to me. You run the risk of becoming addicted. Of needing to be turned or facing insanity. You might not survive the turning."

"But none of those things are certain, are they?" Becca said.

"No."

"But it is certain that if you are not bonded, and you die, you will not rise. That's what you're telling me, isn't it?"

"Yes," Jody said quietly.

Becca felt the distance between them widen, even though neither of them had moved again. She could let the chasm build. That would be the smart thing to do. The safe thing to do. So many things she didn't know. So many things Jody didn't want to tell her. *I'm doing this for your own good*, she'd heard so many times as the invisible bars closed around her life. But Jody sought not to ensnare her or capture her or enslave her. Jody sought to keep her free. And what was freedom, if not the ability to choose?

"Every time we've touched, that's been real, hasn't it?" Becca asked. "No thrall?"

"Yes."

Becca stepped across the divide and, pressing full-length against Jody, kissed her. "Can I feed you again?"

Jody skimmed her fingertips over the contours of Becca's breasts and whispered against her mouth, "Not so soon."

"Then call someone, I'll be all right." Becca opened Jody's shirt and trousers and skated her hands over Jody's chest, caressing her breasts, her smooth abdomen. "Do it now, Jody. I don't want you endangered because you're weakened."

"Not yet. I want you." Jody unbuttoned Becca's shirt and pushed it off her shoulders. She unclasped her bra and disposed of that as she backed her toward the bed. Becca's knees hit the mattress, and they both went down in a jumble. Jody stretched out over her, and their bare breasts met in a surge of heat. Becca arched at the electric shock of pleasure.

"Oh God." She skimmed her hands down Jody's back and pushed at her pants. "Take these off." When Jody lifted away to strip off the rest of her clothes, Becca quickly got rid of her own pants along with her panties and everything else. Her skin was scorching, and all she wanted was the cool press of Jody's body. Pulling Jody back down on top of her, she wrapped her calves around Jody's thighs and fused their centers. She was swollen, hot and hard and throbbing.

"Can you feel me?" Becca gasped. "How ready I am for you? How much I want you?"

Jody's eyes flickered between midnight and flame, her lips slightly parted, her incisors flashing like ivory daggers in the dim lamplight.

"You play with fire, Becca," Jody warned.

"Apparently, I do." Becca caressed Jody's tight-nippled breasts. "And I don't plan on stopping."

Jody groaned and circled her pelvis, working her center over Becca's. She traced her tongue over the pulse in Becca's throat.

Becca whimpered. Her clitoris felt like it was going to explode.

She so wasn't ready to come, but she wasn't sure she could stop it. *Think.* Thinking always helped her hold on to her control. "Can you come without feeding?"

"Sometimes," Jody murmured, her mouth against Becca's neck now. "If I'm full, the blood makes me potent for a while."

"I want you to come with me before you feed from anyone else." Becca tightened her legs, thrusting her hips, forcing Jody to follow suit. "I'm going to come…" She gasped and struggled to focus. She just needed to hold on a little bit longer. Until Jody couldn't escape. "I'm going to come, and I want you to come with me. I want you to drink me. I want you to be one with me." She pushed her tongue into Jody's mouth, and just as she planned, Jody's incisor opened a thin line along the side of her tongue. Her blood flowed into Jody's mouth, and Jody reflexively swallowed. Jody's hormones flowed into her mouth and Becca drank. Jody jerked in her arms, and then more blood flowed, binding them.

Jody reared back, yanking her head away. "Becca, no."

"I know what I'm doing," Becca gasped, gripping Jody's shoulders. "I know what I want. Give me your blood."

"Forgive me," Jody moaned and slashed her incisors across her wrist. Crimson rivulets dripped from her marble forearm onto Becca's lips.

Becca opened her mouth, her gaze locked on Jody, and swallowed. Her body ignited, an explosion of pleasure so intense she screamed. Jody was everywhere—in her mind, in her body, in every corner of her being. She came and came, drops of Jody's blood searing her tongue.

CHAPTER TWENTY-FOUR

As Andrew pulled the Rover into the huge parking lot of Mir Industries situated on the outskirts of Albany, Drake scanned the sprawling research and pharmaceutical complex. Even at five thirty in the morning, the parking area was half-full. Lights burned in many of the windows. Sylvan directed Andrew to park in the rear by a private entrance.

"Wait for us here," Sylvan said to the *centuri.*

Drake and Sylvan loped toward the rear of the building. Before they reached it, an unmarked steel door opened and a black-clad, auburn-haired female with broad shoulders and narrow hips stepped into the doorway. An automatic rifle rested in her right hand, canted down by her side but clearly in position to swing into readiness in an instant. She inclined her head. "Alpha, Prima. We did not expect you."

"Good morning, Chris," Sylvan said, brushing the backs of her fingers lightly over the guard's jaw.

Chris glanced toward the Rover as if expecting to see the *centuri* emerging. When no one did, she said, "I will call an escort for you."

"That's not necessary," Sylvan said. "We are not expecting any trouble, but nevertheless, raise the alert status to level three."

"Yes, Alpha." Chris closed the door behind them and issued orders into her radio. "I'll accompany you to the elevators."

They traversed the halls in silence, nodding to the Weres who snapped to alertness as Sylvan passed, until they reached the private elevators in the research wing.

"You can return to your post, Chris." Sylvan brushed a hand over the guard's shoulder as she stepped onto the elevator. "Thank you."

"An honor to serve you, Alpha." Chris's face glowed with pleasure and pride. She nodded to Drake, her gaze level with Drake's shoulder. "Prima."

"Chris," Drake said quietly. The reverence extended to her as Sylvan's mate would take some getting used to. The doors closed and they were alone again. "You seem quite sure Leo and Nadia will be here."

"Yes, I can sense them. But I expected they would be here, since they usually are. Or they would be soon."

Drake leaned against Sylvan's shoulder, enjoying the contact. The frenzy that had ridden her so hard for the last few days had abated after their last mating. The urgency in her loins still simmered, but she could think. Her skin no longer felt as if it were being stripped from her muscles, inch by inch.

"You're better?" Sylvan asked.

"Yes, I think so. Can you feel the difference?"

Sylvan settled against the back of the elevator and pulled Drake against her chest, back to front. Threading her arms around Drake's waist, she rested her chin on top of Drake's shoulder and nuzzled her neck. "I still hunger for you, but I can wait. This time yesterday, I couldn't."

"I think the breeding frenzy has passed. How long does a heat usually last?"

"Several weeks," Sylvan said. "We don't conceive easily—it often takes continuous joinings."

"More than we've had."

Sylvan hesitated. "Yes."

"An aborted heat, then." Drake sighed. Although she was glad that both she and Sylvan would soon be able to function without the constant urgency to tangle, the disappointment cut deep. She'd never given a great deal of thought to raising a family. She'd never really anticipated having the kind of relationship that would lead to permanence or expected to love anyone the way she loved Sylvan. She'd never expected a mate. Now, when the opportunity to conceive appeared to be beyond her, she ached for what she wouldn't be able to share with Sylvan, with the Pack. Sylvan's mouth was warm against her neck, comforting. Drake reached behind her and stroked Sylvan's face. "I'm sorry."

A rough warning growl rolled from deep within Sylvan's chest. "Why would you say that to me?"

Drake turned in Sylvan's arms, letting her thighs rest against Sylvan's, and kissed her. Sylvan's mouth tasted like a summer night—charged with heat lightning and life. "I know what you need, Sylvan. You're Alpha. You need to breed for the good of the Pack. And because your DNA carries the strength of generations of Were Alphas, you must have an heir." She kissed Sylvan's throat. "That's your destiny, your birthright. I love you for it."

Sylvan's eyes slid from blue to gold so fast, Drake caught her breath. She forgot sometimes how close Sylvan's wolf prowled to the surface. The shift was so swift she couldn't tell the moment when the bones in Sylvan's face elongated, when her jaw grew heavier, when her canines slid down in a show of dominance and power.

"You are my mate." Sylvan's voice was lethal, and the power that rolled from her made Drake's legs weak. "I've chosen you, my wolf has chosen you. Do you choose me?"

"Of course, God, of course I choose you." Drake framed Sylvan's face, rubbing her thumbs over the sharp crests of Sylvan's transformed face. "You're everything to me."

"Do you regret being turned?"

Drake smiled. "Not only don't I regret it, I love being Were."

Sylvan's eyes flashed, and her features softened infinitesimally. "Don't ever apologize to me again for things you cannot control."

Resting her forehead against Sylvan's, Drake rubbed Sylvan's shoulders and stroked her back. Now was not the time to distract Sylvan from the dangers that faced them by bringing up future challenges. "Don't scare the scientists. Calm down, love. Tell your wolf to rest."

Sylvan grumbled again, but her power receded like the tide from shore, leaving heat playing over Drake's skin—lingering ripples in the sand.

"I love you," Drake said. "I would give you anything—"

Sylvan covered Drake's mouth with hers. Her kiss was hot and hard and demanding. Drake could no more resist Sylvan's call than she could stop the breath from moving in her lungs. She closed her eyes and let herself be dominated, for in the belonging, she found safety and purpose and contentment. Sylvan's legs went rigid against her, and she heard a hungry groan rise from Sylvan's chest.

"Not now, love," Drake murmured and pulled away. "You said you could wait, remember?"

"I said I *could*," Sylvan grumbled. "I didn't say I wanted to."

Drake laughed softly despite the persistent pain in her heart.

"Good, I wouldn't want you to find waiting comfortable. But you're still going to need to." Behind them, the elevator doors slid open. She backed up, pulling Sylvan with her out into the hall. "You have business to attend to, Alpha."

Sylvan snarled softly. "You test me, Prima."

"Oh, I hope so."

❖

Becca slowly became aware of lying on Jody's bed with Jody in her arms. She swallowed and tasted the dark tang of Jody's blood. A rush of power and pleasure coursed over her. No wonder humans and Weres flocked to Nocturne. Sex with Jody stirred every one of her senses, and though she doubted any other Vampire could have touched her as deeply or as powerfully, even half of what she'd just experienced would have been mind shattering.

"I can't feel my arms and legs," she whispered. "I don't think I've ever come like that in my life. For a few seconds, I don't think anything separated us—nothing physical, nothing mental, nothing emotional."

Jody rubbed her face against Becca's neck, her mouth hot as it brushed over her throat. "The blood joined us, Becca. I've never…"

"You must have exchanged blood before."

"Yes. Sometimes unintentionally. Sometimes to heighten a host's pleasure."

Becca's eyes narrowed. "I'm not a host."

"No," Jody said softly. "No, you're not. I've never exchanged so much. Never felt so much." She caressed Becca's face. "Never lost myself in anyone that way."

"Good." Becca smiled, supremely satisfied, and stroked Jody's back. Jody's skin was cool. Too cool. Becca gently pushed Jody over onto her back and leaned up on her elbow to get a good look at her. She was beyond pale. Her hair clung to her neck in wet strands, her breathing was ragged and rough, and shudders racked her body. She hadn't fed nearly enough.

"Did you call someone to host?" Becca asked.

Jody shook her head.

"Why not?" Becca cupped Jody's chin and forced her to meet her eyes. "What are you trying to prove?"

"I don't want anything between us. Not yet."

"You don't get it, do you, Vampire?" Becca shook her head and kissed her. Even her lips were cold. "Nothing will come between us that we don't let between us. But I'm not going to watch you suffer because you can't tell the difference between taking what you need to survive and giving me what I need to be secure and satisfied." She covered Jody's heart with her hand. The beat was slow and sluggish. A streak of terror raced through her. Was it possible that Jody could actually die from not feeding? "What I want is in here. If you feel anything for me, if you—"

Jody silenced her with a kiss so possessive, every thought fled her mind. Jody's tongue filled her mouth, stroked over hers, and she knew only an unbearable force scorching through her and a wanting so deep she trembled. "God."

"I don't have the right words," Jody murmured.

"You don't need them." Becca rubbed against Jody, fitting the curves of their breasts and the arches of their hips together until there was no space between them. "Call your host, do it now."

"You can wait next door," Jody said. "I won't be—"

"I'm not going anywhere."

A knock sounded on the door, and Jody stared at Becca. "Are you sure?"

"I'm very sure. I won't run from what you are. I have no reason to."

"Enter," Jody called without taking her eyes off Becca.

The door opened and closed, and a gorgeous young man in his early twenties—thick black shoulder-length hair, longish sideburns, olive skin, brown eyes—approached the bed. Handsome. Young and virile, bare chested and barefoot, wearing only loose, dark sweatpants.

"You called a man," Becca murmured. "Somehow I thought you would want—"

"I want you," Jody said. "I am only feeding from Carlos. I can't help what happens—"

"I know that. I don't expect you to." Becca didn't usually go in for public displays of affection, but there was so much she needed to say, and she had no idea where to start. The young man stood patiently a few feet away. She kissed Jody again. "I want to hold you while you feed. I want to be the one to make you come."

"You already did." Jody frowned and looked confused, an expression so rare Becca's heart nearly melted.

"Don't tell me a Vampire as powerful as you is a one-shot wonder," Becca said, grinning.

Jody's brows drew down. "It's very dangerous to insult a Vampire."

"Oh, believe me, I know." Becca brushed her fingers through Jody's hair. "Do it now, baby. Do it now."

Jody turned her back to Becca and murmured, "Carlos."

The young man smiled and stretched out on the bed, facing Jody with a foot or so of distance between them. His eyes were clear but seemed to be focused on something far beyond them. Becca wondered what vision Jody had created for him. What memory she had embellished or what fantasy she had brought to life. Clearly, wherever he was, whatever he was experiencing, he was happy. Happy and unafraid.

Becca slipped one arm under Jody's head and the other around her waist. When she fitted herself against Jody's back, the curve of Jody's ass nestled against her stomach. Burying her face in Jody's hair, she stroked her breasts and her belly.

"Carlos," Jody murmured, "are you ready?"

"Yes, please, Liege," Carlos said softly.

Becca felt Carlos move closer on the bed and looked down. His hand rested on Jody's hip. His touch was not intimate as much as familiar. Becca continued to caress Jody's chest and abdomen as Jody cradled Carlos's chin and turned his head away from her. Exposing the jugular vein, Jody slid her incisors neatly and cleanly into his neck. Carlos jerked, a gasp of pleasure escaping his throat as his back arched and his pelvis thrust forward.

Jody's ass tightened against Becca's belly, and she groaned. Beneath Becca's palm, Jody's heart raced wildly like an animal thrashing in a cage. Jody was holding back, fighting the bloodlust.

"Don't fight it. Don't fight who you are." Becca caressed Jody's stomach and slipped her hand between Jody's legs. Jody was hot and slick and so beautiful. "I want you to come."

The instant Becca cupped her, Jody's hips jerked, and her orgasm burst against Becca's hand. The thrill of feeling Jody come in her arms nearly set Becca off again. She pressed her cheek to Jody's shoulder and closed her eyes, battling the arousal spinning through her. She was in bed with a Vampire in bloodlust, and Jody could just as easily take her after finishing with Carlos. She *wanted* Jody to take her. She wanted Jody's mouth on her throat. She was desperate for the mind-dissolving eruption of pleasure that followed fast on the shining pain of Jody's bite. But if Jody took her now, in the mindless throes of lust, she would hate herself for endangering Becca. Her Vampire lover was very complicated. Becca shuddered and kissed the back of Jody's shoulder. She's asked to be here, damn it. She'd just have to hold on.

Jody fed for what seemed like a long time, the only sounds in the room the steady measure of her swallowing and Carlos's deep groans, as if he were in pain or terrible pleasure. Becca never stopped her caresses, feeling Jody's orgasm crest over and over again. Eventually, Jody stopped drinking, and her hips quieted.

Carlos fell onto his back, his eyes closing. He let out a long sigh and slipped into a post-orgasmic daze. Jody turned to Becca, her dark eyes tortured.

"Becca, I couldn't stop—"

"I think you're beautiful," Becca said. "I love your power. I love your tenderness. I know you don't think of yourself that way, but you are. So tender." She pulled Jody on top of her. "Touch me. I need you to make me come."

"I want you." Jody slipped her fingers between Becca's thighs and entered her.

"Oh yes." Becca's belly tightened as Jody filled her and slowly worked her way deeper. She gripped Jody's shoulders, riding her hard until she exploded. "Yes, yes, mine."

"Becca," Jody groaned. "You make me helpless."

Becca smiled shakily. "I was rather hoping I would make you strong."

"I never knew what true strength was until you. Without you—"

Becca feathered her fingers over Jody's mouth. "I'm not leaving you. Not ever."

"Forever is not the same for us."

"Maybe. Maybe not." Becca kissed her. "But I know what matters—I know what I want. I'm yours, and remember this, Vampire— you are mine." She turned her head and bared her neck. "Take my blood. Give me yours. Make our connection unbreakable."

Jody traced a line down the side of her own neck and bright red blood slicked her flawless skin. Cradling Becca's head, she pulled Becca's mouth to her throat. "With this blood, I bond us."

Becca sealed her mouth to Jody's throat and drank her in, power and pleasure detonating in her depths. *I love you. Oh God, I love you.* Too soon, Jody pulled her mouth away and bit Becca's neck, and Becca was lost in their joining.

Chapter Twenty-five

Metal scraped on stone, and Gray jerked upright in her restraints. The guards were coming. It must be morning. No light penetrated the depths of her cell from the corridor beyond the bars. The murky air enclosed her like a heavy fog, clouding her mind. Footsteps drew closer. She shook her head, mustering her strength. Shimmering particles danced in the air, hazing her vision. Or maybe her exhaustion had her imagining things. Shouldn't the air be clear? Somewhere in the ceiling, fans whirred continuously, and constant currents wafted across her bare skin. Maybe they were filtering it or recycling it or poisoning it. Could you poison air? Maybe that's why she couldn't control the rage or the frenzy. Her belly rumbled. Hungry. Her stomach cramped, and she started to double over, but the chains on her arms stopped her. Hurt. Belly hurt. Razor blades gouged at her insides. Her wolf. Her wolf was winning. She didn't care. Too sick and hungry and tired to fight.

A dark form took shape in front of the cage, and she blinked. One. Only one. Where were the others? Even a single human could best her now. Fury rippled along her spine, and she readied herself. She was a Timberwolf Were. She would not fail the Alpha. She would not fail her Pack. She let her wolf come.

"Stay quiet."

She recognized the voice. The guard Martin, the only one of her jailers who had not tortured her.

The soft clink of tumblers falling as a key turned, and then the cell doors opened silently, and he slipped inside with her. So, he had finally come to take his pleasure with her. Pelt bristled beneath her skin, and her claws and canines abruptly extruded.

Claws tore through her fingertips, and her sex swelled.

Katya's warning whispered through the gloom, below the range of human hearing. "Gray, no. I know you want to shift, but don't. Don't."

Gray snarled, her jaws snapping on air as she struggled for freedom.

"Listen to me," Martin said, his voice low and urgent. "You understand me, don't you?"

Gray growled. Her wolf was close now, so close.

"I know you understand me. I'm trying to help you."

The dark menace of a stun baton glinted in his right hand. Pain. Shock. Pleasure. Release. She thrashed, her head rocking from side to side, her canines ripping at her lower lip.

"Damn it." He pushed his hand through his hair. "They've got more tests planned for this morning. I'm trying to buy you time."

He grabbed her shoulders, something none of them had ever done before. She could rip his arm off if she angled her head just right. Even the restraints would not hold her back. He shook her. "Listen to me. I'm on your side."

"You imprisoned us," Gray rasped, her voice rusty and rough. "You torture us."

"I don't want to! Jesus, I'm not one of them," he said.

His scent was different from the others. They always smelled like sex and fear. His scent was a warning call, signaling danger. Different. But she didn't trust him. She bared her teeth and tried to shrug his hands away.

"I didn't know what they were going to do." He looped the baton into his belt and held his hands up just out of range of her teeth, as if he trusted her not to hurt him. "I didn't know what this place was. I didn't know what they did here. When I found out, I couldn't do anything, or they would've discovered I'm a spy."

Gray struggled with her wolf's imperative to destroy him. Think. The Alpha would want her to think. *We are not animals, we are Weres. We are hunters and warriors. We are swift and strong and smart.* Her chest hurt so much. Her stomach cramped. Her sex pounded with pain. "Who are you, then?"

"One of a group of humans trying to find out who's behind these atrocities. To stop them."

"Can you get us out?" Gray stopped struggling, but she couldn't quiet her racing blood.

His face contorted. "No. Not without giving myself away, and I'd just end up getting us all killed."

No one in this place had befriended her, and she wasn't going to trust a human now. "Tell the Alpha where we are, then. She'll come."

"I can't," he said. "I don't *know* where we are. They transport us here by bus for our tours. We're scanned when we enter and leave. No cell phones, no beepers, no cameras, no chance of carrying a tracking device."

"Then let us loose. We'll fight our way out."

"You'll get killed." He glanced down her body, then into her eyes. The humans hardly ever looked into her face. Her wolf grumbled at the challenge, but she let him examine her for a second. Then she allowed her wolf to show in her eyes, and he averted his gaze. "They're getting impatient. Stepping up the frequency of the tests. If they don't get what they want, I'm afraid they'll go after someone else. You need to delay today's test. Every hour helps."

"How? I can't do anything." Gray rattled her chains. "If you let me loose when the other guards come, I might be able to overpower them."

He turned his back, his shoulders tightening. Then he spun around. "If you kill them, they'll just bring someone else in after they kill you both. But if you don't have anything to give them during the tests, they'll have to reschedule."

"The *victus*. That's what they want." Gray snarled, rage pouring through her.

"They can't make you give what you don't have." He rubbed his face. "God…Look, I can release your hands. If they don't have specimens to analyze, they'll have to delay whatever they're going to do. Can you—if I free your hands, can you, you know, get rid of it?"

Gray shook her head. "No. I can't—not all of it. Not enough."

"I can't risk bringing the other female in here. To help or whatever. Jesus, I won't watch."

"It's not possible," Gray said. "That's not how it happens. We have no need to release that way."

"Then at least don't fight them. Just give them what they want."

"No. We will never help them." Gray didn't see that she had many choices. If they resisted, their captors might take more females. If they cooperated, they could hurt the Pack. This human was right. Time was her only weapon. If she had nothing to give them, they would have to wait. "Stun me."

"What?"

"Stun me long enough, and I won't have anything for them to collect."

"Oh good Christ." Martin paced in a rapid circle. "I don't know if I can."

"If it keeps them from getting what they want, if it gives us more time, do it." Gray wasn't afraid, not of the bright stabbing pain or the searing electric shock. She knew what would happen when he shocked her. She feared the surge of excitement roiling in her loins and the eager pulsing in her clitoris.

"Are you sure?"

"Just do it," she rasped, her sex readying painfully.

He pulled a stun gun from his holster and fired. The darts struck her abdomen, embedded deep in her muscles, and a jolt of electricity ripped through her. Her back arched, and her arms and legs flailed. She growled, straining in her shackles. The current escalated, burning through her blood, and her clitoris abruptly exploded. Roaring with ecstasy, hips jerking wildly, she emptied in heaving spasms until the electricity abruptly disappeared.

"I'm sorry," Martin muttered, jerking the electrodes from her belly.

Gray dangled from her restraints, spent and hollow.

❖

Drake waited while Sylvan rang the buzzer outside the airlock connected to Leo and Nadia Revnik's multimillion-dollar Level 4 research lab. Sylvan completed the retinal and digital print scans to confirm her identity, and a closed-circuit camera above the computer-controlled chamber door slowly panned across their faces. The door whooshed open, and they entered a six-foot-wide, ten-foot-long corridor, shed their clothes, and stepped through a portal that emitted low-level radiation to sterilize their skin. Decontamination complete, they pulled scrubs down from the shelf next to the inner door. Sylvan didn't bother with a shirt. The pressure in the chamber equilibrated, the inner door opened, and they walked out into the lab.

Leo and Nadia Revnik were alone, surrounded by cutting-edge instruments and equipment, some not even available in government installations. With their unlined skin, clear blue eyes, lustrous blond hair, and athletic bodies, neither looked older than their daughter Sophia.

Even in scrubs and white lab coats, they both appeared as strong and lethal as any of Sylvan's soldiers.

"Alpha," Leo said, his gaze moving rapidly from Sylvan to Drake. "Prima. We weren't expecting you."

"Sophia?" Nadia asked anxiously.

"Sophia is fine," Sylvan said.

Nadia sighed. "Forgive me, Alpha. I—"

Sylvan shook her head. "You're a mother first. I understand."

"Prima," Nadia said, turning to Drake. "How are you?"

"I am well, thank you," Drake said with a surge of affection. Leo and Nadia had conceded to her wishes to take more extensive biopsies than Sylvan might have agreed to, and she was in their debt. They had pushed the limits of their comfort zone in circumventing their Alpha's orders. "Do you have any results?"

Leo said, "We have completed most of the assays and have some very good news, Prima. Your muscle biopsies and biochemical analyses are all normal. Your mitochondrial DNA is indistinguishable from any other Were's."

Sylvan gripped Drake's hand. "What does that mean?"

"The Prima's transformation was total," Nadia said. "We've detected no mutagens in any of the tissue samples."

"Then I'm safe?" Drake asked. "There's no chance that I could transmit any kind of antigen through the mate bond and endanger Sylvan?"

"No, none that we can find."

Drake sagged against Sylvan, grateful for her solid presence. She would be destroyed if her love for Sylvan ever hurt her. "Thank you."

Nadia and Leo both grinned. Leo said, "We don't often get to deliver such momentous news. You're very welcome, Prima."

Sylvan rumbled and kissed her. "I told you there was nothing wrong. I'm your mate. I know."

"Yes, Alpha," Drake murmured, nibbling on Sylvan's lower lip. "But sometimes a scientist needs hard evidence."

Sylvan snarled softly. "You try me."

"So you've said." Drake took a deep breath and turned back to Leo and Nadia. Knowing she wasn't a danger to Sylvan relieved most of her fears, but not all of them. "What about the viability of my eggs? Am I sterile?" Her heart faltered at the prolonged silence. "Just tell me what you know."

Leo flicked a quick look at Sylvan, then swallowed. "We can't tell,

Prima. Our reproductive process is more complicated than in humans. The hormonal mix, the deregulation of the suppressor RNA, initiating the mitotic cascade—there's no way to simulate it in the lab. If we knew how to do that, we could potentially enhance the fertility of our species and protect ourselves from the threat of extinction."

Drake nodded. "I understand. If you could control the regulator proteins, you could improve our reproductive capabilities. And if anyone could reverse that process, they could potentially destroy the species."

"Yes, which is why our research is so carefully guarded." Leo frowned. "It would be difficult to disrupt the process, however. Someone would need to develop multiple immunoglobulins or antigenic proteins to counteract the reproductive cascade."

"Agreed," Drake said. "Although there are theoretically numerous points at which antigens could block the neurotransmitters and pheromones in the *victus*."

"Even so," Nadia said, "deactivating the mitochondrial receptor sites would almost certainly not be one hundred percent successful."

"But anything that significantly impairs our already low fertility rate could effectively catapult the species toward extinction," Leo added.

Drake pulled at the thread that had been mentally teasing her ever since they'd learned of the females' disappearance. If Were scientists were studying this phenomenon, then maybe their enemies were too. That would explain the abduction of adolescent females whose reproductive potency was nearly peak. The process would be lengthy, though, and keeping the whereabouts of the females secret would be a top priority. "If someone kept a Were in a negative-flow environment, so that no scent could escape, could the Alpha's awareness of the Were be impeded?"

Nadia sucked in a breath and glanced at Sylvan, then quickly away. "The Alpha's connection is more than physical. Her ability to sense us might be impaired if some of the physical signals were blocked, but I don't think it would be total."

Drake paced across the room to where a coffeemaker was tucked into the corner of a long counter. Since she'd turned, she wasn't really susceptible to the caffeine effects, but she couldn't break the habit of drinking it while mulling over a problem. She wondered if the Revniks kept it for the same reason. She leaned her hips against the counter and sipped the excellent brew. Sylvan remained on the other side of the room with the Revniks, proof enough that their breeding frenzy was over. Until just a short while ago, they could not have tolerated that much separation. The pangs of disappointment returned, and she ruthlessly shoved them away. She rotated the ceramic mug in her hands, watching the dark liquid circle in the cup.

"What if a physiological barrier were created in conjunction with the negative-pressure environment? That might effectively block all of the Alpha's connections."

Leo frowned. "But what?"

"Silver," Drake said. "Perhaps aerosolized, injected intravenously, or even impregnated in the substance of the structure. Maybe all three."

"It's possible," Nadia said. "Silver nonspecifically and irreversibly binds to multiple cellular receptors sites, deactivating them. It essentially neutralizes many of our subcellular systems, and that translates into organ failure and death. The brain would be affected as much as any other part of the body."

"How many facilities in a hundred-mile radius would be capable of creating that kind of environment?" Drake asked.

The Revniks looked at each other.

"We have one here," Leo said. "Every Level Four facility should be capable of adapting those kinds of barriers. It would be expensive, and time-consuming."

"All right. So even if a facility had initially been built as a standard Level Four, it would need to be modified." Drake looked from Leo to Nadia for confirmation.

"Yes," Nadia said vigorously. She turned to a nearby computer and began rapidly inputting data. "Let me see how many are in the search area, but that still won't tell us which one."

Sylvan said, "What about tracking new construction or the movement of large amounts of materials? Can you draw up a list of what would be needed to modify the facility?"

"Of course," Leo said, "but it's unlikely Weres are behind this. Humans may be moving the materials by rail or boat or truck."

Drake glanced at Sylvan. *Becca or Jody might be able to help us.*

Sylvan nodded. "Nadia? Anything?"

"I found three facilities in addition to ours that could be readily modified for this kind of...experimentation," Nadia said, sending information to a nearby printer. "One not far from here, another in Vermont, the other in Massachusetts."

"We'll start with those," Sylvan said. "Expand the search just in case those prove fruitless."

"Yes, Alpha," Nadia said.

"I'll get the materials list," Leo added.

Drake set her coffee cup on the counter and returned to Sylvan. She might not have the desperate need to be in constant contact with her, but even without the primal force of breeding frenzy, she wanted, needed, to touch her mate. Sliding an arm around Sylvan's waist, she said to Leo, "I'll need you to run some more blood assays on me."

"What are we looking for?" Leo asked.

"Reproductive hormone levels and circulating antigens to my genetic material."

"Why?" Sylvan growled.

Don't worry, love. Drake rubbed Sylvan's back. "I may appear to be genetically Were, but it's possible my human immune system created antibodies to the Were reproductive hormones even while I was transitioning. My body may attempt to breed, but I may already be programmed to destroy any possibility of that happening."

She didn't need to say what they all already knew. If she couldn't give Sylvan and the Pack offspring, then they needed to make plans for Sylvan to find another way to fulfill her destiny.

CHAPTER TWENTY-SIX

Veronica held up one hand, signaling for Adam to wait while she finished her call. He stopped in the doorway of her office, looking a little bit like an animal with its leg caught in a trap. She swiveled her high-backed leather chair toward the windows that looked out over the Green Mountains. "As I told you in my interim report, I expect concrete results very shortly."

"You do understand our urgency."

The familiar, modulated voice grated as it usually did, whether in bed or in the boardroom. How she detested bureaucrats. Regardless of their politics, their philosophy, or their station, they were all parasites who lived off the brains and initiative of others. "I totally understand your situation. Your needs are always my priority, in every way."

He chuckled dryly. "And you, Dr. Standish, know exactly how to exploit a man's weakness."

"As I recall," she purred, "there's nothing weak in your repertoire."

"There doesn't seem to be where you're concerned," he said. "So I can tell my associates to expect something soon?"

"Very soon."

"Dinner on Friday? The Governor's Benefit for the Arts?"

"Of course, darling. I wouldn't miss it." Veronica disconnected and swung her chair back around to her desk. She pulled a stack of paperwork in front of her and asked, without looking up, "What is it, Adam? I have reports to review before this morning's session."

"That's what I came to tell you," he began hesitantly.

Veronica slowly set the budget summary aside, a chill settling along her spine, and eased back in her chair. He seemed to flinch when her gaze met his. "What?"

"I'm afraid she's not ready."

"What do you mean, she's not ready?"

Adam swayed in place, as if he wanted to flee but his feet were nailed to the threshold. "The guards went to retrieve her forty minutes ago so we could get her prepped." He licked his lips. "They radioed that she appeared to be in a weakened state, so I went to check on her."

Veronica frowned. "Ill? I saw her last night, and she seemed in fine form. Besides, they're animals. Their physiology prevents them from contracting human diseases, and these subjects haven't been exposed to anything else. You *are* monitoring the serum silver levels, aren't you?"

"Yes, three times weekly, per protocol. The last biopsy specimens showed the expected diminished cellular activity, but no evidence of tissue death."

"Well then, she should be well enough for what we need." Veronica returned her attention to her reports.

He cleared his throat awkwardly. "It's not a systemic issue, it's…"

Veronica tossed her solid-gold Waterman onto the desk and rose abruptly. "I don't have the time or the inclination for riddles. What is the problem?"

"There's evidence she had a nocturnal emission. A substantial one. We aren't going to be able to get appropriate specimens from her today."

"Let me see if I understand this." Veronica straightened her gray silk pencil skirt and walked around her desk in measured steps. She locked onto his face as she crossed the room. He paled, a fine sheen of perspiration coating his forehead despite the air-conditioning running full force. She'd wager the follicles on the back of his neck were standing up. His penis certainly was—he displayed all the adrenergic signs of an animal trapped by a predator. She nearly smiled and didn't stop walking until she was so close to him his erection brushed against her thigh.

"We've had them how long?" she began conversationally. "Several months, isn't that right?"

He nodded, his pupils flickering wildly.

"We've never had a problem collecting specimens. But now you're telling me that's impossible. On the day I expressly stated I needed to have results?"

He swallowed, and his Adam's apple quivered like a small animal lodged in his throat. He was either about to wet himself or ejaculate in his underwear. "Yes, I'm afraid so."

"Do you have an explanation?"

"We've...ah...never observed this behavior with any of the subjects before. They aren't known to have spontaneous emissions, but apparently she did. She's somnolent, and even with moderate stimulation, we can't produce any kind of erectile response."

Veronica lifted her brow. "Stimulation?"

"As you know, if physically challenged, their response is in part sexual. Low-level electrical current will always produce engorgement of the genitalia." He grimaced apologetically. "Nothing is producing a response this morning."

"What about the second one?"

"We could certainly use her," he said eagerly. "She hasn't produced the sample volume the other one does, and the chemical mixture seems to be altered, but—"

"They're not equivalent specimens, that's what you're telling me. What kind of scientist willingly accepts inferior data? Are you suggesting I'd be satisfied with less than—"

"No, no, of course not." A bead of sweat trickled down the side of his face.

"We have yet to determine why there's a variation in the hormone profile between two clearly dominant females." Veronica stepped even closer, her body invading his personal space, the taut plane of her skirt pressing his erection back against his abdomen.

"But then," she said softly, "we don't know very much at all, do we? Because we haven't, despite all our efforts, despite all the money and resources we have thrown into this project...we haven't been able to answer any of the critical questions, have we?"

"I'm sorry," he murmured.

"Are you?" she whispered, her eyes boring into his. He looked like he might whimper, and his nearly palpable fear made her clitoris pulse pleasantly. She slowly smoothed her hand down the front of her skirt, the backs of her fingers brushing over the ridge in his trousers. He sucked in a sharp breath.

"I need you to take care of this problem, Adam," she said gently, almost apologetically. She leaned a little closer, her mouth inches from his. Her pelvis grazed his. Slowly. Firmly. "Can I count on you? Can I count on you to take care of this problem?"

"I will. I will—oh God—I..." His hips lurched and his face contorted.

A satisfying warmth spread through the pit of her stomach as she watched him struggle to regain his balance, his chest heaving. He always did have a tendency to ejaculate too quickly. "Reschedule for tomorrow."

"Of course," he said hoarsely.

She turned away, paused, and said over her shoulder, "E-mail me a printout of the log book for the isolation corridor airlock. Let's see what made last night so different."

"Yes," he said, backing out into the hall. "I'll do that right away."

She sat down at her desk and retrieved her gold pen. "That's wonderful. I knew I could rely on you."

As soon as he disappeared, she pressed a button under the edge of her desk, and a wall panel slid open to her right. A bank of eight monitors showed video feeds from various areas of the complex. She programmed in a download for the data from the cameras outside the holding pens in the restricted area of the research wing, congratulating herself on having kept the presence of the cameras a secret. In her business, it paid to trust no one.

❖

Becca was pulled from sleep by the ringing of her cell phone. She snatched it up before the "William Tell Overture" awakened Jody. Chagrin and the faintest bit of sadness gripped her for an instant. Jody wasn't sleeping, and she wasn't going to be awakened by the phone ringing. Jody's breathing was so slow, at first Becca had been terrified she might actually be dead. Only after lying perfectly still for several minutes and shutting out every extraneous thought, even blocking out the thud of her own heartbeat, had she finally been able to detect the faintest sound of Jody breathing. When she'd pressed her hand beneath the curve of Jody's breast, she couldn't feel a heartbeat. She'd bitten her lip so hard to keep from crying out she'd tasted her own blood. Then, there, at last, Jody's distant heartbeat had fluttered against her palm, such a fragile tremor her own chest had ached.

Jody was somewhere beyond Becca's reach, but she lowered her voice and rolled over on her side away from Jody all the same. "Becca Land."

"Ms. Land," Sylvan said. "I'm sorry to disturb you."

"That's quite all right, Alpha. Is something wrong?" Her pulse immediately started racing. What if they were in danger? God, what if they were attacked? Jody was so vulnerable, lying there naked and helpless. Jody had assured her she would rouse if threatened, the way a bear in hibernation instinctively reacted to its cave being violated, but Becca didn't see how Jody could possibly react in time. A fierce surge of protectiveness rushed through her. "Is there danger? Should I get Niki?"

"No, forgive me. With Niki on guard, you're safe. I didn't mean to worry you."

"I'm sorry," Becca said. "I'm not usually this nervous, but—"

"I take it you're still with our Vampire friend."

Becca stroked Jody's hair and rested her fingers against Jody's cheek. She was as cool and beautiful and lifeless as a statue. "Yes, I'm with her."

"You won't have to leave her for what I need."

"How can I help?"

"I need some information, and I was hoping you might have sources who could provide it."

"Just a minute. Let me make some notes." Becca carefully rose from the bed and found her purse on a chair on the far side of the room. She tucked her phone against her shoulder and rummaged inside for her notepad and pencil. "Go ahead."

"I need to know if any construction permits have been filed for major renovation on three locations during the last two years. These would not be minor repairs, but major expansions. Perhaps licenses or plans were filed with the state or municipalities or—"

"Don't worry. That's all pretty standard. I know where to check," Becca said. "Give me the locations." She scribbled down the information. "Okay, what else?"

"This may be trickier. We're looking for orders for large volumes of certain building materials. The list is not long, but we're not sure how they were shipped."

"So I may need to access bills of lading through the port or trucking manifests," Becca muttered. "Can you e-mail me the list?"

"Yes."

"Good. Read it off to me just so I have some sense of what I'll be looking for." Becca made more notes as Sylvan listed various construction components, some of which seemed very strange. "Wait a minute. Did you really say nuclear exhaust fans?"

"Yes, the type used for cooling and circulating the air in nuclear reactor silos."

"What exactly do you think these people are building?"

"Prisons."

Sylvan's fury reached out to Becca over the phone lines and chilled her heart. She imagined how she would feel if anyone attempted to harm Jody, and the rage settled deep inside her. She didn't have the physical strength of the Weres or the mental power of the Vampires, but she had her brains, and she had her will, and she knew how to fight. Now more than ever, she had something—and someone—to fight for.

"Don't worry, Alpha, I'll have the information for you by nightfall."

❖

"Once Jody rises tonight," Drake said when Sylvan disconnected the call, "she may be able to access additional databases through police headquarters."

"Yes," Sylvan said. "I think we've done all we can for now. In case Becca can't help us narrow the possibilities down to a specific location by pinpointing which facility has been modified, we'll put surveillance around all three of them today. If they're operating a clandestine research lab with living subjects, they're going to need a lot of supplies and extra personnel."

"You may have to get someone inside to be sure." Drake assumed Leo and Nadia could hear their conversation, but the two scientists appeared to be engrossed in conversation on the far side of the lab. "Their security is going to be tough to breach."

"We'd need someone with enough scientific expertise to be able to identify what we're looking for." Sylvan sighed. "Sophia would be our best choice."

"I could do it."

"No."

"Sylvan, you can't expect me to sit—"

Sylvan was in her face so quickly Drake sucked in a breath of surprise. She narrowed her eyes and thrust her chin forward. "What was that for?"

"I will not place you at risk." Sylvan grumbled, but backed up a step. "You are as important to the Pack as I am. You have to learn to accept that."

"You put yourself in danger every day without concern for *your* position in the Pack." Drake clenched her teeth to keep her voice down. She'd fought her way out from under the weight of double standards when she was ten years old. She wasn't about to embrace them as an adult, especially when her mate put herself in danger every time she left the Compound.

"My position in the Pack is to go to battle for them," Sylvan said. "Yours is to preserve order and stability by showing you trust my judgment."

"That's convenient," Drake snapped.

The corner of Sylvan's mouth flickered. "For me, it is." She traced a finger over Drake's lower lip. "You're a warrior, I know that. But not every battle is fought with tooth and claw. The Pack needs more than I can give them. A calm center. Unwavering strength. You are our heart now, Prima."

"Damn you," Drake whispered. "*You* are my heart."

"And you are mine." Sylvan kissed her. "I promise, when the time comes for you to fight, I won't stop you. But this is not that fight."

"You make it hard for me to argue."

"Then don't." Sylvan grinned. "All I do, I do for you and the Pack."

"I know. And that needs to include staying safe." Drake gripped Sylvan's shoulders and drew Sylvan's gaze. She was the only one who could look into Sylvan's eyes and see all that she was—defender, protector, fearsome fighter, tender lover. "I love you."

Sylvan stroked her face. "I love you."

"Let's go home," Drake said. "We're going to be busy tonight."

"Yes," Sylvan said, her eyes flashing with wolf. "Our females are not going to spend one more night in captivity."

Drake kept her silence as they strode into the airlock. Regardless of how Sylvan saw their roles in the Pack, she would never let Sylvan stand alone. She would risk Sylvan's ire, she would risk anything, to keep her safe. Tonight would be soon enough to wage that battle.

Chapter Twenty-seven

Francesca pushed the blinking red light on her office answering machine, scrolled through the messages, made notes for her aide, and replayed the fourth one.

"Good evening, Viceregal, I hope you slept well," the sensuous female voice began. "I have need of assistance, and I immediately thought of you. I'd like to borrow one of your trusted Vampires for a few hours tonight. I promise they'll enjoy themselves. Call me."

Francesca pressed Erase. She knew the return number. Veronica Standish was an interesting human. If she'd been a Vampire, Francesca might have been worried about her motives, but even for a human, Veronica wielded too much power to be underestimated. Francesca didn't trust the scientist, but then she didn't trust anyone, except Michel and the wolf Alpha. Michel had been by her side longer than any Vampire, knew more of her secrets than any other creature, and her loyalty was unassailable. And Sylvan. Sylvan was honest to a fault. Someday, Sylvan's honesty and integrity would be her downfall. When that day came, she would be sad—she was very fond of Sylvan. But sentiment did not keep one in power.

She dialed the number. "What can I do for you, darling?"

"I take it this is confidential?" Veronica said.

"Isn't everything between us?"

"I need one of your Vampires to assist me in a study."

"That sounds wonderfully mysterious. Assist you in what way?"

"I'll skip all the very boring parts and get right to the summary," Veronica said, as if her experiments were of no real consequence. "I want to quantify the effects of the Vampire feeding hormone in a Were."

"Is this the study I'm not supposed to know about? You have Were subjects?"

Veronica laughed. "The secrecy was never my mandate, so I have no problem ignoring it for you. Yes, some of the work I'm doing for the group involves Weres."

Sylvan's missing females, no doubt. These humans were very foolish. Francesca murmured, "I can't see you ceding authority to any master."

"You're my role model in that," Veronica said playfully.

Francesca smiled. She wasn't susceptible to seduction by humans. They were satisfying to feed from, nothing more. "You flatter me."

"Not at all. I think we both know if we allow the males of our species to control us, we are no better than the animals we study—controlled by biology rather than our higher faculties. Don't you agree?"

To Francesca's way of thinking, every species with the possible exception of the Weres was inferior, but that didn't mean she could ignore their potential threat. "Of course I agree. If I didn't, we wouldn't be having this conversation. Let me see if I understand. You want a Vampire to feed from a Were while you—what? Study them both?"

"Actually, I'm interested in analyzing the Were emissions during orgasm. I'll only be collecting samples from the Were. Your Vampire can take as much blood as they want, short of death, of course."

"Naturally. I'll give it some thought and get back to you."

"I've moved my test up from tomorrow to this evening to accommodate your nocturnal needs."

"How thoughtful." Francesca disconnected and considered the request. She had yet to see the research facility, and sending someone inside would be to her advantage. Veronica *said* she wasn't interested in studying Vampires, but even if the scientist was telling the truth, she could easily change her mind in the future. Any Vampire Francesca sent must be capable of guarding critical secrets about the Vampire species. There was only one Vampire she would trust with such an assignment.

Senechal.

A moment later her office door opened, and Michel entered. "You have need of me, Regent?"

"I have a job for you I think you're going to enjoy."

❖

Jody opened her eyes, fully conscious, with no transition from deep somnolence to total awareness. Usually the soldiers escorted the selected hosts from the safe house to her lair just before sundown, securing the tunnel entrance and remaining on the doors until she was awake. Her hosts often waited beside her in bed for the moment when she arose, knowing her hunger was greatest after the long period of daytime unawareness. The body beside her was not a host. She rolled over and pulled Becca into her arms. "You shouldn't be here right now."

"Why?" Becca kissed her.

Becca smelled fresh and alive, a hint of shampoo still clinging to her hair, her natural scent unmarred by any other fragrance. Her body was warm from the shower, her skin soft and flushed with the rush of her blood beneath her skin. Becca's blood pumped strong and hot, and Jody's mouth filled with feeding hormones. She wanted to taste her. She wanted to drink her.

"My hunger is greatest right now, and my control is the weakest." She nuzzled Becca's neck. She couldn't help herself. Her body tightened, her entire being focused on the promise of strength and power flowing mere millimeters from her mouth. She groaned. "Becca, please. You must go."

Becca pushed Jody over onto her back, something no host had ever done. When Becca stretched out on top of her, Jody's sex did not respond—she didn't have enough replenished blood circulating for that to happen—but she felt arousal just the same. Not bloodlust, desire. The reaction was so foreign, she was able to ignore her hunger long enough to gather the threads of her control. She brushed her fingers through Becca's black curls. Becca's eyes were so bright, her lips so full and moist. Jody ached for her in her mind, in her heart, in her depths. "I want you."

Becca grinned. "Why do you sound so surprised?" She moved against Jody's leg, coating her skin with the slick, hot evidence of her desire. "Feel that? I want you too. I thought I'd combust before you woke up. I'm glad you didn't call a host, because I'm not sharing this time."

Jody frowned. "You don't understand. I want *you*. Not just your blood."

Becca's eyes widened and then grew impossibly soft. "Really."

"Yes, but I—"

Becca leaned down and kissed her, playing her tongue over her lips.

Becca tasted hot and sweet, and Jody chased the promise of pleasure with her tongue, sweeping inside Becca's mouth. When Becca's hips sped up on her leg, Jody pulled her head away, cursing.

"What?" Becca braced herself on her arms, her breasts swaying teasingly over Jody's face. "Why are you aggravated?"

Jody looked down the length of their bodies, hers so stark and hard, Becca's a dusky gold suffused with the faint rose of healthy blood. "I can't respond to you the way I want to. My body can't—"

"Your body needs blood, doesn't it?" Becca murmured. "For you to become physically aroused."

Jody turned her face away, embarrassed. "Yes. Without it, I'm not able—"

Becca stopped her confession with her mouth, sliding her tongue over Jody's incisors as she moved on her again. Becca moaned into Jody's mouth, her hips thrusting steadily. Jody jerked, excitement surging through her, not the way she was used to, not the involuntary orgasm that accompanied her feeding, but intense, aching arousal rising from every corner of her awareness. She rolled Becca over, under her. Becca's excitement was real, and so was hers. She answered Becca's passion with a hard, demanding kiss and slid her hand between their bodies. When she stroked through the wetness between Becca's thighs, Becca gave a shocked cry. Starving for her, Jody pushed herself down the bed and kissed Becca's stomach.

Becca twisted and pressed against her mouth. "Oh God, Jody. I want you so much."

And that confession, offered freely, with no thrall, no plea for her bite, no mindless addiction to the feeding hormones, gave Jody the strength to hold her hunger at bay for a few more minutes. "I want you too. I want you, Becca. All of you."

Becca's hands came onto her shoulders, pushing her lower. "Please. Take me in your mouth. Make me come, and when I do, bite me. God, Jody, bite me then."

"No," Jody groaned. "You've already given me blood today. I don't want to take more."

"I need you to. Please. Let me feel it like this."

Jody couldn't fight both Becca's need and her own. She kissed the insides of Becca's thighs, her moist lips, her hard clitoris. She tasted her, drank her, and finally took her into her mouth. Becca's shoulders jolted off the bed, and her fingers dug into the muscles of Jody's back.

"Please, yes, please, yes," Becca gasped, over and over again.

Jody was helpless to deny her. She sucked her, licked her, and pressed inside her. Becca stiffened, shaking uncontrollably, and climaxed.

"Oh please, now," Becca moaned.

Jody's incisors slid down, and she carefully, gently, pierced the wide vein running on the inside of Becca's thigh. A flood of power and pleasure stormed through her. She released the erotostimulants with every pull.

"Oh my God," Becca cried out, jerking against Jody's mouth.

Jody drank until she was strong enough to break free from the bloodlust and slipped out, sealing the wounds in Becca's thigh with several slow swipes of her tongue. Gasping, she collapsed, her cheek against Becca's stomach.

"I love you, Becca," Jody murmured.

Becca laughed softly, weakly stroking Jody's face. "Oh, Vampire, oh, you surely do."

❖

The bedroom door opposite Niki opened, and she went on high alert. Jody emerged wearing pressed dark trousers and a pale gray open-collared shirt. Her gaze was sharp, and her skin glowed. The Vampire had fed, but Niki hadn't seen any hosts since the guards had escorted the man with the dark hair to and from the bedroom early that morning. Jody must have fed from the human. Niki pushed aside a swell of jealousy. She wasn't there for her own pleasure, she was there to carry out the Alpha's orders. Safeguard Lara. And the Vampire. And the human. During the long hours of standing guard, she'd managed not to think about who would feed the Vampire when she awoke hungry, but she hadn't been as successful controlling her body. Watching the host arrive that morning, hearing the groans and cries of ecstasy, had brought on a frenzy almost as intense as running with the Alpha. Just seeing the Vampire ratcheted up her need.

"Lara hasn't stirred yet," Niki reported brusquely.

Jody nodded. "She will any moment. How are you?"

"I'm fine." She wasn't, but she could hold. The Vampire was powerful, and her need permeated the surroundings. Being inundated with the pheromone-laden air in the underground lair had Niki full and ready. But she had plenty of practice absorbing that kind of stimulation, and she would not admit to this Vampire that she throbbed for release.

"Let's see to Lara, then," Jody said, passing Niki without commenting on the damp sheet of sex-sweat coating her body.

Niki appreciated the Vampire allowing her to preserve some dignity, and stepped aside so Jody could enter first. She followed her into Lara's room and secured the door behind them. Lara was as she had left her, curled in the center of the bed, naked, covered by just a sheet. Niki ached to see her so alone.

"She should be with Pack," Niki grumbled.

Lara turned her head, and Niki's heart jolted. Lara's eyes were a clear, bright amber. All wolf, healthy and sharp. "Lara?"

"Niki," Lara whispered. Her gaze flicked to Jody, and her face hardened. "And what should I call you? Master?"

"You may call me Liege," Jody said, bending over the bed. She grasped Lara's chin in her hand, and Lara quivered.

Niki tightened, her wolf bristling at the affront to her Packmate. The Vampire was rolling Lara's mind, enthralling her, and to her wolf, that spelled danger. Danger meant fight. Niki held her place, waiting, wary, watching.

"You are strong, young Vampire," Jody murmured, straightening.

Abruptly, Lara sat up and shook herself vigorously, as if throwing off rain after a hard run through a thunderstorm. Her naked body looked hard and lean and hungry, like that of a lone wolf who had hunted for days and had yet to find prey.

"I still hurt." Lara grimaced and rubbed the center of her chest. "Will it always be this way?"

"Yes, but you'll notice it less as time goes on. Right now, you need to feed."

Lara shuddered and her incisors abruptly extruded. "Yes. Yes. Now." Her gaze shot to Niki.

Niki's stomach tensed and her sex pulsed. "Let me feed her."

"It's after dark," Jody said, "and the threat to us is less now that I am awake. But if you feed her, you will be weakened, and your Alpha may need you tonight."

"I am a Were," Niki said, never looking away from Lara. "I can feed her and be recovered by the time we leave this place." She didn't want to beg, but she was close to it. She needed her connection to Lara, to Pack, and she needed the release Lara's Vampire bite would give. "Lara needs a wolf tonight, not a human."

"All right," Jody said, stepping back to the door. "But I'll need to stay. Lara is not yet ready to feed alone."

"Then stay. You've seen it before," Niki said bitterly. Her weakness—everyone had seen it now. She'd always prided herself on her control, on being able to absorb the strongest of the Alpha's call and still stand strong. She couldn't any longer. She was already on the verge of bursting, and she could not defeat her need. With a groan, she leapt to the side of the bed and ripped off her shirt. Panting, she shredded her pants.

"Now," Lara snarled, crimson bleeding through her amber eyes.

"Yes, yes," Niki whispered.

Lara grabbed her with more strength than Niki had ever felt from her and pulled her down onto the bed. And then she was under Lara, where she would never have gone for any wolf but the Alpha, and she was willing. Willing to be taken, open and needy.

"Please," Niki moaned.

"Niki." Lara's grip gentled and she kissed her. "I've missed you."

Niki scented wolf, scented home. She lifted beneath Lara, and Lara's sex pressed to hers. The pleasure was only that, no pain, no humiliation, no domination. This was Lara. She was Pack. Niki closed her eyes, felt pine needles under her pads, the cool mountain air rushing through her pelt, her heart thudding in her ears as she hunted free. She was wolf. She was strong. When Lara's teeth slipped into her neck, all she knew was joy and the contentment only Pack and a wolf who loved her could give.

Chapter Twenty-eight

Sylvan pulled Drake closer into the curve of her body and reached over her for her cell phone resting on the table next to their bed. Her cabin was quiet, the night outside the open windows just starting to cool. She scented Andrew and Misha close by—standing guard in the forest. Drake's naked body was a warm comfort against her own. The phone vibrated again.

"Sylvan."

"Alpha," Max said, a hint of apology in his voice. "Sorry to disturb you. Detective Gates is on the line."

"That's all right, put her through."

Drake stirred and grumbled beside her. "What is it?"

"Jody." Sylvan stroked Drake's chest and belly. Her mate had been unusually restless and agitated when they'd arrived back at the Compound, and Sylvan had insisted they sleep. Drake had finally fallen into an uneasy slumber, but even now she vibrated with tension, as if sensing danger. "Rest a bit longer. All is well." Into the phone, she said, "Vampire?"

Jody said, "Have you made any progress finding your females?"

"We have suggestive activity at two locations," Sylvan said.

"Becca may have found something more for you."

"What do you have?"

"The Green Mountain Center for Progressive Studies outside of Bennington, Vermont, underwent significant expansion a little over eighteen months ago. An entire new wing was constructed. That's a matter of public record."

"That's cat territory," Sylvan snarled.

"I thought they were too disorganized to be a threat?" Jody said.

"They were, but everything is different now. If they were offered part of our territory to help overthrow us—who knows?"

"It would seem we can no longer rely on previous assumptions," Jody said.

"What else did Becca discover?" Sylvan would worry about the cats when she had her young home.

"She found some preliminary architectural specs buried in a slew of environmental filings that show underground tunnels."

"Perhaps an underground installation?" Sylvan's wolf surged along with her fury. Abducting her wolves was a killing offense, but if they'd been harmed, she would make sure the death of anyone involved was slow and painful. Pack law ruled where protecting her wolves was concerned, and as Alpha, she was judge and executioner.

"Very possible."

"Who owns it?" Sylvan sat up, bracing her back against the sanded log walls. Drake rolled over in the nest of tangled sheets and rested her head in Sylvan's lap. Sylvan combed her fingers through Drake's hair, soothed by the satisfied rumbling in her mate's chest.

"We don't know that yet. I've made a few calls. Discreetly. I may be able to track down the filing papers, but my guess is we're going to find a shell corporation or a series of them. Eventually we may be able to sort out who owns it, but not within any reasonable timeframe."

"I posted watchers at all three potential sites this morning," Sylvan said. "We've seen significantly more personnel arriving and departing throughout the day in six-hour shifts at this place. Thank you for the information. I am in your de—"

"Wait a minute," Jody said. "You're going to need me and my Vampires."

Sylvan said, "I told you before, I don't need Vampires to protect my Pack. Wolves don't fight with Vampires."

"That hasn't always been the case," Jody said. "We've hunted together before against common enemies. And you could use us if the place is warded with silver."

"How is it I can't get rid of you, Vampire?"

Jody laughed. "Sometimes, Wolf, necessity creates strange bedfellows."

"How *are* my wolves?"

"Niki is a worthy second. As to Lara—" Jody chuckled. "*My* Vampire is amazingly healthy. She is strong, Sylvan. She's very strong."

Sylvan heard pride and perhaps a trace of worry in Jody's voice. "Can she come home?"

"She will never be just a Were again," Jody said quietly, all hint of arrogance gone from her voice. "There are still things she needs to learn. Powers, if I'm correct, that will manifest soon and that will be difficult for her to control. She needs to be with my Vampire seethe, with my aides, until we know whether she will eventually be more Were or more Vampire."

"She will never be separate from Pack," Sylvan said. "I feel her connection as strongly as I ever did."

"Nor can she be separated from me. At least not for very long." Jody sighed. "It seems yet another compromise is necessary. If she needs to be around Weres, you can station your wolves in my lair. But they must be willing to host or be able to resist the thrall if the other Vampires here wish to feed from them. I won't ask my Vampires to ignore their needs for the comfort of Weres."

"Agreed," Sylvan said. "What about Niki? I need my second to come home."

"Understood," Jody said. "She can supervise those you station here, if you wish. She's an excellent liaison, despite her resistance to the idea."

Sylvan laughed. "She is not bred for diplomacy, but Niki will do what is needed. What about Lara—if you are with us—"

"We will come to you tonight. Lara will be secure for the night in the Compound if she has fed."

"Very well."

"And, Wolf," Jody added, "if I am to have Weres in my lair, I will send Vampires with Lara when she is in your Compound. I protect my own as well."

Sylvan snarled. "We have never had Vampires in the Compound."

"No, and I have never had Weres in my lair who were not here for my pleasure."

Sylvan grumbled and silver pelt shimmered beneath her bronzed skin.

"Easy, love." Drake rubbed her fingers in light circles between Sylvan's breasts, reaching deep inside her, soothing the fires of temper.

Sylvan drew a breath and covered Drake's hand with hers. "On your word as Liege that these Vampires will not take an unwilling Were host in my Compound."

"You have my word, Alpha."

"Then we have an alliance," Sylvan said.

"Even if that alliance puts you at odds with the Regent?"

"I hope I never need to choose. If I do, you must know that I will choose what is best for the protection of my Pack."

"Of course," Jody said. "That, I never doubted. One more thing."

Sylvan growled and Jody laughed.

"I'm bringing Becca to the Compound with me tonight. If we are going hunting, I want her protected."

"On my honor."

"Then I and my Vampires are at your service."

"I heard that last part," Becca said, leaning in the doorway leading from Jody's bedroom to the bath. "Exactly what do you plan to do with me? I'm not going to hide somewhere so the big strong Weres and big bad Vampires can babysit me every time you think there might be danger."

Jody pulled a black shirt out of her closet, shrugged it on, and tucked it into her black trousers. With her speed she was nearly invisible to human perception, but in a fight, any advantage was welcome. She glanced at her blood mate. Fortunately looks could not kill, because the daggers Becca was sending her way might very well have proven lethal. She smiled at Becca. "You look good in my clothes."

Becca scowled and flicked a hand in the direction of the slightly too large maroon silk shirt and the decidedly too tight blue jeans that one of Jody's servants had brought her. "Somehow, I can't even see you in blue jeans. You're too elegant. And you're avoiding the issue."

"Too elegant?" Jody laughed. "A strange phrase to describe a Vampire."

"That's because you have no idea how you appear to others."

"Oh, I know how others see us," Jody said, remembering after the Exodus when humans had demanded that Vampires be exterminated like a contagion. Only a joint appearance by her father and Sylvan's on international television had convinced the heads of the powerful human governments that the Praeterns could control their predatory urges—that the humans had nothing to fear. Even now, organized human factions called for the destruction of the Vampires. "Because we feed on humans, we're viewed as the greatest threat of all the Praeterns.

We've been labeled monsters. Unnatural. Undead—isn't that what they call us? Not worthy of rights because we're not really alive?"

Becca moved so quickly Jody was startled. Nothing ever startled her, but then Becca constantly surprised her. Becca's warm hands were on her face, and Becca's hot mouth was on hers, and for a fraction of a second her mind was blank of everything except Becca. She pulled Becca close, drew her in, let Becca plunder her mouth. Finally she moved her head away. "Careful," she murmured. "I'm still potent."

Becca swayed in her arms, laughing. "Darling, your potency has nothing to do with whether you can get physically aroused at the moment or not. You are always arousing to me, and don't think you can use not having fed as an excuse to put me off if I want you. Ever."

Jody's clitoris stirred, but the arousal went far beyond the merely physical. Unlike anyone in her experience, Becca reached her in places she could not name.

"You make me feel," Jody whispered, still astonished by what she had never imagined.

"Is that bad?"

"In some ways. You make me afraid, and I have never in my existence been afraid."

Becca skimmed her fingers over Jody's face. "What do you fear, my darling Vampire?"

"The one thing I have no control over. Losing you."

"It must be terribly hard," Becca said with utter sincerity, "for you, who can so easily control others, control your own desire, control your own destiny, to love me when I'm so damn uncontrollable."

Jody laughed. "I'm not sure I like being so well understood."

"You'll have to get used to it. And here's something else you're going to have to get used to." Becca kissed Jody lightly on the mouth, looped her arms around Jody's waist, and leaned back so their eyes met. "I love you. I don't want you only when it's safe. I want you when it's dangerous. I want you when you're threatened. I want you when life is uncertain. Whatever is coming for Sylvan or for you or for us, I want to be there. I want to be by your side."

"Isn't it enough that you're in my heart?"

"No. It isn't." Becca sighed and kissed her again. "That you love me is everything, but only if you let me love you back."

"You're not a warrior. You can't fight the way we can. I'm a cop, and you don't expect to take to the streets with me." Jody grimaced.

"Well, actually, you do, but that's just because you're unreasonably stubborn and—"

"Careful"—Becca pressed her fingers to Jody's mouth—"you're getting in deeper by the second. I expect to do whatever I can to be part of your fight, whatever form the battle takes, and that does not involve sitting back somewhere safe with armed guards around me."

"For tonight, come to the Compound with me," Jody said. "We'll find out what Sylvan plans." She glanced at the computer where Becca had adeptly gathered all of the information that had pinpointed the most likely location of the imprisoned Weres. "You're very good at finding information fast. At communications."

"That's what I do."

"Then that's how you'll fight."

Becca nodded. "It's a start."

❖

Drake sat up in bed next to Sylvan and caressed her mate's chest. "What time is it?"

"Just about seven p.m."

"Do we have them?"

Sylvan gave a satisfied growl. "I think so."

Drake warmed with a surge of relief and a hotter wash of fury. "Then we'll take them back. Tonight."

"We will. The Vampire is bringing her soldiers." Sylvan stroked Drake's back. "I'll take Niki and Max in with me. A small, swift hunting party. I'll bring them home."

Drake straddled Sylvan, braced both hands against Sylvan's shoulders, and pinned her against the wall. She dipped her head and nibbled on Sylvan's lower lip. "All of us will bring them home. I'm going with you."

Sylvan stiffened for an instant, and Drake could practically hear the argument forming in her mate's mind. In fact, she could *feel* the argument pushing against her senses. She bit a little harder and slid her tongue into Sylvan's mouth, stealing the words and replacing them with her own desire. Sylvan groaned.

"All of us," Drake repeated, then worked her way down the bed and between Sylvan's legs. For the last few days, their mating had been wild and hungry and hard and hot, and every joining strengthened her bond to Sylvan. But now, she wanted something else. She wanted to show Sylvan how much she loved her and how much they belonged together. She wanted Sylvan to know Sylvan owned her heart as well as her body, her soul as well as her passion. Now, on the eve of battle, she needed her to know. She took Sylvan into her mouth, held her there in the warm haven as Sylvan hardened for her, grew wet for her.

"Drake," Sylvan whispered hoarsely, trembling with the effort to give Drake control. "I need you."

The words speared Drake's heart. The only words that held more power over her were *I love you*, and she wanted Sylvan to feel her need *and* her love. She sucked Sylvan slowly at first, letting the tension build, even though she knew Sylvan was instantly ready to release. She wanted to satisfy her, but more than that, she wanted to please her beyond the primal bonds that made Sylvan hers and her Sylvan's. She reached up, brushed her fingers over Sylvan's chest, felt Sylvan's heart beating strong and sure. Sylvan's breasts swelled, her nipples tightened. Drake dragged her fingers down the center of Sylvan's tense abdomen, feeling muscles contract. Sylvan quivered, her body drawing tight. When Drake owned Sylvan, body and soul, she pulled her in deeper, licked her faster, sucked her harder. Sylvan jerked, the warning growl of her impending release starting deep in her chest and filling Drake's heart with power and wonder. When Sylvan groaned and poured all that she was into her, Drake was more than satisfied. She was complete.

"I love you," Drake whispered.

"You are my life," Sylvan said, drawing Drake up beside her. She licked Drake's neck and kissed her. "You are Prima of the Timberwolves. If I fall in battle, you will become Alpha—"

"You won't fall," Drake said sharply, refusing to consider the unthinkable. "Not tonight, not ever. Remember what you told me—the Pack needs us both. Besides—I don't want the job. I hate politics."

Sylvan smiled and rested in Drake's arms, absorbing the strength of their bond. "As you wish, Prima."

Chapter Twenty-nine

Niki stood on the landing of the Vampire's town house and sniffed the air. Nothing unusual—the park was across the street. Dogs, humans, squirrel and other prey. A faint scent of Were, a few days old. Vampires were hard to scent under the best of circumstances, and she was surrounded by them. If a Vampire assassin lay in wait for them, she might miss them. She growled unhappily. A dark-haired Vampire, female, in black fatigues and boots, an automatic strapped to her right thigh, appeared beside her and echoed her visual scan of the street.

"I can't scent any Vampires," Niki said, because pride had no place when duty was at stake. "Can you?"

"No sense of any other than ours," the female murmured.

"You feel each other?"

The Vampire regarded her blankly, and Niki stared back. The female smiled after a second. Her incisors gleamed. "Yes."

"Handy," Niki said thoughtfully.

A black limo pulled to the curb. Gates waited in the foyer with Lara and Becca.

"Clear," Niki and the female Vampire said simultaneously. They flanked the group as everyone moved down the stairs toward the now-open rear door of the idling vehicle. A male Vampire, the driver, stood by, his black suit jacket unbuttoned, a holstered weapon on his hip.

After everyone was in, Niki climbed into the back of the limo, and the female Vampire got into the front along with a male Vampire dressed in combat gear. Lara curled up in the corner a foot from Niki. Gates and Becca settled across from them. The vehicle was luxurious— leather seats, a recessed mini-bar, phone, satellite radio—and it was also armored with reinforced side panels and smoked UV-filtering glass.

"This vehicle will have trouble off-road when we reach the Compound," Niki commented.

Gates smiled. "I believe it will manage, Wolf."

All three Vampires in the front were dark haired and dark eyed like Gates. Niki had difficulty telling the age of the ageless and didn't understand the bloodlines, but one thing she recognized. The carriage of warriors. They weren't just bodyguards, they were soldiers. From the practiced ease with which they had maneuvered the car up to the house, covered the street, and escorted Gates and the others from the house to the vehicle, they were Gates's personal guard. Gates was more than just a detective. Why the Vampire put herself at risk, working with humans, unprotected, unguarded, made no sense. Why anyone would let her made even less sense.

Niki would never allow the Alpha to be so vulnerable. Where was the Clan allegiance to this Vampire, that they allowed her to be so alone? Or were they all so singularly focused, they cared only for the one who held power in that moment? At least the Vampire had guards now, and something else. Something strange. The human—Becca— kept her hand on the Vampire's leg, something Niki had never seen before. She had been in Nocturne many times with the Alpha, and she'd seen how Vampires acted with their retinue of blood servants. She'd witnessed possession, domination, and primal passion, but she'd never in her memory witnessed tenderness. She'd never seen a human, or a Were for that matter, put claim to a Vampire. Gates slid her hand over the human's, and their fingers intertwined. Niki raised her head and found the Vampire watching her, a speculative look in her eyes. Niki stared back, but felt no challenge. Rather, she read an acknowledgment of what lay between the Vampire and the human and sighed inwardly. She supposed she would have to continue with the Alpha's directive to protect the Vampire and the human as well as Lara. She leaned back and closed her eyes.

Before the Exodus, she'd understood her place in the world, in the Pack. She was born to protect Sylvan, the Alpha, the heart of the Pack. She was needed, she had purpose, and she was proud of who she was. Now she was riding in a limousine with a Vampire, a human, and one of her Packmates who had somehow been changed—not taken from them, but made *other* all the same. The Alpha was mated to a *mutia*, something not forbidden, but something that would soon become a problem. Suddenly, everything she thought she knew about life, about her duty, about herself and her own value, had changed. But one thing she knew with absolute certainty. Her heart would always belong to Sylvan, to the Pack, and to her Packmates. She would die for any one of them. She reached across the space separating her from her Packmate, pulled Lara close, and kissed her.

"We're going home, *centuri*. We're going home."

"Be careful tonight, darling," Francesca said, watching Michel get dressed. "I don't like you going in alone. I don't like Standish sending a car for you either, but if I insist on having guards accompany you, she'll think we fear her power."

Michel tucked her blood-red shirt into her tight black pants and pulled on knee-high black boots. She looked like a bloodied blade, sharp and dangerous and beautiful. As she slipped a silver cufflink into her sleeve, she crossed the room and kissed Francesca on the mouth. "We don't fear her, we will never fear humans."

"Let me do that," Francesca said, taking the second cufflink bearing her crest from Michel. "Roll up your sleeve, darling." Michel complied, and Francesca strapped a sheathed stiletto to her forearm. "You're right, of course, humans are not our equals, but even a pack of jackals can take down a lion if there are enough of them and the lion is alone. I will not have you harmed." She inserted the cufflink, slid her fingers into Michel's hair, and kissed her deeply. "Eternity would be so very boring without you."

Michel stroked Francesca's face and laughed. "Regent, I don't believe your heart or your bed would be empty for very long without me, but I promise you, as long as you call, I will be there."

Francesca tapped Michel's mouth with a scarlet-tipped finger. "See that you come back undamaged."

"What do you think the human really wants?"

Francesca shrugged. "What everyone wants. Power. Humans mistakenly believe their numbers provide them the strength to control us. They only *admit* to wanting dominion over the Weres, but I am sure they feel the same way about us. They'll be looking for our weaknesses. Take care not to show them any."

Michel shrugged. "What do you think I would reveal while feeding from a Were?"

"One of the reasons I'm sending you is I know you can think through the bloodlust. For those few seconds when we are lost in the lust, we are vulnerable. Take care that doesn't happen tonight."

Michel's eyes narrowed. "Regent, it's been centuries since I lost myself to bloodlust. Since I hosted for you, before my turning."

"Do you regret it? That you didn't remain blood-bonded?"

"If I'd thought you loved me, I would have remained your bonded host for as long as your power allowed me to survive. But you didn't, so I chose eternity at your side instead."

"Should I say I'm sorry?" Francesca said, stroking Michel's breast beneath the scarlet silk.

"No, Regent." Michel caught her hand and kissed her palm. "I am pleased with my existence, and honored to stand as your second." She laughed, but the blue of her eyes darkened for a second, and Francesca felt the wave of sadness Michel usually kept buried.

"You're a romantic, darling," Francesca said, "though you hide it well. You should take a lover—a human, perhaps, who would shower you with devotion."

Michel shook her head. "I have the satisfaction of feeding at your side, of sharing your body when we share hosts. I have the honor of pleasing you. I am well contented."

Francesca nodded, believing Michel believed her own words. Believing also that a day would come when Michel would want what she had never been able to give her. When that day came, she would have to decide if she still held Michel's allegiance, because Michel knew far too much were that not the case.

She kissed the only being with the knowledge to destroy her. "Take care, darling, and at sunrise, I promise you we will celebrate."

❖

The three guards came for Gray and Katya as they always did, laughing, sneering, taunting. Gray had no idea what day it was—without windows, without sunlight, without air, she couldn't judge where she was in the world, and without contact with the Pack, she had no way of finding herself.

The guard, Martin, did not look directly at her as he released the shackles on her wrists and legs, but he kept his body between her and the other two guards. The thin one who smelled like rotting prey, the one who liked to stun her until she twisted on the floor in her own fluids, reached around Martin and gripped her breast. Martin shoved him aside.

"Damn it, Elliot, don't rile her up. You heard what the supervisor said. He wants her delivered pumped up and ready to go. You get her pissed off enough, we'll have to stun her, and then we'll pay for her not performing in the lab."

"Oh fuck," Elliot sneered. "They're just gonna do the same thing in there to get her juicing. A little poking, a little jolt. We might as well get a head start. Fucking job doesn't have any other perks. We get treated like we're the prisoners. Scans and body searches. Fuck."

"Look," the third guard said, "the money makes my old lady happy. And when she's happy, I get more pussy. So leave this one alone. I need the job."

"Fine," Elliot snapped. "I'll go get the other one ready."

Gray didn't want Elliot molesting Katya. She snarled and thrashed and snapped when they tried to collar her.

"Damn it—Ames, get that collar on her," Martin said. "Elliot, hit her with a low dose. I mean it—low."

Gray roared when the current arced over her skin, but she stayed standing. The jolt left her teetering on the edge of release, but she held herself together. Ames clamped the electric shock collar on her neck.

Martin snapped, "I'll get the other one."

A minute later, the guards dragged her and Katya down the hall through murky air that stung her chest and shoved them through the metal doors into the harsh glare of the laboratory. She blinked and tried to clear the fog from her eyes, but her vision was worse than it had been earlier that morning, and much worse than the day before. The glaring overhead lights were ringed with smoke, and the faces of the men and women who tugged her to the cold steel table and tied down her arms and legs with metal restraints that burned her skin swam in and out of focus. She strained to see where they had taken Katya and saw her only a few feet away. A loop of thick black cord wrapped around her wrists and suspended her from the ceiling. Her body was stretched upward in a tight arch. Their eyes met for a second, and Katya's green eyes flashed bright with wolf. Gray's wolf started to prowl.

Somewhere a door whooshed open, and the low murmur of approaching voices penetrated Gray's dazed mind. She recognized the scent and the low sultry voice of the human female who had stood outside her cage and taunted her with her body and her words just… When? The day before, the week before, an hour ago? Gray wasn't certain how many times the human had come, how many times she had been baited into losing control, and the rage swelled again. She snarled, her vision flattening, sharpening, as her wolf clawed to the surface. And this time, Gray let her come.

❖

"This one," Veronica Standish said, pointing to the blonde suspended from an overhead pulley, "is dominant, but less aggressive. The other one would not be as much to your liking."

Michel surveyed the two Were females. Both were underweight, both appeared dazed and disoriented. The one in four-point restraints on the table already showed signs of shifting. She wondered if the humans recognized how close to going feral that one was. A thin line of dark pelt bisected her tight, hollow abdomen, and her canines protruded. Her lips were drawn back in a snarl, and blood tinged the tips of her fingers where her claws extended. That one would shift before long, and when she did, those restraints were not going to hold her. The one they had prepared for her, the one the human called Katya, was full-breasted and well-muscled even though thin, and young. Just barely beyond adolescence. Not virginal, none of the Weres were inexperienced once past early adolescence, but Michel doubted this one had ever experienced thrall. Even physically depleted, her Were blood would be invigorating.

"You're right," she said to the scientist, smoothing her hand over the Were's face, down her neck, over her chest. "She's quite appealing."

The Were snarled and tried to pull away, but with her arms extended over her head and her feet barely touching the floor, she had no purchase, no way to escape. Michel ensnared her mind, projected the scent of forest and mountain breezes to soothe her. If the Were fought her, she might hurt her when she fed, and that was of no benefit to her task. The Regent requested she study the facility, and thus far she'd learned some valuable new information. The extensive underground facility was accessible by a single elevator, keyed to the scientist's retinal scan. She couldn't tell how many subjects might be held underground, but she'd seen half a dozen windowless, computer-locked doors that could easily lead to holding pens. Holding areas that might have been built with Weres in mind, but which could just as easily be adapted for Vampires. If there was an enemy in this room, it was not these Weres.

"How can I help you, Dr. Standish?"

Veronica studied the Vampire who always seemed to be by Francesca's side. Michel was beautiful in her androgyny, exciting in her aloofness, dangerous by nature. Veronica found nothing more arousing than danger, and danger combined with beauty was even more appealing. The combination stirred her mind and excited her body. She was wet, and that fact alone was a challenge, considering Vampires enthralled their prey with sexual allure. How very exhilarating. She imagined the Vampire could scent her arousal, and she didn't mind. She wasn't a victim of her desire, not when she could control it and use it to control others.

"I want you to feed from her and ensure that she orgasms. We'll collect specimens throughout. You, of course, are free to enjoy yourself in any way you desire."

"And if she's not enough for me?" Michel slowly smiled at Veronica Standish and loosed her thrall. The Regent had not expressly forbidden her from engaging the human, and what better way to determine a human's secrets than in the throes of passion?

The Vampire's scarlet gaze cascaded over Veronica's body, heating her skin and tightening her sex. She shivered. So, that was a little taste of Vampire thrall. Definitely powerful. No wonder the species was so resilient despite their small numbers. Veronica had never been with a Vampire, but she would certainly find the opportunity to do so now. "Perhaps when we have completed the experiments, you and I can retire somewhere a little more private and discuss the outcome."

Michel slipped her hand around Veronica's arm. "Let's finish this part, then, so I can spend my time with someone more worthy of my attention."

Veronica smiled and let her fingers graze the Vampire's chest. "Indeed, I couldn't agree more."

CHAPTER THIRTY

Max parked the Rover on a forested ridge overlooking the Green Mountain research facility—an easy run through the woods in pelt. While he and Niki scouted the route down, Sylvan and Drake found a clearing in the trees and scanned the grounds and surrounding woodlands with a night scope. The sprawling facility was surrounded by a high chain-link fence topped with razor wire. A deterrent for humans, but easy to leap over for Weres. Covered kiosks at regular intervals marked sentry points. In addition to the perimeter security, the trees had been clear-cut for twenty yards beyond the fence in all directions, leaving no cover and preventing a stealth approach.

"This is no research facility," Sylvan said. "This is a paramilitary installation."

"How can they keep something like this secret?" Drake asked.

"Money," Sylvan said. "And political connections."

"We need to find out who's behind this place," Drake said.

"We will," Sylvan said, "after we find our young."

"We need to send a message," Drake said, "that our wolves will not be victims."

Sylvan showed her teeth, and her eyes flashed gold in the silver moonlight. "We will."

Drake caressed Sylvan's bare shoulder. "Good."

"Sentries in the woods at twelve, three, six, and nine," Sylvan said, handing the scope to Drake.

"Perimeter guards walking post, also," Drake grumbled. "They don't move like humans, but they don't look like wolves either."

"I don't think they are," Sylvan said darkly. "I think they're cat Weres. Probably mercenaries. It makes sense if the humans are trying to keep what's happening here a secret. The fewer humans they involve, the better. Especially guards."

"How do they fight?" Drake asked.

"They're quick, and they go for the eyes and the belly. A big cat can take out your throat with one quick slash, so don't hesitate on your approach." Sylvan caressed Drake's back. "We have strength on our side. Go in low, use your body weight to take them down, and clamp your jaws on the throat."

Drake nodded, still surveying the installation through the night scope. "Getting to the sentries in the woods shouldn't be difficult, but the guards on that perimeter fence have the advantage. Crossing that no-cover zone will be difficult, even in pelt. They'll see us coming."

Sylvan laughed softly. "Not true for our Vampire friends. Their speed renders them nearly invisible."

"Then it's a good thing they joined us," Drake said.

"Not something I plan on telling them," Sylvan muttered.

"There's no way we're going to breach these defenses without bloodshed," Drake said.

"Are you prepared for it?"

Drake kissed her quickly. "Yes."

"Stay close," Sylvan said.

"Always."

They returned to where Jody leaned against the right fender of the Rover. Her soldiers, Rafaela and Claude, stood a short distance away, automatic weapons slung over their shoulders. Niki and Max appeared out of the woods.

"A dozen outside," Niki said. "The facility is isolated inside some kind of much larger complex. If we can cut the communications from that building before we go in, we'll buy ourselves time."

"We should be able to eliminate the guards in the woods without the perimeter guards being aware of it." Sylvan glanced at the Vampire. "Can you take out the sentries on the fence quickly enough to prevent them from alerting anyone inside?"

"We are four," Jody said. "Six humans is no challenge." Jody glanced at Rafaela and Claude, the two Vampires in combat gear, and the driver, who had shed his suit coat for a black windbreaker. "Silent approach. No weapons fire."

"Yes, Liege," they all said at once.

Sylvan turned to Max. "I want you to disable the hard lines and jam wireless communications."

"Yes, Alpha. It would help if I could see a grid of the area."

Jody said, "Becca can pull that up for you." She handed Max her cell phone. "She's ready to relay images. Press One on the speed dial and tell her what you need."

"Go with the Vampires," Sylvan said to Max. When he started to protest, she growled at him, and he ducked his head. "We need you to block their communications and disable security on the door. When we arrive, I want to be able to get in immediately. The Vampires will clear the way for you."

"Yes, Alpha." Max walked a few feet away and spoke into the phone.

Rafaela glanced at Niki and winked, her incisors sparkling like shards of glass in the moonlight. "Should be fun."

Niki grinned.

"Good hunting," Sylvan said as the Vampires misted into the darkness. She turned to Niki and Max. "Research facilities do not require armed guards. There are no innocents here. Take them down, and if they resist, kill them."

"Yes, Alpha," Niki and Max said.

Sylvan let her wolf rise, flooding the clearing with her call. Niki shuddered and tilted her face to the sky, shifting effortlessly in a flurry of red and gray. Sylvan glanced at Drake.

"Are you ready, Prima?"

Drake breathed in, absorbing Sylvan's power, and let her own power flow. "Yes, mate."

They shifted together, silver and black, lethal and wild. Niki took a position on their flank, and Sylvan led the war party into the night.

❖

The moon was nearly full, and Drake felt the strength of the Pack gather inside her in a way she never had before, not even running with Sylvan at the height of their breeding frenzy. Cool air redolent with life flowed in and out of her lungs. Her heart pumped and her muscles churned. She had never been as strongly attuned to her wolf as she was then, cutting through the trees by Sylvan's side, swift and sure and strong. Sylvan tilted her muzzle into the air, sniffed, and nudged Drake with a snap of teeth. With a low growl, Sylvan inclined her head, gold eyes glinting, indicating prey off to their right. Drake pulled back her lips and showed her teeth in understanding.

Be careful, Prima.

You too, love.

Drake cut away into the denser forest, and Sylvan led Niki on. Drake slowed, padding softly through the thick layer of pine needles and crushed leaves on the forest floor. She stayed downwind of where they had sighted the first guard from the ridge above. A cat Were's senses were as acute as a wolf's, and she needed surprise on her side.

Fortunately, the guards would not be expecting them, and definitely not from a rear approach through the mountains. She smelled him first, gamey and pungent. Male cat, aggressive and half-feral. Drake growled quietly in anticipation, her hackles rising.　　　　　　　•

She was nearly on him when he swung in her direction, raising his automatic rifle with a curse. Airborne, she hit him in the chest with all fours, taking him down onto his back. He flung the gun aside, and by the time they landed with a bone-shattering thud, he had shifted. He was a big cat, a mountain puma, eight feet long with six-inch canines. He pulled his rear legs up to his belly, attempting to rake her underside with his lethal claws. He slashed at her muzzle with his teeth as she went for his throat, but she clamped her strong jaws down on his trachea. His rear claws caught her in the side and razor-sharp slashes of pain exploded, but she held fast, whipping her shoulders from side to side. Blood welled from her shoulder and his throat, the copper tang flooding the air. She hoped Sylvan was far enough away not to scent it. She did not want her mate distracted in the heat of her own battle. He thrashed, but without air, he was weakening. She bit deeper, jerked her head right and left, and snapped his neck. Panting, she dropped his lifeless carcass, spun around, and retraced her path until she caught the scent of Pack.

Racing through the forest, leaping over thick underbrush, skirting around trees, and bounding over fallen logs, she quickly detected where Niki had split off. She followed her mate's trail, as strong a beacon as if the path were illuminated by electric lights. Fiery pain exploded in her front leg and she almost fell. Sylvan. Sylvan was hurt.

Drake burst into a clearing vibrating with savage growls and ferocious snarls. A dead cat lay just in front of her, its throat a gaping cavern. A little farther away, Sylvan was down, pinned by two huge mountain lions. Drake smelled blood. Her mate's blood. With a roar, she launched herself into the battle.

She landed on the back of a female cat just as the cat raked her canines across Sylvan's exposed belly. Blood welled on Sylvan's silver pelt. Drake sank her teeth into the cat's neck and tore it open. A geyser of hot blood shot out as the cat screamed and fell beneath her. She held the Were down long enough to be sure she was dying, then spun around just as Sylvan slashed a hole in the belly of the cat who straddled her. The cat screeched and released its hold on Sylvan's neck. Sylvan's canines flashed and the cat's scream died with it.

Drake dragged the heavy Were off Sylvan's body.

Sylvan!

I'm all right, Prima. Sylvan staggered to her feet, her head down, her chest heaving. Blood dripped from her belly and her shoulder onto the ground.

You're not. Drake licked Sylvan's face, then nosed at her shoulder. She licked the blood away. A deep gouge ran into the muscle. *Let me see your belly.*

Sylvan rumbled. *No time. It's not bad.*

Niki burst into the clearing and raced to Sylvan's side. She nosed her, whining and shivering.

I'm all right. The rest of the cats?

Niki's ears flickered and her eyes glinted.

Good. Sylvan leaned against Drake's shoulder and rested her muzzle on Drake's back.

Draw strength from me. I am here for you.

As I am for you. You're hurt, Prima.

Drake felt Sylvan reach out to her, felt the power of their connection flowing between them. Niki crowded close, and the connection deepened. Drake's pain receded. Sylvan took a deep breath and pulled away, her shoulder healed, her eyes bright and clear.

Once over the fence, follow Max and the Vampires inside.

Drake stayed close on Sylvan's heels as she raced into the forest. She wasn't letting her mate out of her sight again. They would fight the final battle together.

❖

Michel held the young Were around the waist, lifting her effortlessly, taking the tension off her suspended arms. The humans would not be able to tell Katya's feet no longer touched the floor. Katya arched her back and rubbed her breasts against Michel's chest, her whiskey eyes soft and seductive, her full lips a sensuous invitation.

Michel brushed her face against Katya's neck, breathing in the scent of female and nature and primal strength. The Were's blood pounded in wild expectation, and Michel's mouth filled even as the hollow agony overtook her. Hunger slashed through her body, burning her consciousness to crumbling cinders. Hunger, destroyer of sanity, annihilator of reason. Her incisors plunged from their sheaths, and she swiped her tongue along the broad vein in Katya's neck. She pulled Katya deeper into her thrall, aching to fill herself with the fire and vitality the young Were's blood promised. She had been so empty for so very long.

Katya whimpered and rolled her pelvis against Michel's crotch. Heat poured through the tight fabric of Michel's pants, stirring her dormant flesh even though she had not yet fed. The Were was potent, powerful, and Michel's hunger nearly obliterated her senses.

"Don't lose any of that specimen," Veronica Standish said from somewhere nearby. "Get the device on her."

Michel felt Katya stiffen in her grasp and sensed the other Were in the room snarling, struggling, shifting. She flooded Katya's awareness with the scent of Pack, and Katya quieted. A chorus of startled voices rose, sounding some kind of alarm. She had time, must have time. Needed this Were. Needed. Hunger. Need. Michel slid her incisors through the golden skin.

"What's happening?" she heard Standish demand. "Watch that other one."

But she no longer cared about specimens or experiments. She had to have this Were now, had to taste her, had to fill her vacant, aching flesh with vibrant life. She penetrated deeper, and the Were's blood poured into her, an inferno of power igniting her lust. Her cells, tissues, organs pulsed with energy, and her sex pounded to life with primal potency. The Were writhed in her arms, her skin burning, a roar of ecstasy trapped in her chest.

Sucking, swallowing, growing stronger with each taste, Michel stroked her palm down the Were's rigid abdomen, felt her struggling for release, felt the agony in her body. Michel's fingers brushed over cold metal—silver—and she dragged her mouth away from the Were's neck. She whipped her head around and captured Veronica Standish's feverish gaze.

"Take it off her," Michel snarled, letting her thrall flow. "Now."

Standish's eyes grew wide, then glazed. "Ames, remove the pump."

Katya whimpered, her need incinerating her, and Michel stroked her damp face.

No one will harm you now. Soon, soon I'll bring you pleasure.

For a fraction of a second, the Were's eyes cleared, and she met Michel's gaze.

"Please," Katya whispered, "the pain. Help me fight the pain." She shuddered and her eyes rolled back.

Bloodlust crashed through Michel's senses, ripping away her control. Her predatory drive ascended, and she thrust aside the foreign hands invading the Were's body.

"She is *mine*," Michel growled, cupping Katya's swollen sex, claiming her prey.

"Please, now," Katya cried out, and Michel struck deep into her neck, flooding her with hormones. Katya burst in Michel's hand, and Michel came in a blinding, insane blast of heat and power.

A wild roar filled the room, and Standish shouted, "Oh my God, what is she doing! Shoot her—for God's sake, shoot her!"

CHAPTER THIRTY-ONE

Sylvan, followed by Drake and Niki, bounded over the twelve-foot fence outside the research facility, landing soundlessly on the concrete surface of the deserted lot. The motionless body of a sentry taken down by the Vampires lay in the shadows behind a nearby guard tower.

This way! Sylvan raced across the brightly lit lot toward the shadows of a loading dock with tall, windowless steel doors. Max ghosted out of the shadows and disabled the security locks by the time they leapt up onto the platform. The doors swung open, and Jody and her two Vampire soldiers appeared beside them.

"All clear on the perimeter," Jody said. "I estimate five minutes before whoever is manning the security command center inside will notice that communications are down."

Sylvan dipped her head in understanding. To Max, she telegraphed, *Do you know where our young are being held?*

"Becca dug up preliminary schematics from the renovations. We've got a general idea," Max murmured as he pressed his fingers to an earbud attached to his phone. "She's sending the images now."

Sylvan growled and paced impatiently in front of the door, her wolf straining to hunt, to find her young, to kill. Drake rubbed against her and nipped at her ruff, as if to remind her the most successful hunt was a methodical, smoothly orchestrated chase with the Pack working in concert. She did not have to fight every battle alone. Grumbling, Sylvan swung her head around and closed her jaws over Drake's muzzle. Their eyes met.

I can't feel them.

Drake eased her muzzle free and licked Sylvan's face. *They're here. We'll find them.*

"Whatever they've done in the underground portion of the lab, it's blocking you," Jody observed. "Otherwise, you'd sense your females even if they were dead."

Sylvan whipped around, searching for challenge in the eyes of the Vampire who knew too much.

Jody grinned and shrugged with nonchalant ease. "There's no other explanation for why you haven't found them already. Your secrets are safe, Wolf."

Sylvan snarled, but she relaxed her aggressive posture. She resented the Vampire in her territory, but in the absence of challenge, she would not fight her. Yet.

"There's a single elevator shaft at the far end of the building," Max said, squinting at the image on his phone. "It does not seem connected to the rest of the complex."

"That's got to be the access to the underground labs," Jody said. "That area will undoubtedly be heavily guarded. What about maintenance tunnels, utility conduits? There have to be other ways in."

Max grunted and turned the phone for everyone to see, tapping the surface with a blunt finger. A schematic appeared. "The ventilation shafts are huge. We can get through them."

"I'll take my soldiers down the main route and clear the halls on your flanks of any security personnel," Jody said, studying the rough plans of the underground wing. "They won't see us until we're on them."

Sylvan tilted her muzzle in agreement.

Rafaela reached down, scratched behind Niki's ear, and tugged on her thick red-gray ruff. "Having fun yet, Wolfie?" She laughed when Niki jerked around and snapped at her hand, missing her by millimeters. "Watch your pretty tail doesn't get singed in there."

Niki snarled but briefly rubbed her muzzle against Rafaela's thigh.

Sylvan ran in a quick circle, her tail elevated, her eyes flashing at Max. *Shift now. Take us there.*

"Yes, Alpha." Max shifted in a blur of black and white. The Vampires were already gone, moving too quickly for anyone to see.

The Vampires do have their uses, Drake said.

Sylvan shot her a look. *We're outnumbered, even with them. Don't take any chances, Prima.*

Trust me, I won't. Drake nudged her side. *Stay safe for me, Alpha.*

❖

Gray smelled Katya's fear and the thick tang of her Packmate's blood. The silver manacles burned deep into the flesh of her wrists and ankles, and her belly pounded with a terrible need for release. Bones slid and grated beneath her skin, her canines and claws burst out, and her wolf fought her way free. Gray couldn't hold her anymore. Didn't want to rein in her rage and fury. She wanted to rip and tear at her tormentors. She wanted to drag down the predators who tortured her and her Packmate and rip out their throats. She wanted blood. She wanted vengeance. Her wolf howled in an agony of rage and frenzy. Her shift took only a few excruciating seconds, and then she was free, finally free.

"Holy crap!" a male shouted. A claxon sounded, hurting Gray's ears with its piercing ring. "It's getting loose. Run!"

Gray wrenched her legs from the restraints and leapt to the cool tile floor, swinging her head in a swift arc, assessing the position of her enemies. Closest to her were two humans in laboratory uniforms. They were the ones who pushed needles into her body, drugged her, shocked her, humiliated her. Right behind them, the two guards who tortured her stood protectively in front of the female who smelled of sex and excitement. Martin, the one who tried to warn her, was gone.

The female stared at Gray with a mixture of fear and amazement. Her mouth, ringed in crimson, curved over bright white teeth, and Gray's stomach tightened with the urge to take and taste and claim. She snarled and crouched to spring. The female screamed, "Shoot her! Shoot her!"

Gray hungered to kill. She would take that female soon, but first, she needed to help her Packmate. Katya hung limply in the grasp of a dark-haired Vampire, scarlet rivers running down Katya's throat over her bare chest. The Vampire was covered in Katya's *victus*, and her eyes shimmered like a bloody sunset when she smiled at Gray.

Gray stalked her.

Careful, Wolf. A cool, smooth voice reverberated inside Gray's hazy brain. *Don't make me hurt you.*

The two guards shouldered their rifles, and half a dozen security officers in combat gear streamed into the room. The Vampire's hand closed around the back of Katya's neck, and she dragged Katya, still swinging from her restraints, behind her.

From somewhere close by, the click of metal made Gray's ears stand up, and she whirled into a crouch, teeth bared, preparing to spring. The big guard Ames, the one who always collared her, the one who shocked her, held a rifle to his shoulder and pointed it in her direction. The human technicians scuttled for safety. Gray uncoiled her muscles, propelled herself from the floor, and drove for his throat. The guard fired. The tranquilizer dart skimmed beneath her stomach and bounced off a piece of equipment with a hollow clang. She struck his chest with her forelegs extended, and he stumbled backward, going down beneath her. She locked her jaws around his throat as they rolled together, his arms beating on her head and neck, her claws raking his torso. Flesh tore beneath her teeth, blood welled from between her jaws. Her eyes locked on his, and she saw terror wash through them. She took her prey quickly with one rapid thrash of her head. His dying cry was silenced by her growl of triumph.

"Oh fuck," a hoarse male voice whined, "Jesus, somebody do something."

The beautiful human female who made Gray's belly hurt shouted, "Use your bullets. Don't try to stun her, you idiots! Kill her. Kill her."

Blood dripping from her muzzle, her mind a red haze of rage, Gray slunk under a table and circled behind the group, seeking her next prey. Elliot. The one who hurt her, humiliated her. First the one called Elliot, then all the others.

❖

"Get down," Michel shouted, pushing Standish to the floor and dragging Katya out of the line of fire. She had no allegiance to the human, but Standish was the Regent's ally.

The guards and security officers, who had taken cover just inside the door, all fired wildly, catching Standish, Michel, and the Weres in the chaotic crossfire. The escaped wolf Were flitted in and out between lab benches and equipment, striking at anyone within reach.

Standish crawled behind a huge computer console and disappeared. A bullet tore into Michel's shoulder and another struck her thigh. The burning pain was fleeting. The wounds weren't dangerous. She forcefully extended her right arm, and the stiletto dropped from its sheath into her palm. She slashed through the rope suspending Katya from the ceiling and caught her as she fell. The Were was weak from blood loss and the poison in her body. With another quick slice of the blade, Michel cut the cord on the Were's wrists. Katya struggled to escape her thrall. "Don't fight me. I'm setting you free."

"My Packmate," Katya gasped. "I need to help her."

"Get out of here. Through the door behind me. Go."

Katya shivered, her whiskey eyes shifting to gold and the bones in her face elongating. Golden pelt flowed over her torso.

"No!" Michel captured Katya's gaze and rolled her mind, halting her shift. A Were so young could not fight the thrall of one as old and powerful as she. Michel grasped her around the waist and carried her toward the door. "You can't fight them all. You'll die with her."

"I won't leave her," Katya protested weakly. "Please."

"She's feral. You can't help her."

Three Vampires materialized just inside the door, blocking their way. Michel stared into the cold dark eyes of Jody Gates. Neither of them should be there, and they both knew it. Stalemate. Michel thrust Katya toward Jody Gates. "Take her. The elevator at the far end of the building is accessible."

"Are there other Weres in here?"

"A feral wolf, already shifted." Michel smiled at the pre-animate, wondering if Gates would survive this night. If she did, she would be a formidable adversary for the Regent. And for her. She misted past Gates and her soldiers into the hall, calling out in her wake, "Another time, Liege."

❖

Sylvan, Drake, and Niki dropped down the airshaft, through a vent in the ceiling, and into a hallway in the underground complex. Gunfire, growls, and panicked shouts emanated from a room at the far end of the deserted corridor. Sylvan bounded toward the open doorway. Her lungs burned with every breath, as if she were inhaling liquid fire. Her vision swam, and her legs churned clumsily. Poison. Silver. The air was thick with it. The longer they stayed, the weaker they would all become. She must find her young.

Gates appeared through the doorway with a motionless Were clasped in her arms.

Katya! Sylvan's heart swelled even as a growl burst from her chest.

"Half a dozen with automatic rifles left inside," Gates said smoothly, never breaking stride. "My soldiers will assist you, Wolf.

You've got a feral young in there somewhere and maybe a minute before more guards show up. I'll take this one out."

Sylvan didn't want to trust her young to a Vampire. She studied the Vampire's eyes, saw nothing but strength and certainty. She drew back her lips, rumbling her assent as well as a warning, and raced on. She streaked into the room, belly low, homing in on the nearest target. She leapt for the kill. So did her mate and her second. Three of the enemy went down amidst a clatter of weapons and frantic cries. Drake slashed open one's chest, Niki clawed another's belly, Sylvan ripped open the throat of a third. The rest, disorganized and firing blindly, scattered or fell before the swift assault of Gates's Vampires.

Panting, Sylvan sniffed the tainted air and smelled her young. Fear sweat. Pheromones heavy with rage and sex frenzy. A young Were, blooded and out of control.

Secure our flanks, she ordered Drake and Niki. *I'll get the young.*

Across the room, unmindful of Sylvan's stealthy approach, Gray stalked her prey. Her hackles were raised, foam frothing from her mouth, her wolf's eyes wild and riveted on a thin, balding human who fired an automatic pistol at Gray while stumbling backward, bumping into carts and poles with sloshing IV bags. His shots went wide while Gray prowled inexorably closer and closer. A dead human lay not far away, his throat torn out, a pool of black congealing blood streaming from beneath his body. The adolescent's muzzle was caked with gore. Gray had taken human prey, something even the most seasoned Were warriors rarely if ever did. After that kind of kill, the instinct to remain wild would be overpowering.

Sylvan howled her fury. She would not surrender her young to madness. She would not kill this wolf.

Sylvan soared over a metal table covered with instruments and syringes and probes to land beside Gray. The shouting behind her quieted, and all that remained was the harsh, rapid breathing of the thin, ashen-faced human with his back to the wall ten feet away. He smelled like her young—he was covered in Were sex hormones and fear scent and rage—he'd hurt her young. This one, this one would die.

Fall back, Wolf, Sylvan instructed her young.

Beside her, the adolescent female swung her head from side to side, saliva dripping onto the floor, her chest heaving. The air stung Sylvan's eyes, and her muscles felt as if they were tearing from her bones. No more time. *Gray! Do as I command.*

The young white-and-gray wolf cut her eyes in Sylvan's direction and stared, uncomprehending and unafraid. Challenging. Sylvan growled a warning. She couldn't control Gray until the danger from the guard was neutralized.

Drake, she called, *corner this young and hold her.*

Sylvan didn't wait for an answer. She trusted her mate. She covered the distance to the guard in one long, powerful leap, her eyes fixed on those of the human male who had violated her territory, her Pack, her wolves. He would pay in blood.

The human grasped his gun in shaking hands, fired blindly, and turned to run. Sylvan twisted in the air, the bullet passing wide, and landed high on his back. She buried her canines in the back of his neck and took him face down to the floor, her heavy body pinning his torso. She closed her jaws, one millimeter at a time, her hot breath heavy in his ear. He scrabbled and scratched, panted and screamed. Slowly, methodically, she clamped her powerful jaws tighter and tighter. Muscle tore from bones, ligaments popped and ripped, bones crushed to dust. Blood welled up as arteries and veins disintegrated. His voice became a wet gurgle as she strangled him, unhurriedly and painfully and without mercy. When he lay still, she dropped him and swung her heavy head around. Her duty was done. Now she needed to see to her wolves.

Drake had Gray backed into the far corner and held her there with snapping lunges and angry growls. Gray's ruff stood on end, her lips were drawn back in a feral snarl, and she challenged Drake with a steady rumble deep in her chest. Gates's two Vampires had subdued the last of the security officers and disappeared. Whoever else had been in the room had escaped. Only the dead remained.

Sylvan bounded across the room and stopped a shoulder's length past Drake, putting herself between her mate and the feral Were. Drake eased away but did not go far. Niki appeared on Sylvan's flank.

Alpha, Niki said, *let me give her a merciful death. Let me do this for you, for the Pack.*

No. Sylvan poured her power into the foul air, drenching the Weres in her pheromones. Niki shivered, a low whine torn from her throat. Drake rumbled, her hackles rising.

On your belly, whelp, Sylvan snarled, staring into Gray's eyes. *Do it now. Do it now or you die.*

Gray shuddered as if a great force thundered through her, and her eyes rolled wildly. Her ears dropped back, her tail trembled.

Sylvan rushed her, teeth snapping. *Now. Down!*

Gray hesitated and Sylvan grabbed Gray's throat in her jaws and dragged her down onto her back, straddling her with all fours. She shook her until the breath stopped in Gray's chest. When Gray went limp, she let go but remained over her, poised for the killing strike.

Gray shuddered, growled softly, and opened her eyes. She gazed up at Sylvan, and the madness in her eyes gave way to a weary peacefulness. She turned her head and bared her neck to her Alpha. Sylvan gripped her throat gently, shook her tenderly, rumbled a welcome. When she released her, Gray licked Sylvan's face.

You did well, Gray. Sylvan nuzzled her and nipped her ear. *I'm proud of you. Welcome home.*

Katya? Where is she? Gray struggled to her feet.

On her way out. Come, we'll find her.

The staccato rap of automatic weapon fire cut through the silence, and Niki and Drake crowded around Sylvan, shielding her.

It's not in here. Sylvan streaked toward the door with her wolves close behind. *It's coming from down the hall.*

❖

Jody and her Vampires raced toward the elevator thirty feet away. Bullets strafed the hall from the direction of an open stairwell up ahead. Jody drew her weapon, shielding the Were in her arms as much as she could. The adolescent had stopped struggling and was either unconscious or on the verge of succumbing to whatever poison had been fed to her.

"Let us take the Were, Liege," Rafaela urged, moving in front of Jody. "Turn back until we neutralize the ones in the stairwell. You will be safer with the Weres."

"Too late. Clear a path to the elevator for us, Rafe," Jody ordered. "We're going out now."

"Yes, Liege." Rafaela cut down the first two figures who burst out firing from the stairwell.

Twenty feet.

Jody took out another, Claude two more.

Ten feet.

Rafaela caught a round in the side and staggered, momentarily thrown off balance. Before Claude could step into the gap in front of Jody, a black-clad figure in full combat gear dropped through the ceiling of the elevator and fired through the open elevator doors. Jody had only two choices—return fire and leave the Were in her arms unprotected or pass the Were to Claude before the bullets struck. Faster than the bullets traveling toward her, Jody pushed Katya into Claude's arms. "Cover me."

She knew it would be too late, but she raised her gun and shot him in the head. A crater appeared in the center of his forehead at the same time as a crimson geyser erupted from her chest. She stared down at the fountain of red, felt her heart falter. Too late. Too late for so many things.

CHAPTER THIRTY-TWO

Claude, secure the stairwell!" Rafaela dropped to her knees next to Jody. The Weres, most in skin now, crowded around behind her. "Liege! How bad?"

Jody tried to pull air into her lungs. An agonizing inferno raged in her chest, her vision wavered, and crushing pressure made it impossible for her to speak.

"A blood mate?" Rafaela asked urgently. "Are you bonded? Where should we take you?"

Jody gathered the last of her power, projecting her will with the force of her ancient bloodlines. There could be no mistake. Only seconds left. So little time. Eternity stretched before her. The cost. Who would pay? *Not* Becca. "No. No one. Take my body to the manor head."

And then the blackness came.

Sylvan asked, "What happened?"

Rafaela turned flat hard eyes to her. "My Liege is dead. We will take her now."

"Wait a minute." Niki knelt on the other side of Jody's body. "She'll rise, won't she?"

Rafaela's sculpted face set into hard unreadable lines. Her voice was cool, all the playful arrogance gone. "That is not your concern, Wolf."

"The hell it isn't." Niki leapt over Jody and snarled in Rafaela's face. "She fought beside us. She saved Katya. We all saw it. They're firing silver!"

Pain flickered in Rafaela's eyes before they became impenetrable. "She is not blood-bonded. We will take her now for proper burial."

Niki grasped Rafaela's arm. "She *is*. She is bonded. And her bonded mate is at the Compound."

"No formal announcement has been made," Rafaela said. "No official notice has been given. My Liege denied a bond."

Niki whirled around to Sylvan. "Alpha? I've seen them together. I know they've exchanged blood."

"Jody must have her reasons for denying the blood bond," Sylvan said, "but if Becca is her blood mate, she deserves to be involved." Sylvan took Katya from Claude. "Let's get everyone to safety." She lowered her voice and growled at Rafaela. "The Vampire comes with us."

Rafaela hesitated for a second, then nodded curtly. "As you wish, Alpha Mir."

❖

Becca checked her phone for the tenth time in five minutes for word from Max or Jody. Why hadn't someone called? They were supposed to have been in and out, a rapid stealth attack. And Jody should have called her. She was going to kick her Vampire ass when she got back from this little adventure.

The door to the small library in Sylvan's headquarters, where she had been using the computer to track down specs on the research center, opened behind her. *At last.* She jumped up and spun around. "It's about time you got ba—"

"I'm sorry." Elena came in and closed the door. "I need you to come to the infirmary with me."

Becca's stomach tightened, and icy dread slithered down her spine. "Why? What's wrong?"

"The Alpha just called. They'll be here in a few minutes. You're needed."

"Why? What's happened? Tell me now. Please." Becca gripped the back of the chair to hide the trembling in her hands. Jody hadn't called. "Just tell me."

Sadness and compassion filled Elena's eyes. "I'm sorry. Detective Gates was shot and killed during the raid."

A gray curtain dropped, suddenly blocking all the light in the room. Becca struggled to catch her breath. Please, this couldn't be. They'd had so little time. So many things left to say, to do. The years of her life stretched before her like an endless night. Endless dark years.

Becca fought back against the despair. "She's a Vampire. She'll rise. She's not dead. It's not the same thing. She's not dead."

"I don't know," Elena said gently. "I only know the Alpha said it was urgent, and you needed to be there."

"Take me there." Becca grasped Elena's arm. "We're blood-bonded. Someone must know what to do. I'm not letting her go."

❖

The treatment room door banged open, and Sylvan strode through, Jody in her arms. Behind her, Niki carried Katya. A white-and-gray wolf padded close beside them.

"Jody!" Becca rushed forward. Jody's white shirt was drenched with blood. Becca grasped Jody's hand. It was cold, beyond even the cold when Jody had not fed for a long time. "God, oh God, baby. What have they done to you?" She looked past Sylvan to Rafaela and saw nothing in her eyes except resignation. "Tell me what we need to do." When the Vampire didn't answer, Becca grasped Sylvan's arm. "Please. Help me. I can't lose her."

"Elena," Sylvan said, shaking her head at Niki when Niki made a move to pull Becca's hand from her arm. "Katya and Gray need attention."

"Take them next door," Elena said to Niki. "I'll get Sophia."

"Niki, stay with them."

"Yes, Alpha."

Becca clutched Jody's hand as Sylvan laid Jody carefully on the bed. Jody's lips were white, bloodless. Her eyelids were nearly translucent, her thick dark lashes like smudges of coal against her stark white cheeks. Becca kissed her. "Jody, hey. I love you." She looked around the room and found Rafaela. "How much time do we have? What do I need to do?"

Rafaela shifted her gaze away.

"Please."

"Tell her what you told us," Sylvan said gruffly.

Rafaela drew a breath and let it out slowly. "My Liege said she did not have a blood mate."

"That's not true," Becca said. "If you don't believe me, ask Francesca." She turned her head, pointed to the faint puncture marks low on her neck. "She's fed from me and given me her blood. We *are* bonded. I will not let her die."

"How recently?" Rafaela said, light flaring in her onyx eyes. "How recent is the bond?"

Becca glanced at Sylvan, saw the same compassion in her eyes she'd seen in Elena's, and her heart started to pound so rapidly her chest ached. "Yesterday, last night. This morning. Why? Why does it matter?"

Rafaela pushed a hand through her dark, disheveled hair. "It's too soon. Even if her organs accepted your blood, there hasn't been enough time for your body to create a sufficient quantity of compatible ferrin. A safe volume of your blood will be insufficient to sustain her."

The room swam, and Becca grasped the cold metal bed frame for support. "What are you saying? That we just let her go? She's mine! I'm not letting her go."

"She denied the bond," Rafaela said flatly. "She did not want to rise."

"No. That doesn't make any sense." Becca's reason gave way under a wave of grief and rage. A black abyss opened in front of her, and she felt herself sliding into it. Too much. The pain was too much.

No! What was it Jody had said? *Your strength is your mind. That is how you will fight.* Becca forced herself to focus. Her vision cleared, her mind sharpened. She stared at Rafaela. "What do you mean, a *safe volume*? You said a safe volume of my blood wouldn't be sufficient."

"In order to counteract the tissue death, you might have to give her so much blood you could die in the process. She'll drain you."

Becca laughed harshly. "My life for hers. That's my choice? Is that what you're saying?"

"Possibly."

"Well, that explains it, then, doesn't it?" Becca brushed trembling fingers over Jody's hair. "She's so stubborn. Of course she wouldn't let me risk sacrificing myself for her. Because, after all, who could love her that much? Who would ever think she was worth it?" She leaned down, kissed Jody again, and murmured against her mouth, "You have so much to learn, Vampire. We're going to need a lot more than a few years before you figure out what I mean when I say I love you."

She straightened, her fingertips resting on Jody's cheek, and looked Rafaela in the eye. "I am Jody's bonded blood mate. Whatever has to be done, do it now."

Rafaela studied Becca for a long moment, then dipped her head. "If we start, I am not sure if we can stop should you change your—"

"You don't know me very well," Becca said impatiently. "How much time do we have?"

"Ordinarily, at least a day," Rafaela said. "Because your bond is new, and potentially weak, I don't know."

"Then we're wasting time. You need my blood." Becca held out her arm. "Take it."

Drake stepped over next to Becca. "I can infuse you with saline, keep your intravascular volume up. That will help avoid shock, at least for a while. We have all the equipment here."

"Outsiders cannot witness the ceremony," Rafaela said.

"Make an exception," Becca said. "Jody brought you here to fight with these Weres. They're not outsiders. Not to her. Not to me."

Sylvan said, "Drake will stay, the rest of us will stand guard outside. You have my word whatever happens here will never leave this room."

"All right," Rafaela said. "My Liege trusted you. So will I."

When the others left the room, Rafaela removed Jody's clothes and turned to Becca. "Lie down next to her. It would be best if you disrobed."

"Fine," Becca said and quickly shed her clothes. Her lover was naked, dead, a foot away. She wasn't going to worry about modesty now. Pulling the sheet aside, she stretched out beside Jody. God, she was so cold and still. "Hurry."

Drake set up an IV bag and quickly inserted an intravenous catheter into Becca's right forearm. While she taped it in place, she asked Rafaela, "How much blood does the reanimation require?"

"Usually no more than two units."

Drake frowned. "Even that is a lot for a woman Becca's size. Three units and she's in danger of hypovolemic shock. Any more than that—"

Becca grasped Drake's arm. "I want your word that you won't interfere until this works."

"I can't stand by and let you die trying to save her," Drake said quietly.

"Then I don't want you in this room. Leave now." Becca covered the horrible gunshot wound in Jody's breast with her hand, as if hiding the violation would somehow undo it. "Rafaela will do what needs to be done. This is Vampire business, Drake."

Drake's jaw tightened, and she rumbled dangerously. "Becca, Jody wouldn't want you to—"

Becca whipped her head around and glared at Drake. "What would you do, Drake, if Sylvan was lying here like this, and you could save her? What would you give?"

Drake's eyes flashed to wolf and she snarled. "I would give anything. Everything."

"Then don't deny me the same. I don't intend on dying, but I'm not living without her." She settled down beside Jody again. "Rafaela, do what has to be done."

"She has to drink it," Rafaela said.

"How?" Becca's throat felt like sandpaper. "How can she swallow?"

"Hold her face to your neck," Rafaela said. "Her mind is not gone, only deeply dormant. If she recognizes you as her bonded mate, she will drink."

Becca laughed shakily. "She damn well better after all this, or I really will kick her ass." She pulled Jody into her arms and cradled Jody's mouth against her neck.

Rafaela drew a short, double-edged blade from a sheath on her belt. "Are you prepared to provide eternity to our Liege Jody Gates, to bind your body and your blood and your life to her as long as she rises?"

"I am," Becca whispered.

Rafaela gently grasped Becca's chin and lifted, exposing her throat, and pressed the edge to Becca's jugular vein. A frisson of fear skittered through Becca's stomach, but she quickly squelched it. "Don't stop, Rafaela. Bring her back to me."

Rafaela incised the vein in one swift slash, and dark, thick blood cascaded into Jody's mouth.

❖

"How are they?" Sylvan asked when Drake emerged from the treatment room. Niki stood guard in front of another door a little farther down the hall.

"Becca's very weak. Jody is still…unresponsive. I don't know if she'll rise." Drake wrapped her arms around Sylvan's waist and leaned into her. She was tired and worried, and the battle had left her needing to connect to her mate. "How are the young?"

"Sophia is with them now. I had to force Gray to shift to skin, but she obeyed me."

Drake sighed. "They've been through hell."

Sylvan snarled. "I know. Everyone in the Pack will take care of them."

Drake skimmed her fingers along Sylvan's jaw. "You found them, you freed them. That will help them heal more than anything else."

"But I didn't find who was behind it. Killing their jailers is small justice for what was done."

"We won't stop until we find out who was in charge of that lab, and who they reported to." Drake kissed Sylvan. "But tonight Gray and Katya will sleep with Pack. And their Alpha will sleep with me." She licked Sylvan's neck and smiled at the rumble gathering in Sylvan's chest. She skimmed her fingers down Sylvan's torso and tugged at the open waistband of her jeans. "I'm glad we brought clothes with us on the raid, but I'd rather you got rid of these soon."

Sylvan nipped Drake's ear. "I want Elena to look at you. Then if we can leave Jody, I want to run. I want you alone, all over me."

Drake settled between Sylvan's thighs. "I don't need to see Elena. I'm fine. All I need is you."

Sylvan raised her lip enough to show the tip of a canine. "That building was filled with silver. I want to be sure everyone is healthy."

"Oh yes?" Drake scraped her claws down Sylvan's bare chest, leaving faint blood-streaked scratches behind. "And I suppose Elena has already checked *you* out?"

Sylvan's hips jerked, and her canines extruded farther. Her eyes shimmered between gold and midnight blue. "You challenge my judgment, Prima?"

Drake licked the feather-thin trickles of blood from Sylvan's chest and pressed her mouth to the mate bite above Sylvan's breast. The pelt line on Sylvan's lower abdomen thickened, and the rumble that had been gathering in Sylvan's chest morphed into a warning growl. Drake smiled and sucked the faint mark left by her teeth. "I don't know, Alpha. Do you feel challenged?"

Sylvan backed Drake against the wall and caged her in with her arms and legs. She raked her teeth down Drake's neck and bit the thick muscle at the juncture of shoulder and neck. Drake groaned and tilted her head back, giving Sylvan more access. Her belly tightened and her sex throbbed.

"Sylvan," Drake warned. "If you tease, you're going to get more than scratched."

"You'll have to catch me first." Sylvan rolled her hips between Drake's thighs.

Down the hall, Niki whined softly. Drake gripped Sylvan's hips and shot Niki a concerned look. Niki shook her head and grinned.

"Soon," Drake murmured in Sylvan's ear. "Soon we'll run, we'll tangle, we'll heal our young. And then we'll go hunting again."

❖

Becca waited, lying beside Jody, Jody's hand in hers. The sun would be up soon. If Jody didn't rise in time to feed, she might be too weak to ever rise. She stroked Jody's face, kissed her mouth. Jody's body beneath the crisp white sheet was so terribly, terribly still.

Weak, weary, Becca rested her cheek between Jody's breasts and wrapped her arm around her waist. The silence beneath her ear echoed the horrible emptiness inside her. She closed her eyes, her tears scalding her cheeks and falling on Jody's cold, perfect breast.

"Please, baby," Becca whispered. "Please come back. I need you. I love you. And now I'm stuck on you, damn it." She laughed through her tears. "You were so worried about blood addiction. See? You're not always right. It's my heart that can't survive without you."

At first Becca thought the warm flutter through her hair was a breeze floating through the open window. She held her breath, her ear to Jody's chest, listening, listening for the only sound she ever needed to hear again. *Please. Please.*

And then it came. Slow, steady, strong. Every few seconds, a heartbeat.

Becca jerked upright, afraid to hope but needing to believe so desperately. Jody's eyes were open, the familiar midnight black as infinite and deep as the heavens, only shot through now with shards of crimson. Different, but still beautiful.

"Jody?" Becca asked softly. "Jody?"

"You never listen to me," Jody said softly. The timbre of her voice was a little deeper than it had been, but it still flowed over Becca's skin like warm honey.

Becca's body shuddered as if caressed from the inside out. Her heart rose into her throat, and she had to swallow before she could speak. "If you'd stop trying to make up my mind for me, I might listen to you." She raised Jody's hand and kissed her palm, then cradled Jody's hand against her cheek. "You scared the hell out of me, Vampire."

"How did this happen? Why did Rafaela disobey me?"

"Because I told her to." Becca wanted to ask a million things.

Jody had never had time to explain any of this. She didn't know what happened when a Vampire rose. She thought of Francesca and Michel—avariciously sensual but so…so empty, somehow. Would Jody still be Jody? Would Jody still love her? "How do you feel?"

"Strong."

Becca traced the spot where the bullet had torn through Jody's chest. The skin was flawless. "Good."

"Why did you do it?"

Leaning up on her elbow, Becca frowned down into Jody's eyes. "Maybe we weren't quick enough with the reanimation, because your brain doesn't seem to be working right."

A flicker of a smile crossed Jody's lips. They weren't pale anymore, but flushed with blood. Her blood. Becca leaned over and kissed her. Warm. Alive. "I missed you, for starters."

"How do you feel?" Jody asked. "How much did you—"

"It doesn't matter. I'm here. So are you. I love you."

Jody's eyes flared a deeper crimson, more Vampire now than Becca had ever seen, even when Jody was in the throes of bloodlust. "Did they tell you that risen Vampires don't feel anything except hunger and power?"

A stabbing pain lanced through Becca's heart. If she had lost Jody, if Jody could no longer love her, at least she had not lost her to death. "No, no one told me that."

"I'm glad." Jody skimmed her fingers through Becca's hair. "They would have been wrong. I feel. I feel what you taught me to feel. I love you."

Tears raced down Becca's cheeks, carrying away the agony of loss, as cleansing as a warm summer rain. With a sigh, she curled up with her head on Jody's shoulder. Jody's arm came around her, and the world righted itself. She was too tired to argue, which might have been a first in her life. "I'll take credit for how you feel, if you want me to. I just want you. I want you in my heart, in my body, in my soul."

Jody trembled. "Becca, part of what you feel is the blood bond. If you're not sure—"

Becca thumped Jody lightly on the shoulder. "It isn't chemistry holding us together, Jody. Chemistry or biology or, hell, Fate might have been what brought us together, but what's keeping me here, and what will keep me here for as long as we have, is in my heart. I fell in love with a Vampire. I want you exactly the way you are."

Jody rested her cheek against Becca's hair. "My heart is yours."

"All of you is mine." Becca searched Jody's face. She looked strong, healthy in a way she never had before, but her eyes burned with new fierceness. "You must need to feed."

"I do, but you can't so soon—"

"I know I have to replenish my blood, but I want you."

"Once I feed again, I'll achieve my full power. When you drink from me, you'll regain your strength and more." Jody kissed her. "I want you too. I want you to taste what you've given me."

Want hit Becca hard. After almost losing her, she couldn't get close enough now. She caressed Jody's chest, down her abdomen, and lightly clasped between her legs. "Let's feed you quickly. I can't wait much longer."

"I'll need to call for hosts."

"No, you won't. There's a line of Weres outside the door. Everyone knows what you did. There are more volunteers to host for you than I think I want to know about."

Jody laughed. "Will you stay?"

"Just try to get rid of me."

CHAPTER THIRTY-THREE

Just before dawn, Francesca, wearing a black silk dressing gown held loosely together by crisscrossing black satin laces from her breasts to below her navel, met Michel at her bedroom door. Raising an eyebrow as she took in the bloody tears in Michel's shirt and pants, she kissed her and caressed her chest with both hands. "How badly were you injured?"

Michel pulled off her shirt and tossed it aside. The hole in her shoulder had closed already, leaving only a faint circular indentation. She unbuttoned her pants and removed them along with her boots. The gunshot wound on her thigh had stopped bleeding and would soon disappear as well, but she'd lost blood and needed to feed. The hunger screamed inside her. "Nothing serious. They were aiming to kill the Weres, but they were incredibly incompetent."

Francesca drew Michel to the bed, stretched out on the crimson sheets, and pulled Michel down beside her. "Tell me."

Michel propped her chin in her hand and lightly traced the contour of Francesca's full breast. Francesca's nipple tightened as she rubbed it with her thumb. "The Weres discovered the abductions, somehow got the location of the lab, and chose tonight to liberate the subjects."

"Sylvan?" Francesca pulled the laces on her gown and let it fall open, guiding Michel's hand inside.

"Sylvan, her mate, and her second." Michel cupped Francesca's breast and squeezed gently.

Francesca laughed. "A formidable force."

Michel kissed Francesca's throat, and lifting Francesca's breast to her lips, lightly bit her nipple. Francesca arched, a sigh escaping her.

"They had help," Michel said. "Jody Gates and two of her soldiers."

"Ah," Francesca said, caressing Michel's ass. "Jody always has been unpredictable."

Michel tugged Francesca's nipple between her teeth and stroked lower on her abdomen, teasing her fingers through the silky curls at the juncture of Francesca's thighs. "She saw me."

"Mmm, and you saw her." Francesca guided Michel's hand lower.

"You fed," Michel murmured, caressing Francesca's full clitoris.

"Just enough to be ready for you. I promised we'd feed together." Francesca kissed Michel languidly, rocking on Michel's fingers. "What about Standish?"

"She may have gotten away," Michel said, slipping inside. The clench of hot muscles around her fingers made her aware of the cold center of her being, and she pushed deeper, suddenly desperate for warmth.

"Ah, careful, darling"—Francesca stilled her hand—"you might be able to make me come even now."

"Then let us feed, so we can both feel it."

"In a minute." Francesca stroked Michel's face and kissed her again. "Is Standish likely to think we betrayed her?"

"I don't think so. I helped her escape."

Francesca's hips picked up speed. "Very good, darling."

"I wonder if Gates will tell the wolf Alpha about me," Michel murmured, following Francesca's pace. Her hunger raged, but she would feed at the Regent's pleasure.

"Jody's actions are often difficult to interpret, but her allegiance has always been clear. She is a Vampire. She'll come to me first for an explanation before exposing us to the Alpha."

"What will you do?" Michel guided Francesca onto her back and knelt astride her thigh, thrusting into her faster and harder.

"You are very good, my darling enforcer." Francesca's body arched. "And very bad. Now you're going to make me come."

"Yes," Michel said through gritted teeth. Francesca's power skittered around the edges of her consciousness, but until she had fed, until her own power had risen, she could not join her. Even then, she could never be one with her. "What will you do, Regent?"

"I will do what I always do," Francesca said breathlessly as her orgasm crested. "I will secure my Dominion in any way necessary."

Michel kissed her, the taste of Francesca's power a taunting promise of pleasure yet to come. Francesca's power would always come first, at any price, no matter who must pay.

❖

Growling steadily, Sylvan paced just inside the door of the treatment room. Elena had commanded her to stay out of the way, and her mate had sent her a look that said to heed the *medicus*. To please her mate, she obeyed the directive, but every time Elena touched Drake, her wolf threw herself around inside her in a frenzy. She'd never been this agitated, this possessive, even when they'd first been mated. Not even in the throes of breeding frenzy. She'd already half-shifted and could barely control the surge of hormones skittering through her system. If she lost control, she'd be dangerous, even to Elena.

"Are you almost done?" Sylvan demanded, absently rubbing the ache in her stomach.

Across the room, Elena turned, her hand resting lightly on Drake's shoulder. "Just about."

"Don't touch her." Sylvan snarled and her pelt shimmered.

Elena slowly withdrew her hand. "Prima, you can get dressed."

Drake slid down from the treatment table and pulled on her jeans. She didn't bother with a shirt. "Something wrong, Elena?"

"I don't think so." Elena looked from Sylvan to Drake, her expression quizzical. "We'll rush the blood assays, just to be sure there's no evidence of silver in your bloodstream, but I can't find anything amiss."

"Something is off," Drake said with a shake of her head. "I feel more aggressive than usual, and look at Sylvan. She's so agitated she's about to shift."

"That's normal under the circumstances," Elena said.

Sylvan vaulted across the room, her canines stabbing down. "*What* circumstances?"

Elena shot Sylvan a stern look. "If you would control yourself, Alpha, you could answer your own question. Take a few deep breaths and quiet your wolf."

Sylvan growled. No one but Elena ever talked to her that way. After her mother, Elena was the only wolf, other than her mate, who would ever be able to dominate her. Her skin vibrated with the need to drag Drake away to their den, away from everyone.

Because it was Elena, and because Drake would want her to, Sylvan forced her wolf to settle. She pulled Drake into her arms and rubbed her face over Drake's neck, immersing herself in Drake's scent. The connection with her mate soothed her, and her wolf finally stopped pacing. Her mate's scent, her pheromones, raced through her system. Quivering, she licked Drake's neck.

"Sylvan," Drake murmured, caressing her back, "you're shaking. What's wrong?"

Sylvan licked Drake again, her heart pounding as if it might burst from her chest. She raised her head and met Drake's gaze. "You're pregnant."

Drake breathed in sharply. "How do you know?"

Sylvan grinned. "I'm the Alpha."

Drake scowled automatically, but her smile erupted and filled Sylvan's soul. "You're sure?"

"Yes," Sylvan said.

"Very sure," Elena said.

Drake gripped Sylvan's hand and searched Elena's face. "And healthy? Can you tell—anything?"

"It's very early, but you're both strong, vigorous Weres," Elena said gently. "You will make beautiful pups."

"Pups—plural?" Laughing, Drake kissed Sylvan. "I love you, but there had better not be more than two in there."

Sylvan buried her face in Drake's neck again, hiding her tears from Elena. War was upon them, and she wasn't certain if she could tell friends from enemies. She had a Pack to protect, a mate to shelter, and now, precious offspring to defend. She felt Drake's warm breath against her ear.

"Together, Sylvan. Whatever is coming, we will face it together. Always."

Sylvan raised her head, and Elena looked away, pretending not to see her tears.

"You honor me with your love, Prima. I want only, always, to deserve it."

Drake pressed a kiss to the mate bite on Sylvan's chest. "As long as you love me, you always will."

Sylvan smiled. "One challenge I gladly accept."

Chapter Thirty-four

I can't believe they overpowered our security and practically destroyed my laboratory." Veronica glared at Nicholas Gregory and paced across the expansive office to the enormous plate glass windows that looked down over the state capitol complex. She could actually see Sylvan Mir's office across the courtyard. How ironic. "They put a *spy* inside my facility. How could this happen? Aren't you supposed to know about these things? Don't you have spies of your own inside those pathetic mutant-loving organizations?"

"We have infiltrated some of the groups supporting Praetern rights." Nicholas's patronizing voice made her want to remind him that without her he had no chance of containing the creatures. "But we need to be careful. Exposure is likely to turn the human population against HUFSI's agenda. This person—Martin—he escaped?"

"Apparently. We're still searching the building. Removing the bodies, cleaning up your mess. Now I'm going to have to relocate my entire lab."

"Clearly we have underestimated our human adversaries as well as the cunning of the Weres. We'll strengthen our precautions at the other facilities," Nicholas said. "We know what Martin looks like. We'll find him and persuade him to lead us to his co-sympathizers."

"Fine. I don't care what you do to him," Veronica said impatiently. "With the specimens I already have, I can continue my work elsewhere until we're able to acquire new subjects."

Nicholas grimaced. "We're going to have some problems there. Now that the Weres have been alerted, they're going to be guarding their adolescents even more closely."

"You know, the timing of this debacle might turn out to be serendipitous. We don't actually want to eradicate these species, we just want to control them." Smiling, she turned from the window and studied the man who financed her work. He had some secret agenda, but for now, their interests were compatible. "You said yourself, you need an army capable of fighting supernatural soldiers. Selective breeding and genetic alteration takes time. For a long-range plan, it's still a reasonable goal."

"And in the short term?" Nicholas asked, sitting forward, his eyes glinting.

"Well, we need to be able to redesign the adults, don't we?" Veronica felt a tingle of arousal. "Human research has already made strides in reverse-engineering mature organisms. We simply need the appropriate material to study."

"Stem cells?" Nicholas said.

"How perceptive of you."

"What exactly will you need?"

Veronica smiled, excitement coursing through her. For the first time since she had run—no, been *driven*—out of her laboratory by a group of subhuman creatures, she felt in control again. Oh yes. She was going to enjoy these next experiments.

"Pregnant females."

Keep reading for a special preview of FIRESTORM,
the new First Responders novel from Radclyffe.

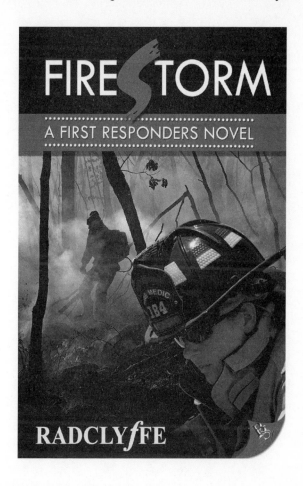

Firefighter paramedic Mallory "Ice" James commands a crew of
smokejumpers—twenty women and men who eat together, sleep
together, and parachute into the face of raging forest fires together.
Discipline and teamwork mean the difference between life and death,
and she's earned her reputation as cool and controlled in the face of
danger. "Hot Shot" Jac Russo never met a rule she wouldn't break
and doesn't plan to stop just because the woman setting the terms is
drop-dead gorgeous and hotter than the blazes they're supposed to be
dousing. Mallory and Jac may not like each other much, but lust isn't
something either can control—and they soon discover ice burns as
fiercely as flame.

FIRESTORM

"Mallory," a gruff male voice called. "Hey, Ice! See you a minute?"

So much for the early shower. Mallory hadn't counted on Sully being up so early, but she should have. He was as much a workaholic as she was—although she preferred to think of her work ethic as thorough rather than obsessed.

"Yo, Sully. On my way." Abandoning her visions of hot steam and suds, Mallory reversed course back to the ops room next to the hangar and stopped in the doorway. Her immediate superior, Chuck Sullivan, was bent over the desk in his cramped one-window office, his arms braced on either side of a haphazard pile of papers and file folders. A huge bulletin board covered with aerial and terrain maps occupied the far wall. A rickety stand in one corner held a Pyrex coffeepot in a dingy white coffeemaker. The room smelled of burnt coffee. He'd been there a while.

Mallory suppressed a twinge of guilt. She knew what this was about—she'd been dragging her feet sorting through all the paperwork that went along with her new job as ops manager of the Yellowstone interagency smokejumping unit. It wasn't like she hadn't told Sully she was terrible at desk work when he'd asked her to take the position suddenly vacated when Phil Reynolds couldn't jump anymore. A bad landing had ended Phil up in the hospital with a crushed lumbar disc. She had seniority after eight years spending May through November fighting wildfires with the USFS, and she had plenty of experience directing activities as incident commander in the field, but ask her to fill out a timesheet—she'd rather spend two weeks sleeping on the ground during the height of mosquito season. "Look, Sully, if this is about filling that last position, I read through the applications last night. I think there are a couple of good candidates—"

"Yeah, about that," Sully said, looking up. His smoke-gray eyes were hooded, the furrows extending out from the corners paler than the rest of his tanned skin, even though summer was still more than a month away. Something in his look made her stomach tighten.

"What?" Mallory said, leaning her shoulder against the doorjamb.

"The last position has been filled."

"That's interesting. How come I don't know about it?" Mallory asked conversationally. Something was off, but whatever it was, Sully wasn't likely to be responsible, so venting her temper at him wasn't going to help. Sully had been supervisor at the Yellowstone site for fifteen years, and Mallory had worked with him for the last five. They got along well and never had any problem communicating. Now he was uneasy and had made a decision that directly affected her for the next half a year without consulting her. She didn't like surprises. Anticipation was her holy grail—she planned, studied, considered contingencies. Orderly, well-thought-out plans brought the team home whole. Fire was unpredictable. Fickle and frivolous. She couldn't afford to be. Not when lives were at stake. "What's going on, Sully?"

"We've been assigned a transfer from Grangeville to fill that vacancy."

"A hotshot?" Mallory tried not to grind her teeth. Hotshots usually worked as part of wildland fire suppression teams on large, long-term fires. They were used to performing as units and often had difficulty making the transition from field-based firefighting to the rapid deployment into remote areas that was the daily fare of smokejumpers. "Geez, Sully. How come I'm just hearing about this?"

Sully straightened and jammed his hands in the pockets of his khaki work pants. His jaw worked like he was still chewing the tobacco he'd given up the year before. Yeah, he was definitely unhappy. "Because I'm just hearing about it myself. I got a call from regional headquarters informing me of the posting. The whole thing was handled a couple levels above my pay grade."

"I've never heard of the higher-ups getting involved in something as basic as hiring a crew member."

"Well, she's not just any crew member."

"She?" Mallory raised an eyebrow.

Sully laughed. "What? You think you and Sarah are the only women capable of doing the job?"

"I know we're not. Except I know all the other female jumpers, and most of the women on the field crews too. None of them said anything to me about wanting to come on board. What's her name?"

"Jac Russo."

Mallory frowned. "Why do I know that name?"

"Maybe because her father is Franklin Russo?"

Mallory stiffened. "Oh, you gotta be kidding me. The right-wing senator from Idaho? The right-to-life, anti-gay, anti-affirmative-everything guy?"

"That's the one. The rumor mill says he's going to give Powell a run for his money for the big house come election time next year."

"Just gets better and better," Mallory said.

Sully smiled a little grimly. "Never knew you were political."

"I'm not. Usually." Mallory shook her head. Sully knew she was a lesbian—so did everybody else she worked with. She didn't make an issue of it, she didn't hide. She was who she was. In the air, in the wilderness digging a line or setting a burnout, no one cared who you slept with. All they cared about was how well you did your job and looked after your buddies. Most of the time she was too busy working to think about what bureaucrats were doing, but she couldn't turn on the television or pick up a magazine or read the news without hearing something about Russo and his campaign to turn the country back to a time when straight white men held all the power. And his vitriol turned her stomach. "This posting is politics, right? Somebody owes somebody a favor and we get to pick up the tab?" She raked her hand through her hair. Her too damn long hair. "Does she even know anything about firefighting? This is crazy. I don't want some pampered politician's daughter, who probably thinks spending six months in the mountains with a bunch of men will be fun and look good on her résumé, on my team. Hell, if she doesn't get herself killed, she'll get one of us killed."

"Slow down, Ice. She's not a rookie. Not quite. She had a season with the Bureau of Land Management in Idaho." He fished around on his desk and came up with a dog-eared file folder. He flipped it open, turned it around, and held it out to her. "Besides, real-life experience is an acceptable substitute for the usual field training."

"She's still a rookie as far as jumping is concerned." Mallory regarded the folder as if it were a rattler coiled in the brush trailside, waiting to strike. There couldn't be anything good inside that file. Smokejumpers returned year after year to the same crew, so vacancies were few and the waiting list long. Somehow, Russo had managed to leapfrog to the head of the list, and that could only mean someone had pulled strings. Anyone qualified for the job didn't need to do that. "Come on, Sully. You know this doesn't make any sense. If she's already on a crew, why move her over to ours? We'll have to train her to jump—"

"You'd have to train whoever joined us to jump, Ice."

"Still, I don't get it."

"Neither do I." Sully gave her a wry shrug and waggled the folder. "I wasn't given the option. She'll be here this morning. You might as well look at this."

Reluctantly Mallory took the folder and glanced at the typed application and color photo clipped to the top of the page. Jac Russo. Twenty-seven—well, at least she had a couple of years on Russo in age and quite a few more in experience. At just thirty, she was young to captain a jump crew and wouldn't have wanted to start out the season breaking in a hotshot who discounted her authority because she was younger or less experienced. The photo was a good one. Even the Polaroid head shot couldn't dampen the appeal of her thick black hair—true black, not dark brown like Mallory's—and dark chocolate eyes. Russo's face was a little too strong to be pretty, with bold cheekbones and an angular jaw. A decent face, nothing out of the ordinary, really. Mallory got caught in the dark eyes that almost leapt out of the glossy surface of the photo—intense, unsmiling, penetrating eyes. Eyes that held secrets and dared you to reveal yours. Okay, so maybe she was a little bit good-looking. The guys would probably be happy to have her around as long as she had even marginal skills. Mallory didn't agree. She couldn't afford to have anyone jumping who couldn't hold her own. No one was coming out of the mountains on a litter on her watch. Not this year. Not ever again.

"I'm telling you right now," Mallory said, flipping a page to look at the work experience Russo had listed, "if she can't cut it, I'm not putting her up in the air. I'm not going to let her endanger my team. I don't care whose daughter she is."

"I wouldn't expect you to," someone said in a husky alto from right behind her.

Mallory spun around and went nose to nose with a stranger, their bodies colliding hard enough for her to feel firm breasts and a muscled torso press against her front. Molding to her—except that had to be her imagination. She pulled back and the brunette took her in with a slow up-and-down perusal and an expression that was half-arrogant, half-amused. Her lips were full and sensuous and unsmiling—like in the photo.

"Jump to conclusions much?" the brunette said.

"Sorry," Mallory muttered. "I didn't realize you were behind me."

"I gathered that." The brunette's smile widened, but her eyes were cool. She didn't hold out her hand. "I'm Jac Russo."

"Yes." Mallory indicated the folder. "I saw the picture."

"Did you also see the part that said I was in the Sierra Nevadas for six weeks on that big burn last year? That I've got search and rescue experience? Can handle explosives? How about the part—"

"I noticed the absence of jump time," Mallory said tightly, "and not much other field work. Basic training starts"—she checked her watch—"in forty-five minutes."

"I'll be ready," Russo said. "And I'm a fast learner."

"We'll see," Mallory murmured.

"What—you've already made up your mind?" Jac's expression tightened and her eyes went flat. "Let me guess. Something you heard on TV, maybe?"

"Sorry, I must have missed the bulletin," Mallory shot back. She lifted the folder. "I was talking about what *isn't* in here."

"Don't be so sure you know all about me from what you read," Russo said.

"I'll reserve judgment till I've seen how you run. You'll be first up this morning."

"Good enough."

Sully cleared his throat loudly. "Russo, I've got some paperwork for you to complete."

"Yes sir, I'll be right there." Jac didn't shift her gaze from Mallory's. "I didn't get your name."

"Mallory James." Mallory smiled thinly. "I'm the ops and training manager. You can call me Boss. Or Ice."

"What do your friends call you?"

"Mallory." She made sure Russo got the message she wasn't planning to fraternize with her. Not that she ever really did with any of the crew. She hung out with them, swapped stories, but she never really shared anything personal with anyone. Breaking away from Russo's probing gaze, Mallory turned and tossed the folder onto Sully's desk. She wasn't sure what besides anger might show in her eyes, and she didn't want Russo to see past her temper to her worry, or her fear. "Roll call at 0600. Don't be late."

"Can't wait."

Mallory snorted and strode away.

Jac watched until the ops manager disappeared into a building across the tarmac. *Well, that was a great start.*

She'd been hoping to slide in under the radar, at least until she'd had a chance to establish herself on her own merits. That obviously wasn't going to happen now. She couldn't tell from the conversation exactly what was behind Mallory James's animosity. Most of the time, a cold reception had little to do with her and a lot to do with her father. The higher he'd risen in national politics, the more airtime he got and the more controversy he stirred up. He seemed to thrive on the reactions his often extreme positions evoked—even death threats didn't bother him. Unfortunately, the more visible he became, the more his notoriety overflowed onto the family. Her mother was an anxious wreck who didn't want to leave the house past the line of protesters lined up across the street and the reporters in the driveway. Her sister Amy was generally humiliated by her parents anyhow, the way all seventeen-year-olds were, and was trying even harder than Jac had to prove she was nothing like their ultraconservative right-wing father by running with a tough crowd of dropouts and delinquents. Jac's solution had been to put as much physical distance between herself and her family as she could, but eventually even the National Guard tour in Iraq had ended. She'd hoped to escape here, but no such luck. She was used to being judged on the basis of her father's latest sound bite, and usually that didn't bother her. Today it did.

She squared her shoulders and faced the guy watching her speculatively from behind the desk. She'd been proving herself all her life—or more accurately, disproving the assumptions everyone made about her. In high school all she'd had to do was demonstrate her willingness to break the rules to crack the mold her family had created for her. Considering that breaking the rules usually involved sex, drugs, and rock 'n' roll—all the things her father railed against—also earned her points with her peers, divorcing herself from her family's politics hadn't been all that hard. Most of the time rebelling had been fun. But she wasn't sixteen anymore, and while she still chafed under the weight of rules and regs, she'd pretty much given up all the rest. The drugs and rock 'n' roll for sure, and the sex most of the time. Of course, sex was what had landed her here.

Realizing the guy was still watching her, still waiting, she said, "I guess you weren't expecting me."

He grinned fleetingly. "You're quick."

She laughed, walked forward, and held out her hand. "Jac Russo. I take it you got that part already."

"Chuck Sullivan. I'm kind of the overseer around here, but Ice calls the shots."

"Interesting nickname."

His gaze narrowed. "None better at the job."

Jac held up her hands. "Hey, I don't doubt it. She just seemed a little fiery there for a minute."

Again the fleeting grin and a shake of his head. "Not much riles her up."

"I'm not sure I'm happy about having that privilege, then." Jac sighed. "I didn't know about this myself until yesterday. I know it's not how things are usually done. I don't blame you for being pissed."

"I'm not pissed," Sullivan said quietly.

Jac tilted her head toward the door behind her. "She is."

"Don't worry about it. Pass basic training, you'll be part of the team."

Too bad it wasn't that easy. Being good at what she did, being qualified, pulling her own weight—all those things helped her fit in, but they never helped her to be accepted. When she was younger, she'd desperately wanted to be accepted. Now she didn't care. At least that's what she told herself most days. The freeze in Mallory James's eyes was nothing new, although usually the disdain was motivated by something other than her showing up where she wasn't expected or wanted. All the same, for the first time in a long time, she'd wanted to melt the icy reception she'd gotten used to receiving.

She wanted this job, sure. She'd wanted it for a long time, but she hadn't planned on getting it this way. But now she was here, and she wanted to stay. She wanted Mallory James to admit she was good enough to stay.

About the Author

L.L. Raand writing as Radclyffe has published over thirty-five romance and romantic intrigue novels and dozens of short stories, and has edited numerous romance and erotica anthologies. She is a seven-time Lambda Literary Award finalist and winner in both romance (*Distant Shores, Silent Thunder*) and erotica (*Erotic Interludes 2: Stolen Moments* edited with Stacia Seaman and *In Deep Waters 2: Cruising the Strip* written with Karin Kallmaker). She is a member of the Saints and Sinners Literary Hall of Fame, an Alice B. Readers' award winner, a Benjamin Franklin Award finalist (*The Lonely Hearts Club*), a *ForeWord Review* Book of the Year Finalist (*Night Call*), and a 2010 RWA/FF&P Prism award winner for *Secrets in the Stone*.

Visit her websites at www.llraand.com and www.radfic.com.

Books Available From Bold Strokes Books

Blood Hunt by LL Raand. In the second Midnight Hunters Novel, Detective Jody Gates, heir to a powerful Vampire clan, forges an uneasy alliance with Sylvan, the Wolf Were Alpha, to battle a shadow army of humans and rogue Weres, while fighting her growing hunger for human reporter Becca Land. (978-1-60282-209-2)

Loving Liz by Bobbi Marolt. When theater actor Marty Jamison turns diva and Liz Chandler walks out on her, Marty must confront a cheating lover from the past to understand why life is crumbling around her. (978-1-60282-210-8)

Kiss the Rain by Larkin Rose. How will successful fashion designer Eve Harris react when she discovers the new woman in her life, Jodi, and her secret fantasy phone date, Lexi, are one and the same? (978-1-60282-211-5)

Sarah, Son of God by Justine Saracen. In a story within a story within a story, a transgendered beauty takes us through Stonewall-rioting New York, Venice under the Inquisition, and Nero's Rome. (978-1-60282-212-2)

Sleeping Angel by Greg Herren. Eric Matthews survives a terrible car accident only to find out everyone in town thinks he's a murderer—and he has to clear his name even though he has no memories of what happened. (978-1-60282-214-6)

Dying to Live by Kim Baldwin & Xenia Alexiou. British socialite Zoe Anderson-Howe's pampered life is abruptly shattered when she's taken hostage by FARC guerrillas while on a business trip to Bogota, and Elite Operative Fetch must rescue her to complete her own harrowing mission. (978-1-60282-200-9)

Indigo Moon by Gill McKnight. Hope Glassy and Godfrey Meyers are on a mercy mission to save their friend Isabelle after she is attacked by a rogue werewolf—but does Isabelle want to be saved from the sexy wolf who claimed her as a mate? (978-1-60282-201-6)

Parties in Congress by Colette Moody. Bijal Rao, Indian-American moderate Independent, gets the break of her career when she's hired to work on the congressional campaign of Janet Denton—until she meets her remarkably attractive and charismatic opponent, Colleen O'Bannon. (978-1-60282-202-3)

Black Fire: Gay African-American Erotica, edited by Shane Allison. *Black Fire* celebrates the heat and power of sex between black men: the rude B-boys and gorgeous thugs, the worshippers of heavenly ass, and the devoutly religious in their forays through the subterranean grottoes of the down-low world. (978-1-60282-206-1)

The Collectors by Leslie Gowan. Laura owns what might be the world's most extensive collection of BDSM lesbian erotica, but that's as close as she's gotten to the world of her fantasies. Until, that is, her friend Adele introduces her to Adele's mistress Jeanne—art collector, heiress, and experienced dominant. With Jeanne's first command, Laura's life changes forever. (978-1-60282-208-5)

Breathless, edited by Radclyffe and Stacia Seaman. Bold Strokes Books romance authors give readers a glimpse into the lives of favorite couples celebrating special moments "after the honeymoon ends." Enjoy a new look at lesbians in love or revisit favorite characters from some of BSB's best-selling romances. (978-1-60282-207-8)

Breaker's Passion by Julie Cannon. Leaving a trail of broken hearts scattered across the Hawaiian Islands, surf instructor Colby Taylor is running full speed away from her selfish actions years earlier until she collides with Elizabeth Collins, a stuffy, judgmental college professor who changes everything. (978-1-60282-196-5)

Justifiable Risk by V.K. Powell. Work is the only thing that interests homicide detective Greer Ellis until internationally renowned journalist Eva Saldana comes to town looking for answers in her brother's death—then attraction threatens to override duty. (978-1-60282-197-2)

Nothing But the Truth by Carsen Taite. Sparks fly when two top-notch attorneys battle each other in the high-risk arena of the courtroom, but when a strange turn of events turns one of them from advocate to witness, prosecutor Ryan Foster and defense attorney Brett Logan join forces in their search for the truth. (978-1-60282-198-9)